Colly Lee
-Rat

Megan
- Nikki Shea

UNDERTOW BOOK 2

STORMFRONT

Listen to
Opeth
Sea Wall
M.J.

K.R. CONWAY

To Jen -
Be a crazy!
woman!

Kathleen R Conway

Bourne MA 02532

Visit the author's website at www.CapeCodScribe.com

First Edition: August 2014

Conway, Kathleen R.

Stormfront / by Kathleen R. Conway – 1st ed.

Summary: In the sequel to UNDERTOW, seventeen-year-old Eila Walker must face the fallout of her past decisions, including a guilt-ridden bodyguard who is determined to keep her from being in danger again, though Eila wants to prove herself as the fighter she was born to be.

ISBN: 0-9897763-2-8 / 978-0-9897763-2-5

Published in the United States of America

DEDICATION

For all the warriors.

Young and old.

Here and gone.

STORMFRONT

Not long ago Eila Walker's choices were limited: death by a bullet to the head, or at the hands of her beloved bodyguard, Raef. Now, five weeks after Raef triggered her power and she nearly leveled a historic mansion, Eila is dealing with the fall-out of her decisions. While she doesn't remember dying in the arms of the soul thief who loves her, she knows that Raef remembers everything about the night he nearly killed her.

Now on the mend and attempting to keep one step ahead of the FBI, Eila and her team of misfits are desperate for a bit of normal. Eila is trying to navigate high school, while her BFF Ana is cautiously hanging with past-boyfriend and soul thief, Kian. Shape-shifter MJ is trying not to piss off his mother, while Raef is coping with his fears that Eila will never be safe.

But just as "normal" seems within their grasp, a powerfully built newcomer arrives. Raef knows the scarred man as a Blacklist Dealer – a soul thief, who peddles the names of humans who deserve to die. Eila, however, knows him as the protective hunter from the woods, whom she nicknames *Thor*. Before long, Raef and Eila realize they've met the same killer, and he has one hell of a story to tell the five friends . . . if Raef doesn't murder him first.

PRAISE FOR STORMFRONT

"The way this author tells a story sucks you in to where you don't want to put the book down – hanging on each word dying to know what will happen next. And let me tell you it is never what you think it will be. This is one author that you can't "figure out" –you won't know where the story is going until you get there, and when you get there it will be something you could have never imagined." – Bobbie Jo for The Reading Diva

"Conway has once again written a very believable story with characters and scenery that will sweep you away to another place. When you come back to reality you will wonder how so much time has passed and what this strange world is you have been dropped into. You actually miss everyone in the book as if they are your real friends and family." Kim Lewis, ARC reviewer

"I believe I enjoyed this book even more than the first, Undertow. Stormfront was able to delve further into the characters, showing their depth. It begins in the snowy Northeast and whisks you away to a tropical local described so well, that any New Englander would eagerly travel to it the middle of winter. Strong new characters are introduced, and like any great read, twists and turns are unexpected and exciting. The end = perfection. Great read!" – YA librarian Lindsey Hughes

Prologue

Newport, Rhode Island
Four weeks before Thanksgiving

THE LARGEST MANSION IN NEWPORT looked like a war zone. At least, that was how Mark Howe remembered the Vanderbilt's historic estate.

He would get another look today if the line ever moved, which at this point seemed doubtful. He couldn't believe how long it took to get a non-foamed, non-whipped, non-mucked-with cup of coffee in Newport. How was it even possible that so many Mercedes-driving blondes managed to squeeze into the corner cafe at the crack of dawn?

He would have left, ignoring his desperate need for caffeine, but his body was literally running on fumes. Since the Newport blast seven days ago, he had gotten the absolute minimum for functional sleep, as the case had become quite the media frenzy. Piecing together what the hell had happened in the boiler room had become priority numero uno for his office in Boston, yet he had not received a final report from forensics on the type of bomb used in the blast.

Yes, "bomb," because it damn well wasn't the boiler.

He was headed back to The Breakers mansion this morning if he ever got a damn coffee.

As he finally reached the counter his phone trilled in his pocket. He quickly gave an order for two large hits of caffeine and snapped open his phone. "Howe," he answered, jostling the phone in the crook of his neck.

"Where are you?" demanded his imposing, seasoned partner of two years, Anthony Sollen.

"Getting us some coffee. You at The Breakers?"

A few faces in the shop glanced at him. The Breakers had Newport in a tizzy and getting the low down on what had happened during the Fire and Ice Ball was the talk of the town. Howe glanced around at his sudden audience and paid the cashier, quickly walking out to his sedan as Sollen talked into his ear.

"Yeah, I'm here, and Forensics wants to talk to us. Now," snapped Sollen.

"I'm on my way. Be there in three minutes." Howe snapped his phone shut, knocking the gearshift into drive.

He managed to swig half of the scalding drink before he pulled through the iron gates of the Vanderbilts' summer home, now being guarded round the clock as a crime scene. He parked in front of the massive entrance and headed inside with his partner's cup of joe.

Numerous members of the local and national historical societies had been the biggest pains in the ass when it came to dealing with the blast scene. They were there, as always, watching every move the FBI made,

2

making sure nothing was further damaged. They were chomping at the bit to start repairs before winter set in and possibly caused further damage to the historic home. Millionaire Christian Raines, whose fundraiser fete had been in full swing inside the mansion during the explosion, volunteered to foot the bill for all repairs. Supposedly he was devastated by the damage to the historic estate.

Devastated my ass, thought Howe. He was certain something was up with Newport's Most Eligible Man.

As he entered the boiler room for the umpteenth time since the night of the Fire and Ice party, Howe was still amazed that the only fatality in the blast was Dalca Anescu, who had been crushed by a piece of the ceiling.

The beastly, cast iron boiler that filled one side of the room looked like a concrete truck had hit it doing 90 mph. The floors and walls of the brick room all sustained structural damage and showed it via hundreds of cracks. A gaping hole in the ceiling gave a clear view up from the cellar through three floors and clean through the roof, where the energy of the explosion had been funneled. Damage estimates were easily in the millions, all of which Raines seemed willing to pay.

Howe thought of the kids from Cape Cod who had survived the carnage. There were the two O'Reilly brothers, deep pocketed themselves, who were the least injured. Ana Lane and the boy, Williams, had minor injuries, but the girl, Walker, was nearly killed and had obvious concussive injuries consistent with close proximity to a blast.

If they were all in the same room, why on earth would they not have all sustained the same injuries?

How in the hell were they not all dead?

3

Something was just wrong with the whole picture and Howe hoped the forensics team finally had a lead on the actual source of the blast. He walked to the center of the room where Sollen was standing with an older, balding man.

"So? I'm right, right? Plastique like C-4 right?" asked Howe handing the coffee to his partner, who nodded his thanks.

Sollen gestured to the man beside him, "Mark Howe, this is Dr. Carl Leeland. He does some work for the DC office from time to time when we are stuck." The forensic geek gave a stiff smile.

Howe reached out and shook the doctor's hand, "We're stuck, I take it?"

"Nice to meet you Agent Howe, though I wish the circumstances were better. I've worked some terrorism attacks for the government when unusual materials are used in bombs."

"So it was a bomb," said Sollen, rubbing the back of his neck, the tension literally forcing his muscles to seize. "Type?"

Dr. Leeland cleared his throat, "Well, that's just it. I cannot find bomb residue of any kind, anywhere in the building, let alone this room. Any explosive that we know of that can create this kind of damage leaves a residue and there is none."

"Couldn't it have burned off?" asked Howe, hopeful as visions of a more simplified end to the Breakers case began to evaporate.

Leeland smoothed back his few remaining hairs as he spoke, "There is no indication of any sort of fire, anywhere. Which tells me that this was not chemical in any way. It had to be a physical bomb."

"Like what? Compressed gas or something?" asked Howe.

"Well, if the blast was far, far smaller, yes. But a blast this huge?"

4

Leeland shook his head. "The only thing that comes to mind that can do this damage without leaving a chemical trail, is nature."

"What?" asked Howe and Sollen, nearly in unison.

"Nature, like a tornado. Although, my guess, in here, it would have been something like a bolt of lightning.

"Why lightning?" asked Sollen.

Leeland looked down at his clipboard as his glasses slipped slightly on his narrow nose. "According to the statements your office took from the guests that night, nearly all said they heard a 'boom' that reminded them of a lightning strike."

Howe shook his head, this idea of lightning being just too damn far fetched and the boiler looking better by the second. "Are we certain it wasn't the boiler? Maybe it actually did malfunction and blow?"

Leeland shook his head. "No. The boiler would be in pieces and right now it is flattened to the wall. Something threw it there with incredible force." Leeland suddenly snapped his fingers, as if remembering something, "Oh! And wait until you see this!" He picked up a flashlight out of a black duffle bag and walked over to the boiler. Sollen and Howe followed.

Leeland flicked on the flashlight and trained the beam of light into the depths of the crushed boiler. The light found its target and Leeland held it steady, "I believe the saying in Boston is 'How do you like them apples?" he asked, triumphant.

Howe squinted as he looked into the darkness at the small, silver object at the end of the light. It was jammed among the pipes within the boiler. "Is that a handgun?" he asked, stunned.

Sollen looked as well, his brow furrowed with lines. "I think that is a

Korth. See the check mark near the end of the barrel. Damn expensive handgun."

Howe knew without doubt that the kids from the Cape knew far more than they were saying. "None of those kids said a thing about a handgun." He shook his head, trying to sort the outrageous intel. "Okay, just so I have this all straight, you are basically saying this was a bomb that causes no fire, but major structural damage, and manages to kill only one person, but levels half of a mansion? Does this sound crazy only to me?"

Leeland tossed his hands, "I'm saying that if this is, in fact, a weapon, then I have never seen it before and it is one hell of a device."

Sollen looked at Howe, lines of stress clearly across his face. Someone had a new type of bomb in the United States and it wasn't the home team.

"What's the chance that Anescu was a brilliant physicist and that this all ends with her?" asked Howe, sarcastically.

"Slim to none," replied Sollen. "Ever been to Cape Cod?"

"Only once when I was stuck in traffic for three hours trying to cross the Sagamore Bridge," replied Howe. "Let me guess – you want some salt-water taffy?"

Sollen, never one to joke, pulled his Blackberry from his jacket pocket. He pressed a button and looked at the screen that showed information on the five survivors of the blast. "I say we pay the charming town of Centerville a visit and start with . . . 408 Main Street. I hear the Walker girl just got released from the hospital and I'm sure she'd love to see us again."

Howe just shook his head. "I hate the beach."

6

Nauset Beach, Cape Cod, Massachusetts
One day before Thanksgiving

I HAD A KILL MARK.

At least, that's what Christian had called it.

He said mine was darker, deeper . . . more distinct, even than my 4th great grandmother, Elizabeth's. From what I had managed to see, the small brand on my back that deemed me a murderer had also begun to change, growing upwards on my spine like a gnarled vine.

Christian said it was normal, considering what I had done a few weeks before. Considering how many I had slaughtered inside the coal room of the Newport mansion. A kill mark, he said, was the badge of the truly lethal and appeared only on those like me - those who could torch soul thieves and nearly flatten a national treasure, though I was sure my

7

wrecking-ball capability was a shocker for Christian.

I've got to say, I could do without it.

In fact, I could do without the whole assassin gene in general. It would be awesome if we were given a chance to choose our gene pool. A chance to mull over the options and pick what we wanted and what we would pass on, like the ability to channel the energy of souls and thus, fry soul thieves.

That would have been a big, fat pass for me.

I remember watching Sleeping Beauty as a child with Mae, and the Three Good Fairies chose what the princess got for endowments. They opted for a fabulous singing ability and babe-worthy good looks. Apparently everyone in the kingdom was stupid, because no one gave the poor girl any BRAINS and she went and touched the damn spindle. I mean, for crying out loud, if you get to choose the genetics ya get, belting out show tunes and rosy lips should be low on the list of must-haves.

Sometimes I felt like I too was destined to screw up and touch the proverbial spindle . . . unless I could torch the spinning wheel first. The only problem was a certain soul thief, who didn't seem too keen on having me test my wheel-frying abilities at all, especially after the Newport fiasco five weeks ago.

I needed a do-over from that night. We all did.

I glanced at Ana standing next to me. The snowflakes had begun to coat the top of her jacket's hood. A few brave flakes descended onto her long eyelashes and she blinked them away as she rolled her lips, willing them to not freeze off.

She huffed out her disgust at our current state, the cold air turning her words into slanted puffs of smoky vapor. "This is the dumbest pastime on the planet. I mean, who thinks up activities like this? Does some moron decide that hypothermia prior to turkey is a great idea and everyone jumps on the bandwagon?" She brutally scrubbed the flakes off her parka, evicting them without remorse.

Truth was, as a Kansas native now calling Cape Cod home, I didn't see the logic of surfing on Thanksgiving Eve either. Especially prior to the Nor' Easter that was heading towards us and churning up some monster waves. That said, however, this brilliant plan to freeze our butts off at Nauset beach was her idea. I decided not to remind her of that bit of info, since she was looking like a fairly pissed Popsicle anyway. I didn't think that the stiff walking boot encasing her left leg helped either.

She wouldn't have the darn thing if it wasn't for me.

Of course, she might not have her life anymore either, if I hadn't done what I did. Luckily, she only had to wear it when we went out of the house for any length of time, as she was basically healed.

"Let's give them ten more minutes, and then we can head back home," I replied, giving her a small smile. She eyed me with a steely glare and then just shook her head, resigned, her eyes going back to the two soulless surfers in the waves.

I must admit that when I first moved to the Cape, nearly three months ago, I didn't think Ana Lane and I would ever be more than classmates. But now? Now I couldn't imagine life without her. Through all the chaos that rained down on our lives over the past couple of months, she became more than just a short-statured blonde with a sharp tongue.

She became my best girl-pal ever.

She became the one I could divulge secrets to, horde chocolate with, and spill my guts to in the dead of night. And we stayed up late every Friday night, watching movies in her room.

Her room, which was now across from mine, since she had moved into 408 Main Street with me and my legal guardian Mae. She was my mother's best friend until the night both my parents were killed in a car accident. I was only two when they died, and Mae had only just graduated high school, but she took me in. She loved me as her own and I have never seen her as anything other than a sister-like Mom whom I have loved for the past sixteen years.

As for Ana, she wasn't just a live-in BFF either. She was also one heck of an asset, especially in our motley crew. She was like an emotional psychic with a super-charged mind. She could understand what a person FELT, deep inside. Pick apart their true desire and either blab about it or modify it. She could take someone who was simply miffed and make her a raging maniac. She could take someone who was shy and make him crumble into oblivion. Or, she could make that one quiet wallflower become a fearless captain.

She was also getting better and better at reading memories. A few weeks ago she was able to link to my mind and view my nightmares regarding Elizabeth's death. A death that happened nearly two centuries ago and that I had begun reliving in my dreams.

Unfortunately Ana couldn't read the future, nor see the train wreck we hit head-on during the Fire and Ice Ball at The Newport Breakers.

Hey – nobody's perfect.

If there was a plus side to my body going nuclear in the coal room of the Vanderbilt's summer mansion, it was the simple fact that the bad guys were dead. Fried into dust by the soul-channeling energy I command.

Well, "command" may be a bit too strong of a word. I think I more or less barfed up a solar flare.

Luckily I didn't remember much of it.

On the downside, I did nearly croak. Plus, I put a hole in the mansion that looked like a comet had struck. And while the mansion and I were finally on the mend, the fallout of what I did with Raef's help was not soon forgotten.

Since the ball, Raef had been treating me with kid gloves and avoiding all physical contact – as if I resided inside a glass bubble. I was also sure he was haunted by the fact that he basically killed me that night in Newport. He never talked about it, which I didn't think helped when it came to his new title: Worry-Wart of the World.

I've gotta say, having the boy who previously could make a kiss scorch right to your toenails, now start acting like one giant mother hen, was SO not sexy.

I missed his touch, his kisses, and the way his face became marked with beautiful black symbols when we were in one another's arms. I missed him, all of him, but he seemed lost in his own painful world and he wouldn't let me in.

In the first days after my weeklong hospital stay, it was a miracle if I was even able to escape to the bathroom alone. Mae was hovering, Raef was obsessing, Kian was patrolling, and poor MJ was semi-grounded. But Ana? Ana found it downright hilarious until she became more mobile and instantly joined my ranks in the dreaded "buddy-system."

See, this was the problem with having immortal semi-boyfriends and an ice-cream wielding shape-shifter as bodyguards – they are great at

11

their jobs, but go a bit overboard. Determined to not have Ana and me in danger again, the boys had devised the "Buddy System," which basically meant we needed a male sidekick wherever we went. The feminist in both Ana and me bristled at the mandatory babysitting and defiantly referred to the boys plan as "BS."

They weren't amused.

So it was with no small amount of arm-twisting that we had managed to get Kian and Raef to go surfing, a whole sand dune and 50 yards of rolling ocean away from us. I think the only reason they finally agreed was because no one else was out here, freezing to death prior to a storm, and therefore the threat was minimized. We were also instructed to STAY at the top of the dune's staircase, where they could easily see us. Of course, such a demand made the devilish urge to go and hide all the more tempting.

Like I said – it was all BS.

I watched as Kian and Raef sat on their new surfboards out in the water. They were talking to one another as they straddled the boards in their wetsuits, though Raef kept looking at me every two seconds. Technically, as immortal soul thieves, they didn't need the protection from the frosty Atlantic, but flinging them out there in just some swim trunks would have drawn attention if anyone else had been as insane as we were.

Luckily, we were the only psychos on the beach.

The thickening storm clouds had blocked out the sun, and the brilliantly blue sky from earlier was now a brutish gray, speckled with hyperactive snowflakes. Ana said that a Thanksgiving storm like this was a rarity on the Cape. Of course, she also had extolled the virtues of surfing prior to pumpkin pie and, well, that wasn't exactly accurate either.

"What do you think they're talking about?" I asked, watching the waves where our bodyguards bobbed up and down.

"Pfft – wadda ya think? What they always obsess about. You. Me. How to lock us up in a tower with ten-foot thick walls and a fully outfitted army." She stepped back slightly and brushed the snow off a small bench to sit down. I noticed Kian and Raef instantly stopped talking the second she moved, and were now watching her and scanning the surrounding area. They really needed to chill.

"How's physical therapy?" I asked.

Ana sighed as she sat, "It's fine. I swear though, they book me more often than everyone else just because of Kian. All the therapists just want to see him leaning against that damn back wall, looking all sorts of sexy. Drives me nuts. And he insists on taking me. Honestly, I don't even think my therapist knows my last name! She sure as hell knows Kian's though. My last session is Monday afternoon, thank goodness."

I gave a small chuckle and she glared at me. Kian O'Reilly and Ana had met the summer before I came to Cape Cod. While both were somewhat tight-lipped about what had happened that summer, I knew one thing for certain: Ana and Kian had been desperately in love . . . until her abusive father had a heart attack and Kian refused to save him.

As soul thieves, Kian and Raef could steal the life force of their victims, but they also could share what they had stolen in a filtered form to heal a human. Kian had told Ana that her father was too weak to be saved and would have turned into a soul thief, like him. Ana didn't believe him, calling him a murderer and banishing him from her life.

A year later, I arrived on the Cape and they collided once again. Kian had returned to sell his yacht, Cerberus, and Raef had come along. Raef soon figured out that I was the 4th great daughter of his former friend, Elizabeth, and he decided to protect me – because he failed to protect her in 1851. Kian had zero interest in the protection detail thing until he realized Ana was hanging out with me and she became a target by association. Pretty soon, I had two immortal guards that were technically my genetic enemies.

Fate works in some crackpot ways.

As for Ana and Kian . . . their relationship was a work in progress. I suspected Raef and I had a long way to go as well.

FIVE WEEKS AGO, I NEARLY KILLED the girl I loved.

It wasn't an accident. It wasn't a mistake.

I did it deliberately, and the feeling of her body weakening in my arms haunts me still, as if branded into my hands. The sound of her last, thin breath replays over and over in my mind, a taunting reminder of what I am capable of and what I had done.

She carries the mark of where I had forced a stolen soul into her - a thin, finger-long scar engraved between her breasts.

She tries to hide it, but I know it's there.

She will carry that scar to her grave, a permanent reminder of who I truly am - a killer, designed by the darker hand of fate.

The scar had bled down her beautiful, fair skin that night, turning the bodice of the white ball gown she had worn into a sickening, mottled pink. In my mind I see her, lifeless, tucked under me as I try to shield her from the pieces of falling stone and wood that rain down around us. Debris that was from the massive hole her energy had drilled through the

15

Breakers. Energy that was unleashed when her body switched to overload, and her DNA hit the self-destruct button because of me.

Her power had wound around us like a snake of light and rocketed through the ceiling only to fall back, collapsing onto us. It had killed the clansman instantly . . . and halted Eila's heart.

I tried to go with her. Tried to poison myself with her life-force by drawing it into my body, but I failed. She wasn't toxic to me – she never was and never could be. I was left alive, desperately trying to restart her heart with MJ and Kian frantically attempting to help. Trying to save this one girl who had so profoundly changed all our lives, and who had sacrificed herself to protect us. To protect me, her historic enemy.

She had whispered into my cheek that she loved me, moments before I caused that scar. I hear her voice speak those words when I stand, alone at night, watching over her home. Praying I will catch anyone who means her harm before they come too close.

Before they have a chance to take her life . . . as I had.

I watch her now, standing with Ana as the snow swirls around them. She seems happy, healthy, and against all odds, alive.

She has told me, repeatedly, that it wasn't my fault. That we had no choice, that night in Newport, surrounded by Mortis who wanted her power. She said she was dead no matter what, but at least she could give the rest of us a fighting chance at survival.

But I was, and am, her guard. I should have been more careful, more vigilant. I should have known, somehow, but I didn't see a friend's betrayal coming. None of us did, and it was Eila who paid the price, and I the one who demanded the ultimate payment.

She was, is, my everything. My need to love her is like a physical

16

demand that must be met for my survival, and for that reason, the fear that I may hurt her again is crushing. The terror that I may fail her again, as I failed her grandmother a century and a half ago, weighs more than the world.

She trusts me, loves me, and I *will not* lose her again.

But to protect her, I know I need to be stronger. Faster. A perfect killer. I needed a Dealer, no matter the cost, no matter the risk. I would do it for her.

I wasn't sure if I could tell Kian, because he may try to stop me, though he had no problem picking off a few people if it were necessary. And Christian I still didn't quite trust, though I was certain he had the right connections to introduce me to the darkest corners of our kind.

So for now, I do what I can. I am hyper-vigilant, I try to stay nearby, and I try not to breech the wall I have built between us. A wall that is a necessity, because when I hold her, kiss her, and run my hands down her slender frame, I forget who I am. In her soft lips and breathy gasps I lose myself, and in doing so, she becomes vulnerable. Unprotected, because I am entirely distracted when she presses her beautiful body against mine. That wall, however, was beginning to feel more precariously erected with every passing day. As Eila grew stronger, my will to keep her at arm's length weakened.

In the hospital we had made a deal: keep our hands off one another until she could use her power like the dangerous weapon it was designed to be and protect herself. I assumed I wouldn't worry so much about her if I knew she could defend herself and I could draw her into my arms once again. Unfortunately, I overlooked one thing: I would NEVER stop worrying about Eila Walker. Even if she could crush the planet, I would still worry.

As I watched her in the center of the swirling snow, her chocolate hair twisting around her face, I knew I was in trouble.

She wanted to fight. I wanted her safe.

As she grew stronger, she began talking about training more and more. She wanted to attempt to call her power again and see if she could control it. But I had seen her power nearly kill her and take out half of a mansion. I saw it kill her grandmother, Elizabeth.

Kian, traitor that he was, told Eila it was her birthright to learn about her gift and protect herself. I wanted to stab him, even though I knew he was right.

But I couldn't let her use her gift again, for I feared what her power could do to her. What if it collapsed on her again, and this time I couldn't restart her heart? What if she practiced when I wasn't there, and it injured her? Or even worse, what if she failed to protect herself from one of my kind and she was killed? The vision of her dying at the hands of a Mortis ran a bitter knife through my heart.

"What's going through that thick head of yours?" asked Kian, rapping his knuckles on the edge of my board. A froth-tipped swell raised us a few feet and then dipped us into a watery valley, obscuring Eila from my view for a moment. I craned my neck to see her.

"She's fine Raef. If you stare at her any longer, your eyeballs are going to burn a hole through the atmosphere."

I glanced at Kian, his blond hair swept back from his face, and wondered how he could be so calm. Ana had nearly died two days before the Fire and Ice Ball, attacked by a Mortis who had gotten into Eila's house and threw her down a flight of stairs. He too knew what it was like

18

to watch the girl he loved nearly fade from this world.

He had saved her life by sharing his pilfered life-forces with her, nearly ending his own in the process. She didn't know how far he had pushed himself to save her that day and he didn't want her to know. I knew he had wanted to also heal her leg, but Eila's energy release inside the Breakers had temporarily disabled our ability to heal . . . both ourselves and others. Thus, Ana was on the mend the old fashioned way, which bothered Kian more than he let on.

While there was no arguing that Kian could be a complete egotistical ass, he was loyal to our dysfunctional crew and endlessly devoted to keeping Ana safe. And because Ana went where Eila did, he guarded them both, and for his help, I was truly grateful.

To say we were tight friends however, would be seriously overstating our relationship. We tolerated each other, disagreed on most things, but when it came to Eila and Ana, we were in perfect sync.

I also knew that his mind drifted to Ana like mine did to Eila. How far they got physically last summer was something he did not discuss. Yes, he was a jerk on occasion, but he also protected Ana's privacy. God help the man who ever dared to touch Ana wrong . . . or Eila.

My Eila.

Not long ago, a drunken footballer named Teddy Bencourt nearly took something from her that she wasn't willing to part with. I was almost too late, and seeing her fight him off caused the killer in me to burn like an Olympic torch. She had calmed me and I had yet to see the kid again, but if I did . . . not good.

"Do you hear me, man? You've got to ease up a bit. You look like roadkill."

19

I turned to him, giving him an unmistakable gesture with a certain finger.

He glanced over at Ana. She was talking to Eila and dusting off the pine bench near the top of the dunes. She moved to sit down and we automatically shifted our gazes to watch her and scan the area for any threat.

He looked back to me. "I'm serious though. When the hell was the last time you slept?"

"The night before the Breakers," I replied, fully aware that even for my kind, 35 days without sleep was pushing past our supernatural limits. It was also the one and only time I had slept beside Eila. The memory of that night rushed into me and I closed my eyes to clear my head.

Complicating my fatigue was the fact that I wasn't hunting animals very often. I never liked leaving Eila in anyone's care but mine, but not stealing animal life-forces on a regular basis was wearing me down. When I was truly desperate for a hit, injecting myself with corpse blood, which contained traces of a human life-force, would work. Briefly.

But what I really needed was a pure hit of power. I needed the soul of a living person.

"You are some kind of stupid, you know that?" grumbled Kian, shaking his head, which caused his board to subtly bounce in the water. "I know you are obsessed with her safety, but you are going to crash and burn at this rate, and you'll be of no use to anyone. Get it together before you become a liability."

I shook my head, "I'm okay. I'll be fine."

Kian looked at me and his face was serious, "No you're not, and soon you won't be."

I knew he was right, but more importantly I knew that only as my true self could I ever be Eila's savior. Only as a killer of mankind could I fully protect the girl I loved.

Which was why I needed to find a Dealer . . . and soon.

3 Eila

BY THE TIME WE GOT BACK to my house, the snow had really begun to fly. Thankfully my awesomely awesome Wrangler navigated the white roads easily. Our secret service duo followed us in Kian's new Range Rover, complete with surf-boards strapped to the top.

It looked entirely ridiculous.

They were about as stealthy as a hippo riding a tricycle.

Kian had bought the black, rock-stomper of a vehicle soon after his immortal ex-girlfriend, Collette, had taken his Corvette. It was a trade he grudgingly agreed to in order to acquire designer clothes for all of us when we went to the Fire and Ice Ball. The clothing was fantastic, but Kian was pissed about the loss of his fast machine. Luckily, he still had Cerberus – his multi-million dollar yacht that had become, briefly, our home away from home. It was the ultimate clubhouse, rolling on the sea.

Cerberus, however, had been shipped down to West Palm Beach for the winter and I honestly missed the yacht and the memories it held. MJ was supposed to check on it while visiting his family in Florida for Thanksgiving – lucky.

The yacht also became our salvation when my house was breeched by an uninvited visitor with lethal intents. While Cerberus was technically just a boat, it was also a weird sort of pal and we all missed her fabulosity.

I pulled my Jeep up to the side door of the house and cut the engine. The boys pulled in behind us just as I was getting out of the car, and I watched as the two killer bodyguards stepped out of the Rover and walked towards us in the falling snow. Their presence seemed almost surreal – my whole life did.

I was the owner of a magnificent Sea Captain home on Cape Cod, built by my 4th great grandparents, including Elizabeth who was one of the fiercest rebel fighters the Lunaterra and Mortis had ever known. I had inherited her dangerous talent, plus that of her guard and lover, Christian Raines. Supposedly I was a hybrid – a mix of two warring enemies, thanks to their forbidden affair.

Unfortunately, all I really wanted to be was a Barnstable High School senior and not look like an idiot in my school picture. Instead I was a rare, zillion-watt light bulb. I bet if I shook my family tree hard enough, Big Foot, Nessy, and even the Sea Witch would come tumbling out and squash me.

I got up close and personal with the Lunaterra side of me when I went all "mega-bomb" inside the Breakers. The Mortis part, however, didn't seem to show itself. I had no desire to suck the soul out of anyone, and I wasn't fast or strong . . . or immortal. At least I didn't think I was immortal. I was 17, soon to be 18, and "immortal" was decades away.

Raef and Kian were thankfully immune to my power, though they did

23

have a few dings and dents after my epic light show. We had known they were unaffected by my power since they had witnessed Elizabeth's death when she called on the limitless energy of the Core within the Web of Souls. Her lightning-like energy incinerated nut-job, Jacob Rysse, but didn't kill Raef or Kian – a fact for which I was extremely grateful. Her death sparked the local town myth that claimed she was struck by lightning.

Yeah – not quite.

It was entirely possible that the healing ability of the Mortis part of me allowed me to survive the Core collapse of my power inside the Breakers. When Elizabeth had tried it in 1851, she had been killed. Christian said he had found her, lifeless, in the harbor square after she had eliminated Rysse. He said he took her body and buried her and sent her necklace back to the young woman named Katherine who had altered it for her.

A necklace that unlocked Elizabeth's diary, and was now in the hands of my most loathed classmate: Nikki Shea.

I could kiss that sucker goodbye.

I slammed the driver's door shut and walked around the back towards Ana who was sliding out her side. Her walking boot was awkward, but soon would thankfully be retired. She wobbled slightly on the slick ground, but Kian was quickly next to her, one broad hand on her back.

"I am not a total klutz you know?" she protested, cursing the slushy driveway.

Kian slid her a sly smile. "Yeah, well . . . knowing your luck, you will slip and break the other leg and then I will be giving you piggy back rides

24

everywhere. Actually, I could get down with that arrangement."

Ana punched him in the arm, but then slipped. He grabbed her quickly and pinned her to his side. "Jeez woman! It wasn't a dare!"

"Will you just help me get inside already?" she sighed, gripping the front of his leather jacket tighter as she slowly made her way across the slick ground to the door. I followed, trying not to smile as she and Kian continued to argue about everything, including the size of the snowflakes.

Raef stepped in next to me, his hands in his black coat pockets. "So Kian and I are going to head back to Torrent Road briefly, get changed and then we'll be back."

I nodded, but a biting wind tore around the house and I tried to tuck my face down into my coat. Raef moved in front of me, shielding my face and body from the brutal gust. The treetops slashed back and forth violently in the gale, as if an invisible giant was pounding through the woods, but just as suddenly as it started, the wind died, and I was mere inches from Raef's chest.

He looked at me while he dusted the snow from my jacket hood. "I have a feeling we might lose power tonight. I'll make sure the fireplaces are ready to go, just in case."

"Mae will appreciate that. Thanks, Raef," I replied as we finally made it through the side door to the house.

Mae appeared from the laundry room, a basket of folded linens in her arms, her crazy red hair pinned up in a bun. "Hi Guys! How was the surfing?" she asked, sliding the basket onto the counter.

"Excellent, Ma'am," replied Kian, helping Ana to sit at the table. He knelt before her and started unstrapping the walking boot from her leg. Ana, never one to be pampered, immediately leaned forward to help, but

25

instead cracked heads with Kian. She bit back a swear as Kian sat back on his heels, "Can you just sit still for two seconds?"

"I can do it," she demanded, rubbing her head.

"I KNOW you can, but there is snow caked in the buckles. Just chill for one moment. Please."

Ana slouched, resigned, as Kian continued working on the boot. I hung my jacket by the door as Raef walked over to Mae. He smiled at her as he reached for the basket. "The waves were terrific. Perfect swells. Do you want this on the second floor landing as usual, Ms. Johnson?" he asked, shifting the basket in his hands.

"For the twentieth time, it's Mae. Please. And you don't need to do that. You and Kian have already done so much these past weeks. I would have been lost without you. All of you. Even Mr. Raines."

Ugh. The way the word *Raines* curled off her lip, I knew she had a serious crush on my soul-stealing, ultra-great grandfather.

I laid down the law with Christian Raines weeks ago; Mae was off limits. And while Christian had obeyed, having him a few miles away at his new Torrent Road home was causing quite the kerfuffle in both our house and throughout the town. He was, after all, Newport's Most Eligible Bachelor three years running, and now he was living in a massive stone villa known to the locals as the Island House, though we called it simply Torrent Road. Mae had no clue about Christian's darker side – or mine for that matter.

MJ argued that Raines should be disqualified from Newport's hot-hunk competition, since he was a Mortis. Soul-sharks, he said, had an unfair advantage in the looks department and as I studied Kian and Raef, I knew he was absolutely right.

26

Raef, with his very dark-blond hair, chiseled physique, flawless face, and stunning deep blue eyes, looked as though he fell off the front of a Hollister shopping bag. Kian, equally perfect, was taller, with blond hair that fell straight near his broad shoulders, as if he was a posterboy for a surfing company. Like Raef, his deep blue eyes hid a blackness that could blot out the blue, and his hands, so gentle with Ana, were capable of incredible violence. I saw him kill someone in front of me with those hands and witnessed the rage that encompassed his body when he did so. No remorse, no regret, but he saved my life and Ana's.

I wasn't super keen on having Christian so close, especially with the adoring stars in Mae's eyes. But Christian had helped us, enormously. He paid all my medical bills and he opened his house to both Kian and Raef, who needed somewhere to stay now that Cerberus was in southern waters for the winter.

Christian had also managed to charm the crap out of MJ's folks, convincing them that he would be an excellent silent partner at the Milk Way – basically he was their personal bank at a zero-percent interest rate. I'm pretty sure he did it to smooth over MJ's mom, whose anger about her son being involved in my crazy life was still at Code Red level.

Raines's home was also where all the books and papers from Dalca Anescu's shop, the Crimson Moon, were stashed. A shop that no longer existed, because Kian and Raef had burned the building to the ground, after removing any shred of evidence that could reveal our world to the FBI.

Torching the building was a risk. FBI Agents Mark Howe and Anthony Sollen had visited me in the hospital and several times at my house. They asked many questions, over and over, about what happened

27

in the Breakers and if I knew what happened to the Crimson Moon. I was worried that somehow, some way, they would realize I was the cause of the damage to the Breakers. But who in their right mind would ever believe that a teenager could channel a mythic power so brutal that it shattered a large portion of a famed, national treasure?

Yes, the FBI was sniffing around, but they were also chasing their tail.

I nodded to Ana, who was finally free of her black boot. "Want to go change? It's a fuzzy-pjs kind of day."

"Hell yes. I'm frozen," she replied as Kian pulled her to her feet. He pouted and Ana gave him a questioning look, "What?"

He shook his head, "I don't have any fuzzy PJs. I'm bummed." He gave her a smile and she shook her head, but a twisted grin escaped her lips. He turned to Mae and began chatting about the storm as Ana and I followed Raef out of the kitchen and up the main staircase to our rooms.

Raef set the basket of laundry near the door to the bathroom, which Ana and I shared. I pushed open my bedroom door as Ana did the same across the hall from me.

"You feeling okay?" asked Raef, as he leaned back against the wall next to the bathroom. To anyone else, Raef acted like a polite, helpful high schooler, which was what made his true identity all the more chilling. A Mortis was impossible for anyone to identify until it was too late. Mortis couldn't even pick out one another from a crowd, just as humans can't identify a convict in a room full of bikers.

"I feel good. I'm going to get into some cozy clothes and help Mae prep some food for tomorrow. You know she expects you and Kian to come to dinner, right?"

He nodded, "Yeah. Not sure how we are going to work around the food thing though." The reality was, Mortis didn't eat food. They noshed on life-forces, and the turkey downstairs in the fridge was definitely lacking in that department.

"Just come. You guys can make up an excuse – some strange fasting for an unknown religion or something. She is so excited to have company for Thanksgiving. We never do. It's always just the two of us, and Ana hasn't celebrated Turkey Day or Christmas since her dad died."

"I haven't celebrated either holiday since 1850," replied Raef, a smile pulling at his mouth. He stepped over to me and leaned down so he was eyeball-to-eyeball with me. "I'm actually looking forward to it."

"Really?" I squeaked. I was super excited to be having the holidays in my new home with my friends, Mae, and Raef. Sometimes I even laid in bed, thinking about finding that ideal tree with my four friends. Of course, Ana and MJ would argue over which evergreen was perfect, and she would make him spin each frothy spruce about 100 times, but I was silly-giddy about the whole season. I shook my fists dweebily and started to squeal, thrilled that he was happy.

"Okay – well it's not THAT exciting," he laughed and I couldn't help it – I crossed our hidden line and hugged him.

He stilled for just a moment and my heart damn near stopped, but then he wrapped his arms around me and pressed me into his solid chest. My throat tightened and I managed to whisper, "Don't take too long at Christian's."

He pulled back from me, just enough to see my face and my glassy eyes. "Am I ever gone long?"

I laughed, "No, I guess not. Am I just that addictive?"

He swallowed and looked more serious, "I'd say that's an understatement."

I heard the door click shut across the hall, and Raef released me, turning to see Ana in a pair of mis-matched PJs. Raef nodded to her fuzzy pants, covered with a certain green, Dr. Suess character. "Is that Elmo?"

Ana looked horrified, "Elmo? Are you color blind? Elmo is red and this . . ." she pointed to one of the emerald faces, " . . . is THE GRINCH! You know, for someone who has been around for almost two centuries, you really are lacking in your furry-monster identification skills."

"I'll be sure to work on that," replied Raef, amused. He looked back at me as I bit back a smile. "I've got to go so I can get back before the storm really hits. Do you two want anything while I'm out?"

"Christmas Tree Peeps!" said Ana, raising her hand.

"What in the world is a Peep?" asked Raef.

Ana slapped her hand to her forehead, "Oh my god, you guys are like aliens. How do you not know what Peeps are? Are you from another planet?"

Raef just shrugged, "I don't exactly go the grocery store."

"It's okay, Raef. Ana and I are going to help Mae, and maybe overdose on some cookie dough, so forget the Peeps," I smiled.

"Okay then. I'll be back, sans Peeps . . . whatever they are." He turned to Ana, "And I'll see you soon as well, Elmo."

He headed downstairs, while Ana protested fiercely, "IT'S NOT ELMO!"

I CROSSED THE LINE. Ran clean through my wall.

But the worst part was, I didn't care, because for one moment I had Eila in my arms. As Kian and I drove over to Torrent Road, I reran how she felt against me over and over. Allowing myself to be distracted by my feelings for Eila could only lead to disaster, but I could feel how desperately she held onto me. How could I ever rebuild the wall between us without breaking her heart?

I looked over at Kian, and realized he had done it. He had left Ana last summer, despite how much he loved her. He left because she told him to, knowing that there were random Mortis trolling the Cape waters for victims. How was he so sure she could defend herself?

"I know I am way better looking than your sorry ass, but staring is annoying," said Kian, never taking his eyes from the road. I gave a clipped laugh.

He ran a gloved hand over the Rover's black steering wheel. "Did you kiss her?" he asked, never one to skirt the issues.

"No," I replied, refusing to ever divulge details of what Eila and I shared when we were alone. I protected her, privacy included.

"Liar. You came down from her room like a man reborn. I heard something about Elmo, but I sure as shit hope that has nothing to do with your lighter mood." When I didn't reply, a knowing, devious grin curled onto his lips and I wanted to punch him in the head, though that desire was nothing new. "You bloody well kissed her. You have zero self-control."

I turned slightly in my seat, anger slowly rising inside me. I had more self-control than Kian could ever drag out of every cell in his body. "Is that what allowed you to leave Ana behind? Self-Control? Or did you just not really give a damn last summer at all?" Okay – I knew that last part was a lie, but I just wanted to piss him off.

Kian's head swung sharply in my direction and his glare was like steel, "Don't you ever accuse me of not worrying about Ana. She is all I care about. All I think about."

"Oh really? Because you seemed to walk away last summer without looking back." I was on a roll, frustrated and angry, and Kian was an easy target.

"Because it was what she wanted!" he hissed back, as he hooked a left into Torrent Road. Christian's home appeared like a crouching giant at the very end of the lane.

He pulled up to the front entrance and slammed the shift into park, turning to me. "Yes, I left her because she wanted me gone. But in the time I had with her, I showed her how to protect herself. I encouraged her to practice her psychic abilities and use them as a defense system,

32

which you are NOT doing for Eila. I still worried, every second of every day, but I loved her enough to believe in her, and I left her with all the knowledge I could."

I growled in frustration as I rubbed my forehead. Deep down I knew Kian probably climbed the walls once he left Ana behind. There was one huge contrast between the girls though. "It's different with Eila. What if I encourage her to train and she kills herself?" I questioned, staring out the snowy windshield at Christian's house.

"Then I guess we better figure out how to train her without her dying. You put her in danger when you show no confidence in her and leave her with no weapons. Right now, YOU are her biggest safety threat, Raef. She was strongest going into the Breakers because you believed in her and the two of you didn't try to box away that freaky connection you both share. You've cut her off from your confidence *and* your love, moron. I would never do that to Ana." He yanked the key from the ignition and stepped out of the SUV, slamming the door shut in his wake.

I sat in the silence of the Ranger's black interior and watched Kian walk through the snow and up the granite stairs to Christian's house. Could he actually be right? I liked to think I always knew best when it came to Eila's protection, but what he said did make some sense . . . and holding her again was a lot more appealing than keeping her at arm's length.

Could we have both? Did strength and courage only grow when we were connected? Maybe she only needed me, backing her up and believing that she could be a brilliant fighter, just like Elizabeth.

Elizabeth, whom I watched die.

33

I literally felt ill when I remembered back to what Elizabeth looked like, dead on the cobblestone street in 1851. Eila had looked so similar that night at the Breakers.

My stress level jumped clear off the chart at the thought of Eila attempting to call the Web of Souls' energy. We had no clue how a Lunaterra commanded the Web. The disaster in the Breakers was an overload of her power and entirely uncontrolled. An allergic reaction to what I had done to her.

Through the windshield I saw Kian staring at me. He thumbed back at the house, signaling me to get inside with him. I growled as I pushed out the passenger door and walked through the snow to where he stood. I was exhausted, hungry, and angry that I didn't know how to help the girl I loved.

Kian was still glaring at me as the snow fell around us. His look was hard, but he finally sighed and ran his hand down his face. "Look, man, we'll figure it out. We have all of Dalca's crap here and Elizabeth's diary. Once we get the necklace back from Bitchy-Pants and unlock the book, I am sure there will be a written recipe for frying soul thieves inside that Eila can follow. Until then, we just keep an eye out for anything odd and give the girls some self-defense training, human-style." Kian grinned, "Plus, rolling around on gym-mats gives me a chance to pin Ana to the floor."

"Ana knows all about your wandering hands. She'll neuter you before you can even call for mercy," I replied.

"Yes – but then hopefully she will be guilt ridden, and pamper me."

I just shook my head. Even though Kian and I were living at Torrent Road, we didn't get to just talk much. One of us was usually around

Eila's house, so we barely passed one another. Our days and nights were filled with searching through Dalca's books and papers, tracking the occasional visit from F-B-Irritating Agent Howe, and keeping a watchful eye out for any visiting Mortis.

Christian, who had a larger presence in the soul thief underground than we did, also kept tabs on any possible chatter related to the Breakers. He was concerned that if other Mortis realized the explosion was due to a Lunaterra, Eila could be targeted for elimination. There were many soul thieves who had fought against the Lunaterra and would no doubt freak if they knew one lived.

Christian, I had to begrudgingly admit, was an asset.

I, however, was becoming a liability. I hadn't hunted since the Breakers and I needed to hunt. Now.

Kian was about to unlock the deadbolt, but I stopped him, placing a hand on the mahogany door, now lightly painted with snow. "I'm in the mood for dinner on the run. Care to come?"

Kian looked at me, surprised for an instant, but then a cocky smile spread on his face. "Hell yeah. Sandy Neck?"

I snatched the keys out of his hand. "I'll drive."

5 Raef

THE AREA KNOWN AS SANDY NECK stretched miles along the northern coast of the Cape. While some portions were accessible by four-wheel-drive vehicles, most of the land was an untouched, sandy forest. It also contained herds of deer and packs of coywolves. For soul thieves trying to stick to an animal diet, it was an excellent place to hunt Bambies, since the carcasses would be finished off by the hungry, coyote-wolf hybrids.

On the downside, animals were harder to sneak up on than people. Animals could sense our approach – could sense that though we smelled and looked like humans, we were anything but human. They sensed the void of a soul, unlike a human whose higher brain function was too busy processing the world around them to comprehend our true, dangerous intent.

But unlike an animal, a human soul was the purest hit of power. A rush, like injecting adrenaline and cocaine into your heart at once.

Those Mortis who killed people on a regular basis were able to seamlessly control the voids of light that the human world saw as shadows. To a Mortis, a shadow looked like a transformable liquid midnight – a living smoke that whispered temptations to us and obeyed our demands. It could coat our skin in blackness, enabling us to hide where the light did not breech.

True Mortis, who killed humans, were perfect stalkers and untouchable in strength. They were living nightmares, both intoxicating and deadly. They were whom I feared the most when it came to Eila and Ana, because as I was right now, I doubted my ability to kill one in a fight.

Hunting deer would give me short-lived strength and energy, but if I wanted to be an equal match to the most dangerous Mortis, I needed to return to my roots and seek out a human hit. It was something that I knew Eila would *strongly* object to.

Kian and I had been walking through the scrub pines silently, checking for signs of deer in the landscape. Hunting was something we both had done when we were human, though back then we both favored a bow as our weapon of choice.

Nowadays we favored our bare hands.

I heard the soft snuffling of something farther in the woods – a noise far too quiet for human ears, but easily heard by both of us. I slowly crouched to the ground looking in the direction of where the deer was foraging. Kian backed up slowly into the shade of a pine and seamlessly called the shadows over his body, disappearing into the darkness.

I knew he shouldn't be able to control the shadows when he supposedly hadn't been hunting humans. I glared at the darkness of the tree where I knew he stood, now almost completely invisible, and understanding took hold, fueling both my anger and envy.

Kian had apparently been sneaking around killing people – a tidbit of critical information he had not shared with me. I was going to force a confession from his lying lips, but right now I needed the life-force of this one doe who was pawing at the underbrush below the snowy blanket.

The animal turned slightly from me and I saw my chance. I bolted across the small clearing, moving at a speed that was nearly impossible for an animal or human to track. The doe caught scent of me just as I was upon her, but I swung up and over her back before she could flee, grabbing her soft neck and hauling her to the snowy ground with a crash.

She had no chance the moment I touched her.

Holding one hand to her chest and the other to her muzzle as she wailed, I immediately began drawing her life-force from her, weakening her quickly and calming her pleading calls. While velvet fur covered much of her graceful body, the area around her eyes showed the soft ripple effect of gentle light that pulsed beneath her skin as I pulled the energy from her body. Her free-running soul, her essence, felt like fire in my veins.

My own skin, now covered with Fallen markings, flared like a heartbeat as I drank in her soul through my touch alone. Her huge, brown eyes, so terrified when I first touched her, now softened. Her breathing slowed and her body relaxed as she weakened towards death. I pulled from her gently, doing my best to control my need, which urged me to brutally rip her life from her. To sate my hunger instantly, rather than in slow, controlled drags.

38

I could cause bone-breaking pain if I wanted to. I could make the last seconds of life be the most terrifying, excruciating final moments for my victims, but I tried to take out my targets with compassion. I had to survive at their expense, but I didn't want them to suffer needlessly. But every once in a while, I failed to control my need and my victims . . . paid dearly.

I could feel the current of the doe's life-force trickle down to a thin stream as she exhaled one final time and stilled, her eyes seeing no more. The pulse of my own marks slowed and faded from my skin as I finished off what she had to offer.

I felt strong. Alive. As if a weight had been lifted from me. I felt like I could fly, high off the power the deer had given me.

"Feeling better?" asked Kian, walking up to me and the dead deer. It took me a moment to regain my balance. I had been starving for so long, I hadn't realized how severe it had been. I was actually light-headed, and my vision was near blinding. My body, finally resetting after such a long run of deprivation, felt incredible. Strong, healthy, and dangerously powerful.

Finally I turned to him, my look hard. "Since when did you start offing people?" I asked, angry that he had left me out. I had thought we were on the same page with regards to hunting, and now I was just pissed that I hadn't gone with him, so I could have taken a few lives as well. How quickly my moral center shifted when it came to protecting Eila.

Kian gave a knowing grin. "I never really stopped, just more-or-less went on a diet," he said, stepping closer to me, a glint of the devil in his eyes. "But the animal-only diet sucked, and once the Breakers happened, I jumped off the wagon. Care to come on one of MY hunts next time?"

I didn't even need to debate my answer. Eila was everything to me and if it meant that I needed to claim the life of a man or woman to protect her, so be it. Not to mention, I wanted the hit. I craved it.

"Absolutely," I replied.

Kian grabbed the keys back from me. "I'll drive, Miss Daisy. You do know the speedometer makes it over 50, right?"

I didn't reply, the adrenaline in my veins running wild. With the deer's life-force flowing through me, I felt reborn. Only one thought blazed in my mind: getting back to Eila and wrapping myself in her breathy laugh and luminous smile.

I needed to calm down before I saw her, however. After so long without a kill, the new power flowing through me was fraying my self-control. I would get used to the soul-high once I started hunting regularly again, but at the moment every dangerous cell in my body was demanding that I ravage Eila the instant I got to her house. And this kind of ravaging would definitely lead from breathy laughter to breathy gasps, and a decided lack of clothing.

In my current state I was very, *very* unsafe for Eila.

Kian stepped in front of me, one knowing eyebrow raised. "Yeah - there ain't no way I'm bringing you back to Eila when you are this cranked-up. You need to run-off the excess, lover-boy."

"Race you to the car?" I offered

"Try to keep up Granny," replied Kian, and he shot off in the direction of the Rover at a break-neck speed. I, however, beat him to the vehicle, and thus was the first to notice that our run was about to get a whole lot longer.

Someone had slashed the tires of Kian's SUV.

"JESSE SAYS THE GAME HAS been postponed to Sunday night," announced Ana, closing her texting app and sliding her phone behind her. She sat on the kitchen counter in her Grinch pants, licking the last remnants of cookie dough from an oversized spoon. Her bare feet bounced to the radio station's hour-long set of Christmas songs.

I sat cross-legged on the kitchen floor near one of the ornate heat registers, keeping myself toasty warm. The hot cocoa in my JAWS mug gave off the most delicious double-chocolate aroma, which was probably the reason why it was disappearing so fast. "I've only been to a couple of football games at my old school, but they were usually the ones earlier in the season."

"Cold-phobic?" asked Ana, dropping the clean spoon in the sink.

"I'm happily frying griddle marks on my rear end thanks to the radiator, so yeah – I am definitely allergic to anything below 40."

Ana snorted as she hopped down from the counter. "Well, you've

41

got to go, especially since Jesse keeps reminding me *constantly* that you *need* to come. I am just about ready to give him your cell number, because this secretary gig is getting old."

"Oh – please don't," I moaned. "He's really a nice guy, but I don't want him to think I'm interested in him when I'm not."

Though he was busy as captain of the football team, Jesse Vale had managed to coordinate all my missed schoolwork from the two classes we had together. He would hand off his copied notes and papers to MJ, who would dutifully bring them to my home. While I was hoping he did it purely out of friendship, I was starting to worry that he was developing feelings for me, and I didn't want to accidentally lead him on.

But he had been my schoolwork gofer and I owed him, so when he asked that I come to the football game, I agreed. I was actually looking forward to the high school's annual rivalry game with another town, but then I realized that there would be two other people in attendance who I did NOT want to bump into: Nikki Shea and Teddy Bencourt.

Nikki wanted to slowly kill me, and Teddy almost drunkenly assaulted me. Talk about a bad combination.

Unfortunately, I had already promised Jesse. Plus, Ana had assured me that she would bring along her pepper spray, which had been a gift from Kian last summer. She said she would happily spray first, ask questions later, which was not a good idea with Ana.

She'd spray just about everyone.

So, I did the only thing I could: I sucked it up. No fear, live hard, and all that jazz. Plus, I would be in the bleachers with a zillion other screaming fans, who would be witnesses if needed.

Of course, I was praying there would be no incidents, period, and therefore no need for witnesses. I was also going to demand a guard-free football game, because Ana and I needed to show the boys that we could be fine on our own.

Kian and Raef had returned from Torrent Road a while ago, but on foot. Apparently some jerkface thought it would be fun to vandalize the Rover's tires, and Kian was not pleased – and no doubt would kill the fool who mucked with his ride, if he could find him.

After a few phone calls, Kian managed to locate a tow company that was able to go get the Rover and replace the tires. Initially they had said the vehicle wouldn't be ready until after Thanksgiving, but then Kian mentioned a sizable bonus to any mechanic who had the Rover repaired and delivered to 408 by the day's end. Sure enough, Kian's vehicle was back at my house within 90 minutes and one underpaid mechanic was a grand richer.

While they had been waiting for the car to arrive, Kian and Raef had started moving the firewood from the barn out back, to the side of the house for easy access. The wind and snow had picked up as the storm bore down on the Cape, and the lights had flickered inside 408 a few times.

While the boys did their thing, Ana and I had helped Mae make cookies and prep the pies for tomorrow's feast. Mae was on cloud nine that she actually got to entertain a real group of friends for Thanksgiving. Ana and I had hung out in the cookie-scented kitchen, chatting and waiting for Kian and Raef to be done. Mae eventually headed upstairs to sew little lace leaves on cloth napkins.

Yeah . . . she was just a wee bit excited.

"I'm in the mood to zone with a movie. Wadda ya say?" asked Ana, pulling a bottled water out of the fridge.

"Movie sounds good. Can I take my butt-warmer with me?"

"Uh . . . no. But when Raef comes in I'm going to tell him that you have a new radiator marking on your rear. Think he will want to examine that one as well?"

I blushed hot. Raef had seen the kill mark on my lower back the night he pulled me from the Town Neck River. I was raised believing that the mark was a radiator burn from childhood, but I was wrong. My mark was a sign of my dangerous lineage and it had changed since the Breakers. Christian said it would evolve every time I killed, just as Elizabeth's had.

The side door swung open and a blast of snow raced into the room, smacking me in the face. I squealed and scrambled to my feet as Raef came through the door, his arms loaded with wood. Kian followed, his arms equally full, and kicked the door shut behind him. A dusting of white littered the tile, but was quickly melting.

"Sorry E!" called Raef, as he headed into the parlor with the wood.

"It's okay!" I called back as I grabbed a rag from the counter and started wiping up the floor. Once done, I tossed the rag to Ana, who pitched it in with the dirty pile in the laundry room that was attached to the kitchen. We headed into the parlor and watched as Raef and Kian stacked the wood beside the ornate fireplace. Soon the boys had a luminous, orange fire crackling.

I sat on the floor near the couch as Ana riffled through the movies under the TV. Raef slid back to sit next to me, his long legs kicked out in front of him.

"So how is Christian?" I asked, admiring how the wood popped and

44

crackled under the flames. I had yet to actually go inside Christian's new Torrent Road home. It just felt weird that he was my grandfather, especially since he looked like he was only in his late 20s. Even more insane was that he was technically my FOURTH great grandfather. It was taking a while to adjust to those time-warping details.

"We didn't actually see Christian. We ended up heading to Sandy Neck to go hunting. That's where Kian got the flat tires." Raef leaned his head back slightly, resting it against the couch cushions.

"I can't believe someone would flatten his tires. Some people are such . . . such . . . poop-heads!"

Raef looked at me, "Really? Poop-heads?"

"I'm trying not to swear too much. I need to work on my creativity, obviously."

Raef smiled, "Maybe just a little."

"I'm glad you went hunting. I mean, you did seem kind of beat. I take it you're feeling better?" I leaned my head back as well, and our eyes were even with one another.

"Yeah. It's good . . . I didn't realize how rundown I was. I haven't hunted in so long."

Had he starved himself? Good grief, why? I furrowed my brow and sat up quickly. He followed suit. "You haven't been hunting? Why on earth not?

He shrugged, "I just didn't want to leave you alone. And I have hunted, just not that often. It's not a big deal, really."

"It is a big deal, Raef! Don't starve for me! And I am safe. For the thousandth time, no one is hunting me down."

"Except the FBI."

45

I smacked him in the arm, pissed that he would deny himself the one thing that kept him alive in order to ensure my survival.

His mouth tipped up, amused at my pitiful punch, so I went to whack him again, but he snatched my wrist, holding it snuggly in his wide palm. My skin tingled softly where he touched and he tugged me towards him, bringing my face closer to his.

"I just want you safe, E. And I realize now that not hunting enough actually makes me more of a liability. But don't worry. I'll hunt more."

I looked at his storm-blue eyes for a moment, allowing myself to enjoy our close proximity. I could hear the voices of Kian and Ana discussing which movie to watch, but their conversation barely registered in my head. I was as close to Raef as I was the night he first kissed me, and thus my brain wasn't functioning too well anymore. I swallowed and finally pulled myself out of my momentary stupor.

"We had an agreement that you have not honored. If you really want me safe, you will help me train," I whispered.

His face tensed and his grip on my wrist tightened. "I know. And I'm sorry I haven't supported you on that. But I will – I promise. Just let me figure out where we can train and how. We can't risk attracting any more government goons. And we do it in stages. Basic self-defense first, okay?"

"Ana comes along as well," I demanded. It wasn't a question, but a statement of fact.

He gave a quick nod, "The Elmo groupie learns to kick ass too."

I snorted a laugh, "It's not Elmo!"

"All furry monsters are the same in my book," replied Raef, finally releasing my hand.

"I'm telling MJ you said that!" I chided, knowing that MJ, whose ability to shift into a massive, black dog was ridiculously cool, would be highly insulted. MJ, once in his dog-form, was one formidable fighter and pretty darn lethal when matched against a Mortis. In his human form, however, he was just a big, lean goofball.

Raef smiled, but then his face grew more serious. "There was another part to that deal we had."

Holy chicken nuggets, I didn't think he would bring that up. Uh, yeah there was another part to the deal, regarding his lips and mine. My voice came out a little hoarse, "Yeah. I remember the other part. Are you thinking we should entertain a few revisions?"

"Maybe just a few," he grinned. "But only if you're okay with it."

"YES!" I shouted in his face. It was so uncool, but the shine in Raef's eyes spoke volumes.

Ana's head popped up, a DVD in her hand with two elderly actors on the front, "Really? You want to watch The King's Speech?"

Raef and I both turned to her and Kian, "The King's Speech? What? No – pick something funny – or scary, Ana."

"I thought his stuttering was both unnerving and amusing," added Kian, pulling another DVD from the boxes under the TV. I felt Raef's hand graze my own as he got up, and suddenly these random touches once again meant something to me. Not just an accidental connection, but a stolen moment of affection we shared. Suddenly, I was heading back in the right direction with the boy I adored.

A holiday freakin' miracle for sure! What the heck did he hunt, and where can I find him more?

Raef slid up next to Ana and poked around the box, finally pulling out a greenish colored movie. "How about this?" In his hand was *How The Grinch Stole Christmas.*

My cheer for the furry green villain movie quickly dissolved into a pissed-off groan as the power flickered and finally cut out.

"Terrific," protested Ana as Kian muttered a small thanks to the weather, which spared him the rhyming abilities of little Cindy-Lou Who. He stood up and pulled Ana to her feet, "Come on Klutzy. Let's go find the flashlights."

"Call me Klutzy again and I'll key your new Range Rover," she replied smoothly. I heard Kian demand that she stop pinching him as they left the room, with Kian leading the way as he saw easily without the light.

In the fire-strewn darkness I could make out Raef's strong, golden outline as he pushed the DVDs back into the cabinet and moved next to me. "Not afraid of the dark, are you?" he asked quietly.

I smiled, his blue eyes nearly black in the room's shadows. Outside, the wind sounded like an angry dragon, raging against the antique beams of my house. Inside however, the fire coated a small perimeter of the parlor in a haunting light, outlining the stunning profile of the devoted killer beside me.

"With you next to me Raef, I fear nothing."

THE SMELL OF CINNAMON AND COFFEE lured me out of my

warm cocoon of sleep. I blinked into the early morning sunlight filling the parlor and listened to the echoing quiet of the house. The soft drip of Mae's coffee maker confirmed that the power had returned and the brilliant blue outside the window revealed a crystal clear sky. I realized I must have nodded off in front of the fire last night, because I was still camped out on the floor, but somehow I had acquired what felt like a pillow. It was a bit too firm though.

I moved slightly and realized the pillow was attached to a perfectly sculpted forearm . . . and hand, which had my long hair gently woven through its fingers. Something warm and solid tightened around my waist and my eyes widened as I realized Raef was tucked against my back, one of his arms supporting my head and the other clasped around my waist.

Sweet baby dolphins everywhere, Raef was SPOONING me, his chest pressed firmly against my back.

49

Now acutely aware of my surroundings, I could feel his warm breath on the back of my neck as he slept. I wanted to turn to him, but I was terrified he would wake and realize he had jumped headfirst into those revisions we had briefly mentioned last night.

Heck, he was WAY MORE than touching me. He was holding me as if I would disappear - as if I would fade into the molecules in the air. I swallowed and stayed still, taking inventory of his hard body against mine, and how we seemed to fit so perfectly together.

A metal pan scraped against something in the kitchen, breaking the silence of the house, and I felt Raef take a deep breath and stretch ever so slightly.

Then he froze.

Crap.

I stayed still, hoping he would think I was asleep. Hoping he wouldn't suddenly shoot across the room, taking with him the warmth and safety I felt in his arms.

He didn't move for what felt like forever, keeping his arm around my waist, but then I felt him softly spread his fingers out over my stomach. It took everything I had not to spontaneously combust.

I felt his forehead touch the back of my neck and he drew a slow, deep breath against my shoulder blade. It sent electricity fanning out from my skin and down my arm. All ability to control myself fled my body and I dragged in a shaky breath.

He loosened his grip and I rolled onto my back, his arm still behind my head and his hand just below my belly button. His fingers grazed the area of my skin that was now exposed thanks to a too-short tanktop.

God bless the discount rack at Abercrombie.

"Uh . . . good morning," I said, my voice a little dry.

"Good morning," he replied, quietly. "I didn't mean to wrap myself around you like that. I don't even remember doing it."

Pfft . . . no worries!

"You just needed a snuggle-buddy," I replied, flashing him a knowing grin, but my face started to flush. Oh my god . . . that was so lame.

Raef gave a soft smile and was about to reply, but a paisley pillow shot up from behind him and wacked him in the back of his head. "HEY!" he protested.

"Will you two SHUT UP!" moaned Ana who was sprawled on the floor as well. "I think I might actually throw up in my mouth. *Will you be my snuggly-swuggly pooh bear?* UGH! Seriously – I'm gonna barf."

I blushed hot and sat up as Raef's hand fell away from my tummy. He slowly got to his feet, tossing the pillow that attacked him onto the couch. He stretched, looking really well rested for the first time in weeks, and his black t-shirt rode up just enough to torment the heck out of me.

He looked down to where I sat on the floor, scrambled hair and silly PJs most likely making me quite the sight to see. "I'm going to go bring in some more wood and see if Mae needs anything," he said, taking his fine self and walking into the kitchen. I heard him greet Mae, though Mae returned a clipped *Hello*, and then the side door closed.

I turned to Ana who was still sprawled on the floor with pillows and blankets. "What the hell woman?"

"SNUGGLE BUDDY? That's all you can come up with after not having your hands on him for how long?" laughed Ana.

"Hey – at least I could speak. I was so shocked that he was with me, I thought I was hallucinating. Did you fall asleep down here too?"

51

"No. I went to my room, but was freezing by one in the morning. Kian and Raef were down here talking while keeping the fire going, and you were drooling on the floor, so I figured I'd camp out too, minus the unsexy drooling of course."

"I do not drool!" I laughed, horrified.

"Well, maybe not, but you do have a line indented on the side of your face from how you were sleeping," she smirked.

"I do not!" I protested, but then felt my cheek. Sure enough I had a long groove running the length of my face.

Terrific.

Mae appeared in the parlor doorway, her arms crossed over a stained plaid apron. "I need to talk to both you girls. Now, please."

That didn't sound very promising. I glanced at Ana, who gave me a curious look, but we followed Mae back into the kitchen where feast preparations were in full swing.

"Sit," Mae instructed as she poured herself a fresh cup of coffee. She added some sugar and slowly turned to face us as she stirred the caffeine. The soft clink of her spoon against the cup seemed to echo ominously in the silent room. What was she up to?

"Um – did I forget to take the trash out or something?" I asked, daring a nervous glance to Ana. Mae cleared her throat, a sure sign of whatever she was about to say was not going to be enjoyable.

"Raef and Kian are lovely young men. They've helped me out enormously while the two of you have been laid-up, and I am very grateful for all they have done. However, what I am about to say is non-negotiable."

Oh please – don't say it. Don't go there.

"Sex should be between two people that are in love and are mature enough to understand the ramifications of such an activity."

Yup. She went there. I'd bet the deed to the house it was because Raef had been curled around me, too.

The color drained entirely from Ana's face.

"Mae – you really don't . . ." I started, but she raised a hand to silence me. It was very possible I would never recover from this conversation. I was sure Ana's ears were shriveling off her head as Mae spoke.

"I am not so naïve that I do not see how you four act around each other. It's obvious that there are feelings that go far beyond friendship between you two and the boys. All I ask is that you girls are careful, use your head. Don't do something you're pressured into. And for heaven's sake, if you are determined to do it, DON'T do it under this roof and always, *always* be protected."

Silence descended on the room, as if a black hole had opened up on the table, sucking all gravity and sound from the kitchen.

Mae stood there, glancing at the two of us.

I was so mortified. I slid my eyes to the kitchen door that Raef had passed through minutes ago. If he was still anywhere near the side of the house, his supernatural hearing would have just offered him an earful. Kill. Me. Now.

Ana, no doubt ready to perform a self-inflicted mental exorcism to erase the past few moments, hopped up from her seat as if she had been scalded.

"Right. Good talk. Will keep it under advisement. Gotta get dressed," she declared, bolting from the room. I think her little feet actually left a smoke trail in their wake. Her leg was definitely all healed.

I glanced at Mae and she eyed me over her steaming cup of coffee as she took a sip.

Somebody save me.

THE INSTANT I MADE IT OUT the side door I gasped for the icy air to fill my lungs. I tried to right my head, tried to get my thoughts back into order, but somehow I had wound myself around Eila last night and slept. Really, REALLY slept. It was the best night's rest I had had in years. Not just in the last few months, but in decades.

I remember laying down next to her when she began softly talking in her sleep. She was saying my name, but she seemed frightened, the dream apparently threading its way into a nightmare. I couldn't understand all that she said, but I began talking to her quietly, telling her I was with her. Telling her she wasn't alone and praying I wasn't the monster in her dream.

At one point she moved and rolled onto my arm, and her fears seemed to fall away when she made contact with me. Not wanting to disturb her, I laid there, on the floor next to her, letting her use my arm as a pillow.

Then I fell asleep . . . and woke up wrapped around her.

As I reran the evening in my head, Kian came around the side of the house, an axe hanging easily from his hand. He swung it lazily into a large stump near the steps and it lodged itself at a perfect angle.

"So, correct me if I am wrong Raef, but wasn't there some ultra-dumb idea that you and Sparky had about NOT touching each other? Because what I saw this morning didn't seem to line up with my understanding of the Keep-Away game."

"Yeah – that was an accident."

Kian just laughed. "Keep telling yourself that and maybe some sucker in another galaxy will believe you. You guys are just too –"

I held up my hand to quiet Kian's irritating speech as I heard Eila's voice in the kitchen. We both could hear her easily through the walls of her home, a perk of being a soul thief. She was talking about trash, and then Mae started talking about us and . . .

Damn.

Apparently when she wanted to be, Mae Johnson was nothing if not direct. Kian and I stood frozen in place in the driveway, listening.

After what had to be the worse anti-pep-talk ever, Ana excused herself abruptly and Eila managed to get away a few seconds later. Kian opened his mouth to say something, no doubt snarky, but then just shook his head as he walked away. Mae Johnson had left Kian O'Reilly speechless. I needed to buy her a trophy.

A few seconds later, my phone pinged and I pulled it from my jacket. Eila had texted me:

~~ OMG. Did U hear that?

I winced. I took a moment before responding. Honesty I supposed was the best policy . . . just not this time.

Hear what? ~~

~~ NEVERMIND!

I couldn't help but laugh. The reality was, getting involved with a human in *that* way wasn't a good idea and Eila knew it. Humans were breakable, and Mortis? Mortis played rough. We stuck to our own kind in that arena. Plus, Eila wasn't just human – she was Lunaterra and she didn't know how to control her power yet. That could go very badly for both of us. It would probably result in a real burning bed.

That whole idea would not be wise. Crazy even. I was supposed to be protecting her and going in that direction with Eila was the polar opposite of playing it safe. I wasn't even supposed to be touching her, though I blew that rule right out of the water last night. Thank goodness Eila seemed okay with me next to her. Plus – she seemed onboard with the "revisions" idea.

I loved that about her. She just went for it – for life, for new experiences. She was fearless and didn't hold back. She gave of herself freely, never expecting repayment. She loved fiercely, lived fiercely, and consumed my universe like an endless star.

Of course, Eila wasn't just Lunaterra. She was also Mortis . . . like me. She existed because a Lunaterra and a Mortis had a child together, which brought me back to the whole idea of her and me.

We shared something – a warped but potent electricity, which wove between us in an intoxicating way. I saw it spark inside her when I was close to her, and felt it like a beautiful, icy burn when I kissed her. But to go *that* far with her? No. No way.

Suddenly I tensed as a horrible thought, dark and possessive, took hold inside of me. What if a boy *had* used her and then left her? What if some boy took her sweet, wild nature and shattered her heart? When I met her, she never mentioned a boyfriend in her past, but then again, we never discussed such *details* as we were preoccupied with running from a clan of Mortis who wanted her as a weapon. But what if some boy had seen her as a brief fling and tossed her aside? He could kiss his life goodbye if he had.

My phone pinged and mercifully snapped me out of my way-too-vivid imagination.

~~ **Ana and I are going to the cemetery.**

Not alone they weren't.

K – I'll drive you. ~~
~~ **You don't have to.**

I'll just follow you anyway. ~~

~~ **Sky falling, Chicken Little?**

With you? Always. ~~

I stared at the screen a moment longer. Ana was going to visit her father's gravesite, which Kian would definitely want to know. I walked around the side of the house, where Kian was leaning against the wood stack, his face turned into the sun.

He heard me coming and sighed, "I miss the south. I can't understand why anyone would willingly stay in this frozen wasteland. I sure as hell haven't done so for more than a century. New Englanders have a screw loose, I swear."

When I didn't respond he opened his eyes and looked at me. I must have had a strained expression on my face, because he got serious fast, "What is it?"

I held up my phone, "Ana and E are heading to the cemetery, I'm going to drive them. I just thought you should know." Kian pushed away from the woodpile just as the side door to the house banged open. He moved quickly past me and I followed. Ana and Eila were coming out of the house, Ana making a beeline for the Jeep.

She looked upset. Ana Lane never looked upset.

She was the text-book definition of a locked vault.

Kian saw it too and quickly got next to her and started walking with her. He was as distressed as she was, "What's the matter? What's wrong?"

"I'm okay," she said quietly as she continued to head toward the Jeep, her bottom lip trembling ever so slightly. She was holding it together, but barely. What in the world was going on?

Kian got right in front of her, but was careful not to touch her, as if doing so would cause a chain reaction in Ana. In some ways, Ana's father was in the ground because of him, a fact that would always hang over the two of them. "You're not okay. I can see you're not. Please, don't shut me out."

Ana couldn't seem to force any words through her mouth, no doubt afraid that her faltering strength would crack.

"Pix! Talk to me – what is it?" pleaded Kian. Ana halted in her tracks, blinking a few times, apparently stunned. Kian even seemed a bit floored at what he had just said, but then she pushed past him. As she moved towards the car, I could see the pain in Kian's face mirror Ana's.

I could feel his agony even at a distance.

Eila walked by me, a sad but determined look on her face, and squeezed my arm while handing me the keys to her Wrangler. Ana was already flipping the passenger seat forward and climbing into the back. She slammed the seat back into place and wiped at her cheek with a mitten-covered hand, keeping her eyes focused out the plastic side window. I walked past Kian as Eila climbed into the seat beside the driver's.

I shut the door for her and came around the hood, but Kian intercepted me. "Text me when you get there and let me know what's up. You keep my girl safe, Raef." It was a command, not a request, and I understood his need to know Ana was alright. I nodded and climbed into the Jeep.

As we backed down the driveway, I glanced back to look at Kian. He was standing in the driveway watching us leave, his hands in his jacket pockets, left behind and forgotten.

9 Eila

ANA HAD GOTTEN THE CALL from one of the cemetery workers when she was changing. The groundskeeper had told her that a tree had come down during last night's storm and landed on several grave stones, including her Dad's. Apparently it was smashed.

I had never seen Ana so withdrawn. So hurt.

The way she carried her pain almost looked like guilt.

Honestly, I was angry that she was called at all – she's eighteen for crying out loud and it's Thanksgiving! But then I realized that there was no one else *to* call. It was just Ana – no parents, no relatives, no trust fund to ensure she could make it in this world.

She had nothing, but she did have Mae and me. She had Raef and MJ, and most importantly she had Kian.

Kian, who she wouldn't even say a word to when we got in the car. I felt so bad for him.

I was sure he thought he had done something wrong, and in his face

I could see the worry that Ana was going to pull away from him once again. I couldn't even begin to fathom what they had experienced together the summer they met. The ultra-highs of true love falling away to the devastating lows of her father's death.

She even admitted that she had called Kian a murderer. I knew she now regretted what she had said to him, but Ana was still on the mend. She was strong and determined, but I suspected that one cruel summer had changed them both, and not completely for the better.

I looked over my shoulder to Ana as Raef drove through the town's winding roads. She was looking out the window at the homes that slipped by, many packed with out-of-state cars. They belonged to family members from all over the country, who were coming home for Thanksgiving.

No one, from anywhere, would come for Ana. But she was home now, with us. She would always have a family with us, as strange and unlikely as we all were together.

As I turned back to look out the windshield I caught Raef's eye and he mouthed the words, *You okay?*

I nodded and he laced his free hand in mine over the center console of the Jeep. His thumb traced a small, endless circle on my hand as we drove.

After a few minutes we finally made it to the cemetery, and Raef asked Ana where her father's plot was, but Ana, her eyes glassy, just shrugged. "I haven't been here since he was buried. Everything looks different. I should have come before. It took a tree falling on his stone for me to come out here." She sniffed.

I leaned back toward her. "Hey – your Dad understands. Life gets in the way and it's hard to come here. He doesn't want to cause you pain," I said, but the second the words came out of my mouth, I wished I could take them back.

Ana gave a choked, brittle laugh, "You definitely didn't know my father, Eila."

Raef cleared his throat. "I'll go find the groundskeeper. He can tell us wherever we are supposed to go."

Raef got out of the Jeep and headed for an office-like building, and soon he was walking back with a map in his hands. He climbed in and shut the door against the cold, handing me the map so I could direct him. Ana stayed silent in the back, her eyes trailing over the many stones, some as old as Raef's time. Something occurred to me then.

"Do you think any of your family is buried here, Raef?"

He gave a shrug. "Maybe. Possibly. My parents and my sister moved to Virginia before I was turned, however. I would think they would be buried down there."

"Did you never contact them after you were turned?"

Raef gave me a look that questioned my logic, "No. By the time I was able to control the more dangerous side of my new personality, it had been more than a year. My parents assumed something had happened to me, though I did hear they were trying to find me. But then I realized I would never age. I would never eat, marry, or have children. The son they knew was dead. Contacting them was not an option. They eventually sold our farm to another family who renamed it CatBird Farm."

CatBird Farm was where MJ's family bought all the supplies for their ice cream shop. I was stunned. The land had belonged to Raef's family? I was about to reply, but Ana's small voice spoke up.

63

"This looks familiar," she said, tapping her finger against the window. Stacked against the fencing of the cemetery was a pile of freshly cut tree trunks and not far from them, the carnage of what a massive spruce could inflict when it fell.

Raef slowed the Jeep to a stop and we all got out. By some instinct, I knew Ana just wanted me with her, so I asked Raef to wait by the car. He didn't argue and seemed to understand.

Ana and I slowly stepped through the stones. This section of the cemetery had only flat stones that lay flush with the frozen ground. Many were crushed beyond recognition, but we still went through them, brushing snow from the engraved letters to read the names.

One stone, heavily caked with snow, had been split into three pieces. I stopped next to it and started working away the snow when I caught sight of an "L" and "A." I worked faster, pulling off my gloves so I could fit my finger into the grooves within the granite that formed the name. When I was done, Ana's father's name was facing me.

"Ana!" I called. "He's here."

She jogged her way through the snow and stopped next to me. The words on the stone, now split and twisted, were simple:

Harold Lane
June 3, 1968 – September 2, 2012

Ana just stood there, looking down at her father's gravesite for a long time before she spoke. "I . . . I didn't have money for a nice stone," she said quietly. "I barely had money to bury him, so the guys from his work kicked in to help."

Tears started to silently trace her fair, wind-kissed cheeks, and my heart clenched, thinking of what she went through alone. Of what Kian

64

went through, knowing how much pain she was in. I couldn't help it, and soon my own tears came just as quietly.

Ana sunk to her knees on the icy ground and began pushing the snow farther away, attempting to fit the broken pieces back into place, as if doing so would fix the past.

I had to look away and saw Raef, watching me, his arms crossed. He saw my tears and his arms fell to his sides, concerned, and he began walking toward me, but I shook my head for him to stay where he was.

I had nothing to offer Ana in that moment except my unfailing love as her friend, and I got down next to her to help. When we were done, the pieces fit roughly together, but I knew Ana's heart was shattered.

When we finally got back to my house, Mae was spinning with activity. She had pulled me aside as soon as we arrived home, asking why Ana looked so upset. I filled her in on what had happened to the stone, and though she was very sad for Ana, we didn't have a few thousand dollars to replace it either. According to the cemetery, it would take more than a year for their insurance to order a new plaque, and that weighed heavy on Ana.

I stayed in the kitchen, helping Mae with the food, but Ana went up to her room and closed the door.

Raef had texted Kian when we were at the gravesite, letting him know what was going on. Kian however, didn't reply. At first I thought he might not have gotten the message, because when we got back to the house, he was gone. Raef tried to get him on the phone, but he wasn't answering. Dinner was supposed to be in a few hours and no one could find him.

Frustrated that I couldn't locate Kian or ease Ana's sadness, I called the one person who could find the sun in the worst of a hurricane: MJ. He picked up after just a few rings.

"WOMAN! How the heck are ya? Happy Turkey day!" he yelled as soon as he answered the phone.

"Happy Thanksgiving weirdo! We miss ya! How's Florida?" I asked, my entire mood lifted just by hearing his voice.

"West Palm is 'da bomb, well except for my Aunt Lois and her strange casserole. I took two bites and decided death-by-food-poisoning was not the way to go. Don't ever eat what she serves you. Seriously."

I started laughing as I tucked the phone into my shoulder so I could continue lining up the ladyfingers in the pan for tiramisu. Mae glanced at me. "Is that MJ? Tell him I said *hi*," she prodded.

"Mae says *hi*," I dutifully reported.

"Tell that wonderful woman that I miss her and her excellent culinary skills. Tell her to send a care package to me . . . or better yet, drive it down here!"

I looked back at Mae, "He says your cooking is lousy."

"WHAT? I DID NOT!" he howled into the phone, loud enough so Mae could easily hear. She just laughed and waved a dishtowel at me, continuing to clean the wine glasses. She had so many glasses out I was wondering if she was planning on getting everyone hammered.

I placed the last ladyfinger carefully in the pan, knowing that the only people who'd actually be eating were Ana, Mae, and me. We were going to have enough leftovers to feed the whole neighborhood.

I left Mae to her glasses and headed into the living room talking to MJ as I walked. "So Ana dragged us to Nauset yesterday so the guys could surf, even though there was a snow storm. Are ya jealous?" I asked, knowing MJ loved to surf.

He snorted, "Not likely. I went surfing too, the only difference was I could wear my swim trunks and not freeze to death. Eighty-eight degrees Chicky! And the women . . . I don't even think those strings they were wearing could be classified as swimwear!"

"You can stop right there, thanks. I get the gist." I flopped into the sofa and kicked my feet up onto the coffee table. "Did you get to check on Cerberus?"

"Kian's elaborate dinghy? Yeah, yeah – not sure he could put it at a more snooty marina though. I nearly got tossed on my ass when I got to the gate. Tell him that down here, Cerberus is far from the biggest fish in the sea. I think I even saw Usher!"

"You did not see Usher. You're hallucinating." I laughed.

"I am not! Just make sure you tell Kian about his boat or he will start hounding me."

I shifted forward on the couch, the stress of today starting to weasel its way back into my body. "So, uh, listen. I can't actually find Kian right now." There was a moment of silence on the other end of the phone.

"Seriously? Where did he go?"

I sighed and filled MJ in on what had happened. He listened intently, never once interrupting me, which NEVER happens. Finally I heard him take a deep breath.

"I'll call him," he said, in a determined voice.

"He won't answer."

"He will for me."

I sighed, feeling less than optimistic. "Hey MJ – there's one other

67

thing. He called her *Pix*. It seemed to freak her out a bit. Do you have any clue what that was about?"

The silence on the phone felt endless as I waited for MJ's reply. Finally his voice breathed through the wireless connection, "Yeah, I know what it's about. I gotta go. Love you, Eila. Tell Ana I will be home soon and I miss her."

"I will – love ya too," I replied as the call disconnected, feeling totally left out of whatever was *really* said between Kian and Ana.

About an hour before we were to have dinner, Kian returned. He gave us all the briefest of greetings and went straight up the stairs to Ana's room. Raef and I heard the door open and close and then nothing.

Curiosity was going to kill me.

Thirty minutes later Kian and Ana walked into the dining room. While the light hadn't returned to her eyes, her mood did seem better. She had pulled herself together, probably with the help of Kian, and was ready to rejoin us. Rather than make some emotional scene of hugging her, I offered her a pile of plates. "Help me set the table?" I asked.

"Sure," she replied and took the dishware. I gathered up other table items and the boys asked if they could help. Mae set them to various tasks and soon the kitchen and dining rooms were a hum of voices, laughter, and the rich scent of Thanksgiving.

A knock on the door a short time later alerted me that Christian had probably arrived. Why Mae had to invite him was beyond me, but I sucked it up and tried to be a gracious host. The reality was Christian didn't really bother me, but I didn't know him very well either. I also didn't know how to treat him – as a friend? A stuffy business man? A watchful grandfather? A sex symbol?

Okay – that last one was a definite *no*.

In the end, we were probably both trying to navigate how our relationship would work.

I got to the front hallway, Raef following me closely, and opened the door. There, standing on the porch with a bottle of Cristal champagne worth more than my Jeep, was Christian. A flawlessly cut suit framed his perfectly sculpted body and stunning face. No wonder Elizabeth fell for him and Newport named him Most Eligible Bachelor.

He gave us a brilliant smile. "Eila. Raef. Happy Thanksgiving. May I come in?" He always asked, even though I had granted him permission nearly a month ago.

As a Mortis, he could only enter a house if the owner granted him passage. I would never forget the day I invited Kian and Raef inside my home, though they had been inside 408 many times when they were human. Raef had helped build my home, including some of the furniture, including my four-poster bed. He had been a friend to Elizabeth, who had hired him as a young, gifted carpenter. The fact that he failed to protect her that night in the harbor haunted him, but he had been turned into a Mortis back then and didn't recognize her as a friend.

"Please come in. Mae will be pleased to see you," I said, stepping aside so he could enter. Raef, still unsure of Christian, moved slowly out of the way. The two soul thieves sized each other up, but then Christian held out his hand to shake Raef's.

My guard didn't move.

"Raef - I am forever grateful for all that you do for Eila, and understand your reluctance with me. I'd want you to be wary of anyone that comes close to her. But I want nothing but the best for her, and that includes the men she loves. You should remember that when your mind wanders to certain things not related to her safety."

Did he just slam Raef? Bastard – I think he did!

"Excuse me? You have no say in who I do or do not love. You need to rethink what you have just said," I whispered, angry. I was seriously pissed.

Raef, unmoving and unflinching, wore a mask of stone. I couldn't read him, but felt the tenseness of his body next to me. When he finally spoke, his voice was low and crisp, "You have been invited by Mae and she expects you, therefore I can't toss you out into the snow. But you hold no rights to Eila's life, nor can you dictate her free will. My goal is to keep her safe, so that she may lead the life *she* chooses, with whoever she deems worthy."

My throat tightened at his simple, yet elegant, pledge to me.

Christian, never loosing his cool, simply tipped his head graciously. "I think I will seek out the hostess. Please excuse me."

He left us, standing together in the hallway, as he walked toward the parlor and the kitchen beyond. I heard Mae greet him with an enthusiastic hello, followed by a more subdued pair of greetings from Kian and Ana.

Raef looked down at me, a devilish gleam to his eyes, "Sure I can't just kill him?"

"I'll think about it," I replied, with a wink.

An hour later, between bites of turkey and potatoes, I learned that Mae had accepted a job working for Christian as an antique real estate scout for North Star Historic Estates. She would get to travel all over the country and though she had some concerns about leaving me now and again, I could tell she was entirely thrilled.

I swallowed back my unease over Mae being so close to Christian and prayed it would all work out. Having Mae work for a Mortis would either keep her safe . . . or put her directly in the crosshairs of my messed up family tree.

10 Eila

DURING MY RECOVERY FROM MY stellar performance in the Breakers, my physician had recommended a physical therapy that could help strengthen my core muscles.

Most of her suggestions sounded downright annoying until she mentioned horseback riding. I had ridden most of my life in Kansas and loved the feel of a horse under me, the rocking motion being its own form of mediation. I jumped at the chance to ride again, and Mae was able to find me a barn that could aid in my recovery – Blackstone Acres a few towns over from my house.

Raef hated the idea. I didn't know why until he revealed that he couldn't be around animals. He said that as soul thieves, neither he nor Kian could safely come with me, or the horses might bolt and throw people in their panic. So MJ had stepped up to the plate and accompanied me in his human form.

Unfortunately my last riding session was today, the day after

Thanksgiving, and MJ was still in the land of palm trees and scantily clad women. I had no problem going alone, especially since a quick one-on-one with Mae's new employer, Christian, revealed absolutely no talk of the Breakers in the New England Mortis community. In the last five weeks, not a single soul thief came after me.

Plus, it was the off-season for Cape Cod, and when the tourists left, the soul sharks often did as well. Without swimmers in the water, hunting on the Cape became more of a liability for a Mortis. Hiding bodies on such a small peninsula wasn't easy, but swimmers would just appear to have drowned.

So when the beachgoers vacated the cold Atlantic water, the Mortis did too. They favored the southern parts of the country, or the more remote Northern woods, where bodies would be taken care of by bears. How nice – I lived in their summer hunting grounds. Just peachy.

I assured Raef that I would be riding in the indoor arena, as always, and he finally accepted the fact that I was going. He knew he couldn't dictate what I could and couldn't do – no one can hold that power over you unless you let him. Sure, I could have skipped riding just to make him happy, but I loved riding. Plus, I wanted to prove to Raef, once and for all, that I could go places without him and come home in one piece.

By the time I got over to Blackstone it was early afternoon. I had agreed to meet sweet (but air-headed) Sarah, another rider and part-time instructor, around 2:30.

I pulled my horse, Porter, from his stall and brushed him down, checking him over for any ticks or stones in his feet. By 2:45 I was tacked up and ready to ride.

Sarah, however, was nowhere to be found.

This was a problem since I didn't have her phone number.

I looked around the barn. I could see a girl about 12 stalls down from me cleaning a saddle. I yelled down to her, "Hey – do you know Sarah's phone number?"

The girl looked up from the leather she was polishing, "Does she own the mental-case Arabian?"

"Yeah. That's her. Do you have her number?"

"No, I'm sorry," called back the girl.

"Okay. Thanks," I yelled back. I looked at my watch. It was now 2:50pm.

"Screw it," I muttered to myself. I wasn't about to not ride because I was stuck without a riding buddy. I led Porter out of the barn and toward the indoor arena, but Saddle Girl called down to me, "The indoor is closed for now. They are going to be dragging it with the tractor to level the ground in about 10 minutes."

Terrific. I looked to the tree line and the clearing where the trails started. It was a beautiful day and the air was not that cold. Most of the snow had melted over the past 24 hours and the ground was no longer frozen.

I made a split decision to trail ride and lead Porter into the shadows of the trees. I swung myself on and adjusted my reins. "I just won't tell Raef, that's all," I said to Porter, who was tossing his head excitedly. I took one last look at my watch, noting approximately how much time I had before the sun set, and rode off into the tall pines.

Blackstone had roughly 30 acres of trails that wound through fields, forest, and cranberry bogs. Bisecting the expanse of land was a long,

74

straight dirt track that ran for miles. It was where the old railroad used to come through on its way to another part of town, but had long since been unused. The actual railroad tracks had been removed and all that remained was a dirt lane, perfect for racing a friend on occasion, or so I'd been told.

As I came to the railroad lane, I crossed over it and continued on into the woods that led to the cranberry bog. The air smelled clean with a hint of brininess from the sea breeze. All I could think of was frozen saltwater taffy.

Porter enjoyed our leisurely pace, occasionally trying to pluck a dried leaf from a passing branch. It felt so fantastic to be back in the saddle, that simple rocking motion, and the rhythmic bounce of Porter's head. It was easy to let my mind wander.

I started thinking about all that had happened to me since learning of 408 Main Street. Of how different my life was now, and the simple fact that I was starting to really enjoy my new existence here (disaster in Newport excluded). Some people would say that the house was more like a curse than a gift, but I'd disagree.

I was born a Lunaterra, whether or not I returned to the Cape. And maybe, had I stayed in Kansas, I would have lived my entire life never knowing what I truly was. Never running into Mortis like Raef, Kian, and Christian, and probably never finding friends like Ana and MJ. Yes, moving here brought with it some catastrophes, but being here, surrounded by my friends and Raef, made me stronger.

MJ brought laughter and comfort to my life. He was that sweet kid who you knew could be counted on to make you laugh or save you from the side of the road when you ran out of gas. He was a genuine, good soul – a rare find in a jaded world and I knew he would be a lifetime pal. Plus . . . he was a dog. I mean, seriously – how COOL is that? In his dog form, he was an incredible fighter and the boys trusted him to protect Ana and me without question. As the lanky high school senior that he really was however, he'd be snapped like a pretzel.

Then there was Ana. Despite her best efforts at being non-emotional, she too was someone who could be counted on to have your back. Though she occasionally protested about the fluff in life and dressed as though she couldn't identify a skirt, she was a beautiful, honest person. She cut you no slack, but at the end of the day, her brutal honesty was what made you a better person. Her gifts as a strange sort of psychic left me awed.

Kian I had judged unfairly when I first met him. He had seemed arrogant (okay – he still does), but was also a man of few words. In some ways, he was, and is, very similar to Ana – another locked vault. I couldn't say I blamed him though – he, like Raef, had no competition in the good-looks department. But in my eyes, Kian redeemed himself a thousand fold when he saved Ana and me months ago. He did it selflessly, with no regard to his own safety. Every once in a while he would let me see him as he truly was – a man, damaged, but with a big heart.

And then there was Raef. Though I had hoped to make a friend or two once here, I never dreamed I would find a boy like Raef. He was handsome, strong, intelligent, caring, compassionate . . . come to think of it, I wasn't sure he actually *had* any faults, aside from the whole "soul thief" thing. We had become so entwined with one another, that I could never imagine a future without him. To lose him would be to lose a huge part of who I had become. I was a better, more compassionate human being because of him.

Because of them all, really.

I continued to think back to the events of my rapidly changing life and rode on towards the cranberry bog. I must have lost track of time because once I had ridden around the bog, the sun seemed to have gone down alarmingly fast. I realized that I had dawdled a bit too long and might be picking my way through the woods in the dark. The idea was not appealing as I had visions of Porter getting tripped up on tree roots. I urged him into a fast trot and we headed back into the woods from the bog.

The sun had dipped below the horizon, but the ambient light still gave me enough visibility to navigate the woods at a trot. Soon enough, with the light fading fast, I came out to the railroad tracks. If I followed the same route I came in on, I would get to the barn a little faster, but the woods would be far darker than the open lane. The railroad tracks would lead me out to the main dirt road that could also access the barn. It was a bit longer, but a lot easier to see the ground.

I turned Porter down the dirt tracks and picked up a peppy trot. We had been only heading down the tracks for maybe a minute when Porter suddenly bolted to the right. I fell forward against the saddle, bracing my weight on his neck. I managed to quickly regain my seat, as Porter stood stone still and tense. He snorted at the woods and his ears were pricked high. I stroked his neck. "Easy, boy. Easy," I soothed, now slightly uneasy myself. I scanned the woods, but the colors were seeping out of the tree line as the darkness started to set in.

"It's okay Porter. Let's get going and get home. How's that sound?" I said, trying to act calm. Porter was not a spooky horse by nature. In fact, I would call him "bomb-proof" – nothing scared him. The fact that something startled him badly enough to nearly dump me was worrisome. His sense of smell was far better than mine and I worried that there might be a larger animal out there in the darkness.

I tried to remember the wildlife section of the guidebook for the Cape I had picked up in Kansas. I didn't recall bears to be on the list and quite frankly, bears were the least of my worries.

I gathered my reins and turned Porter back toward home. Just as I did so, I caught sight of it to my right: a blur of blackness and speed, moving fast between the trees about 40 feet into the woods. Porter saw it too and reared high, causing me to lose my seat. I tumbled out of the saddle, across his back, and slammed onto the dirt track, knocking the wind from my lungs. My ears were ringing and through my blurred vision I could see my stalwart steed hightailing it down the track. I was pissed that I lost my horse, and pretty sure I landed on a sharp stone, but then reality set in.

I wasn't alone.

With my back and chest screaming, I rolled onto my stomach on the cold ground and blinked away the fuzzies in my sight. I scanned the tree line and slowly, gingerly dragged myself to my feet. I listened, carefully, for any revealing sound.

Then I heard it – something in the woods headed towards me. Something large. I braced myself for whatever was coming, but was shocked when the biggest man I had ever seen burst through the tree line.

He wore a long, dark jacket – almost like a trench coat with a hood

78

pulled up over his head. He scanned the lane and then his eyes settled on me. His coat drifted open in the breeze and under it he wore a leather vest, crisscrossed with lacing, but his bare skin was showing under it, and he was scarred. It was as if he had been in a knife fight that went really, REALLY wrong. He had tattoos as well, all different symbols which no doubt meant something to him, though they looked faded and old. As if he had given up on them long ago.

He was basically *that* dude, from those creepy movies where you end up screaming at the dumb actress to run before he kills her. So not good.

He started walking towards me and I stood frozen for a moment, searching every inch of my body for a reaction to this huge man. In the past, my body would sometimes give a strange sort of warning signal when I came close to a soul thief, almost like a twisted form of mental goosebumps.

But with this guy? Nothing. I got zip.

Not even a regular tingle of wariness if this dude was just some teen-stalking pervert, which was damned odd. And there was no way I was walking away from this guy in one piece if he meant me harm. He looked like a cage fighter for crying out loud!

All my cockiness about being able to handle myself without one of my guards was quickly shriveling up like a Shrinky Dink in a thousand-degree oven. I nearly launched myself clear out of my skin when he finally spoke.

"Are you all right? I saw you fall," he asked. His voice was deep, velvet, but with a rugged quality. It held an aged, graveled undertone that spoke to the life he had lived. He looked to be in his late 20s and he reminded me of a warrior - rough, confident, and a bit worn through. He

79

was Thor . . . if Thor came from the worst part of L.A. and hung with the Hell's Angels.

"Did you hear me? Are you alright?" he asked again, slowing his approach and stopping well out of arm's reach. He pulled his hood back, revealing a wide-set brow, chiseled jaw edged with a short beard and goatee, close-cut dark hair, and huge neck. He was good looking – handsome even, almost like a military man from those romance novels. Thanks to Mae, we had quite a few of *those* books lying around the house.

"I, uh, lost my horse," I mumbled like an idiot, but then I remembered why I got dumped in the first place. "Something spooked him." I scanned the wood line quickly, recalling the black shadow that tore through the woods. I didn't care how big Thor was, if there was a Mortis around, life was going to get seriously ugly.

Of course . . . where did this guy come from? I eyed him warily.

As if reading my mind, he shifted slightly where he stood and offered an explanation, "That may have been me. I was hunting and startled a deer. I'm very sorry." I looked him over carefully. If he had been hunting, where the heck were his weapons?

"Where's your gun?" I asked suspiciously, straightening slightly. This was not a good situation for me to be in. Aside from the fact that this guy could probably tow my Wrangler with his teeth, being alone with him also reminded me of the night at the beach. A night when I had been caught alone with another big guy – Teddy Bencourt – who tried to force himself on me.

Panic started to creep into my bones, and I shivered at the memory of being pinned to the sand, nearly unable to draw breath to scream. My visitor must have recognized something on my face, and he stepped

80

back, his hands at his sides. "I left my bow back in the woods. I came running when I saw you fall. I'm not going to hurt you."

Sure you're not. I needed to get the heck out of here.

Now.

Thankfully the silence of the darkened woods was cut with the sound of people yelling my name, searching for me. Porter must have wandered home, hungry for dinner and riderless, which was a sure way to panic a barn full of equestrians. Thank you Porter for your greedy gut!

Thor turned his head in the direction of the voices and I caught a glimpse of something peeking out from under the wide strap of his vest. It was a raised mark – a brand, which looked weirdly familiar though I couldn't see all of it.

He turned back to me, "I've got to go find my things before it gets too dark. Will you be okay?"

I nodded, the sounds of my searchers getting closer. I yelled in their direction and they shouted back. I turned back to Thor, wanting to thank him, but he was already pushing his way into the shadows of the woods.

Even with his wide frame, he soon blended seamlessly into the darkness, and disappeared.

11 Raef

WHEN I GOT THE TEXT THAT EILA wanted to meet me at Torrent Road, I was instantly worried.

She had never even been to Torrent Road, avoiding it at all costs. For her to meet me there was not a good sign.

To make matters worse, I had been grazed by an arrow while hunting on Sandy Neck. Granted, I was just about to take down a deer, which was no doubt why I got nicked, but archery season had ended. Whoever had the eyesight of a turtle was also hunting illegally.

I didn't bother tracking him down as doing so would raise too many questions about why I was out on Sandy Neck, wrestling the local herd with my bare hands.

The gash over my bicep would have required stiches if I was human, but my accelerated healing would leave nothing more than a faint line in a few hours. By tomorrow, there would be no line at all and no one would ever know I had been hit – especially Eila, who'd obsess about it.

While she took her own safety with little more than passing interest, she had a dogged determination to protect everyone else. I had no desire for her to know I had been hit by a hunter's weapon.

Mindful of how quickly she would arrive, I bandaged the wound to keep it from bleeding, and changed into a shirt that would cover up the damage. I tossed the bloody shirt into a waste basket in the corner of my room.

The space Christian had offered me was a large, second floor bedroom filled with dark woods, leather, and brass, as if it was modeled after a first-class room on the Titanic. It had a massive floor to ceiling curved window that looked out over the harbor, though I was so rarely at Torrent Road, I didn't have much time to admire the view. I suspected that would change now that Mae was more wary of Kian and me around the girls.

We had been at 408 daily when Ana and Eila were injured, helping Mae with whatever she needed. But now that the girls were well, our presence meant something else entirely to Mae. Of course, if we told her about the killer shadows who would relieve a person of their soul, she might change her mind about having us around. She would probably still lock up E and Ana though.

While the timing was less than ideal, I was grateful that Eila was finally coming to Torrent Road. If we wanted any time together on any sort of regular basis, I knew it was going to be here, and she might as well get used to Christian's home.

As soon as I heard the tires of her Jeep pull into the driveway, I headed downstairs and opened the massive entry door. She looked as she always did – stunning, with her wild, dark hair contrasting beautifully against the fair skin of her face. Just her presence filled me with such a rush of longing that it was a miracle I ever left her side at all.

As she stepped from the Wrangler however, I immediately knew something was wrong. She moved slowly, carefully, as if some part of her body was causing her pain. I was at her side in an instant.

"What happened?" I asked, offering my hand as I shut the Jeep door. She waved off my help, however, which was typical of her.

She swore, angry at herself, "I got thrown. Landed on my back. It was stupid."

As absurd as it was, I was furious at the horse. "Okay – let's get you inside. Do you think you broke anything?" I prayed she had not broken anything. I couldn't heal her like a normal human because of what she was, and the thought of seeing her in pain for any length of time made my stomach twist.

"No, no. I think I just have a nasty bruise. I didn't want to go straight home like this because Mae will instantly be in my face about it. If it's okay, I just want to hang here for a bit. I think Mae is going out later anyway, to a book club meeting. I will call her from here and then sneak back home when she is gone."

"Your level of duplicity is a bit alarming," I said, opening the door to the house for her, but then I paused, scanning the long driveway and the trees that lined the road. I thought I had heard something moving through the brush, but when I looked, all that twitched were the branches in the light breeze.

I kept my eyes scanning the area as Eila stepped inside the towering entrance and paused, taking in the expansive space. I shut and locked the door behind us, brushing aside the sounds of the wind in the trees, and watched as she took in all the details.

Opposite from where we stood was a wall of glass set behind a huge sunken living room, complete with an ornate billiard table and large stone fireplace. A curving staircase climbed up to a second floor balcony that overlooked the entire room and a chandelier that was made of wrought iron and amber glass. Outside, the view captured that of the ferry making its way past one of the channel markers.

"It's . . . ummm. Impressive?"

"I'd say ostentatious," I replied.

Eila looked back at me with a flinty smile on her face. "Yeah, maybe just a little bit."

She started to unsnap her coat, and I helped her slide it off her arms, as twisting too far made her wince. The back of her navy shirt looked damp and I gently touched the fabric, and then looked to my fingertips. Red. Blood.

"Eila, you're bleeding," I said, my stress level jumping higher. She seemed okay, so the wound couldn't be too severe.

"Are you kidding me?" she demanded, looking down at my fingers. "Well that's just peachy. I must have landed on a rock or something. Do you have a shirt I can borrow?"

"Of course, but I need to check out what maiming you have inflicted on yourself first," I said, brushing a cold strand of hair out of her face.

She slowly crossed her arms, a pitiful act of being pissed. "I didn't maim myself. I'm a very good rider."

I smiled at her, slowly releasing my initial fear that she was badly hurt. "That's what they all say." I got a finger jabbed at my side for that remark.

I held her hand as I led her to my bedroom, which thankfully had its own bathroom. Eila could at least get cleaned up in some semblance of privacy, especially if Christian was lurking in the house. Thankfully he traveled often, keeping his massive company functioning. He also kept many homes, including an exclusive Beacon Hill apartment in Boston. Unfortunately, he rarely forewarned us of when he would be around, and this place was so huge that sometimes I had no clue he was inside.

Eila sat down in an upholstered wingback chair near the window and attempted to take off her boots, but bending over that far caused her to suck in a tight breath. I got down in front of her, and started unlacing them. "So besides your detour to the ground, how was your ride?"

When she didn't answer me, I looked up to her face. She had a weird, conflicted look to her. "What's the matter?"

She kept looking at me and her face scrunched in thought, "Are you sure my mark just means I have the ability to zap soul thieves?"

"What?" I asked. I didn't even know what spurred the question. "I believe so, yes. That's what the legend says. And Christian called it a kill mark, so I am assuming that we're correct. Eila – what made you – ."

"What if it means something else? Or something more?" she asked, her eyes animated, but then her face suddenly looked more fearful.

"You're freaking me out a little, E. Where's all this coming from?" I was trying to figure her out. Her sudden fear made me uneasy.

She sighed and leaned forward ever so slightly, bringing her forehead in contact with mine. "I'm sorry. I just was riding and my mind was running with a million thoughts. You and Kian thought I was the only Lunaterra left, but the world is a big place. There may be more of my kind and what if they are hunting down Mortis, like you? Good guys, who don't hunt humans. We just don't know."

All of her points were valid, but the one thing that stood out in my mind was the fact that she called me a good guy because I didn't hunt humans. That was going to change soon. It needed to change because I needed to be at my best to protect her. Only a human life-force could do that for me. And what if there were more Lunaterra? What if they did find out about E? Would they hunt her down? Attempt to steal her away from us?

Good grief, the sky *was* falling. I needed to pull it together. She was safe with me, and our friends. There had been no Mortis in the area and her ride, aside from her fall, was uneventful.

"I'm sorry," she breathed, her voice causing delicate icicles to dance across my face. "I'm being obsessive. I'm just tired and my back hurts."

"It's okay. We all get to freak out once in a while, especially after falling off a horse. How about you take a hot shower, and then I will check you out? I MEAN, check out your back."

Damn . . .

Eila pulled back from me, but kept her face close to mine. Her eyebrow wiggled upward as she eyed me, knowingly. "Mr. Paris, just exactly what type of a girl do you take me for?"

I didn't hesitate. "The best type. A one-of-a-kind warrior who is kind enough to be my friend," I said, trying to fight against the darker memories I had of her.

Eila leaned a little closer to me. "You are far more than a friend to me," she said quietly. For a moment I saw her again, bleeding on the floor of the coal room. But then the fear slowly gave way as I breathed her in, alive and beautiful in front of me. I could feel the tingle of the

87

Fallen marks beginning to rise to the surface of my skin and I wanted to kiss her, fiercely. My mutinous markings were letting her know it.

She drew a cool finger down my cheekbone, following one of the marks, and a beautiful chill followed the path of her touch. She flashed me a breathtaking smile, "Do these mean you feel the same?"

I grabbed her wrist softly, halting her exploration of my face. Her smile fell away as I spoke, "Never doubt my feelings for you, Eila. Ever." My voice lost its smooth quality, roughened by a want I could no longer hide.

I studied her brown eyes, and in them I could see the connection that we had denied each other for too long. In her face was a love that ignored the darkness that I was, accepting me as a killer and trusting me as a savior.

She bit her bottom lip, and all sane thoughts fled my head. Every decent reason I had for keeping her at arm's length vanished, and I gently smoothed her lip with my thumb. She released a shaky breath, causing a fever-like need to shatter the wall I had so carefully maintained between us.

I slid my hand to the back of her neck and pulled her close, admiring the autumn colors of her eyes. "I want to kiss you. I know it is not part of the deal, but I want to. Can I . . ."

Before I could finish my question, Eila closed the small gap between our lips, igniting a riot of sensation that coursed through my body. It was as if the sun finally blazed in the sky after centuries of frozen night, and I took her face in my hands as I kissed my raven-haired angel for the first time in forever. Our lips met gently at first, but the more I tasted her and felt her bewitching burn, the more my self-control frayed.

She ran her delicate hands over my shoulders and down my back, balling the edge of my shirt in her fingers. Small gasps escaped her when I would break from her for an instant to kiss her silken neck and flushed cheeks. Those little sounds she made could kill a lesser man, and drove me absolutely mad, sending me higher than any human soul ever could.

I wanted to feel her, alive and vibrant, and my own hands began to boldly wander, sliding around her waist, skirting the edge of her shirt and her ribs. She slid forward on the couch, forcing our bodies into greater contact, and I forgot myself entirely.

I ran my hands under the hem of her shirt, feeling her graceful lower back slide easily under my palms. Everywhere I touched teased my skin, like icicles drawing along my palms. I pulled her tighter, wanting to feel her electric reaction to my touch intensify, and I raced my hands up her back. But then she gasped. Really gasped, in pain.

Her body stiffened, arching away from my touch and I snapped out of my momentary insanity. "Damn it – I'm so sorry, Eila," I growled, ashamed I had forgotten about her abused back.

She looked entirely flustered, as if she got caught crawling through the window after curfew. "It's okay, Raef. Seriously." She tried to look away from me, rolling her lips tightly together, her cheeks pink.

I turned her face gently back to mine. "Are you . . . embarrassed?" I asked, now worried I went a little too far. I had never kissed her, nor touched her, so recklessly.

A sheepish grin slid up her face, "I think I ignored our rules. Sorry about that."

"I hate rules," I whispered, relieved as I kissed her again, softly this time, tracing my lips over the curves of her own. I knew I needed to get

89

up – get away from her for a few moments, otherwise I might never let her leave the room again.

Reluctantly, I pulled myself back to functional sanity, and I left E in my bathroom with a fresh t-shirt and towels. I headed down to the kitchen to find her some food, debating the possibility of throwing myself out into the harbor to calm down. As I turned the corner, I nearly collided with Kian.

"Hey – you're here," I announced, which was not the smartest move. Normally I would barely acknowledge him, but Eila's lips had rattled my brain.

Kian eyed me warily, "No. I'm a figment of your boring imagination. Of course I'm here! What is wrong with you? You have some weird look on your face - like you're high or something."

Oh, I was high on something, and she stood about five and a half feet tall and was in my shower. I just shrugged, trying to safeguard Eila's privacy if she didn't want anyone else knowing she was here.

"I went hunting again. Took down a buck and a doe. Well, almost a doe. That's all – excess energy, is all."

"Would that excess energy also involve a fair skinned brunette who could double as a disco ball? Because her Jeep is parked outside."

I had forgotten about her car and couldn't quickly come up with a good excuse. I tightened my jaw and quietly gave in to the truth. "Fine. She's upstairs taking a shower. She fell riding and messed up her back. She didn't want Mae to see."

"Messed up her back riding, huh? Sure she doesn't just have rug burns from you?"

Anger cut through me instantly, and my fist connected with his jaw before I even realized I swung. The punch sent him staggering back until he hit the edge of the doorway that led to the library, where all of Dalca's things were kept.

I began to come at him again, enraged that he dared to imagine Eila in such a degrading way. To even visualize her in such a manner. I went to swing, but he caught my curled fist, striking me in the jaw with his free hand. The hit felt like a steel bat and sent me sliding along the marble floor into the sunken living room. I had forgotten that Kian had already begun hunting humans. His hits would be harder, faster, but I didn't care. He had insulted Eila in a way that burned me right through the gut.

I shook my head to clear the ringing, and began to go after him again, but then I heard Eila's voice behind me. I turned, and she was coming down the stairs, her stained t-shirt and old jeans still on. Kian and I immediately switched to a more neutral stance so she wouldn't know we had just tried to start our own Fight Club.

"Oh," she said, halting on the stairs, "I didn't know you were here, Kian. Everything all right?"

He glanced at me, then to Eila. "Of course. I was just going to keep digging through Dalca's journals. Ana might join me later."

"Really?" she asked, genuinely surprised and happy.

He shrugged. "It will keep her mind busy."

She nodded, "That's a great idea. Thank you, by the way, for helping her yesterday."

He shifted, looking more uncomfortable. The subject of Ana's father was never mentioned around Kian.

"I'm going to leave you two, so you can get back to whatever it is you have to do. I'll be in the library." Kian eyed me once last time as he

91

turned to leave.

I looked back to Eila and she gave me a shy smile. I came to the stairs and walked my way up to her, "You didn't take a shower?"

"I can't raise my arms enough to get my shirt off. Do you have scissors? 'Cause I'm just gonna cut it off – it's old anyway."

"Christian probably does somewhere, but I'd need to find them," I replied, stepping closer to her and taking the edge of her t-shirt in my hands. "Turn around," I instructed and she gave me a curious glance, but obeyed, turning her back to me.

With one good pull, I tore the t-shirt straight up her back, turning the top into a smock.

"Better?" I asked.

"Uh . . . yup," she replied with a breathless squeak.

12 Eila

I SPENT THE VAST MAJORITY of Saturday up to my eyeballs in guilt.

I hadn't told Raef about Thor for multiple reasons, though none could ease how bad I felt about leaving him in the dark. But there was something about the man from the woods that nagged at me. I couldn't place my finger on it yet and I needed a chance to figure it out.

If I told the guys that some giant had approached me in the woods, I would immediately be placed back in the horrible Buddy System. Additionally, I was certain that Raef, Kian, and MJ would try to track the hunter and spy on him, or worse.

So I kept my mouth shut, pushing Thor to the back of my mind, which wasn't too difficult after the scorching kiss that Raef had given me.

Holy, ever-loving crab cakes.

Sure, I had kissed Raef before, but last night? Last night made every liplock I had swooned over in the movies look like a kindergartener's crush. Last night I *felt* how much he wanted me, and it shocked me, leaving me with both a stratospheric high and a deep-set panic.

And then there was the whole shirt-modification move.

Dear heavens.

But he was also a complete gentleman when he checked over my back, putting ointment on the few small cuts I had from hitting the road. But all I could think about while he tended my bruises was that kiss and the nerves it brought with it.

Maybe I was freaking out for no reason - Raef would never push me into something that I wasn't ready for. But *that* kiss wasn't the end-of-the-road type kiss, but a turn in the road that led to a new place. A place I knew I wasn't ready for.

Plus, Raef had lived for nearly two centuries, and had loads of experience with female soul thieves. While I had never met one, I could only imagine what they looked like. I mean, if the guys looked as insane as Raef, Kian, and Christian . . . yeah.

And it wasn't like I picked apart my flaws in the mirror, but hell – Mortis females? The contrast between the women Raef was used to and me was like comparing a Stealth bomber to a paper airplane. For the first time in my life, I doubted how I looked.

Plus, I had no experience with guys and my idea of undie excitement was a plaid sports bra from the discount store. Somehow I doubted that is where the killer chicks selected their intimates.

Actually, I did kiss another boy once in second grade. He dared me over a bag of M&Ms and I had a chocolate addiction. That kid was so not worth the candy. Raef, I knew, was completely worth the calories. Me, however? I probably was more along the lines of artificial sweetener,

94

which is never as good as the cane sugar.

By the time Sunday night rolled around, I had twisted myself into such a knot of stress that even Ana knew something was up. She eyed me carefully as we shared the bathroom mirror, getting ready for the football game.

"So are you going to cough up the details on what happened at Christian's on Friday or not?" she asked, running her hands through her short cropped blonde hair. I had already given Ana the whole story about falling while riding, and how I went to Torrent Road to avoid Mae.

I shrugged, hoping I could deflect her questions. "I already told you. I just took a shower, had some dinner, and came back here."

Ana twisted her body and hopped up onto the counter, leaning right into my line of sight, as a devious smile curled onto her pale pink lips.

I laughed, trying to push her out of the way, but Ana was like a bloodhound, hot on the trail of something. "Eila Walker, you better spill! I know I am not getting the full details – your emotions are all over the map and I definitely get an undertone of LUST in there!"

I blushed hot and my mind went to a vivid flash of Raef's hands running across my back. Ana's eyes widened, no doubt catching the heated emotion rolling off my body. Only I would have a human lie-detector for a BFF, making secrets entirely pointless. But then I panicked, worried she would somehow get a hint about what really happened in the woods.

Ana's face instantly fell the moment my attitude changed. "Eila – what happened?" she asked, now serious, concern written all over her face. I sighed, dragging a brush through my hair yet again.

95

"He kissed me. Or rather, I kissed him. Actually, we basically kissed each other." I tossed the brush in a drawer and dug around looking for a hair elastic.

I could feel Ana's eyes boring a hole through the top of my head as she watched me look through the drawer. "And you . . . didn't like it?" she questioned, clearly trying to sort out why my emotions were all over the map.

"Oh no. I liked it – a lot. I think he did too," I replied, finally recovering a wayward hair tie. I refused to meet her eyes, choosing instead to study my reflection in the mirror as I pulled my long, dark hair to one side of my neck and began braiding. Primping wasn't my thing. Like, ever. Basics. I liked the basics. I WAS basic.

Ana scooted over slightly, giving me more room, "So then why do I KNOW I am missing some vital piece of intel?"

I glanced at her, refusing to answer and her eyes narrowed. She huffed, crossing her arms. "Fine then. I'll just guess. Umm - his breath stank?"

"What? NO!" I laughed.

"Too much tongue? Too little? None at all?"

"WHAT?" I screeched.

"His hands were too rough? Too adventurous?" she demanded, and I was laughing while trying to make her stop. I finally gave in, "ALL RIGHT! ALL RIGHT! Stop!" I choked.

She gestured for me to get on with the details. I looked at her for a long moment. "The kiss was amazing. It was, but . . ."

"BUT?"

I sighed. "Have you ever seen a female Mortis?" I asked.

Ana looked completely confused. She shook her head, "No. Why?"

I finished braiding my hair, wrapping the tie to the end. I walked out of the bathroom to my room and Ana followed. I began rummaging through my closet for a sweatshirt to wear.

"Well?" demanded Ana from her perch on the corner of my four-poster bed.

I sorted through my hanging clothes, finally answering her. "The kiss was killer and, I don't know, felt different. More . . . uh, you know – heat between us. But afterward I got to thinking about how Raef is, ya know, experienced . . ."

"And you're not," finished Ana. "I get that. I do. But Raef isn't expecting you to be experienced, so don't feel like you should be a smooching superstar."

"No, I know that," I continued, yanking a gray sweater from a hanger. I walked out of the closet and changed into a tank top while I continued talking. "It's just that I could really feel what he wanted – really wanted. And I am not ready to go much beyond the kissing thing. Yet. What if that drives him nuts?"

Ana pulled her feet up under her. "Even if it does drive him nuts, Raef won't go much past the kissing part anyway, and never without your say-so. Kian wouldn't with me either – it's too risky, so stop stressing about that," she replied, suddenly finding the details in the engraved wood of my bed SUPER interesting.

I glared at her, recognizing avoidance when I saw it. "Exactly how far did you and Kian get last summer?" I asked, now suspicious of the petite blonde on my bed.

Her face started to flush. "We, uh, got around most of the bases, just no homeruns," she said, finally flashing a huge grin, but it slowly slipped away. A sadness crept into her body and she picked at the wood. "One night we did go pretty far, but . . ."

"But?" I demanded, now dying to know all the details of last summer.

"But my Dad had a heart attack," she said quietly.

I knew the rest of that story and I felt bad that I had dragged her mind back to those painful days. Ana slid off my bed, her mood quiet.

"Ana . . ." I started, but she just shrugged.

"It's okay, Eila. I know," she said with a pale smile as she left my room, heading to change. Suddenly my worries with Raef seemed so small in the grand scheme of life.

I grabbed my puffy coat from the desk chair and headed down the stairs, sliding my hand along the smooth cherry handrail that poured effortlessly towards the first floor. I yelled up to Ana's room as I reached the last step and grabbed my keys from the hall table, "I'll start the car – it's freakin' cold out!"

"Wimp!" I heard her yell back through her bedroom door.

I fished in my coat pockets for my gloves as I walked through to the kitchen and pulled side door open to leave. Just as I did so, Agent Howe's fist nearly connected with my forehead.

"Holy shi . . . WHAT the heck!" I demanded, pin-wheeling my arms as I narrowly avoided his gloved hand knocking on my skull.

"Whoa – sorry Ms. Walker! I was just about to knock," he replied, the apology slipping away into the freezing night like smoke from a cigarette. His young face was pink from the ocean breeze biting his cheeks, and he squeezed his chin further down in his plaid scarf.

Sometimes I looked at Howe and thought he could pass as a college student, given how young he looked. And yeah – he was cute in a semi-disheveled, CSI sort of way, especially with his wayward auburn hair. Unfortunately his constant nagging deleted any positive points he had, and made me want to poke him in the eyeball every time his freckled face appeared.

I looked out into the darkness and saw his blue sedan sitting in my driveway. "Does your damn car come with stealth mode? I didn't even hear you pull in!" I accused. I was so aggravated that I was once again facing the FBI. Couldn't they just leave me alone? Toss their hands in the air and scream Uncle over the whole Breakers thing? What ever happened to the appeal of a little unsolved mystery?

Howe apparently wasn't a fan of loose ends – as a kid, I was sure he debunked Santa and the Tooth Fairy in the same day, no doubt sharing his horrifying discoveries with the other small kids on the playground.

I pushed past him and headed for my Jeep, keys in hand.

"Ms. Walker – I really do need to talk with you and your friends again. When can I meet with all of you?" he asked, following me over the crushed seashell driveway. I heard the house door slam and looked up to see Ana glaring at Howe as she exited the house.

He glanced back and almost winced, "Oh – Ms. Lane is here too." His voice was barely a whisper and I was pretty sure I saw him shiver.

I bit back a smile, remembering the last time Ana was face to face with Howe. She had mentioned that his ability to fetch coffee was divine, and she couldn't understand why his partner Sollen only allowed him to handle the drinks. Surely he could also move up to take-out orders. She may have also mentioned that men in the FBI as young as him needed a job that was full-time since they had no love life.

Yeah – Ana was his least favorite suspect, no doubt because she ruthlessly stomped out any spark of self-worth he had, reducing his confidence to a smoldering heap of ash . . . repeatedly. She came striding over to the Jeep as I unlocked the door and cranked the engine to life. Howe took a step back as she approached, the fire in her eyes glowing brightly.

"You again? Jeez man, you need to get a life. I mean look at this," she said gesturing to his outfit, plaid scarf and all. "No wonder the ladies run in the opposite direction. Plus – you nag, like all the time. It's annoying. You're like a Cabbage Patch doll with a pull string, except you yank it yourself and repeat the same inane questions over and over again." She slammed her arms across her chest.

Howe gave her an exasperated look, "Ms. Lane. Lovely to see you, as always."

"Yeah, well, the feeling ain't mutual," she replied.

Howe tried to twist down a smile, "I'm sure. I was just telling Ms. Walker that we all need to meet up again. For a chat." Ana dramatically rolled her eyes and slid into the car with me. Howe shut the door for her and then walked around my side. I wondered if I would go to jail for a long time if I just ran him over.

He leaned down near my window and rapped on the glass, so I rolled it down. "What?" I snapped.

"Dalca Anescu's shop was vandalized last night – well, what remains of the shop. Would you know anything about that?"

I gave him a ridiculous look, "Are you kidding me? Hell no. Probably some moron decided it would be fun to wreck the place further on a dare." It was the truth, though it made me uneasy that anyone would set foot inside the Crimson Moon again, especially in its current state as a burned out shell.

Howe looked at me for a moment and my unease grew. He finally pulled out a photograph from his jacket pocket. He held it out to me and I gave him a curious glance as I looked down to the picture of a gear with a white, glassy finish. It had a strange, looping symbol engraved into its surface. "What's this?" I asked, taking the photo from Howe.

"We uncovered a safe built into the floor of the Moon, after it was ransacked last night. When we got it open, this gear was inside it in a wooden box. You don't know anything about it?"

"Do I look like I know anything about gears?" I asked, losing my patience. "No. I have no clue what the hell this is."

Howe handed me another photo as he replied, "Then maybe you can explain why the lowest scar on your back matches a drawing that was also found with the gear. Care to explain that?"

I looked down at the second photo and the air stilled in my lungs. Just as he said, my kill mark was drawn on a faded piece of paper that had been photographed in some well-lit room, most likely at FBI headquarters. I could literally feel Ana frozen beside me. We had been trying like crazy to distance ourselves from Dalca Anescu and this was definitely not the way to do it. Not to mention, I had no clue what a gear had to do with me – or my kill mark. I managed to choke out a question as Howe plucked the photos from my hands, "How do you know what the scar on my back looks like?"

"Photographs from the hospital, Miss Walker. Seeing as you and your friends are under investigation for your role in a possible bombing, we

101

had access to all your medical records. Tell me – why does your physician believe the scar on your back is a burn from babyhood?"

"Because it is," I whispered, knowing that was TOTALLY a lie. "It's a radiator burn."

Howe placed the photos back inside his pocket and looked me dead in the eye. "And yet the exact same design is on a paper that was inside a hidden safe in the home of Dalca Anescu. A woman who happened to be killed during the Fire and Ice ball, while the rest of you survived."

"Eila nearly died," hissed Ana.

Howe simply pushed away from my car, heading for his own as he yelled over his shoulder, "I'll be in touch soon, Ms. Walker."

I sat there in the Jeep, listening to the radio play a rock band softly as Howe walked back to his car. I turned to Ana who looked paler than usual. "Well, crap."

13 Eila

ON THE RIDE TO THE HIGH SCHOOL, I called Raef to fill him in on Howe, the drawing, and the gear. He and Kian had no answers either, but weren't thrilled that there was now a link between me and Dalca. He was also concerned as to why anyone would ransack Dalca's former shop, though he was proud that both Ana and I managed to keep our cool when questioned by Howe. With Raef's assurances that we would figure it out and come up with an excuse, I shoved Agent Howe and his pestering questions to the back of my mind.

At the football field, Ana and I had managed to squeeze through the throngs of fans to the top bleachers on our home-field side. I felt as though nine million people had greeted both of us, happy we had finally come back to school, though I suspected they just wanted to see if we looked damaged and possibly confirm the Newport rumor.

Ana and I however, showed no outward marks except for her walking boot, which probably fueled the rumor mill that we weren't actually at the ball. We people-watched from our high perch above the football field and my eyes soon found the most curvaceous and loud cheerleader in a five-block radius.

Nikki Shea, with her body built for badness, was causing a near riot with the male fans as she shook her red and white pompoms. Ana caught me watching her. "You know, I was actually looking forward to getting back to classes, but now I'm not so thrilled," she moaned, sticking her tongue out.

I chuckled. "I'll just avoid her. I already switched classes, so I rarely see her anyway," I reasoned, refusing to give the irritating twit the satisfaction of my social agony. Plus, she had Elizabeth's necklace, which just plain pissed me off. Seeing her face reminded me that I didn't have the one item that could unlock Elizabeth's freakin' diary, and that drove me nuts.

Ana stared at Nikki with a focused intensity and I shuffled uneasy in my seat. "What are you doing?"

"Shhh!" she snapped, waving a multicolored mitten in my face.

I leaned closer, whispering, "What are you doing?"

"Trying to convince her to flash the crowd so she gets expelled."

"ANA!"

Ana sat back laughing, "Chill woman – I'm not that brilliant."

"You are pure evil, you know that?" I laughed, but my giggles were cut short as a snowball whizzed past Ana's head and smacked into the back of a heavy-set woman in front of us. She turned, the tight red curls on her head framing a face that could freeze the sun. She glared at the two of us and I shook my head, raising my hands to prove we didn't just nail her with a snowball. She looked like she had a mighty short fuse and angering her would probably lead to an early grave. She slowly swiveled back to the field.

What moron was tossing snowballs?

We glanced at the crowds milling around, but saw no guilty snow-hurler anywhere. I looked at Ana and she gave a confused shrug just as another snowball whipped past her and nailed the woman right in the back of the neck. Oh dear.

This time the woman got to her feet and turned on us. "What is wrong with you?" she snarled.

"I swear – it's not us!" I pleaded.

Ana, never one to be wrongfully accused, crossed her arms defiantly, "Lady – do you even see any snow up here in the stands? It isn't us!" Ana apparently wanted us both to die a slow and painful death.

The woman started unwedging herself from the two other people in front of us, their looks wishing us well in the afterlife as their popcorn was jostled all over their laps. This was how we were going to go out – not at the hands of a talented Mortis, but broken into itsy-bitsy pieces by an enraged, middle-aged football fan.

Just as she was stepping over the steel bench to pummel the two of us, I heard our names being called. Crazy lady stopped as Ana and I searched for the source of the voice.

Finally I spied the name caller – MJ, tall and lean with a giant smile on his face and a snowball in hand, was standing just off the side of the bleachers.

"MJ!" screamed Ana, delighted. I waved down to our long-lost pal, but then turned my attention back to the angry redhead. "I think the snowballs were meant for us – our friend just can't hit the broadside of a barn."

I wanted to suck the words back into my mouth the moment I said them.

Her eyes grew wide as she realized I suggested (unintentionally) that she was bigger than a barn. Knowing she was about to grind me into the silver paint beneath our butts, I grabbed Ana's hand and yelled down to MJ, "We're coming! Stay right where ya are!"

"What?" asked Ana, turning her attention back to me as I yanked her arm to get her moving. "We aren't watching the game?"

"We will – just from somewhere else!" I hauled her down through the bleachers and out of the glare of the woman, who no doubt was plotting ways to dismember us if we ever came near her again.

We finally reached the bottom of the bleachers where MJ was strolling towards us. Ana launched herself at him and he grabbed her up in a bear hug, her petite frame glued to his long torso. She was squealing in his ear and MJ was laughing at her craziness. He finally put her down, keeping one arm around her as he reached out and hauled me into his chest. His long arms curved around both of us, hugging us tightly. "I know, I know – ya missed my fabulosity. But have no fear, the cool dog is here."

I snorted into his chest. "Yeah, sure ya are," I laughed. He began wiggling his fingers into our sides and Ana and I started yelling at him to stop tickling us. We were writhing around in his arms so much that he finally had to release us or risk toppling into the band – all of whom were watching our antics with great amusement.

Ana had tears in her eyes and MJ's face faltered as he gave her another hug, and kissed the top of her head. "Missed ya, babe," he said softly into her blonde hair.

"You're forbidden from leaving ever again," she whispered.

He held her tightly and rubbed her back. "You got it . . . though all those hot chicks in West Palm are going to be bawling their eyes out."

She started laughing and MJ pulled her over to sit in a few open seats toward the end of the bleachers. I followed and Ana and I boxed in our dear friend, drilling him with a thousand questions about Florida. Having him with us was like coming home to a warm fire and perfect cup of cocoa. While I would never see MJ as anything other than a friend, I loved him. He was the brother I never had – for both Ana and me.

The game finally started and Barnstable dominated the field. I watched as Jesse led the team through play after play, fighting their way into the end zone and racking up the points. As they scored, Nikki's voice would ring out in the cold night, working the crowd into a thunderous roar. It was contagious, and soon I was on my feet with my friends, screaming for our classmates battling on the field. I was shocked to find myself truly enjoying the game, the atmosphere – the entire event. I glanced around and noticed one girl cheering from the warmth of her boyfriend's jacket. She had leaned into him, her back to his chest, and he had pulled his coat tightly around them both, cheering along with her.

Watching them, I missed Raef's warmth and I wondered what he was up to tonight. I wondered if he would be as insane for the football game as our classmates.

The buzzer rang out, signaling half-time, and the team jogged from the field. I noticed Jesse scanning the crowd as he ran and when his eyes swept towards where I was, I waved. He saw me, and his face lit with a brilliant smile that contrasted sharply against his dark skin. He waved and disappeared into the field house.

I turned back to Ana and MJ and found them staring at me. "What?" I demanded.

"He LIKES you," purred MJ.

"He's just a friend," I replied, looking sternly at my disbelieving pals. "HE IS!"

14 Eila

WHEN THE FINAL POINTS WERE LIT on the scoreboard an hour later, it was obvious – very obvious – that we had one heck of a football team. People were high-fiving and yelling and shouting. The cheerleaders had joined the players and fans on the field, in their own victory-induced party.

The crowd finally grew silent as a mic was handed to the coach who named Jesse the MVP of the game. Everyone went wild again and Jesse graciously accepted the game ball and the mic and the crowd hushed to hear what he had to say.

Ana, MJ, and I were scanning the masses, looking for familiar faces as I listened with one ear as Jesse thanked his coach and praised the hard work of his teammates, saying victory was only accomplished when everyone worked together. I was only half listening when he began talking about being MVP, "So while I am very flattered to receive the game ball tonight, I'd like to hand this off to another winner of sorts.

109

One who defied the odds, and came back from a no-win situation to be with us tonight. Eila Walker – can you join me on the field?"

I turned slowly toward Ana whose mouth was hanging open. MJ had an equally stunned look on his face. I started to shake my head *no*, but the crowd finally saw where I was and started to clap. Ana and MJ tried to shrink away but I grabbed them. "If I have to go out there, you are both coming with me," I hissed.

Ana moved with near wooden legs, but MJ slipped easily into rockstar mode, waving to people. As I walked across the field, the crowds parted, opening an alleyway to Jesse and the team. On my left I saw the vibrant pompoms of the cheer squad and I passed dangerously close to Nikki, who gave me a lethal look, her eyes tracking me. I glanced over my shoulder back at her, worried she was about to literally stab me in the back.

MJ and Ana hung back as I made my way up to Jesse, who held the football easily in his wide hand. I swallowed as I finally reached him, daring a glance at the massive crowd around me.

Jesse leaned toward me, "You look a bit pale."

"I am a bit freaked, thanks," I replied.

"Don't pass out."

"I'll try not to."

Jesse brought the mic back to his lips and spoke to the crowd. You could hear a pin drop and I wanted to crawl under the AstroTurf.

"Most of our class knows Eila here. They know she, along with Ana Lane and MJ Williams, survived the disaster at the Breakers a month ago. She has fought hard to come back to us – a sign of a true warrior's heart. It is with great honor that we – the entire team – bestow the winning game ball to her tonight. She won against impossible odds and that makes her our MVP – Most Valuable Person – of the night."

Jesse handed the ball to me, and I looked down at its thick leather hide and tough outer shell. It was a ball that had gone through hell tonight and weirdly, I knew how it felt thanks to the Breakers.

My football and I weren't all that different.

Realizing the rumor mill just spun completely off its track thanks to Jesse's revelation, I managed to whisper a semi-sincere thanks to Jesse. I then turned to the crowd, which looked like a sea of millions and Jesse tipped the mic toward my face. I swallowed and said the first thing that came to my mind as I held up the ball, "To all the warriors, big and small."

The crowd went insane and the team grabbed me and pushed me up onto the shoulders of Jesse and another player. At first I was completely horrified, but as I looked out over the sea of people, jumping and cheering, as a rock song pumped out of the speakers, I suddenly felt like an average high schooler.

No deadly gifts, no shadowy killers, and no family history of murder. I held the ball high and just let myself be a teenager.

Eventually I was able to make my way out of the crowd, though Ana and MJ were still in the thick of it. I tucked the cold football under my arm as I walked to the Jeep, rubbing my hands through my gloves in a vain attempt to warm them.

For the life of me I couldn't figure out how in the heck the football team didn't freeze to death playing in weather like this. Kansas could be really cold, but the Cape air had a rawness that cut through your body and froze the marrow inside your bones. It was brutal, and I couldn't wait for the warm weather to come back. It was going to be a long, LONG winter.

I glanced back to Ana and MJ who were talking with some classmates. They were accustomed to the cold air that rolled in off the ocean, but me? Forget it. I wanted to crank the heat in my Jeep and crawl inside the air vents, which was my plan.

Finally reaching the driver's side of my vehicle, I placed the football on the hood against the windshield. I fished my keys out of the thick parka, but I fumbled with them and they dropped by my feet. I muttered a curse and reached down to get them when I heard a familiar male voice glide over the hood of my vehicle.

"Nice ride."

I snatched the keys from the frozen ground and popped back up, narrowly missing the side-view mirror.

Leaning against the bumper of my Jeep was Thor, now dressed in jeans and a mariner's jacket. What. The. Heck.

Why was this guy here? Was he one of the player's older sibling? He was definitely built for football, including his biceps, which I was fairly certain I couldn't even get my arm around.

"Thanks," I replied as I subtly flipped each key on my key ring between my fingers, turning them into little daggers. If Thor decided to flip the crazy switch and turn pervert, my keys would become angry little weapons, although . . . jumping me in front of the BHS football fans, and team, would be unwise. We were, after all, surrounded by people milling around their cars, talking, and cheering. I eased my iron grasp on my keys as I realized I was safe here.

112

Plus, I wasn't above stabbing him in places the sun doesn't shine if he came at me.

"Can I help you?" I finally asked.

Thor didn't move a muscle as he replied, "I saw that you earned the game ball. That's quite impressive. Doesn't the game ball go to the most valuable player of the night?"

"I, uh, couldn't say. I don't normally watch football," I replied, rubbing one sharp key with my thumb.

"But you are here, teeth chattering and all," he replied, a small smile crawling onto his lips.

"I was invited by the captain." My confidence was slowly growing. "I never caught your name the other night, Mr . . ."

"Blackwood. Rillin Blackwood," he replied, tilting his head ever so slightly in a chivalrous salute. "I was on my way to Boston, but then I saw the game. I swung in to watch, but then heard over the speaker that Eila Walker was being given the game ball – as a welcome back gift after the Newport incident. You must be the girl that survived the explosion in Newport. You look amazingly well for such a massive blast."

"It isn't that impressive," I said slowly.

Son of a nugget, was this guy FBI? I was so sick of the Feds and the work involved in keeping them misdirected. If this dude was yet another agent, I might just scream.

My visitor cocked his head ever so slightly and studied me with a strange intensity, making me shift on my feet, uneasy. I felt like he was trying to commit my face to memory, which was downright weird and definitely scumballworthy.

Suddenly his gaze moved past me and he nodded to an area behind

113

me. "You seem to have company headed this way in a hurry."

I watched Thor, er, Rillin, for a moment more, then dared a glance behind me. As if the night couldn't get any more screwed up, Teddy Bencourt, number 44 on the football team, was pushing his way through the crowd and waving at me.

I so didn't want to deal with him right now.

After drunkenly falling on me during the senior beach bonfire in October, he had jettisoned his mind and started manhandling my parts without permission.

Actually, I recalled screaming at him to get off me until Raef grabbed his sorry butt and nearly flung him into the next town. If Jesse hadn't been there as well, it was entirely possible Raef would have killed the linebacker.

Jesse had apologized to me about his teammate's stupidity, but Teddy had yet to beg my forgiveness. I had been able to avoid him thus far as I hadn't been back to school since that night, but I knew he was going to want to talk to me as soon as I set foot on school grounds. He wasted no time, apparently.

I needed to escape.

"Eila!" Teddy yelled as he worked his way through the high-fives and pats-on-the-back.

I quickly turned back to my car and swore under my breath as I tried to fumble my key into the lock.

"Not a fan of Double Digits?" questioned Rillin, amusement in his voice. I was stuck between irritating guys, neither of whom I wanted to friggin' deal with, but at the moment I'd take the dude glued to my bumper over the baller headed my way.

114

"Let's just say our understanding of 'no' varied between the two of us," I muttered, my breath creating clouds of vapor.

I mercifully heard the lock pop and I swung the door open, but I could still hear Teddy calling my name. I glanced at Rillin, but the amusement he had moments ago was gone. His face was dead serious as he watched Teddy approach and I was shocked to recognize a protective anger begin to grace the face of this strange man.

Who the hell WAS this guy?

I cranked the Jeep to life and Rillin pushed off my bumper coming around to my side of the vehicle. I stiffened, unsure of what he was doing. He grabbed the football off my windshield and came around to my door before I could shut it. He leaned down in the open door frame and I got a clear view of his face – deep blue eyes, rugged skin, and another faint scar that flirted with the edge of his brow. His life showed in the lines of his face, giving him the air of hard-won elegance. I slowly took the ball from his offering hand, unable to make heads or tails of this strange man.

"You are not the type to run from what scares you," said Rillin quietly, his face hard and serious.

Uh, yeah – okay, psycho.

I opened my mouth to reply, but Rillin suddenly strode away toward Teddy and stuck a hand out to shake his. He began talking to Teddy, who was torn between looking at me and at this new man, who was congratulating him on a great game. Rillin then said something that grabbed the footballer's full attention and Teddy grinned from ear-to-ear.

I sighed, relieved. Teddy had effectively been distracted by Rillin Blackwood, whoever the heck he was. He began to slowly guide Teddy back into the throngs of people and out of my sight.

I looked back down to the football, but nearly jumped clear through the fabric top when Ana pounded on the passenger side window. My heart racing, I reached across to her side and popped the lock for her.

She slid into her side, "I don't think I ever had so many people talk to me at once. My brain is in melt-down mode!" She turned to me, smiling that sly knowing smile of hers. "And looky-looky who got the game ball from Jesse Vale! Could it be that the mighty captain is crushing on you?"

I rolled my eyes as I dared a glance toward the crowd where Teddy and Rillin had been. "Jesse is just a friend."

Ana laughed, "Yeah – and that's what you said about Raef and boy was that a whopper of a lie."

I shook my head. "That's different. I tried lying to myself, and you guys about Raef, which was pointless. Jesse though is REALLY just a friend."

"To you maybe," replied Ana. "But Jesse may have other ideas."

I prayed Ana was wrong. I would be back in the halls of BHS tomorrow morning, among my classmates. As it was, I would be dodging Teddy, who I luckily didn't have any classes with, and Nikki, who I was sure daydreamed about running me down with her convertible Mustang.

Jesse, however, wouldn't be so easy to avoid. He sat across from me in English and behind me in Ecology.

"MJ had to head out, but he wanted to know if you think you will come back and see another game sometime soon?" asked Ana, who was pressing her mittened hands against the dashboard heater.

"Maybe," I said, as I tossed the ball to Ana and backed out of the

116

parking space, scanning the lot for my strange stalker. Once again, however, Mr. Blackwood had disappeared, taking with him my brief stint as an average teenager.

15 Raef

THE PART OF BOSTON WE WERE IN was not known for its stellar bar scene, but it was quite possible that Kian and I had landed in the worst dive on the planet. While I didn't dig for details as to how he located a dealer, even Kian seemed to question the logic of where this Mortis hung out. You could probably take your pick of patrons inside and they most likely all deserved to be on the Blacklist. In a place like this, who needed a dealer?

"You know – this would be a heck of a lot easier if we just went on our merry way and simply picked off some random degenerate," muttered Kian.

I peeled the label on the bottle of beer in front of me. Though neither of us drank, we bought the beers so we looked like we fit in.

At least, that was the intent.

We were surrounded by gangbangers, drug dealers, and a handful of bikers who looked as though they could chew the tires off my Harley. "If we're going to start doing this, we are making sure who we target deserves what they have coming," I replied.

Kian gave me a knowing look and gestured to the entire room, as if to say *take your pick*. I shook my head *no* and Kian growled, aggravated. "Figures you would have a moralistic psyche."

He leaned back from the bar and scanned the dark, dingy space of the Lucky Lady. His eyes settled on three pool tables stuffed towards the back. All were occupied by various, suspicious individuals, most likely fresh out of prison or headed there.

Kian leaned closer to me, "Okay – so here's the deal. We need to take over the last pool table on the right with the chipped leg. Once we do that, we need to drop the seven-ball in the corner pocket near the wall and wait."

"You're not serious . . . are you?" I asked, floored that we needed to partake in Cloak and Dagger nonsense to get our hands on some names. Kian nodded and headed for the table. I sighed and followed.

Five minutes later, the table was ours thanks to a hundred dollar bill I offered the two leather-clad players. I dropped the seven-ball in the specified pocket and Kian racked the balls. "You first," he said, casually scanning the room for our potential dealer.

I pulled a stick from the wall and set up my shot, the smooth rock maple sliding easily through my fingers.

"Think the girls are having a good time at the game?" he asked, no doubt trying to quell his fears that Ana was alone with Eila. Of course, we did contact MJ who had gotten home earlier in the day, and asked that he spy on them.

Eila would shoot me if she found out.

"Hopefully, though Agent Howe showing up did not get the night off to the best start."

Kian slid his luke-warm beer farther down the edge of the pool table, "Yeah, that wasn't such a grand development. I bet they were super pleased to see him again. What's with the gear though?"

"My guess is it's a remnant from the Lunaterra," I said. "Maybe something the Rysse clan followers gave Dalca for some reason. I mean, they did entrust her with the ashes of Rysse himself, so maybe the gear was a trophy of sorts – something Rysse had that had belonged to one of the Lunaterra he killed. I guarantee the drawing was so Dalca could identify Eila as Lunaterra."

Kian shook his head, "Maybe. Either way, it's not good that the Feds found either. We need Howe getting bored, not more interested. I still vote for making him disappear." Kian's pipe dream of killing Sollen and Howe was starting to become mine as well. We could absolutely make them disappear, but doing so would draw attention to all of us. Murdering an FBI agent was not an option . . . unfortunately.

Kian stretched his spine and swung the pool stick around the back of his neck, letting it rest across his shoulders as he hitched his hands over either end, making him look like a scarecrow. "I don't know about the girls, but football ranks up there with watching paint dry for me. I'm actually glad I didn't go to that funfest," he said.

I glanced up at him. "Did MJ text you?"

"Yeah – he had located them before the game had started. They were in the bleachers," he replied as I called my shot and aimed, sinking the ball as I predicted. Pool was one of the ways I killed time over the years and as such, I could clean the table in a matter of minutes. I had used

Christian's billiard table a few times at Torrent Road, often when I was trying to keep my mind from drifting back to the boiler room in Newport.

I easily took out the next three balls when Kian finally cleared his throat, swinging the pool cue off his back. "Think I can play as well, or am I stuck here watching you all night?"

I smiled, the devil in me thoroughly enjoying watching Kian stand by like a lawn ornament. I finally stepped back and he finished off the game, an obvious pro as well.

We played for several hours and as midnight rolled around, I had just about given up hope on the dealer, but then a hand appeared on the edge of the table.

I traced the muscled arm up to its wall-sized owner. He walked the length of the cherry wood, a black wool coat fitted tightly over his wide shoulders. A navy blue t-shirt underneath revealed faded tattoos that laced his neck. He pulled the seven-ball out of the pocket and tossed it on the table with a resounding thump.

He turned and looked at Kian and me, and Kian gave a small nod, his hand twisting tighter around his cue. It was then that I noticed the dealer had a faint scar that ran down the side of his face. I didn't know what would leave a scar on our kind – we always healed. He pulled a cue stick from the wall and rubbed the tip with blue chalk.

"Mind if I join you?" he asked, his voice rough as he seemed to study my face as if to commit it to memory. He seemed to focus on me more than Kian, and his weird attention made me suspicious.

"If you must," replied Kian, with a twist to his mouth.

Our new player gave him a knowing smile as he racked the balls again, turning his attention to me. "Where you two from? Originally?" he asked, fishing for details on who he was going to do business with, and I expected the inquisition. He took his shot, the hit nearly cleaving the ball in half.

"Barnstable." I replied. "What about you?"

The dealer looked surprised I asked him. "Around."

He knocked another ball in, and then tilted his head towards the back wall and the shadows. Kian and I followed, casually pretending to take a swig of beer. The dealer leaned against the wall, pool stick still in his hand.

"Here's how it works. However many you buy, you have exclusive rights to those names for one week. You don't use them in the seven days allowed, the names go back on the list. No refunds. And sloppy work – anything that remotely is questionable by the cops – and our friendly relationship will end. Permanently. Those are the terms."

I couldn't believe we were discussing people like drugs. We were going to buy the names of those who deserved to die – people who were proven to be worthless humans and had done some vile things. Rapists. Wife beaters. Drug dealers. Murderers.

Technically we were doing the human world a messed up form of public service, but buying someone's death sentence climbed up my spine with chilling clarity. But I needed the strength held captive in a human soul to protect Eila . . . and a long time ago, I killed humans with ease.

"Agreed," I replied. Kian added his consent as well and we got down to the money aspect. While drugs could be bought for a few hundred dollars, a human life was at least ten-grand a hit. Kian and I decided to start with one each, and the dealer slid two envelopes with the target details inside – where they lived, worked, drove, etc.

Kian had already sorted the money into a tightly rolled wad and handed the dealer our cash. No one in the bar even cared, as they most likely were all there for various forms of illegal activity.

A few of the patrons were listening to the news that played above the bar, but I had ignored it until the word *Newport* caught my attention. On the screen was a picture of the Breakers, with a female newscaster speaking. Kian saw that I had turned to watch and he did as well. We listened to the blonde reporter as she spoke to the camera,

Authorities have yet to issue a final report on the explosion last month at the historic Breakers mansion in Newport. Billionaire Christian Raines, who federal officials questioned earlier in the month, has been cleared as a suspect. Mr. Raines, whose company North Star was using the mansion for a fundraiser the night of the explosion, has offered his financial heft in repairing the building. Mr. Raines has also been credited with saving the lives of several party-goers the night of the explosion. In other news . . ."

I turned back to the dealer, and was surprised to see that he had also been watching the report. He shook his head slightly, as if disgusted. It was a move that concerned me. None of our names had been released to the press, thanks to the FBI and Eila's age, but the dealer's reaction made me uneasy.

"Something amusing?" I asked.

The dealer just shrugged. When he realized I was looking for an actual answer, he offered up his thoughts, "I just think Raines knows what went on that night. I'm sure he does."

Kian turned to the dealer as well, now on edge like me.

"Why is that?" I asked, trying to act casual.

The dealer eyed me carefully for a moment, obviously debating whether or not to fill us in. Finally he spoke, "He had been drugged prior to the explosion, which tells me someone didn't want him interfering with whatever was going down."

The dealer's revelation was like a blow to the gut and it took every ounce of control I had to not show my utter shock. Even Kian was doing all he could to keep it together. No one knew that Christian had been knocked unconscious by one of the clan members except the five of us. We knew because we saw it happen. How the hell did this guy know?

Kian, realizing I couldn't speak, piped up, "Seriously? How'd you find that out?"

"His dealer told me – said he was shot up with arsenic."

Christian had a dealer? And here Kian and I were trying to sneak around, locating one of our own. We could have just asked Christian, though now we had uncovered something far more disturbing than a soul thief who dealt in . . . souls. I looked at the dealer, "Arsenic?"

The dealer gave me a weird appraisal for a moment. "Yeah – doesn't last long, but arsenic will knock out our kind for a few minutes. It's an old school way of taking down a soul thief, but it works." The dealer walked to the wall rack, pushing his pool stick back into place. "Christian is an idiot though. He should have never helped that girl."

Kian stepped over to the table and leaned casually against it, clearly aware that I was about to lose it. "I don't follow," he said.

The dealer turned to us, "Think about it. He has taken some strange interest in this human. If I were a Mortis who wanted to get rich quick, I would aim for the one thing that Christian Raines seems willing to pony up the dough to protect."

"The girl," I breathed. The dealer nodded.

Dear god. How did we not see this coming?

"Like I said – stupid move on his part. Someone will grab her up, hang onto her for ransom, and make Christian cough up that obscene wealth he has, only to kill her in the end. I'd give her a week or two at most, before someone pegs her for the walking lottery ticket that she is."

Kian stood straighter, "No one knows who she is. The FBI never released her name."

The dealer slowly rolled the seven-ball into a far pocket. My nerves flamed inside my body and I dug my fingers into my palms to control my panic.

"True . . . but how long can that last?" he asked casually.

He was right. I couldn't hide her forever. Cape Cod was so bloody small, that her name was bound to get out. A hurricane of terror started sweeping through my body. We needed to get back to Eila's house. NOW.

The dealer watched my reaction carefully, aware that I was a bit too interested. I needed to calm down. I couldn't think straight. She was most likely asleep and warm in her bed.

"You feeling all right?" he asked.

"Yeah – I must need a hit more than I thought," I replied, trying to pull it together.

The dealer nodded and extended his hand to shake mine, "Remember - you've got seven days, just like the ball says, or you forfeit your purchase."

16 Raef

KIAN AND I HAD RACED BACK TO 408, consumed by a horrific fear that we had left the girls unprotected. It was foolish and shortsighted of us both, and we drove in silence, the anger at ourselves toxic. In the dead of night, we were unable to reach MJ or the girls, all of them no doubt asleep.

We hoped.

Our belief that they were safe could have cost them their lives, Mae included. But when we finally got to 408, I saw Eila's Wrangler parked next to the house, and relief slowly surfaced. With the key she had given us, I got into the house and flew up to the second floor.

That's when desperation set in, hard and fierce.

Eila was not in her room.

Kian had followed me inside and checked on Ana, who slept soundly in her bed. Mae, whose suite was on the top, 3rd floor, was also asleep, but Eila was missing.

126

I tried not to panic, and when I heard the TV, I followed the sound of Jimmy Stewart's voice into the living room, finally laying eyes on my E who was snuggled into the couch.

I had nearly dropped to my knees in relief.

She had drifted off in front of the TV, which played softly throwing a ghostly light over her relaxed form. A few magazines were strewn around the floor and one rested open across her stomach. Her chest rose and fell gently, and her curved lips were parted as she dreamed, probably of a world that was far safer than this one and didn't include my kind – or hers.

I slowly walked over to her and picked up one of the magazines. She had written inside the glossy pages and circled a few items. Then I saw my name, written in the margin, and I realized she had been making a list. A Christmas list – for me.

Some of the items she had circled, she had gone back and scratched out – a nice scarf, a pair of leather gloves – even a stuffed Elmo, though the red little monster did have a heart next to it.

I swallowed back the emotion that was beginning to crush me. I had left her alone, defenseless against the world once again. My poor planning in Newport, my assumption that we would be safe, nearly cost her everything.

But despite all that I had gotten wrong and how thoroughly I had failed her before, Eila had spent the evening trying to pick a Christmas gift for me. She had fallen asleep paging through ideas that might make me happy, when all that ever brought me joy was her effortless smile.

I looked away from her sleeping form for a moment, blinking away the building tears in my eyes, willing myself to rein in the emotions that were about to suffocate me. I was nearly two centuries old and designed to be a heartless, driven soul thief, but all of that became muddled, confused and splintered, the day I came face to face with Eila in the halls of Barnstable High School.

Because of her, I now ran a fine line between being a bodyguard who would kill without question, and a man who adored her like a lovesick teen. But what we had wasn't a crush – it wasn't even a Romeo and Juliet love. What we shared moved beyond all those human terms to something else. A fire and ice that bound us together, linked us like magnets and the polar opposites that we were, inscribed on our very DNA.

For me, the world held no other person I could ever love as much as Eila, and whether my desire to be with her was encoded during Elizabeth's death or not, I didn't care. I would tear down the world to keep her safe and nothing would get by me, nothing would come near her that was remotely threatening ever again.

Unfortunately, I suspected Eila would do the same for me, which made me worry constantly that she harbored a self-confidence that would get her killed. No one walked away from a Mortis who wanted them dead, and an untrained Lunaterra like Eila might as well just be your average high school girl.

My kind would kill her before she even had a chance to scream.

I heard her take a deep breath and I looked back to her, grateful beyond words that she was resting on a garish red couch and not inside a coffin . . . or lifeless on a cobblestone street like her grandmother.

I got down on my knees next to her and carefully tucked her dark hair away from her porcelain skin. She blinked and then a slow, sleepy smile spread on her face, her brown eyes warming with the life that flowed through her. A life that I was so fearful of losing again.

"Raef?" she whispered. "What are you doing here? What time is it?"

I stroked her soft cheek and leaned close to her, whispering. "It's late, but I just wanted to see you. I hope that's okay."

"You are so weird," she mumbled, but her smile grew and she snuggled against my palm. The pain of how much I loved her cut through me like a bullet on fire and I couldn't help myself as I leaned down and kissed her softly on the lips.

She raised a delicate hand in response, running her fingers through my hair. "Good thing I like weird," she whispered, a sweet grin on her face.

I drew a trembling breath, trying to push away the words of the dealer as I gathered her warm body to mine. "Let me get you to bed," I said quietly as I rose to my feet, Eila safely in my arms.

She sighed, curling into my chest as her dark hair cascaded down my forearm like a sheet of cold satin against my skin. "Thanks for coming," she yawned as her body relaxed and drifted back to sleep.

I couldn't help but smile and I rested my chin against the top of her head. I carried her up the creaking stairs to her bedroom, laying her down in the bed I had built for Elizabeth, and she curled her body against the cold sheets.

I wanted to climb in with her and warm her skin, but instead I stood there, watching her sleep.

Guarding her like a ghost in the darkness, even while she dreamed.

MONDAY MORNING CRASHED ON TOP of me like a drunken

elephant, thanks to the sound of my alarm clock screeching in my ear. I slapped it off and lay in bed, staring at the dark gray sky outside, a visual reminder that the halls of Barnstable were waiting to consume me.

I slowly kicked down my covers, but then realized I was still in my jeans and sweatshirt. Confusion slowly gave way to the memory of Raef kissing me last night and picking me up off the couch. His scent and warmth still lingered on me and I smiled, squashing my face down into my pillow, a flush of heat flowing into my skin.

I heard my door click open and the mattress bounce as Ana flopped down next to me on the bed. I turned to her, and she groaned into the covers, "The superintendent is a sick individual. High school should never start this early."

I sighed, slowly dragging myself out of my memories and warm sheets. "Agreed. Let's start a petition."

Ana snorted and finally pushed herself off my bed. "Ugh – I'm getting dressed," she moaned, stumbling back out my door.

"Don't forget your walking boot!" I called to her.

"Yes, MOM!" she snarled back.

Thirty minutes later, Ana and I were dressed and in the kitchen, finishing the last of our mismatched bagels. Mae breezed into the room, looking amazing in a tailored blue suit and stone-colored heels.

I choked on my hot cocoa. "Wow. You look terrific," I sputtered, floored at her dramatic change.

Her face beamed, "Do you really like it?"

"Yeah – but where are you going?" I asked, trying to calculate how she got the money for such a stunning piece of clothing.

"My first day on the job, sweetie. I am heading over to Mr. Raines' office. He has a whole separate workspace in that fabulous home on Torrent Road. I am going to be working out of there, and then sometimes at his Beacon Hill office."

"You are going to be working with him *in his house?*" I asked, a bit alarmed. Ana's eyebrows crept up in surprise over this new arrangement.

"Well, yes, but I will be traveling a lot as well. I've got to fly – don't want to be late on my first day!" she said, thrilled that she had her dream job. I couldn't rain on her parade and swallowed back my fears that she would fall for Christian. Why couldn't he just look like a toad and make my life less stressful?

I walked over to Mae and gave her a gentle hug, trying not to wrinkle the fabric she wore, "Good luck."

"Thanks, sweetie! Have fun at school," she smiled, and grabbed her keys, heading out the door.

I stood staring at her minivan as she backed down the driveway. Ana slid up next to me. "Come on – let's get this day started so it can be over already."

When I pulled into the packed parking area of the high school, I scanned the lot looking for Raef, but was surprised to see MJ instead, sitting on the hood of his Bronco, peeling an orange. The morning was foggy, but warm, and many of my classmates were not even wearing jackets. I had grabbed a sweatshirt, but MJ was in a t-shirt that displayed some metal band that I never heard of.

I parked next to him and he hopped off his car, tossing the last of the rinds into the bushes by my bumper. I stepped out of my side while he helped Ana out the passenger door.

"Where's Raef?" I asked MJ as he pitched Ana's bag over his shoulder. He slammed the door shut and Ana wobbled over to me in her walking boot.

"Raef said he and Kian had to go hunting today. They were headed up North – something about Raef's appetite for the local deer population starting to raise eyebrows at the DNR office."

"Oh," I replied, surprised he didn't text me or call. I was so used to him always being there, checking on me. But I had demanded some space and he was obviously honoring that.

MJ looked at me as we all started walking into the school with the sea of students. More than a few breezed by us with a friendly greeting. "Don't worry, Eila – I'm sure you'll see him later," he said, reading my face.

"No – it's okay, MJ. I had asked him to back-off on the protection detail thing. He is probably just following through with my wishes." I squeezed through the glass doors and the halls vibrated with the chatter of hundreds of students.

"Wait – does that mean I can actually go to my last rehab appointment without Kian causing the women to drool?" asked Ana, now brighter and hopeful.

MJ shook his head, "Is it really that bad to have some guys looking out for you? I mean, are you two going to kick me to the curb as well?"

"WHAT? We did not kick them to the curb!" I protested, finally reaching my locker. I spun the lock, but it took a few times to remember the exact combination.

Ana reached up and kissed MJ on the cheek. "We would never be mean to a doggie," she said, smiling.

"Oh thanks a lot," MJ laughed. "Come on, PegLeg – I'll escort you to your locker," he said, looping his arm with Ana's. They gave me a wave as they headed down the south corridor to their respective homerooms.

I watched them leave, shuffling books into my locker, focused on what things I needed for my next three classes. It took me a moment to register that someone was standing next to me, but the bright red fabric finally caught my eye.

"You're back," said Jesse, his red and white varsity jacket hanging open on his athletic frame.

I shifted uneasy. "Uh yeah – I guess, though I am already missing sleeping in late."

"I hear that," he said, leaning against the lockers. A few girls giggled *Hi* to him, star struck by his presence. Jesse could absolutely go into

133

modeling someday and his future was bright as a footballer and genuinely nice human being. The NFL would someday be salivating over him, I was sure.

"Is Raef here?" he asked, looking down the hall. Most of the school knew I hung out with Raef, but no one knew that we were more than friends. In the eyes of my classmates, Raef and I were just tight buddies . . . which meant I wasn't dating anyone.

I swallowed and tried to avoid Jesse's curious eyes as I shut my locker. "No. He's not here today. I'll probably see him later."

"Oh. Well . . . can I walk with you to English?" he asked, reaching down to pick up my backpack before I could protest. I just nodded and shoved my hands into my jean pockets as we walked, angling ourselves between the crowds. Occasionally the tight space would force us together and he would brush against my arm or back. My heart hammered in my ears every time we made contact.

Finally entering the English wing, the crowds thinned some and Jesse cleared his throat. "So, how are you feeling?" he asked.

"I'm fine. Ana gets her cast-thing off today. She is thrilled and I don't blame her. It looks uncomfortable."

Jesse nodded and I noticed his face looked a little strained. He caught me looking at him and gave me a weak smile, but then he stopped and turned to me. I tensed as he glanced down the hallway, as if checking to see if we were alone. He sighed and spoke quietly to me, "I uh, am really sorry about that night at the bonfire. I shouldn't have let Teddy drink."

I did NOT want to talk about this right now. Or ever. I started to shake my head, about to tell him not to worry about it, but Jesse took a step forward and I froze in place.

"It was really messed up. And I know Teddy tried to approach you last night at the game. He wants to apologize, but I get it if you don't want to talk to him."

I swallowed, feeling way, WAY outside my comfort zone. Jesse was looking at me for direction and I finally was able to force the words out of my mouth. "No. I don't want to talk to him. I know he is a teammate, and probably a friend of yours, but I can't be around him. I'm sorry."

"Don't apologize, Eila. And yeah – he is a teammate and a damn good friend, but I'm your friend too."

I just nodded, trying not to replay that night. I focused on the faded tile of the floor, trying to form a coherent design with the speckled pattern. Anything to cut off the memory before it bloomed fully, like an invasive weed.

"I'll keep him away," promised Jesse.

"Thanks" I whispered, and turned to get to English class, hoping to numb my brain with some heavy Hemingway. It was only first period and the day already sucked. That was not a good sign.

Ecology class focused on the issues with the coyotes attacking the deer in greater numbers. Most of the class found it quite fascinating, comparing the new hunting patterns of the coyotes to wolves. I went along with it, even though I knew it wasn't the coyotes. It was Raef.

The coyotes were just enjoying his leftovers. By the end of the winter, they would be the most out-of-shape, lazy mammals on the Cape.

Our Ecology teacher, who was insanely excited about this whole new wolf-mentality, handed us papers on previous hunting patterns of Eastern Red Wolves. As I listened to him talk animatedly about pack dynamics, I began doodling my kill mark from my back, thinking back to the drawing Howe had shown me. I had never noticed how pretty the pattern was, with its twisted lines that seemed to spill inward on one another. It made me think back to the pattern on the gear as well, and I started to try and draw a replica of what I remembered from the photo. I became so absorbed with my makeshift art that I barely noticed when the bell rang.

Jesse tapped the edge of my desk. "You awake?"

"What? Oh yeah," I replied, laughing slightly, embarrassed I had zoned.

"Heading to lunch?" he asked. I replied I was and that I was meeting Ana and MJ. A couple of his teammates called to him from the doorway to hurry up.

"I guess I'll see you tomorrow," said Jesse, looking a bit torn. I felt bad for him, knowing he did probably hope for something more from me. I should have just let him know right then that Raef and I were together, but I couldn't bring myself to hurt him more. Instead I dug my ditch a little deeper and smiled back at him, "Sounds good. I'll see you tomorrow."

He immediately brightened, and his smiled glowed as he headed out to his friends. I was not even dating him and I was going to need to break up with him. It was so messed up and I wished beyond words that Raef was at school.

Lunch with Ana and MJ brought a smile to my face until I realized Nikki was watching me from her throne among the popular crowd. I notice that Teddy also sat at her table and he too glanced my way on occasion.

Feeling the spotlight becoming a bit too scorching, I decided to cut lunch short and head to the library. Ana and MJ understood and told me that we would find a new place to sit in the future, but I told them not to worry about it. I just needed to get used to Nikki's evil eye, like I did before.

Thankfully the remainder of the day rolled by with few speed bumps. MJ and Ana had split during last period since she needed a ride to her final physical therapy session, and I found myself reflecting on the day as I finished sorting my things at my locker after last bell. Finally confident I had all the things I needed for my homework, I headed out to the parking lot, daydreaming as I walked.

"Hey!" yelled a voice behind me. I looked over and Jesse trotted up next to me and fell into step. "So, how was day one?" he asked, shifting his own backpack over his broad shoulder.

"Pretty good. I noticed you weren't at your normal table at lunch."

He shrugged, "Nah. There is actually a smaller café for seniors they just opened while you were gone. I decided to go there instead. You should try it – the food is pretty good and it's a lot smaller."

A smaller, less drama-prone dining experience sounded perfect. "That sounds great. I'll tell Ana and MJ," I replied, making a point of adding two extra people to our table.

We rounded the building and I finally saw my Jeep, with one fabulous addition – Raef was leaning against the driver's door and catching the eye of every female that walked by him. My entire day immediately got better just by seeing him. I gave him a little wave then looked back to Jesse, but his face was not so happy.

He looked over to me, "You two hanging out a lot?"

"We are kind of dating," I said, giving a sheepish smile. "I should really go see what he is up to. It was great seeing you today," I said, now feeling all sorts of weird. I began to speed up to get to Raef, who was watching Jesse and me from his spot by my car.

Jesse however, sped up with me and caught me by the arm, stopping me in my tracks. I saw Raef straighten, his guard instinct roaring to life. It was a credit to his control that he didn't start coming towards us, but kept his place by my Jeep.

Jesse slowly let go of my arm, but concern was written all over his face. "Eila – listen to me. I know Raef seems like a nice guy, but that night at the beach he looked like he might kill Teddy. I mean, REALLY kill him. Guys that react like that usually have some major anger issues that might spill over to other people . . . like their girlfriends."

I was actually insulted, for both Raef and myself. "Raef would never hurt me. And he was furious because of what Teddy almost did. What exactly do you think would have happened if he hadn't been there?"

"We both were there," replied Jesse, not answering the obvious.

"And you immediately apologized for him!" I snapped, catching the attention of a few people walking by. I did not want to be in the spotlight, especially about this.

Jesse backed up slightly, "You're right. I shouldn't have done that, but he also didn't deserve the punishment I saw in Raef's eyes."

"And what did I deserve?" I demanded and I knew I was done talking. I turned and headed for my car, refusing to look back.

IT WAS HARD ENOUGH LEAVING EILA alone at school after what the dealer had said to me, but standing by while she argued with Jesse over his idiot teammate assaulting her was almost impossible. I stood my ground, however, because Eila had asked me to trust her to hold her own, even though I wanted to hurl Jesse under one of the exiting buses.

I had managed not to think about that night for a while, shoving it to the back of my mind, mainly for Eila's benefit. She didn't talk about it and insisted it wasn't a big deal, but when I got to her that night, I saw the fear on her face.

I heard her screams and saw her fight.

And no, Teddy didn't get far, thank god, but I had no doubt he wouldn't have stopped had I not been there.

That type of violence I found to be the worst of the worst. Unforgiveable, by any standard, which was why it was so easy to kill a forty-year-old man a few hours ago. He was a convicted offender, but the justice system was faulty. He had been released and gone back to his old ways, including a tendency to go freshwater fishing after an assault.

That's how I found him – fishing behind his Vermont cabin just as the dealer's assignment said he would be, his victim still unconscious in his decrepit shack of a house. I checked on the young woman, who had a steady pulse, but resisted moving her from the floor where he had left her. I could smell the alcohol and ketamine he had given her, making her an easy target, and would thankfully erase some of the attack from her mind.

Eventually, however, she would wake, and see herself in the mirror, leaving little doubt of what had happened to her. The knowledge of what she would wake up to made my anger all the more pure. When he finally saw me approaching his boat, I turned off any shred of humanity I had left. Unlike the deer, I made his final moments brutal, absorbing every scream for mercy he made as penance for what he had done to each of his victims.

When I was finished with him, I dumped his body, along with his boat, in the middle of the lake and swam back to shore. It would look like he had a heart attack and drowned – a favorite way to cover a soul thief's tracks.

It was the first human I had killed in a long time. I thought it would bother me, taking a man's life again, but it didn't. He had it coming – deserved the end he got, and justice was served in the name of all the women he had attacked.

As I watched Eila, all I could think of was the girl on the floor of a dirty cabin, her life forever changed, and how close E came to a similar fate. I wanted to kill Teddy Bencourt and I was sure his death I wouldn't mourn either.

I watched proudly as Eila told Jesse off, then started walking toward me. She didn't stop until she grabbed hold of me, snaking her arms around my waist and under my leather jacket. I held her tightly to me, and could feel a small shiver go through her body. I glared at Jesse from over her head.

To his foolish credit, he didn't flinch and met my eyes with his own, unwavering. Finally he turned and walked to his own vehicle and I pulled my attention back to Eila, who was resting her head against my chest.

She drew a deep sigh, "Thank heavens the day is over."

"That bad?" I asked, concerned.

She drew back from me and I moved so she could unlock the Jeep. She tossed her things inside and leaned on the open door, "No, it was actually okay. Just getting back into the swing of things is a little rough. I just need to unwind."

"Unwind you say?" I asked with a smile. "I think I have just the thing." I took her hand and towed her around the other side of her Jeep. Sitting in its own parking slot was my Harley – a bike which had become our first date of sorts so long ago.

"Really?" asked Eila, a smile lighting her face. "I thought it was put away for the winter."

"Technically it was just stashed in the garage at Christian's, but the day warmed up so nicely that I thought you would be willing to come for a ride with me."

Eila's smile faltered, "I'd love too, but I didn't bring a jacket. I'll freeze on the bike."

I started peeling off my leather jacket, which would be a perfect windbreaker for her. The cold air wouldn't bother me, even in the t-shirt I wore.

"Are you sure?" she asked, which was a bit crazy. I always would supply her with whatever she needed.

"Of course," I replied, holding out my jacket for her.

"Well, okay – but let me take my sweatshirt off," she replied, starting to pull the blue hoodie over her head. As she did so, it caught on her t-shirt and began to raise the thin fabric, revealing the smooth skin of her stomach and a perfect, oval belly-button. Instinctively, protectively, I reached out and gently grabbed the shirt, tugging it down so she wasn't exposed to the world. She finished pulling the shirt over her head and her raven hair tumbled around her shoulders, like a riot of black party streamers.

She left me breathless and I couldn't pull my gaze from her easy beauty. Eila swallowed as she looked at me and I realized I was still holding her shirt. I let go and cleared my throat, "Sorry – it was riding up."

"Thanks," she replied quietly and I helped her into my jacket. She wrapped her arms around herself, "Oh! It's still warm!"

I smiled back at her and handed her a helmet. She put it on and snapped the strap into place as I climbed onboard the bike. She followed once I had it balanced, and I cranked it to roaring life. She slid down to my back, her arms winding around my waist holding me tightly. Her breathing had kicked up, and I knew the bike had made her nervous before.

"You okay?" I asked as I looked back at her and slipped my own helmet on.

She nodded, giving me a cheeky grin, "Yup! Let 'er rip . . . but not TOO fast."

I laughed, loving her smile and the way her hands curled tighter against me as I torqued the throttle, forcing an angry growl from the chrome pipes. A few of the students turned toward the sound and I saw Jesse watching me through the windshield of his pick-up truck. I pulled down the wind visor of my helmet and gave Eila's small fist a squeeze, signaling her to hold on.

My hand twisted on the throttle and the bike smoothly accelerated out of the high school parking lot, letting the drama of the day blow away from both of us. I made a decision then to not tell her about what the dealer had said – she needed a chance to just be a teenager. I could guard her with the help of Kian, Christian, and MJ and give her the life she so craved – one of normalcy and homework.

As I pulled onto the main road, I felt her tighten her grasp on my torso and I knew, without doubt, I could protect her.

19 Eila

RAEF SHIFTED THE BIKE through the gears, bending easily into the turns, and I pinned myself to him, following the movements of his body.

We were melded as one as he navigated the twists and turns of Old King's Highway that snaked its way through the picturesque area of historic Barnstable. Every once in a while the tall oaks would part, revealing a sprawling saltmarsh and the ocean beyond, a vibrant blue against the winter sky.

I didn't know where we were going, nor did I really care. I didn't want to think about anything but the boy I held myself so tightly to, and the salt-kissed air that rolled past his heated body. If I could live in this moment of freedom forever, I would be entirely content.

Eventually Raef eased back on the bike and turned into a road I didn't recognize. He deftly avoided the aging potholes and excess sand that littered the cracked blacktop. The tall grass and pines that lined the road eventually thinned, revealing a well-worn parking lot and an endless stretch of sand, dotted with beach shacks. It was the definition of Cape Cod and what I had envisioned when I first learned of the house here, before I even moved.

Raef slowed and lowered his legs to balance the bike, shutting down the grumbling engine as he did so. He flipped up the visor of his helmet and I did the same, the raw air instantly making contact with my face.

"This is fabulous. Where are we?" I asked over his shoulder.

"Cummaquid," he replied, pulling his helmet off. He turned more toward me. "Want to go down to the beach?"

I smiled and nodded as I began taking off my helmet. When I finally pulled it off my head, I realized Raef had been watching me.

"Oh man – do I have helmet head?" I asked with a laugh, dragging my fingers through my hair. But then I caught the look on Raef's face and I swallowed, the joking slipping away from me.

Raef leaned toward me, "I love your hair, how dark it is, like coal before it transforms into a diamond. The way it frames your face steals my breath away. But then you giggle like that and all I can think of doing is kissing you until the world crumbles into oblivion."

Dear heavens . . .

I tried to form a single, sensible reply. Something along the lines of *thanks* would've been great, but instead I went all goofy and slapped my hand over my mouth. "Sorry," I mumbled through my fingers, my heart-rate doing way more than the appropriate 60 beats per minute.

He reached up and pulled my hand away from my mouth as he smiled, stealing the air from my lungs. "Don't ever apologize," he said quietly as he leaned in, drawing his lips across mine, sending a delicate flame dancing across my face.

His touch sent electricity fanning out over my body, and I drew a shaking breath as his mouth began to carefully explore my own. He twisted his solid body towards me, but the movement caused the heavy bike to shift and I let out a squeal, breaking our kiss. Raef steadied the bike with a smile, but I was done trying to make-out on a two-wheeler that weighed close to 800 pounds.

"We should probably get off the bike," I offered, though Raef's face was still intoxicatingly close to mine. I slid my way off the back seat and was about to step away to give him room, but he grabbed my waist, and pulled me tightly to him as he remained straddling the bike. He let go of the handlebars and balanced the massive machine with his legs alone as his other hand caressed my cheek.

His touch, while gentle, felt stronger. He felt stronger, as if the granite he was made of had been reinforced with steel. I suspected it was because of the deer hunting he had done while I was at school, but the contrast between how gently he touched me, versus how dangerous he truly was, made my head spin.

He held me there, stroking my cheek, and threading his fingers through the hair that hung by my face. His other hand softly crossed back and forth over my lower back and his look was pensive.

"What's the matter?" I asked, tracing the furrowed lines on his brow with my thumb. He shook his head unwilling to speak at first, but I put my face closer to his. "Talk to me. Please," I whispered, worried for the boy who always guarded me and my heart.

"I'm sorry I had left you alone that night on the beach. I'm sorry you were alone when Ted came by," he said, not able to look at my face.

"Raef – it's okay. Nothing –"

146

"It wasn't okay!" he demanded fiercely and his blue eyes darkened. "It is never okay, and when I heard that idiot Jesse try to make light of it, I wanted to kill him. I still want to end that fool Teddy."

I shook my head, "You can't end Teddy. And Jesse did act like an idiot for a moment, but he is also trying to walk a fine line between being my friend and dealing with Teddy. He's a good guy, and you know it."

I watched Raef's face as his jaw set into a tight line. He looked away over the water as he spoke, "Ted touched you against your will. You told him to stop and he didn't. He crossed the line, drunk or not. It could have ended so differently."

Okay – yeah, that was all true. But Ted was also horny and had enough alcohol in him to pickle his liver that night. I had to hope that his behavior was just a one time, momentary lack of a brain that had him man-handling some of my parts.

Unfortunately, I could still feel his hands drawing down my body, his weight locking me to the beach. I began closing off the memory, securing it away in a place where it couldn't dictate my life. Was it healthy? Probably not, but survival was survival.

Raef took my hand in his and I realized he had been watching me. He looked like he wanted to say something, but was torn.

"What?" I asked finally.

He held my hand tighter and his face looked tense. "Has anyone else ever done that to you?"

"Good grief, no," I sputtered, amazed he would even think to ask.

"No past boyfriend that was more insistent than he should have been?"

I began to blush, "Uh, no. No boyfriends." How lame was that? I

147

was turning eighteen two days after Christmas and I had no flipping boyfriends in the past.

Raef however, looked relieved but then looked weirdly ashamed. "Did I . . . cross a line? At Christian's?"

Did he? Or was I just being an inexperienced freak? I debated my answer, but Raef took my silence as confirmation and his hands dropped away from me. "Eila – I'm sorry. I didn't think for a second. It isn't a good excuse, but I –"

"Stop. Just stop," I said, wrapping my arm around his shoulders and bringing my body close to his. "You didn't cross a line. I just . . . hadn't done that before. Kissed like that or had someone touch me, like, you know. Like that." My face blushed hot as I stumbled over my words.

Raef's face warmed with a gentle smile, and he carefully wrapped his arms back around me. "Never?" he asked. I just shook my head, entirely horrified at my own lack of smoochery background.

"I'm glad you told me," he said, slowly dragging his hands across my lower back. His touch left a fiery trail along my skin and I pulled in a shaky breath. "I want you to always tell me when I come close to crossing a line that you are unwilling to cross. You set the rules, okay?"

I could only nod, watching his beautiful eyes study my own, and then he leaned in and kissed me. It was gentle at first, beautiful in its simplicity, and I closed my eyes as I felt his hands slide around to my hips. His kissing grew stronger and caused heat to swirl inside me, flowing through my veins and weakening my legs. His fingers slid under the edge of his leather jacket that I wore, and he made contact with my skin, grazing my lower ribs. My mind began to fret as his fingers came closer to my belly, and I stiffened ever so slightly.

He pulled his face away from mine and brought his hands back to the unfeeling fabric of my jeans. "Line?" he whispered.

"Yeah," I replied sheepishly. "The kissing thing, though, is well within the boundaries."

He smiled with breathtaking perfection. "Yes, Ma'am," he replied and began kissing me again, lighting a brilliant burn across my lips.

We never made it to the beach. The lot was way too fabulous.

WE ENDED UP BACK AT TORRENT ROAD as dinnertime neared

and I was surprised to see Mae's minivan parked by the side garage. She was still at work, and I just sighed, determined to make the best of a messed up situation.

I slid off the back of Raef's bike and he kicked the stand down, angling the front wheel to ensure the bike didn't fall over. He saw the car as well. "Mae's here?" he asked, surprised.

"Yeah. First day at work," I moaned, heading up the front stairs.

Raef cut me off before I opened the front door. "Wait! What will she think when she sees us together? Remember her fun chat?"

My cheeks bloomed hot, "Oh good grief, you DID hear that! Don't ever mention that again. Please! That was just a complete disaster."

Raef took my face in his hands, "Your cheeks are as red as a candy cane. You need to lose the blush or she will absolutely think we were experimenting with her rules."

My face grew redder.

"Okay – see, that's not working. I said LESS red," he laughed.

"YOU are not helping!" I fanned my face, trying to compose myself. It took a few minutes but my cheeks finally faded to just a wind-kissed pink. "Better?" I asked.

"Much," he replied, finally pushing the door open. Inside I was shocked to see Ana lounging on one of the couches near the massive window along with MJ, who was seated on the floor by her chair. Schoolwork was scattered about them and music played through the elaborate sound system built into the walls. They looked up when we came in.

"WOMAN!" yelled MJ, "Where the heck have you been? We've got pizza from Craigville! It is so damn good!"

Ana poked MJ with her pencil, "Uh huh . . . but the joint also has two hotties that work the counter, and whenever we go there, MJ turns into Flirty McFlirt Master. What are their names again? Tina? Carrie?"

"Tessa and Cassie. And I totally do NOT do that," replied MJ, though he was turning a tad pink.

"Sure ya don't," laughed Ana.

Dear lord, had I fallen into an alternate universe? "What are you guys doing here?" I asked as Kian walked in from the kitchen. He looked at Raef and me, no doubt noticing my extra-pink lips from the kissing session.

He gave a knowing smile. "Ana is celebrating the loss of her favorite mechanical appendage. We are having a cheese-ridden meal to mark the occasion," he replied, handing Ana a soda.

"Hey – what about me?" demanded MJ.

"I don't serve canines - go fetch your own drink," replied Kian, flopping into a chair across from Ana. MJ flipped him an indecent finger.

"So they finally gave you the green light to kick people without the boot?" I asked, delighted for her.

"YUP!" She hopped to her feet and did a weird little dance.

"Woo hoo!" I yelled and joined her, kicking off my sneakers so I could slide easier on the wood floor. I glanced at Raef who was leaning against an ornate pillar and he smiled as he watched me. MJ jammed to the tunes while he stayed seated, flipping through a Spanish textbook.

My dancing came to a halt however, when I heard laughter, Mae's laughter, from the direction of the second floor balcony. I looked up and sure enough, she emerged from one of the rooms with Christian following her.

She saw me below her and waved. "Hi, sweetie! How was your first day?" she called as she rounded the top of the curved staircase.

"Uh – good," I replied as she descended the stairs. "I'm kind of surprised you are still here," I said, daring a glance to Christian, who looked gorgeous in a gray pair of slacks and a white button down shirt. He had left the top two buttons undone and rolled the sleeves up to his elbows, revealing perfectly cut forearms. I wondered if he had any clue what he looked like to a human female – especially Mae.

"Oh, Christian, I mean, Mr. Raines and I were just going over my travel details," she replied, finally coming up to me and giving me a hug.

Christian came up beside her, but kept a respectable distance. "How are you, Eila?" he asked as Raef stepped next to me.

"I'm good. Raef and I just went for a ride on his Harley," I said, knowing that Mae wouldn't be pleased. I said it just to rile her, and

152

immediately regretted it. I was mad she took the job, but she knew nothing about my history or Christian's. I needed to just deal with it.

"Eila. I am not a fan of having you on the back of a bike," she glanced to Raef, an accusing look in her eye.

Christian however intervened, shooting me an irritated look that I had worried Mae. "Raef is an accomplished rider. I am sure he was very careful with Eila."

Both Raef and I stared at Christian for a moment, but then Raef snapped out of his stunned mental lapse. "Yes, Ma'am – I'd never put her in harm's way."

Mae glanced from Raef to me and I could see the wheels in her head spinning. "Eila – I am going to be scouting three estates in Monterey California for Mr. Raines next week. I will be out of town for a few days and I expect certain rules to be obeyed, including no boys in the house."

I sighed, "Mae, I'm not going to . . ."

"NO boys," she stated crisply, ending the conversation. She looked over to Kian and back to Raef, "I assume you boys will obey the rules."

MJ glanced up from his textbook. "Wait – does that include me?" he asked, delighted he was placed in the same heartthrob category as Kian and Raef.

Mae turned to him for a moment, thinking. "No – you're okay, MJ."

I had to stifle a chuckle as MJ tossed his hands in the air, defeated. Ana was trying not to bust out laughing while Kian had an ear-to-ear smug smile on his face. We all agreed to Mae's rules, though I knew they would be broken without a second thought if danger was lurking. Looking at Christian, I wasn't sure he would even allow such a deal. While he and Raef sometimes butted heads, Christian knew Raef guarded me fiercely.

It was strange to have Mae see them as "boys" – teenagers, with hormonal heads. Raef and Kian had lived since the time of my grandmother and they were far from boys. They were grown men, with hundreds of experiences to hone who they were, and dictate their behavior.

While I had spouted the virtues of taking care of myself, being alone with Ana in the house also brought with it a twinge of unease and a vision of Rillin Blackwood.

Rillin, who no one else knew about, and to whom I suspected there was more than meets the eye.

21 Raef

A WHILE LATER, EILA LEFT with Ana, MJ, and Mae.

MJ gave her a ride back to her Jeep at the high school and then tailed her home, without Eila catching on.

He stood now, a look of concentration on his face, as he, Kian, Christian, and I gathered around the massive cherry table in the library. Dalca's books and papers were spread out everywhere, a disarray of literary frustration. We had work to do, but first MJ had a bone to pick with Kian and me.

"All right, so just to make sure I am clear on this, you two went and bought names of people to kill from some beast of a dude at a place called the Lucky Lady?"

Kian shifted back against the table, "Technically it was the Ucky Lady, since the neon L had crapped out. It was actually a much more accurate name."

"I can't believe you bought a person's death," said MJ, shaking his head, truly disturbed at this new revelation.

"Technically we bought two," replied Kian, not flinching in the least. He looked over to me, "Did you cash in?"

I nodded, "During school today. He was where the dealer said he would be. What about you?"

Kian shook his head. "I'm going tonight."

"I CAN'T BELIEVE YOU ARE KILLING PEOPLE!" yelled MJ, disgusted. "No one deserves that type of justice."

"Oh really?" snapped Kian. "Because my meal ticket beats the tar out of his wife and two kids. Sound familiar?" Darkness laced his face and MJ fell into silence. An abusive parent hit way too close to home for both of them, thanks to Ana's father.

Christian waved his hand to get everyone back on track, "So this dealer believes that Eila will be targeted for abduction and ransom because of my ties to her?"

"Yes, and I think he's unfortunately right. It makes sense," I replied, my body tense. I was itching to drive over to her house instantly, especially since her entire protection detail was currently in my company. The only security she had was the house, which barred any uninvited soul shark from entering without her permission. Even if Mae invited them in, they wouldn't be able to cross the threshold because the house was only in Eila's name. She had told MJ she was going to try and finish a chapter of ecology before bed, which meant that she, Ana, and Mae were safely tucked inside the massive walls of Elizabeth's home.

Christian gripped the end of the table, clearly as stressed as the rest of us. He feared for his granddaughter, and it was written all over his face. "So we guard them 'round the clock. Put them with one of us at all times.

I will keep Mae traveling as much as possible. Removing her from Eila's proximity should lessen the risk that she will be associated with Eila. As for Ana and Eila, they go nowhere without a guard."

I rubbed my face, knowing what Eila was going to say.

"Raef, man, we don't have a choice," said Kian, knowing that Ana was going to balk as well.

"What if we do it – guard them – without them knowing?" I offered.

Christian slammed his hand against the table, causing the books to vibrate. "What difference does it make? I don't care if she wants to stand on her own or not. Her safety is not up to her! I will not lose another young woman to a hatred that never ends! Elizabeth will not die because of me – not this time. Not ever!"

MJ and Kian glanced to me, but MJ was brave enough to speak up, "You mean Eila, not Elizabeth. Right?"

A heavy weight seemed to seep into Christian's bones and he loosened his fist that had been pressed to the table. "Yes. I mean Eila. I won't lose Eila – she is all I have left of Elizabeth." He glanced up to me, "Don't repeat my mistakes, Raef. Please, I know you love her. I can see it, but such love can consume you both."

I shook my head, "I won't ever let her die for me. Ever. My only goal is to keep her safe, but honor her wishes for a life. A real life, not trapped inside a fortress, where she can only look through the bars at the world. She deserves more than that. I promised her more than that."

Christian shook his head and walked around the table to me, resting one hand on my shoulder. "Raef – she already *did* die for you, once. Eila is Lunaterra, she is encoded to never back down, to be fearless in the face of her enemies. What she is, on a biological level, is both her greatest

157

asset and what dooms her to fight to the death. You think, because you love her, that she would never choose to leave you. But you're wrong – I've seen it, twice now. Because they love us, and because they are fearless, they will always lay down their lives for us. The only way to protect her is to keep her out of the fight in the first place. Don't repeat my past and don't let her be her grandmother. Don't be me."

Christian dropped his hand from me and the room fell into a painful silence as I absorbed all that he said. Eila was bold. Brave. She hit her fears dead-on, just as she did with Jesse, Teddy, Nikki, and even when we were cornered in the Breakers. I never thought that one defiant personality trait could become a death sentence.

I finally spoke, the words forcing their way through my lips as I knew I was going against her wishes. "We guard them, 24/7, but without them knowing. Eila would always tell me if something was off, so not telling her about the threat shouldn't be an issue. Plus, the girls want some self-defense training, so we will honor that. If we keep them busy, they may not notice we are always with them. When they think they are alone, we are there, in the shadows. We can keep their lives normal."

MJ rubbed his forehead and I knew what he was thinking. "Raef – we can't do this forever though. As long as she has ties to Christian, she will always be a target," he said, glancing to Eila's grandfather.

Christian nodded, the pain evident on his face, "I know. I need to distance myself from her. I wanted to be part of her life, but I see now that doing so brings with it danger, and that is unacceptable. I will move back to Boston, but this house will remain yours to use. I will limit my time here to the bare minimum."

"It's not forever," I said, even though I knew it probably was. "We just need to let things calm down. And at least the news hasn't released her name yet."

MJ winced, "Yeah . . . about that. Jesse kind of announced, officially, that Eila, Ana, and myself were all in the Breakers the night of the explosion."

"WHAT?" demanded Kian. "You're just telling us this NOW?"

"It just happened yesterday! And you two were off buying souls at the Unlucky Lady like a pair of druggies!" snapped MJ.

I shook my head, alarmed but at the same time I knew that most of the high school has suspected Eila had been at the Breakers. Something like that, in a town this small, was impossible to keep under wraps. Mae could have said something. MJ's parents could have said something. Most of the town knew.

"I'm sure most people here knew who was at the Breakers," I said taking a deep breath. "Our only saving grace is that this is a tight community. Knowledge of our involvement in Newport has probably not spread beyond the town and the papers are not allowed to print her name until Eila is of legal age."

"Ana is eighteen," hissed Kian. "Is she not as important?"

"Of course she is – don't be a fool. But the paper will hold its tongue until Eila is eighteen, because Ana lives with her. I'm sure they have guessed who she is by now, especially with Christian helping her. They just legally can't say."

"When is her birthday?" asked Christian.

"Two days after Christmas," I replied, trying not to panic. Once the world got wind of who Christian had helped, the floodgates would open to anyone who wanted to grab Eila. If a Mortis figured out that the

159

explosion was supernatural in nature . . .

Christian seemed lost in thought and began pacing the room. We watched him and he finally turned to us, "I may have a solution to her impending birthday."

"Care to clue us in?" asked Kian, crossing his arms.

"I have a home in the Bahamas. It is remote and perhaps I can convince Mae that a vacation for Christmas break would be good for everyone. We can get her away from the area for her birthday and figure out damage control from the safety of my place."

Kian gave brittle laugh, "It will be a cold day in hell when Mae allows Raef and I to vacation in the same home as Eila and Ana."

"I'll convince her," said Christian. "I can keep her busy island hopping for me, looking at properties. I'll even work on your mom and dad, MJ."

"Yeah – good luck with that," replied MJ, unconvinced.

Christian leaned against the table, his look determined. "For now, we stick to the plan – guard the girls, around the clock and on the sly. I am going to call Mae, see if I can get her to head to my Boston office first thing in the morning. I will have her work out of that office, rather than here."

"Christ, we're splitting up families," moaned MJ.

"It's for their own safety," I replied, but I knew this was hard on MJ. He carried the guilt of our deception with a pure heart, making the load all the heavier for him. "MJ – you've got to be with us on this. The girls can't know about us watching them. We are trying to keep them safe," I urged.

MJ reluctantly nodded his head, "You can count on me."

"Are you two going to buy from this dealer again?" asked Christian.

"We didn't have any plans to do so, but considering what he said, I would put him at the top of our watch list," I replied.

"How do you contact him?" asked Christian.

"We don't – he posts some random listing on the online Want Ad the day he will be at the Lucky Lady. You go and play pool without the seven-ball until he shows up and approaches you. You also have to post a specifically worded Ad on the site when you complete an assigned kill, so he removes the name from the Blacklist. I did so earlier today."

Christian placed his hands on the table and the soft light of the room cast dark shadows on his face. "Keep your eyes on the Want Ad, see if his listing comes up. If it does, go find him and kill him."

I looked over to Kian. The dealer was built like a gladiator, but when it came to Eila and Ana, we could take on Zeus.

"Not a problem," replied Kian, but then he turned his full attention to Christian. "Speaking of dealers, our dealer said that *your* dealer blabbed about you being drugged during the ball. Aside from the fact that your dealer can't keep his mouth shut, why didn't you let us borrow the guy? Do you not like to share?"

Christian looked at Kian, "I will have to discuss the importance of secrecy with my dealer, but trust me - you don't want to meet my dealer." I looked at Kian and we exchanged a curious glance as Christian left the room to call Mae. What was that all about?

MJ grabbed his jacket from the back of one of the leather chairs. "So, what did you think of the football thing?" he asked me, pulling his coat on.

"What football thing?"

MJ paused. "Well – Jesse gave Eila the MVP ball at the game. He called her the Most Valuable Person and crap. You didn't know?"

My jaw tightened and the vision of him arguing with Eila in the parking lot came back to my mind with vivid clarity. "No – I didn't know," I replied slowly, trying to figure out what Jesse was up to.

MJ waved it off, "She probably just didn't think it was that important . . . or she thought you'd freak and go all dark-and-creepy-type-Raef."

Dark and creepy didn't even begin to cover my state of mind.

22 Eila

TUESDAY MORNING MANAGED to be fairly drama free, thank goodness. Mae had left at the hellish hour of 5am to get to Christian's Boston office, which was a request he had made not long after we had left Torrent Road. I suspected he took one look at my face last night and decided having Mae work out of his Cape Cod house was not a good idea.

The day was also one-thousand times better thanks to Raef's presence in the halls with me. Jesse steered clear of us and a homicide was avoided since he kept Teddy far from me as well. Raef seemed more on edge however, and I didn't understand why until he asked about the football game and Jesse's gift during lunch. I told him what had happened and how blindsided I had been by the whole thing.

He understood, but then he asked if anything else had happened, and I knew he was thinking of Teddy or Nikki. I however, could only think of Rillin, and I nearly told him, but then something deep inside me

163

convinced me to keep it buried.

Plus, that mark on his chest had been driving me friggin' insane. I wish I had seen the whole thing, but the small sliver I saw nagged relentlessly at my mind, taunting me to recognize where I had seen it before. I was starting to think it was just a logo from some obscure album that Ana had forced me to listen to. The guy did look like he could have been a former metal-band drummer.

I doodled a rough approximation of the gear's symbol over my notebook as I zoned at the lunch table with Raef, Ana, and MJ. We had come to the smaller café for the seniors and Jesse had been right – the food was better and the atmosphere a lot less toxic.

Jesse sat on the opposite end of the room with a few other athletes. He glanced to me briefly and I gave him a weak smile. He had been thoughtful and nice during Ecology and I knew he was trying to make up for our blowout in the parking lot. He kept silent in English however, no doubt because Raef also was in our class and watched him the entire time.

A few minutes into our lunch, and Nikki walked in, her entourage of adoring mannequins tailing her. I noticed Raef following her with his eyes, tracking where she was going, and she stared him down, venom in her glare.

Word was that Nikki had approached Raef before I arrived at 408 in September. She had used all her powers of flirtatious persuasion to try and garner a date . . . but Raef politely declined. No one declined Nikki and apparently she had not forgotten. She probably also didn't forget my anti-accident of tossing a milkshake in her face, though she did even the score by smashing my face into a goal post during gym.

164

Needless to say, we weren't exactly pals.

Which was why it sucked so entirely that her family had Elizabeth's necklace. Supposedly Christian had given Elizabeth a beautiful, cut diamond pendant for her birthday. Elizabeth had it altered by a friend to act as a key to her diary. When the necklace was fit into the ornate cover, the blank pages inside the book would finally reveal the words that were entirely hidden from view.

No necklace = no words.

No words = no answers.

I pressed the tip of my pencil harder into the lines of my drawing and nearly snapped the tip off, my frustration aimed at the cheerleader across the café and the design, which I couldn't seem to get right. The stupid symbol was all over my paper-clad textbooks, and notebooks.

"Are you thinking of getting a tattoo?" asked MJ, watching me retrace the lines of my drawing. I glanced up at him, noting the curious curve to his brow.

I gave an absurd snort, "No. Why, weirdo?"

MJ touched my drawing as he took a bite of sandwich, garbling his words through the turkey and cheese. "Umm, because you haf dwawn dis atom ting all over you notebook." He mercifully swallowed, "Are you a massive fan of chemistry or what?"

Damn, he was right. My drawing did look like an atom, and I was flipping sure the gear didn't fall out of a nuclear plant. I just shrugged, not really knowing quite what I was trying to replicate. Yeah, it looked like an atom, but at the same time something was wrong with it. Most likely I just sucked at drawing.

Ana reached out and pulled my notebook from me, swiveling it around to look at all the various versions of the same stupid symbol. "You're trying to draw the mark on the gear aren't you? I think it had more lines or something. This looks more like a round cage or a rubber-band ball," she replied, tracing the marks with the tip of her finger. The carbon left a smudge of black on her fair fingertip and she rubbed it along the table, making it fade from her skin.

A round cage? I pulled the notebook back in front of me and stared at all my drawings, realizing it did look a bit like a cage. Raef had shifted his gaze to me and finally noticed the scribblings, all looking vaguely the same.

"When did you start drawing these?" he asked, stilling the pencil that I rolled neurotically through my fingers. The warmth of his palm eased my tension – a tension I couldn't quite understand, but always rose to the surface when I started drawing. It was like I had to get the sketch right, but couldn't. I HAD to, not because I was a perfectionist, but because I just . . . HAD TO.

Freaking weird.

"Eila – did you hear me?" asked Raef.

I finally looked at him, "What? Oh yeah – no I just started drawing it after I saw Agent Howe, but Ana's right – it doesn't look much like the symbol on the gear. Art is not my strong suit." I gave him a shrug, apologetic that I was such a defect, but he seemed unfazed.

He eased the pencil from my hand and started drawing the same shape, but as he did so, tension coiled tightly inside me. With every sweep of his hand, and every drag of the pencil, the stress got worse. I peeled my eyes away from the drawing, and looked around the café, trying to keep my eyes off my notebook and relax . . . but then I looked

166

at Nikki.

She was watching me carefully, but the look on her face was tough to read. Loathing, but laced with something else . . . something more like suspicion. She had always looked at me like a bug that needed to be squashed, but the way she eyed me now was entirely different, causing my nerves to flare deep inside my body. We locked eyes and it was only then that I noticed she had a thin, silver chain around her neck, the end disappearing between her well-endowed chest.

Ever so slowly a small smile played over her perfectly bowed mouth and one delicate finger looped under the chain, as if she was adjusting the thread of silver. She rolled the delicate strand through the crook of her finger and slowly a diamond cut pendant emerged from her cleavage. She let the chain fall from her hand and Elizabeth's necklace landed softly over her tightly fit Hollister top, sparkling in the sun that tumbled easily through the wide picture windows.

"Nikki's got the necklace. She's got the necklace RIGHT NOW," I whispered.

Ana's eyes widened and she glanced over her shoulder at the same time Nikki decided to toss her long, brown hair to the side, smiling elegantly at a few of the football players who had joined her table.

Then she glanced to us, and that perfect smile slipped into a knowing, superior grin that played on her lips. Damn it . . . somehow she *knew* the necklace belonged to my family! I could see it in her cocky smile.

"There's got to be a way to get Elizabeth's necklace from her," MJ mumbled. Raef watched Nikki with the same interest as the rest of us, no doubt thinking of a way to relieve the diary's key from its bitchy

STORMFRONT – K.R. CONWAY

gatekeeper's claws.

Ana, always practical, offered up a solution. "The theater department has a working guillotine. Think we can lure her to the auditorium stage?"

"She is a drama queen . . ." replied MJ, as if chopping her head off was a real option.

On the other hand, crazier things have happened.

After missing five weeks of school, I had been shuffled out of graphic design and into mixed media arts. While my guidance counselor had been sympathetic to my injuries that had forced my long absence, the graphics teacher said she would never be able to get me caught up to the rest of the class. So . . . mixed media arts it was.

By the end of class, I was pretty darn excited that I got my butt tossed out of graphic arts. The sculpting we had started was awesome and I loved how the clay felt through my hands. While I was washing up, Raef texted me. He wrote that he was skipping last period to go meet Kian. He said that they had some errands to run for Christian that couldn't wait, but he would call me later.

I replied "K" with a goofy smile and a blessing to be safe.

As Ana and I walked out to my Jeep after final bell, she was talking about every conceivable way to get the necklace from Nikki. Unfortunately most of her ideas required us becoming criminals or facing murder charges.

"We will figure out something," I said to her as we finally got to my Jeep. MJ had parked a few rows over and waved to us from his beat-up Bronco.

"You two headed home?" he yelled from his spot next to his car.

"YUP," I called back, but then was a bit curious why he asked in the first place. "How come?" I yelled.

MJ just shrugged, then called back to us, "I have to make up some ice cream cakes at the shop and I was going to swing by and hang afterward. Unless you don't WANT ME!" He made a faux sad face, pretending to sob into his jacket. I glanced at Ana, who just rolled her eyes.

"FINE. Come by later," I called back and MJ smiled huge and gave a thumbs up.

I turned back to my car and started to unlock the door. "I thought the Milk Way was closed for the season," I said to Ana.

She was fishing for something in her backpack and finally pulled out a Chapstick as she replied. "It is, but they make specialty cakes during the off season. I usually help him when it gets closer to the holidays. Want to come sometime?" She slicked on a layer of cherry lipbalm and rolled her lips, spreading it evenly.

Just the three of us in MJ's family's decadent ice cream shop? I could totally get down with that idea.

"Sounds awesome. I'd love to come," I said, swinging open the door to the Wrangler. As I stepped forward to climb in, my foot bumped into a hard object under my car. I looked down and saw something round and reddish-brown peeking out from under the Jeep, near the front tire.

I leaned down and picked up the small, heavy ball that fit in the palm of my hand. I rotated the ball and the opposite side was emblazoned with a white circle with a number 7 stamped inside it.

Who the heck had tossed a billiard ball under my car?

"Hello? Are you going to let me in or what?" asked Ana. I lifted the

169

ball up to show her. "Is that a pool ball?" she asked, confused.

"Yeah – it was under my car." Ana just shook her head as I finally climbed in and reached across the seat to open her door.

She got in next to me and gestured for the ball. I handed it to her and she examined it carefully. "I've seen a lot of stuff roll under my Trans Am when I park here, but mostly it's trash or a baseball. A seven-ball is a new one."

"Do you know anyone with a pool table?" I asked, admiring the color of the ball as she handed it back to me.

"Except for Christian? No, but then again I don't go to many parties. Well – I don't go to ANY parties, and since there's like 2000 students here, my guess is that one of them must have a pool table. It probably rolled out of another person's car – or it's a joke."

I just shook my head and dropped the ball to the floor behind my seat with a thunk. I turned to her and smiled. "It can be my new good luck charm," I said, cranking the Jeep to life.

The radio immediately blasted the local station and Ana turned the heat up as she looked at me, "You mean OUR good luck charm. Seven is my favorite number ya know?"

"Works for me," I replied and pulled out of the high school, heading for home, our new talisman rolling around in the back of the Jeep.

23 Eila

THE NEXT TWO WEEKS ROLLED BY without incident, save for one snow day we managed to squeeze in thanks to an overnight storm. I hadn't seen Mr. Blackwood again, Jesse and I were back to normal, and Teddy continued to steer clear of me.

Nikki occasionally wore the necklace, but I managed to ignore it, figuring that her inability to visibly rile me would be the best revenge. Plus, the guillotine had been made of foam.

My refusal to be baited by her behavior and the necklace seemed to work, and she had a stern expression on her face whenever she saw me. Eventually she stopped wearing Elizabeth's fine jewelry and returned to ignoring me, though occasionally I would smile huge and wave to her as if we had been BFFs since the womb. Her look when I did that could melt a hole through an armored truck.

It was completely worth it, though my friends knew I was beyond frustrated that we couldn't get our hands on the necklace, especially since that damn symbol I kept drawing continued to nag at me. Out of sheer desperation, Kian suggested hitting on Nikki, maybe even taking her out on a few dates as a way to get into her home and steal the thing. Ana shot that idea down instantaneously, which I knew made Kian pleased beyond words. She had placed Kian firmly in the "friends" category, though I knew he hoped for more. He hoped they could make it back to what they were the summer they met, which, according to Ana, involved a lot of "bases."

Yes, it was true - the necklace was the bane of our lives, especially since we were all hoping it would give me the details as to how to command my power. MJ tried to spin our situation in a brighter light by pointing out that Elizabeth's diary may just be filled with ooey-gooey love letters to Christian.

Unfortunately *that* idea did NOT brighten my mood.

As far as Mr. Blackwood went, I couldn't make heads or tails of the man who seemed to have disappeared. At night I would rerun our two brief encounters, over and over in my mind, hoping for a clue as to who he was, and why in the world he said that I *wasn't the type to run from what scares me.* Was he just guessing at the type of person I was, 'cause for all he knew I could've only been able to handle G-rated movies.

He was worried about me in the woods.

He shooed away Teddy at the game.

He was like . . . a protector. Well, at least until he up and evaporated.

The lack of Rillin Blackwood was in some ways a good thing, because Mae had begun traveling for Christian, and I didn't really want to deal with a tattooed semi-stalker when it was just Ana and me in 408. Plus, Mae loved her job, which led to a permanent smile on her face, though she was traveling more and more. I was happy for her and, in some small way, grateful that Christian gave her such an opportunity.

Life had begun to follow a familiar pattern, though hanging with Raef became more limited because of Mae and the fact that he and Kian had been doing god-knows-what for Christian. I would ask what was keeping them so busy, but they skirted the exact details, claiming what they were doing was just boring gofer stuff in Boston. I also knew that they had been hunting more often, and they needed to move their hunting areas around, so as not to draw unwanted attention.

Christian had been busy with his own company and he was rarely at Torrent Road anymore, though he let Raef and Kian use the house as their own. With Mae often traveling and Christian rarely at home, Torrent Road slowly became our hang-out, not unlike Cerberus had. I had even put our lucky seven-ball in one of the pockets of Christian's elaborate pool table, believing it deserved a taste of the good life, rather than the nastiness stuck to the Wrangler's floor.

As promised, the guys had begun giving us basic self-defense training, having set up an area of Christian's home as a gym, complete with padded floor mats. I had to admit, having Raef pin me into submission and then show me how to weasel out of his hold, had begun to blur that line of mine. Teaching me how to fight him off made me grow to appreciate my body, rather than pick apart the things I saw as flaws. Soon my reflection in the mirror revealed a body I was proud to call my own, curves and all, and I owed it all to Raef.

He had no idea what he had done for me.

Between training, studying, and school, however, my days were pretty darn busy. On Fridays, Ana and I got to hang with MJ at The Milk Way and attempt to "help" him make ice cream goodies. Helping, from me anyway, was more of a train wreck, but MJ insisted I continue to try.

He watched me now, a crooked smile on his face.

"What in the heck is that? It looks like seagull poop," he finally asked, laughing as he leaned against the stainless steel counter in the back of his family's delicious shop. The apron he wore was the same one he had on the day I met him in September – still stained and ridiculous looking on his tall, lean frame.

My mouth dropped open, horrified. "EXCUSE me – it's supposed to be the beginning of a rose," I protested, holding up the silver nail-like device on which I was piping a sugary flower. Well, trying to at least. I looked at it carefully and it did resemble some sort of white blob. "Okay fine – it does look like crap."

"Literally," snickered Ana, who was cranking out perfectly formed chocolate seashells. She had been making the tasty treats with MJ since she was a kid and her effortless technique was honed on years of practice. My only practice with the sweets and ice cream came from eating them.

MJ shook his head, his smile still huge, and reached out as he took my hands in his. He reset the angle of the nail I was holding, and began turning it in gentle little arcs as he forced the frosting through the bag, squeezing my hand softly as he formed a perfect rose.

"Ta da!" he announced, releasing my hands.

I admired the delicate sugary flower in my hand, which no longer looked like a turd. "Obviously I need more than 'ta-da' to get this right. I think I should just stick to tasting them."

Ana got up from her stool at another counter, a full assortment of

174

edible sea shells on a tray in her hands. She slid them next to a three-tier ice cream cake that MJ had been working on. "Just let her dust them with sugar and color, MJ. That way your cake won't be covered in bird poop."

"Hey now!" I laughed, placing the flower carefully on a tray with others just as the back door slammed open. I jumped and swiveled to see MJ's mom strolling in, her round face and almond shaped eyes taking in the scene of the three of us laughing.

I choked back the remainder of my laugh as I met her unflinching eyes. "Uh, hi, Mrs. Williams," I mumbled, shifting on my feet. MJ's mom thought I was the devil, leading her son down a wayward path of total destruction. Before I arrived, he never missed work, never took off to another state, and damn well never ended up inside an exploding mansion during a million-dollar fundraiser.

Actually . . . I did sort of sound like a one-way ticket to a life of back alleys and prison bars.

Mrs. Williams didn't even answer me, her attention turned to her son, whose humor had fled him altogether. He worked dutifully on the cake, adding Ana's seashells to the tiers with artistic precision.

"That cake should have been done by now Marshall James," accused his mom, using his formal name to reinforce her pissed-off attitude. "I think having visitors here while you work is no longer such a great idea."

"I'm just about finished, Mom, and they've been helping," replied MJ shortly, placing a starfish on the edge of the second tier. He picked up an airbrush and began dusting a blue hue on parts of the cake. MJ had a bright future in the pastry industry if he ever decided that turning into a guard dog was getting on his nerves.

Ana cleared her throat and glanced to me. She placed a hand on MJ's

175

back, "Hey – Eila and I are going to head out, okay?"

MJ stopped what he was doing and looked at us. "I'm almost done. I can come with ya," he said with a bit of urgency. His mother glared at me with even more venom in her eyes, and I swallowed.

I thought MJ's desire to come with us was because of his mom, but I couldn't help notice that for the last two weeks, Ana and I were almost always with one of the guys. Raef and I had a deal about toning down the whole buddy system thing, and I was sure he wouldn't go back on his word. Still, Ana and I had rarely been alone. Of course, we had all been busy doing stuff together as well. I wrinkled my face in thought, but when I looked back at MJ, he widened his eyes and flicked them to his petite mother.

I never knew a little Chinese woman like MJ's mom could look like she could turn my body into a jigsaw puzzle. Man, she was scary. I found it fascinating that MJ didn't look anything like her, but his shifter ability definitely came from his Chinese ancestors.

I finally managed to answer my pleading pal. "Sure. We can wait for you out front," I said thumbing my way toward the small restaurant section of the ice cream shop that was closed.

MJ nodded and Ana and I slipped out of the back room and sat down on the 1950's chrome bar stools out in the front. A light snow fell past the huge picture windows that encased The Milk Way, the street lamps illuminating the flakes' drifting descent. Christmas was only three weeks away, and I had yet to find a gift for Raef. Ana and MJ, however, I had covered with gift cards to the local Indie Rock store. They would be in heaven.

Ana leaned back against the counter, kicking her boot-clad feet out in

176

front of her as she watched the snow fall. Her ultra soft boots had been a gift from Kian when she had finally gotten her walking cast off. It was a gift between friends she insisted, but I wasn't sure it was entirely the truth – I didn't think Ana could say for certain either.

"So, did you get Kian anything for Christmas?" I asked, sliding my finger along the speckled counter. Ana flopped her head in my direction.

"Are you serious?" she asked, her eyes wide. I gave her a shrug. "Well . . . no. I don't even know what I would get him. The man has everything."

Wasn't that the truth? Kian and Raef had plenty of money, which left me confused as to what I could possibly get them. Especially Raef.

"I'm not even sure we are getting each other gifts," said Ana, turning her attention back to the snow. I watched how the light from the street lamp played over her cheeks and the tiny shadows of the snowflakes streamed across her face.

This holiday season had been great for Ana, but also tough. She had stopped celebrating everything after her dad died, so the fact that she was even partaking in the holidays was huge. Add in that she was talking with Kian and spending time with him, and I felt that we all might just enjoy a Christmas miracle after all. Well – except for MJ's mom, who would loathe my butt until the day I died.

Ana sat up and turned to me, "Have you gotten anything for Raef?"

"No, and I have no clue what to get him," I moaned.

"How about you – wrapped up in just a bow?" she asked, a devious smile on her lips. I shoved her, but she grabbed the seat to keep from falling off.

"Listen perv – I bet that Kian put the same request on his letter to

177

Santa in regards to YOU."

"Of course he did. I mean – can you blame him?" she asked, but contorted her face to look like some deformed witch and I laughed.

I heard footsteps behind me and MJ appeared, pulling on his jacket. "I'm done – let's get outta here before she finds something else for me to do," he whispered urgently.

MJ didn't have to tell me twice and we all dashed out of the store and into the flurries. Ana climbed in the Jeep with me, while MJ headed to his Bronco. "Wanna follow me over to Christian's?" he asked, knowing that Mae was once again off on an assignment for North Star.

"Sure," I replied and slammed my door shut, cranking the Jeep to life. The interior of the car was cold, and I willed the heat to come through the vents faster.

"You know – there are a bunch of cool shops on Commercial Street in P-Town. They sell some funky stuff. We could go there and look for Raef," said Ana as she shoved her hands into her jacket, curling the leather tighter around her.

"And Kian too? I mean – come on. He deserves something," I said, watching her.

She sighed and turned to me, giving me the faintest smile laced with hope, "Yeah . . . Kian too, I guess."

24 Eila

WE FOLLOWED MJ BACK TO Torrent Road and I was happy to see the Range Rover parked by the front door. Raef's motorcycle was parked in the garage along with Ana's Trans Am and a brand new pick-up truck. MJ saw the stunning black truck and whistled, impressed.

"Is that . . . Christian's?" he asked, walking to the front door next to Ana and I. Before I could answer, the door opened and Raef greeted us, "Hey guys."

"Hey – how'd you and Kian do, uh, hunting?" asked MJ.

Raef looked at MJ. "Same as usual. Nothing exciting."

Ana pointed to the garage next to the house. "Is that truck Christian's?" she asked as MJ and I walked in past Raef to the warmth of the house.

"No – it's mine. I had to get something that would work in the winter and fit more than just me and Eila," he replied, his hand grazing my leg as I moved past him. Raef was not one for displaying our affection to the world, but he always let me know, subtly, what he wanted. It was a brief touch, a certain look, or how he deliberately passed so close to me that a delicious burn reflected off his skin. The entire effect messed with my brain cells, but I finally pulled myself back to what he had said.

"You bought a truck?" I asked as he swung the door shut and wrapped his warm hand around mine.

"It's not a big deal. I just called the dealership, told them to give me something new and black, and they delivered it. The bike wouldn't work for us during the winter. That one ride we managed a couple weeks ago was probably the last until the spring."

A truck.

He called up and ordered A TRUCK like a freakin' pizza!

There was no way to compete with something like that for Christmas. I mean, I knew that already, but somehow whatever I got him would just seem silly in comparison. Ana's store better have something crazy awesome that will work for my ultra tight budget.

I could hear Kian and Ana talking in the library and MJ interjected something that made Ana laugh.

Raef tugged my arm, causing me to stop before we reached the library and I looked to him, questioning why we weren't walking anymore.

"I'm sorry I couldn't be in school today," he said, pulling me closer as he tucked a defiant strand of hair behind my ear. "No idiots bothered you while I was away hunting, did they?"

My body began to melt under his touch. "Nope. No idiots, though my culinary skills are horrific."

"Good thing I don't eat food then," he replied as we finally joined our friends in the library. MJ had already disappeared into the kitchen, looking for something to munch on. His endless appetite, despite his lean frame, was apparently due to his shape-shifting ability.

At least, that was the excuse he used.

On the ornately carved cherry table at the center of the library sat all the books and papers from Dalca's shop. Much of it had been about herbal remedies and books of old photos. We had found a few more photos of Elizabeth and had given them to Christian, believing he would want anything that was part of her. She was my grandmother, yes, but I never actually knew her. Christian, however, had loved her, and I felt strongly that the photos belonged with him. He had taken them, gratefully.

On the top of one of the library's tall bookshelves was Elizabeth's diary – an elaborately engraved leather-bound book that thus far only showed photos. If we could get the necklace from Nikki, it would also bleed through with the handwritten thoughts of Elizabeth. I tried to reach the book, but it was too high for me.

Kian walked over from where he had been talking with Ana and easily grabbed the book, placing the heavy diary into my hands.

"You know – it hasn't magically change since the last time you saw it, Short Stuff," he said, leaning back against the table.

"I'm average height, thank you. And I know – but I thought I could use it for an art project I have to do. I'm going to copy the cover," I replied. Our teacher had assigned a project that required us to bring in a print of a textured surface and then overlay the design with hand-formed letters. It occurred to me during class that the diary would make for a

181

great rubbing surface for me to practice on, with all its intricate leather carvings.

I felt Raef step next to me, and his hand traced the book's surface, "You are going to make an exact copy of the cover for art class? Is that wise since your mark is on the back cover?"

"No, no. I'm just using this to practice my technique on. I'll find something else to use for the final project," I laughed.

"Thank god," muttered Raef and he reached onto another shelf and pulled down my box of art supplies and papers, placing them on the table for me. I had left most of the things from my art class here, since I spent so much time doing homework by Christian's massive fireplace.

I gathered up the supplies and moved into the living room, where MJ had gotten a beautiful fire going in the fireplace that was guarded by two cast iron lions.

I sat down in front of the fire and MJ sprawled like a relaxed dog in front of me. He tried to tickle my feet, but I warned him he'd get kicked for his efforts. My highly ticklish toes were off limits unless you wanted to be maimed.

Ana came in with another old book and it too had some markings on the cover.

"Alright – what are we doing again?" she asked, and I explained how to lay the piece of paper over the cover, making sure it didn't move, and then take the charcoal and lightly rub over the paper. She tried it, and as she worked the pattern appeared on the paper.

"So fancy!" she proclaimed sarcastically. She held it up for Kian to see as he entered the room, Raef following.

He looked at her design. "It's a masterpiece. Better than Van Gogh," he replied flatly, keeping a straight face. Ana narrowed her eyes and crumpled her paper, tossing it as his head, but he simply snatched it from the air.

Music filled the room as Raef turned on the sound system and he and Kian walked over toward the billiard table and the wide windows that framed the snowfall. They were talking with one another, no doubt about where to hunt next.

I carefully rubbed my piece of charcoal over Elizabeth's diary, admiring the delicate swirls and designs that began to appear and Ana hummed along to the song on the radio as she worked on a new sheet of paper beside me. I heard the thump of hard balls hitting the pool table's slate surface, as Kian and Raef readied the table for a round. MJ heard it as well, and he clamored off the floor to join the guys.

I continued to work at my art project, tuning out the world, but I noticed my rubbing had a weird flaw – little darker lines almost on top of the other marks.

I started to follow one of the flaws carefully with the charcoal, too absorbed in what I was trying to decipher to notice the sudden silence that came from the direction of the pool table. The flaw had breaks in it, but is seemed to form a long, arching curve, which was crossed with another flaw.

I started following the new line and it too became a curving line. There was a shape, or rather a symbol, hidden in the twists and folds of the engraved leather cover – something that I would have never noticed if not for my art teacher's assignment.

I came across another intersection of lines just as Ana elbowed me, breaking my focus. The paper slipped off the diary and I knew I would need to start all over again, but I could have sworn I had been forming the lines of the round cage that continued to haunt me.

Aggravated that I had lost the shape I was following, I snapped at her, "What?"

Ana was taken aback for a moment by my clipped tone, but then pointed a finger at the pool table, where Raef, MJ, and Kian were standing, staring at the balls. Slowly Raef picked up the dark red ball that I recognized as our talisman. I had never told them that I had added it to the table, and now they were so confused because there were two seven-balls.

It was actually quite funny, but the look on their face was weird.

"Did you find my seven-ball?" I called across the room, my voice the only sound beside the pop-star's that flowed from the sound system.

Raef's hand tightened on the ball he held and his voice was dark and quiet, "What do you mean, your seven-ball?"

I glanced at Ana. Was pool really this big of a deal?

"I put it on the table," I replied with a shrug, getting to my feet with Ana. "It was under my car a few weeks ago and I kept it. It's a good luck charm for Ana and I. But I just got sick of it rolling around in my car, so I put it here. I'm sorry – are you mad I added it to the table?"

"A couple of WEEKS AGO?" yelled Raef. I actually jumped at his voice and so did Ana, entirely shocked he was so pissed. He was never angry with me – he never raised his voice to me.

I bristled at his unusually short-temper. "Yes – what's the big deal? Why are you so mad at me?" I demanded sharply.

Kian reached out and took the ball from Raef. "Hey – they don't know. You can't be mad at her. To her it's just a ball."

184

STORMFRONT – K.R. CONWAY

"It's not just a ball," snapped Raef.

Ana and I exchanged looks as we walked over to the table. "If it's not just a pool ball, what is it?" Ana asked. "A POKEMON?"

Raef seemed to have turned into a stone of anger and I found it completely unnerving. I carefully walked over to him and touched his rock hard arm. He finally looked at me and his face fell into a strange sort of confused fear. He dropped the ball and grabbed me tightly into his arms, "I'm sorry I yelled at you, Eila. You didn't know."

Ana looked at Kian, "What the hell is going on?"

Raef slowly released me and he looked at Kian and MJ. "You've got to tell them," said MJ. "If you don't, I will."

Raef rubbed his hand across his forehead and dragged his fingers through his hair. He took a deep breath, "A few weeks back we learned of a possible threat against you. We had met with a dealer in Boston, and the way you signaled him was by removing the seven-ball from the pool table. The dealer said that because of your ties with Christian, you would be a prime target for abduction – and ransom."

Oh hell. "You said dealer. Do you mean . . . drugs?" A chill went up my spine at the idea that Raef and Kian may have an addiction problem.

"No. Not drugs. Souls."

I blinked, confused. "How you can you buy a soul? How is that even possible?"

Raef turned toward the window, looking out over the harbor, his hand at his side curling into a fist. "You can't just buy a soul," he said. "But you can buy a Blacklist name. You can buy the details of a human who doesn't deserve to live, and then you go and . . ."

I felt sick. "You kill them. You haven't been hunting animals, have

185

you?" I asked, anger rising inside me. "HAVE YOU!" I yelled.

Raef couldn't look at me, so Kian took over, "Eila. We have been killing animals, but for us to be strong enough to fight against other Mortis, we MUST hunt humans."

"You don't need to be *that* strong if I can learn how to handle my power!" I protested.

Raef spun around and grabbed me by the arms. "Your power is too damn dangerous! I won't have you risking your life when I can protect you!"

I tried to yank out of his grasp, which was laughable. If he didn't want to release me, there was no way to force him. "I can do it! You just don't think I have what it takes!"

"I KNOW you can do it! I've seen you do it and felt you DIE IN MY ARMS!" he yelled, stunning me into silence. He pinched his eyes shut, his jaw pulsing as he clamped his teeth together, but then he finally took a slow deep breath, calming himself.

He touched his forehead to mine as he eased his grasp on my arms. "I know you can do it, E. Your power is incredible, but we have no way to understand it. No way to show you how to use it, and without the necklace, we can't unlock the details in the diary. If you try to train without instruction, I fear it will kill you and this time, no amount of medicine will bring you back to me. Please, please don't try it. Please, for my sake."

I stilled as I listened to the pain in his voice. I didn't remember my final moments in the Breakers, but those in my company no doubt did. "I don't want you killing people . . . but I don't want you to be defenseless either." I swore, beyond conflicted about the idea of him being a true murderer, but at the same time, if I loved him, I had to accept him for everything he was, killer included.

What happened to our carefree days?

What happened to normal?

"Are you worried this dealer is the problem, or someone else that might think like him?" I asked.

Raef pulled himself back slightly. "Both, but we haven't been able to find the dealer again. That's why I have been away so often – Kian and I have been searching for him. The fact that there was a seven-ball under your car tells me that we are right about him. He got close enough to leave his calling card of sorts and even worse, knows what you drive. That scares the hell out of me."

Kian stepped closer to Ana and looked at her, then me. MJ had been silently listening and looked fairly guilt-ridden and I realized it was because he knew all of this already. He had been glued to Ana and me to keep an eye on us. Sneaky little . . .

Kian took Ana's hand cautiously as he began to confess. "We have been guarding you two and Mae since we found out about all of this. We know you girls want your freedom, but with a real threat out there, you need to be with one of us at all times. Trust me – this guy is huge and covered with tattoos. He looks like he could be serious trouble."

I slowly stepped back from Raef to lean against the table, my mind and heart racing. I knew the dealer. It had to be him.

Raef watched me, worried. "Eila – it's okay. We won't let this guy get near you. I swear." I looked at Raef, his face pledging that I would never come face to face with this man who sold human lives for a buck. Unfortunately, I knew something no one else did.

"It's a little late for that," I said, drawing my arms around me, trying to stop myself from shivering.

Raef gave me a questioning look as I confessed a few small details, "I'm pretty sure I've met your dealer. Twice now, and he has a name."

25 Raef

"YOU . . . WHAT? WHEN? Why didn't you tell me?" I asked, floored at Eila's revelation and the fact that she never mentioned any of it to me. She shifted on her feet, clearly feeling guilty that she had not told me about the dealer earlier.

"I . . . uh, met him for the first time when I went riding."

I swore sharply. "He came in the barn?" I couldn't believe a Mortis would ever enter a barn full of horses. The ensuing riot must have been complete chaos.

Eila fidgeted more and my unease climbed higher. "Well, see, the indoor ring was being dragged by the tractor, so I kinda went on a trail ride instead. Alone."

My stress morphed instantly into anger. How could she have been so reckless? I stepped back from her, afraid I would lose the tenuous control I had on my temper and end up shaking some sense into her.

Eila watched me, and her beautiful mouth slipped into a forlorn

189

frown. "Raef – he wasn't out there to hurt me. I got tossed while riding and he came through the woods and asked if I was all right. He didn't even come close to me. He just wanted to make sure I was okay."

I laughed out loud, dragging my fingers through hair, horrified that she had come so close to such a killer. "Seriously, Eila? Are you kidding me? When did you get so naïve – so stupid?"

Eila reacted to my words as if I struck her, but I ignored her pained face. I just kept seeing her lying dead in the woods, in the boiler room, on a cobblestone street . . .

She was destined to die.

I was going to fail.

I couldn't figure out where to stand, where to place myself in the physical space surrounding the table. I paced back and forth, dragging my hand along the back of my neck as Kian and MJ tried to calm me down. But my fear had bled into rage at the dealer, at Eila's silence, and at the injustice of our situation.

And then it hit me – Eila didn't tell me because she believed I would strip her of her freedom. That I wouldn't trust her to make good decisions and be able to stand up for herself. Eila kept this beast of a dealer a secret because of me.

I turned back to her and MJ had placed himself right next to her, one hand gripped tightly in hers. I met her eyes and she tipped her chin up, an act of bravery daring me to say something even more hurtful than I already had, but her bottom lip trembled ever so slightly. She dragged in a breath, "Are you quite done?"

I couldn't answer her. I just needed to calm down and regain my senses.

Eila took a step toward me, fearless, but definitely injured by my words. Guilt soaked through me, defusing my initial rage. She crossed her arms as she spoke, "I met him twice. Once in the woods and then once at the football game, where he distracted Teddy from approaching me. His name is Rillin Blackwood and I do not believe he is a threat. I did not keep him a secret to be deceptive, but because I believed this man – this dealer – somehow knows me, and you three would have hunted him down. He is tattooed and scarred, but he also has a mark over his heart that seems familiar."

Eila placed her hand over her breast, as if showing me where the dealer's mark was, but all I could notice was how close her hand was to the scar I had caused. I wanted to reach out and touch her, make sure she was still alive in front of me, and not some terrible ghost that I had already lost.

She dared another step towards me, and my fear began to slip away as I watched her brown eyes study my own. "Am I surprised that he is a dealer? Yes, but you said dealers maintain a Blacklist of people who deserve to die. Why bother to make such a distinction, unless you don't want to harm someone who is innocent? Isn't it possible that this beastly soul thief only was looking out for me?" she asked. "Isn't it possible that *stupid* little *naïve* me, may be right?" I couldn't form the words to reply. I was rooted to the floor.

"I thought you could see me as more than a breakable doll in a cellophane box, Raef. I thought you could believe in me," she whispered, a brittle edge to her voice that crumbled into a single tear that traced her face.

I had hurt her, allowing my fear to fuel my anger and I took it out on

191

her. "Eila - please," I begged, quietly, but she turned and walked away from the table and up the staircase.

"Eila, I'm sorry," I called to her, the understanding of how badly I hurt her constricting my words into a hollow shell.

"Just leave me alone Raef. Please," she replied softly, her sweet voice now broken around the edges. I watched as she disappeared into one of the hallways of the second floor, wondering where she was headed. Wondering if I should ignore her request for privacy and follow her. Wondering how I could be such an ass.

"I knew it," said Kian. "They started living together and now Eila is acting like Ana. It's like they have cloned their personalities and grafted them onto one another."

Ana punched him in the arm and Kian barely reacted.

"Excuse me, but Eila had every right to tell him off. He called her stupid for crying out loud!" She turned to me, her short cropped blonde hair a perfect reflection of her in-your-face personality. Leave it to Ana Lane to tell off a killer. "You know, Raef, this whole new lifestyle is not easy for her. She was stripped of her freedom, her sense of normalcy – heck, even her innocent understanding of what she thought the world was. She died for us – you, me, all of us. She didn't do it because it was an accident or because she was stupid, you jerk! Her actions in the Breakers were a calculated decision, her life for ours. That wasn't just brave! That was bloody heroic! What the hell is wrong with you, saying such things to her?"

I turned to Ana, knowing everything she was saying was correct, but she was skipping one crucial detail. "This is new for me too, you know? I was a carpenter, not a bodyguard. A killer, not a savior. I want her to

192

have a life free from threat, where she can take a walk to Craigville Beach not worrying about the shadows coming to life. But I can't lose her again and I am terrified that I will fail her. I don't know what to do or how to balance it all."

Ana looked at me, shaking her head slightly. "Men are such ridiculous creatures. All you have to do is be there for her, back her up, and show her you trust her. She loves you, every aspect of you, and she never tries to limit your life or your decisions. All she needs is for you to do the same for her."

Ana glanced up to Kian, who had stepped in closely behind her. "Are you taking notes?" she asked, looking up into his face as he towered above her. "Because you could still use a few pointers as well."

Kian smiled like a Cheshire cat, "Yes, Ma'am, but I was thoroughly schooled in your ways last summer. I'm a very good student, I think." He gently touched the outside of her arm, but she shifted away, smiling. The fact that she could smile at his touch, when she previously could barely stand to be in the same room as him, left me hopeful for the fierce endurance of love.

"You're a work in progress at best," she teased as she moved away from Kian to MJ, who looped a lazy arm over her narrow shoulders.

MJ looked down at Ana. "Should I take notes as well?" he asked.

"Nah. You're polished and perfect. Now let's go eat while Raef finds Eila and grovels for forgiveness," she replied as they turned and headed to the kitchen. MJ glanced over his shoulder to Kian and winked, gesturing to himself as he mouthed the words *perfect and polished*. Kian just flipped him off and MJ laughed as he and Ana disappeared into the kitchen.

I looked back up the staircase and ran my hand roughly through my hair, frustrated. "God, I can't believe I said that to her. It was bad, wasn't it?" I asked him.

"It was like watching a plane go down in flames . . . and then crash into a volcano filled with nuclear devices," he replied shoving himself away from the pool table. He started toward the kitchen as I continued to look up the staircase, debating my next move.

Kian's irritating voice called back to me, "I thought you were a carpenter? Go fix what you just broke, dumbass."

"I hope I can," I mumbled as I started up the stairs to find the one girl I couldn't exist without.

I WAS PISSED. AND HURT. But definitely more pissed at the moment. Raef gave me only fifteen minutes alone before I heard him slide open the glass door to the balcony that was off of Christian's office. I had escaped to the outside, among the swirling snow, to clear my head and take stock of everything that was just said.

The truth was, I understood why he was so mad.

I had kept critical information from him, information that he should have been given since he was technically my bodyguard. But I was bothered that he called me stupid. I wasn't an idiot, and I sure as hell wasn't naïve. I worried that what he called me in anger was a true reflection of how he saw me. Maybe he did think he knew better, because of his age, his experiences, and what he was. Sure, this whole thing was new for me, but deep inside, I wasn't afraid. I felt like I understood what I was, could feel my need to rise to the challenge, as if it was as simple as breathing.

I believed in myself as I never had before and I refused to be stripped of that self-confidence. Raef needed to accept me as I was, believe in my ability to fight, and have my back when I needed someone to lean on.

"I'm so sorry," I heard him say softly to my back. "Please forgive me. Learning of your contact with the dealer scared me and I spoke out of fear. I snapped at you, and it was uncalled for."

I reached out, over the side of the balcony, and raised my palm towards the night sky to catch the snowflakes on my warm skin. The icy little bites of winter landed along my hand, only to melt away in seconds. The harbor below filled the air with an endless purr as the water lazily ran up the sand and dragged its way back over the broken shells and stones.

I breathed out slowly, watching the vapor escape my mouth as I debated my reply. Finally I turned to Raef, his stunning figure leaning against the glass door, his hands tucked into his jean pockets.

He looked damaged, ashamed, and riddled with remorse. All snide retorts I was going to toss back at him dried up on my tongue. He was truly sorry, and I could see it plainly as he stood there, the snow frosting the edges of his shoulders and hair.

"We need to be a team and you need to trust my instincts once in a while," I said, slowly walking over to him. "I need to know that I can tell you anything without you going all commando and locking me away for my own protection. I didn't tell you because I believe this Rillin guy to be more than he seems, but not necessarily in a bad way. I knew if I told you, you'd freak out – a theory you proved correct just a few minutes ago."

He swept his hand over his head, a sure sign he was stressed out, and the snow dampened his hair, slicking it down in the process. The effect was an even more drop-dead handsome Raef. His deep blue eyes lifted off the floor to me, "What if he's dangerous?"

"Technically, driving is dangerous, as is hanging out with Mortis like you. Sometimes taking a leap of faith and trusting the heart is all that defines our humanity." I stepped closer to Raef and slid my hand up his chest to where his heart resided. "I knew you were more than just a killer when I met you, and look at us now."

He wrapped his hand around mine, warming it from the cold air that surrounded us. I sighed. "This man, Rillin, deserves a chance to prove he is not dangerous. He is a dealer of people whose actions condemn them to die, but he himself may not belong on such a list. We need to find him and question him. He knows more than he says, I am sure of it. I can feel it," I said, looking up to Raef who had pulled me in tighter.

He closed his eyes and I could feel his body tense, but he gave in. "Fine. We will find him and see what exactly he knows. Why he left you the billiard ball and why he told us about the possibility of you becoming a target. But Eila, if he makes a threatening move, I will remove him from the equation. Agreed?" I nodded as he swept the snow from my hair. "E, you are smartest, bravest girl I have ever known. Please, please forgive my outburst as – "

"Stupid and naïve?"

He smiled, "Uh – yeah. That pretty much sums it up."

I pulled away from Raef and headed for the glass door, but he reached past me and pulled it open. "At least let me try to act like a gentleman," he said, standing aside for me to enter first.

"Pushy, pushy . . ." I muttered as I walked into the office, but realized that Ana was standing inside the room.

197

"Jeez that took long enough," she huffed. "We have a visitor downstairs. He wants to talk to us – all of us."

Raef straightened and his face became hard. Ana looked at him and gave him a dismissive wave, "Oh chill, Raef. It's not the dealer. It's Agent Howe, though I will say he looks different."

I gave Ana a curious glance and we followed her down to the first floor where Agent Howe waited. Several boxes were by his feet and a few business envelopes were tucked under his arm. He was dressed in a Red Sox jacket and baseball cap and he looked as though he hadn't shaved in a week. Or slept.

"Agent Howe? You look, uh, more casual," I said, trying to tactfully tell him he looked like a zombie with a hangover.

"Hello, Ms. Walker. I went by your home but no one was there, so I took a chance and came here. Is Mr. Raines home?"

"No, he's not," said Raef, stepping next to me. Ana and Kian joined us and I heard the padding feet of Marsh the dog come up next to me. It didn't surprise me that MJ had phased. As a dog, he was a top-notch shield against anything unsavory. Plus his beastly size and teeth kept most visitors on their toes, including the FBI.

Howe glanced at Marsh. "Uh, nice dog. Is he friendly?" he asked, uneasy.

"As long as you are," I replied with a grin, patting Marsh on the head. "He's just a big 'ol snuggly wuppy-poo, aren't you Marshy?" I crooned. Marsh narrowed his eyes at me and shook my hand off, snorting as he did so. "So, how can we help the FBI this snowy evening? I take it this is you fulfilling your promise to meet up with all of us?"

"Actually, no. I am returning some things to you. I am no longer assigned to your case. I'm actually on suspension, so you don't need to address me as Agent Howe. Mark is fine."

We all stood there, a bit stunned. Agent Howe was like an ultra-annoying Boy Scout and now he was suspended? What the heck did he do? He leaned down and stacked the two boxes on top of each other with the envelopes. "Can I put this somewhere?" he asked, shifting his packages.

"Uh, yeah – just put them on the pool table," I replied, not wanting him heading into the library with Dalca's stolen goods. Kian and Ana swept all the balls, including the dealer's gift, into the various pockets of the table, leaving the green felt clear as Howe walked over and set the packages down on the table.

"So how'd you get kicked to the curb?" asked Ana, blunt and to the point.

Howe looked exhausted and I actually felt bad for him. The FBI had been his life and I knew our case had become his unicorn of sorts – something he was determined to solve and cement himself as a legacy within the Bureau. "Two weeks ago, my partner, Agent Sollen, committed suicide. Hung himself, inside his apartment."

I was shocked, "I'm so sorry about your partner. Do you know . . . do know why he did it?"

"I don't think he did, actually. I think it may have been staged, but I have been removed from the office, so digging further is impossible."

Kian leaned against the table, all our eyes on the former FBI agent. "You think he was murdered? Why?"

"After Sollen's death, his computers were searched. I didn't know why, until they started digging through mine. I found out that he had been selling all the details of the Breakers case to someone. My office was able to retrace where he had gone, including the last place he was seen. He was dead by the next morning, but when they searched his home, they uncovered tickets to Mexico for the following day. He was going to take the money and run. No way he killed himself."

We all were stunned, but Raef spoke up, "So all our details are in someone's hands. Who? Who was the buyer?"

"We don't know. Whoever he dealt with was brilliant at covering their tracks. My bigger concern is WHY he sold them and who would even want such information."

I could think of a bunch of immortal people who would love to dig deeper into the "incident" at Christian's ball. People who would like nothing better than to fully exterminate my kind once and for all. I could see that my friends were thinking the same exact thing. Plenty of money? Good at covering their tracks? Well practiced in the art of making murder look like suicide or an accident? A Mortis had to be the buyer.

Howe scanned the room, completely defeated, but then he looked at me. "Listen – I *know* you guys know what happened in Newport, but after being on this case for weeks on weeks, I am fairly certain none of you are terrorists. None of you had previous plans or knowledge of what was going to happen, but I do know you are all scared of something. Perhaps someone has you all silenced. Whoever you are hiding from may have just uncovered everything they ever wanted to know about you."

I looked to my tense comrades and then back to Howe. "Why are you telling us this? Won't you be in huge trouble? Won't you get, well, you know."

"Suspended? Yeah – already done that, so I figured how much worse

200

can it get for me? They suspended me because of the files being taken from my computer. I know Sollen got into the hard drive, but I am responsible for the safety of the information in my care. I also feel I am responsible for YOUR safety – all of you – and I thought you needed to know that you all may be targets. I'd appreciate it, however, if you tell no one that I was here."

Well, this information was definitely not headed for the plus-side column of Rillin Blackwood. I could tell that my friends believed he probably was the mystery buyer and Agent Sollen's killer. Damn. Maybe I was a bad judge of character. Maybe Raef was right to not trust my instincts.

I pointed to the boxes. "What are these?" I asked as Raef pulled one of the striped boxes with my name on it towards the two of us. Ana pulled another box with her name written on the side towards her as Kian stepped next to her.

Marsh got up on his hind legs and placed his front paws on the edge of the table, looking on. Howe gave him a curious glance, no doubt shocked to see the dog showing interest in the boxes. Either that, or the ex-agent was unsure of the dog's "safety" in general.

He managed to pull his eyes off of Marsh's bear-like presence. "These things belong to you and Ana. They were released from evidence a few weeks ago, but I never had a chance to get them to you."

I slowly lifted the lid as Ana did the same.

"Our dresses," she whispered, slowly lifting the dust-covered, ruby-red gown from its spot in the box. Kian reached around her and let the fabric trail through his fingers, no doubt remembering how it had hugged her curves and left him entranced.

I braced myself, and looked down into the box in front of me. Tucked into the cardboard rectangle was a lush pile of silky fabric, laced with thousands of beads and crystals. I slowly reached in and began lifting the dress, once a beautiful white, but now dusted with the ash from the soul thieves I had killed. But when I saw the brown streaks and blotches covering the beadwork, I gasped, and dropped the dress.

Raef stepped in closely behind me, his chest brushing against my back as he reached around me, one solid hand on my hip as he started to pull the lid back on the box. "Don't look at it," he breathed into the side of my face, but I placed my hand on the dress, stopping him.

"I want to see it," I whispered, pushing the lid farther away and pulling my dress slowly from its resting place in the box. As it emerged in my hands, the dark stains and torn bodice revealed just how gravely I had been injured the night of the Breakers. The bloodstains, now brown with time, ran down from the beaded bodice, fading outward. The elaborately sewn beads and crystals tumbled off the dress into my hands and scattered over the table. The center of the bodice had been torn down the midline, the threads now sticking out at funny angles towards the gap, as if reaching across the divide to re-stitch themselves together.

I heard Ana come up next to me. "Dear god," she breathed, reaching out carefully to the once-stunning dress that had made me feel like a princess.

Raef's arm threaded under mine, his hand open, and I carefully tilted my wrist, allowing a few beautiful beads to fall into his palm like discarded raindrops. His fingers curled around the broken gems, forming his hand into a fist that guarded my gift, "All that matters is that you are alive. The details of what happened back then are not important – only that you are here now."

A lump had formed in my throat and I nodded as he and Ana eased the dress back into its cardboard coffin and slid the lid back on, attempting to shut out the pain and desperation of that night.

Howe, who had been watching us, slid a small envelope across the pool table to me. "This is also yours," he said, and I opened the envelope, pulling my beloved bracelet from the paper.

My voice cracked as I thanked him and Raef helped me put it back on – a beautiful silver bangle with a ball in the center. Raef had given it to me the night of the bonfire and I treasured it. He called it my 'badge of belonging' – a reminder that I was part of the Cape. That night felt as though it was a dream, distant and unreachable after all that had happened.

Howe picked up the two wide envelopes and looked at them for a moment. "The truth is, something larger than what I understand is going on, and I am left baffled by a few things. First of all, I started digging through anything I could find on any of you and was shocked to find a file on Sula Lane." Howe looked at Ana, who had wiggled her way up to sitting on the table, her legs dangling off the edge. I swear she only sat on non-chair furniture.

She looked at the envelope in his hand as she crossed her arms, decidedly not pleased to hear the name of the mother who had left her when she was a toddler. "Terrific – my mother has a criminal record. Why am I not surprised? My Dad said she was an addict and now she is a drug dealer as well."

"Miss Lane, I know that is what your father told you, but this is not a criminal file. This is your mother's agent file. She worked for the FBI," said Howe, holding out the envelope for Ana.

Ana however was frozen in place. Kian realized she was too stunned to move and he gently placed an arm at her waist as he stood in front of her and accepted the folder, thanking Howe. Rather than moving away from Ana, however, Kian stayed where he was, tucked in front of her, and I noticed one of his hands had become interlaced with hers. Ana, however, just stared at the envelope in his hand with disbelief.

"What division?" asked Kian, as Ana braced herself for any information on her mother, who had apparently left her in favor of a job with the feds.

"Sula was a profiler in the serial killer division," replied Howe.

"Was?" I asked, realizing he was talking about Ana's mother in the past tense.

"I'm very sorry to inform Miss Lane that her mother and her associate were murdered sixteen years ago."

Ana didn't move, but her hand turned white as she clutched Kian's fingers tighter. I was sure that Ana had believed her mother was still alive, or at worse, dead from an overdose. But to learn Sula Lane was murdered and her disappearance from her daughter's life was not her fault, was a massive shock for Ana. She didn't burst into tears, however, and she didn't scream or flip out. Instead, she simply closed her eyes and leaned against Kian's wide chest. His arm wrapped around her shoulders and he held her tightly, as if trying to somehow pull the pain out of her and into him.

As I looked at her, I made a silent plea to the universe for mercy and for the past to stop haunting us.

I cleared my throat and looked at Howe. "You said a few things left you confused. What else?" I asked.

"Well, we think we know how Dalca located you," replied Howe, pulling a printed photo from his jacket pocket that was of me from a few years ago. It showed me in a tankini standing by a lake in my old hometown, a few classmates playing frisbee. I was not the focus of the shot, but rather just an extra – someone who happened to be caught by the camera's lens. It was a photo I also had on my bureau.

"When we looked through Dalca's files, she had no previous searches related to your name. But at one point, she came across this photo on one of your former classmate's FaceSpace page. It was only after pulling up this photo, and saving it to her computer, that she started trying to locate you. Eila, your branded scar in this photo and on the paper we recovered, are a match, but the photos of your back taken at the hospital show a far more elaborate scar. Care to enlighten me as to how your scar managed to . . . grow?"

"Maybe it was Photoshopped by Dalca herself?" I replied as I looked at the old photo, trying to stay calm. I knew exactly why this photo stopped Dalca cold. The kill mark that deemed me a Lunaterra showed as plain as day on my lower back, just above my boyshorts.

Howe crossed his arms, leaning into the pool table. "Somehow I don't think Dalca Anescu knew a damn thing about Photoshop, Miss Walker."

Stupid. Social. Networking.

#

HOWE LEFT NOT LONG AFTER dropping the bomb about what he had uncovered in the FBI files. Somehow, Kian had managed to convince Ana to not open the envelope, and in the back of her mind, I was sure she knew why.

Eila, god bless her, managed to get Ana over to the fire and the two girls snuggled together, using Marsh as a pillow. While I knew that MJ wanted to see the file, he sensed the girls needed his warm, strong presence more than anything else.

Eila spoke in quiet tones while Ana absently ran her hand over Marsh's thick, black ears, causing them to fold down and then pop back up. She did it over and over, like a nervous habit that managed to keep her from losing it entirely.

In the library, Kian and I went through the paperwork in Sula's file, all of which appeared to be copies of photos Howe took with his cell phone. I had to give Howe credit – he couldn't take the files from the

FBI's office, nor could he Xerox them, but he was slick enough to make copies via his phone's camera. Mr. Boy Scout had less-than-perfect morals.

Flipping through the pages, Kian and I were looking for anything graphic or violent that would haunt Ana, though luckily there were no photos of the crime scene from her murder. Sula's file was thick, but huge swaths of information had been blacked out. It was all about Sula's murder and that of her partner, whose name was also blacked out. They had both been shot in the back of the head, execution style. The only pages that had not been edited were a few sheets of journal-like paper with some strange numbers and letters she had written in pen. At the bottom of each page, she wrote the same word over and over – *reloaded postmortem.*

"Does it say who killed her?" I asked, looking over the pages.

Kian shook his head as he picked up one of the pages that seemed riddled with nonsense number and letters. "You don't think she was going . . . insane, do you? I mean what is with the *reloaded* stuff over and over?"

"I have no clue," I replied. "And who was her partner? This damn file tells us nothing."

Kian kept peeling back the pages, one after another. Coroner reports, witness logs, more gibberish, a page of scribbles . . .

"Wait!" I grabbed the page of haphazard drawings from the stack Kian had placed aside, my heart freezing in my chest. I turned it over and there, in the upper corner and somewhat faded with time, was Eila's strange drawing. It was an elaborate atom, with curving lines that rotated back on themselves. A round cage, just like Ana had said.

"What is it?" asked Kian, looking down at the paper.

"I saw Eila drawing this at lunch one day. She said it was the symbol on the gear that Howe had shown her," I replied, unnerved by what this could possibly mean. How did Sula Lane, murder victim and gifted profiler of serial killers, have Eila's drawing? A dark, menacing thought curled through my mind – was this symbol somehow related to the death of Sula Lane?

"Sula has the same thing that Eila has been drawing? There is zero possibility that is dumb luck," replied Kian. "I've had enough of this waiting for the right moment crap. I say we just kill Nikki Shea and get the damn necklace from her if we need to. If both Sula and Eila were obsessing about this pattern, and it looks like it was on Dalca's gear, then I guarantee Elizabeth knew something about it as well."

"We are not murdering the captain of the cheerleading squad, no matter how irritating she is."

"She bashed Eila's face into a goalpost not long ago. Did you forget about that?" asked Kian, trying to stress how good it would feel to bump off Nikki.

I gave him an stern glare. Killing Nikki was not an option. Sadly. "What are you going to tell Ana about the file?"

"The truth," said Kian. "She is owed nothing less than the truth. Unfortunately this file only gives me snippets of what happened and no reason why. I'll tell her what I know and if she wants to see the file, she can. I'd definitely show Eila the sketch though."

"I will," I replied glancing out towards the girls and their furry black pillow. "I know what Eila's going to say though."

Kian looked at me, "We need the necklace?"

208

I nodded. "We need the necklace."

A half hour later, Kian and I were walking through 408, doing a security sweep of Eila's home. After the disaster of an evening that was the past few hours, I was really surprised that E and Ana didn't want to just crash at Torrent Road. Mae and Christian were both gone and Ana had once said that 408 could feel "intimidatingly large and creaky" if you were ever there alone.

Alas, they were determined to sleep in their own beds and Kian and I were determined to break Mae's rules entirely. If the girls slept at 408 tonight, we would be there as well.

MJ however could not escape his mother for a full evening and phased back into his lean, two-legged self to head home. He gave each girl a big hug and told them that he would run a patrol past the house during the night . . . and possibly howl to terrorize the neighbors. His ability to make the girls smile, despite how rotten our luck had been, earned him a gold star in my book. MJ was a good guy, plain and simple, and I knew he would have been a friend of mine in my former life.

When I had shown Eila the mark in Sula's drawings, she could barely speak, though she did manage to demand we get the necklace from Nikki, as I predicted. Ana, however, refused to look at Sula's file, instead asking Kian some heart-wrenching questions about her mom – did she feel any pain when she died? Did she know she was going to die? Did he think Sula was thinking of her when she died?

She asked all her questions with an eerie calm and listened while Kian answered as he sat next to her, his fingers brushing her own. He was worried for her and I could see the tension in every move he made

209

through the house. He was waiting for Ana to crumble. To Scream. To do SOMETHING.

Yes, she had not known her mother for sixteen years and she never expected her to return. But to learn that her mother was murdered, rather than just disappearing due to an addiction problem, were two entirely different things. Kian and MJ knew Ana in a way that Eila and I had yet to fully understand, but the way Kian watched her now was more than just sympathy.

He watched her now as if she might become a threat to herself. The reasons behind *why* he would think such things about Ana made me uneasy, and I became acutely aware that I only knew the smallest of details about what happened the summer they met.

Eventually, the girls took showers and headed for their rooms. I came up the staircase after checking the house once again and saw Kian leaning against the doorframe to Ana's room. He watched her as she cocooned herself into her blankets, shutting out the world. She muttered a "goodnight" and "stop staring" to Kian, who reluctantly left her to sleep and headed down the stairs.

Eila's door stood open about a foot and light poured from her room. I eased the door open a bit more as I said her name, "E? Can I come in?"

"Sure," she replied, and I stepped into her bedroom. The air instantly stole from my lungs.

Standing in front of a long mirror in a pair of pinstriped PJs and a cropped t-shirt was Eila, methodically dragging a comb though her wet hair, separating her mane into rail-straight lines. She concentrated on her reflection, making sure not to miss a single ribbon of hair.

As I watched her, I was hit with a desperate desire to touch her and

210

feel her coffee black hair stream through my fingers, leaving a damp, cold trail in its wake. I wanted to run my hand down the side of her neck, tracing the edge of her collarbone that rolled so perfectly under her delicate skin.

When she had been injured, I had come in and out of this room with things she needed, or simply sat and kept her company when Mae allowed. Back then I was filled with a brutal longing to see her well and on her feet again. Now, however, I was hit with a different kind of longing entirely.

She glanced over at me, and I noticed the t-shirt stuck to her shoulder because of a wet blotch from her hair. I envied the blotch . . . and the fabric.

"Are you planning on standing in the doorway like a stalker, or are ya coming in?" she asked, finally snapping me out of my trance. I moved into the room, my eyes drifting over Eila's space as she began braiding her hair.

The silence between us was easy. No longer was it necessary for us to clutter the quiet with words - we could just be in one another's presence and feel at ease. We had both changed so much in the past few months. Everyone had. We functioned as one, looking out for each other, and somehow we became a team.

I trailed my hand over one of the twisted posts of her bed and remembered how I slaved over every smooth turn of the cherry wood and the hours it took to form each engraved spindle. I could still smell the sawdust and hay inside the barn where I used to work on furniture pieces for Elizabeth. This bed was made for her, and though it looked complete, I knew it was unfinished. My life had been stolen away from me before I could complete my vision for the bed, which now was a restful haven for my E.

I hooked one arm around a post at the foot of the bed and leaned against the polished wood. Eila finished with her hair and walked across the room to me, wrapping her own small hand over mine on the post, and I noticed the bracelet I gave her rested gently against her wrist. She smiled up at me, and my world filled with hope. "You have a very fine bed, Ms. Walker."

Her eyes traveled to our entwined hands and her fingers traced each of my knuckles, sending a kiss of ice over my skin. "Mmm hmmm. I hear the carpenter was quite talented with his hands, and I am entirely in love with his amazing ability."

I breathed in Eila, and she smelled like the sweet pea flowers that used to grow by my mother's garden, and the clean air that would cut across the corn fields of our farm. Somehow she had become home to me, a place I thought I had long since bid farewell. She reminded me of my human past and the dreams I once had as a boy.

"It's not finished," I said as I leaned closer to her, and she bit her lip, a sure sign the butterflies were stirring inside her. I loved that I could cause that reaction in her and I prayed it never faded.

"It's perfect the way it is," she mumbled, and I leaned down to her mouth, whispering a reply that I wanted to finish what I started.

My lips gently connected with hers, and all the pain in our world washed away, leaving only the sunlight she brought to my life of shadows and stolen souls.

I T TURNS OUT, CAPE COD is many things in the winter: quaint, picturesque, and loaded with traditions. I personally was a fan of the whole Christmas-trees-strapped-to-the-tops-of-sailboats thing, especially when a fat seagull would park his butt on top like a star. The owners weren't so fond of the makeshift tree toppers though, especially when the birds decorated the boats with their own, homemade ornaments.

Man, I love nature.

But there was one other thing in abundance on Cape Cod in the winter that I could absolutely do without.

BOREDOM.

Boredom could be blamed for why I was experiencing a head-rush of excess blood flooding my brain as I lay upside down on our camelback couch, my fuzzy-socked feet in the air. The new band that MJ had downloaded played through the speakers, and we had been listening to his playlist for the past couple hours. The music wasn't cutting it, even

213

upside down.

Pinning Raef against the wall and kissing him until I lacked oxygen would have been a perfect way to pass the time, only he was with Christian.

Last Friday, Mark Howe had opened a Pandora's box with the revelation about Ana's mom. Since then, Christian had quickly returned, and Mae had been matched up with an unknown "secretary" who would travel with her, though I suspected the secretary might be packing a firearm or two along with her organizer.

Vigilance and security had become the order of the day, resulting in very little time alone with Raef, and thus very little kissing. Cape Cod sucks – SUCKS, in the winter.

I turned toward MJ, whose hair was standing on end as he too hung upside down, though he managed to defy gravity by munching on cheese puffs and swallowing without gagging. "Is Cape Cod always this super fun in December?" I asked with a sigh. My eyeballs felt like they could roll around loose inside my skull.

"Yup. Thrilling isn't it?" he replied, wiping away a dusting of neon orange on the underside of his nose – a reminder that his snack was SO not organic.

"You know, we could have gone with Ana. Why'd you say 'no' anyway?" he asked as he drew his knees forward and flipped backward off the couch and onto the floor.

I let out a deep breath as I looked at him, his hair back to its floppy normalcy. "First of all, she was going to see some slasher flick and I have had my fill of creepy killers, thanks very much. Plus, Kian was going and, let's face it, those two have been dancing around each other since last

214

week. I can't tell what is going through their heads. I swear we should just rig a game of spin-the-bottle and jam the two of them in a closet."

"So you passing on a movie has more to do with matchmaking than bumps-in-the-night?" asked MJ with a grin.

"Look . . . " I replied, rolling off the couch with a less-than-graceful thud. I scooted up to sit in front of him, "I say they deserve a chance. Not to mention she actually let him tag along. When does that ever happen? Hmm . . . let me think. Oh yeah – NEVER."

MJ started picking up bits and pieces of his snack from the oriental carpet, "Technically she only got to go because he insisted on tagging along."

Okay – yeah I did know that, but I was still sure there was an ulterior motive in there as well. Like Ana, I too had a designated babysitter for the night and he was currently licking the tips of his fingers clean. It was the first time, in a long time, that MJ and I got to hang out alone. With Kian and Ana on their anti-date, and Raef at Torrent Road, MJ was my designated keeper.

We were trying to go for "normal fun" such as TV, music, and junk food. Thus far, "normal" was working, right down to being bored out of our minds. Monopoly might literally become an option if I wanted to keep my sanity. MJ seemed to sense my fraying mind. "We could go grab a hot chocolate at The Raven?" he propositioned.

I glanced at the clock. "Doesn't the Chocolate Raven close at five in the off-season?" I asked, noting that it was well past closing time.

"Oh dang it – I think you're right. Sorry, Eila." He got to his feet, gathering up our munchies and drinks and headed for the kitchen. I could hear him moving around as he put things back.

I pulled at a wayward thread in the carpet. "I think I am going to need a library card soon," I yelled so MJ could hear me. "I have a feeling that reading is going to become my one escape during the winter. I wish I had something to read now. Even a brain-candy magazine would do the trick!"

Suddenly the kitchen went quiet. "MJ? Did you hear m . . . AHHHH!" MJ bounded back into the room so suddenly that I toppled backward. "DON'T DO THAT!" I yelled, whacking him in the shin.

"I know what we are going to do tonight!" he proclaimed, eyes like saucers filled with excitement.

"Uh . . . okay. What are we doing?"

"Getting Elizabeth's necklace!"

"Ha ha. No, seriously. What is your plan for tonight?"

"What are you? Deaf? We're getting the necklace! We'll just get into Nikki's place and take back what is technically yours!"

Poor kid had slipped into a state of psychosis brought on by toxic snacks. "We are not breaking into her house," I said laughing as I got to my purple feet. MJ's juvenile ideas were sometimes just hilarious.

"Yes we are!" he argued, grabbing me by the arm and pulling me towards the stairs. "You want reading material? Let's get some real reading material! Let's get that damn necklace and unlock the diary!"

Holy crud, he was serious!

I tried to stop him from dragging me along, but my stupid fuzzy socks acted like little skis and I slid easily along the wood floor.

"MJ! Listen to me! Her place will have a security system to rival the White House. And we don't even know her addre . . ."

"No it doesn't and she lives at 647 Bluestock Lane. Brown house with black shutters. Granite mailbox thingy," he interrupted, giving me one last shove toward the stairs. "Now get your butt upstairs and change into something stealthy, will ya?"

"I'm NOT committing a felony. I'm NOT breaking into . . . wait, how do you know she doesn't have a super security system? And for that matter, how do you know what her house looks like?" I questioned, suspicious as I hung onto the wooden railing.

He shuffled a bit on his feet as he rubbed the back of his neck, his eyes avoiding my glare. "Well, see . . . I sorta, well, kinda . . . already broke in once."

"*What?* Are you FREAKIN' INSANE?" I yelled.

"Chill, alright? I heard that she made the youngest members of the squad do her chores when her folks weren't home. So I did some digging and it turns out that she leaves a key under some stupid stone frog near the back door for her slaves. I tested the theory." He took another step towards me and slowly began prying my fingers from the railing one by one. "We. Can. Get. In."

This was such a bad idea. "I bet she's home, bored like we are, although probably *not* planning a B&E on someone's house." More likely, she was planning a way to torture me just for kicks.

MJ managed to pluck my last finger from the railing and gave me that damn, devilish grin. "Actually, Casa de Shea is empty right now. Nikki is stuck at the hospital's charity event with her folks tonight. They should be gone until at least ten."

He glanced at the hall clock, which defiantly proclaimed it was five minutes to eight. Stupid clock would side with a maniac. "We have plenty of time and we are only getting back what is rightfully yours in the first

217

place. I mean, technically it isn't stealing."

I folded my arms and glared at him.

MJ sighed, "Okay – it may be a teensy-weensy bit like stealing, but we'll get in and out and no one will be the wiser."

I muttered a curse. I was torn between doing the sane thing, which was locking MJ and his idiot ideas in the laundry room, or reclaiming Elizabeth's necklace. A necklace that could very well shed some light on who exactly Rillin was and what the deal was with the atom-thing. Plus, I might finally be able to understand how to channel my ability. I needed answers, which might or might not be inside Elizabeth's diary and there was only one way we would ever know – we needed the necklace.

I moaned as I looked at MJ who waited, hopeful that I would join him in his psychotic plan. I muttered a few choice curses, "DON'T tell Raef or I will jam your furry butt in a zap-collar the next time you phase."

MJ threw his hands in the air, victorious "YEAH! Let's go be criminals!"

God help me.

Forty minutes later, I found myself sitting on the split vinyl seats of MJ's decrepit Bronco. The night was cold, but with a snow-less ground, we could actually creep from our parking spot near the neighborhood florist to Nikki's house about a quarter mile away.

Elizabeth and her neurotic ideas about locking her diary with a blasted necklace was going to lead me right into a rap sheet, I was certain. I silently fumed at her, knowing that she was probably watching us from some ethereal place and laughing at our stupidity.

218

I had dug around in my closet and drawers for MJ's specified criminal clothing and turned up a black pair of yoga pants and a black sweatshirt with a logo of a favorite band on the back. My partner in crime was smoothing a green knit hat down over his ears as he looked around at the abandoned parking lot. Why, WHY did I listen to a kid that liked to shift into a black, stray dog with an endless appetite? "Just for the record, if we DO get caught I am totally throwing you under the bus once we are in police custody. I'm going to say that I was drugged and dragged along against my will."

MJ smiled out the window, "Tsk Tsk – that is completely not something a warrior would do."

"A warrior wouldn't be breaking into someone's house!" I hissed. A car drove by and we both dove down in the wide bench seat, landing nose to nose with one another.

MJ tapped me on the forehead, "Have a little faith, will you? I've got this and I'm dragging you along so you can think like a chick. Show me where Nikki might stash the necklace in her room and whatnot."

I raised an eyebrow, "Did you really just refer to me as poultry?"

"I'm going to refer to you as a full-on chicken if you don't stop stressing and get with the program."

I glanced at the digital clock MJ had taped to the dashboard. It blinked 8:42 in neon green. "A half hour. THAT'S IT! If we can't locate that sucker in thirty minutes, we are gone. Got it?"

"Yes, Ms. Bossy-Chicken-Pants. Jeez."

We slowly sat up, and when the road looked empty, slid from the car and darted into the hedge line, sticking to the shadows as we made our way towards Nikki's McMansion. The neighborhood was built near a

219

resident-only beach, and the air near the water was raw and cold.

The beach, barely visible at the end of the dark road, was supposedly a favorite place to go in the summer for the locals. If I managed to not be incarcerated by June, I would like to visit myself. Of course, I was a friend to MJ Williams, and thus jail-time was a foregone conclusion, apparently.

We rounded the side of her huge, Tudor-styled home and dashed between a four-car garage and a storage shed. Finally we made our way to the back door that MJ had gone through once before. "Grab the frog," he whispered to me.

"What frog? I can't see a damn thing."

He pointed near my feet and I glanced down. Sure enough, the butt of a fat toad peeked out from under an evergreen bush. I bent down and tipped the frog over, officially starting my life as a criminal mastermind.

MJ was so getting a zap collar for Christmas.

Nikki's key lay squished into the dirt slightly, but the silver glistened in the light from the backdoor. I swallowed, knowing there was no going back now, especially with MJ standing by the door waiting for me. I picked up the key and handed it to him while setting the over-weight amphibian back on his tummy.

MJ stuck the key in the lock and it easily turned. He did the same to the deadbolt and within seconds, we were standing in the back-half of a designer kitchen.

"Wow," I whispered, taking in the bright white cabinets, lime green bar stools, and iron chandelier. Marble counters, huge windows, and a stove that could make Rachael Ray envious, finished off the Shea's huge kitchen. The cherry floors looked pristine even in the darkened house.

"We should take off our shoes," I whispered to MJ. He gave me a ridiculous look, but then I pointed to the foot-prints we had already left. He nodded, and we took off our shoes, and I quickly rubbed away any sign that we had stepped on the floor with my sleeve.

Carrying our Reeboks with us, we carefully made our way through Nikki's stunning home. Soaring ceilings, beautiful moldings, and designer furniture was everywhere. My home, while stunning, had a very different feel than Nikki's. We had antique furniture, built mostly by Raef, and it was nowhere near as spotless.

It was then that I realized the real difference between our two homes: my house was lived in, but Nikki's was more like a museum. What was it like to live a life that was so flawless? MJ and I had just been hanging out casually at my home eating cheese puffs. Somehow I didn't see that happening here on the cream-colored furniture and white rugs. Plus, my fuzzy socks would clash with the stark décor.

I wondered if Nikki's perfect life was actually more like a prison.

We made our way around the first floor, being careful not to touch anything. After several sitting rooms, a formal dining room, monster-size pantry, laundry, and a few bathrooms, we realized the bedrooms must be on the second floor. I started heading up the stairs with MJ following, but heard a wooden bang behind me. I spun around and MJ was sheepishly picking up the ball finial from the floor.

"Did you just break the staircase?" I accused through my teeth.

"No! It just toppled off. It must be missing a screw or something," he whispered, setting the ball back on the post at the base of the stairs.

Stealth was not our strong suit thus far.

We headed up the stairs and quickly identified Nikki's room by the one doorknob that was different from the rest – a crystal. I suspected her knob was as much defiance as she could muster with a mother who kept such a pristine and orderly home.

MJ nodded to her door and I pulled down my sweatshirt over my hand so I wouldn't leave fingerprints as I turned the crystal. The door slid open revealing a room that was a jarring contrast to the rest of the house. "Dang," breathed MJ.

Inside Nikki's room, deep colors of black, purple, and gray flooded everything. Charcoal drawings and vinyl records hung everywhere, and black armchairs were tossed with shimmering purple pillows. The effect was insanely awesome, but entirely not the pink princess that I assumed Nikki was. I thought I was going to see wall-to-wall cheerleading confetti and her field hockey stuff. I was expecting to see boy-bands framed on the walls and crystal chandeliers. But this? This was a collision of classic rock and twisted art and it looked sick.

MJ moved past me into the room to one wall that was partially painted as a chalkboard. On it, Nikki had written different phrases and poems, but one took up the center of the black rectangle. She had scrawled it in a dark red and MJ stood still as he read it.

Sometimes I'm terrified of my heart.

Of its constant hunger. For whatever it wants.

Sometimes I'm terrified of my heart. The way it stops.

I looked back to my friend as we stood in front of the blackboard inside Nikki's secretive world. "Uh . . . that's interesting."

MJ pointed to the words, "These are lyrics from a songwriter called Poe. I'm weirdly impressed – and a little alarmed. This seems pretty dark for how she always appears."

I wrapped my arms around me, oddly cold. "Does Nikki really have any friends? I mean, I know people do her bidding and whatnot, but does she have any real friends?"

MJ shook his head, looking both sad and angry, "I don't know. Honestly I spent so much time avoiding her that I didn't really get to know her."

I reached out for his hand and took it in my own and gave it a squeeze. "Tomorrow is another day. Tonight we need to look for Elizabeth's necklace, but tomorrow maybe we can try to say 'hello' to Nikki without her throwing something at us."

"I wouldn't hold your breath about that," replied MJ with a faint smile. He scanned the room. "Where do we start?"

"Well, Elizabeth's necklace was made of cut diamonds. I doubt Nikki would just leave it lying around. If I was her, I'd put it in a jewelry box or safe." I walked over towards Nikki's dresser and started searching the polished wood top, using my sleeves once again. MJ did the same, as he carefully opened little boxes and jars on Nikki's dresser.

I started pulling open drawers, but all they seemed to contain were clothes. I moved over to her bed and got down on my hands and knees and looked underneath. She had tucked away several boxes under the boxspring, so I dragged them out one by one and searched each. Most were scrapbooking stuff – a photo of a little blonde baby being held by a teenaged boy, ticket stubs to bands I'd never heard of, BHS bling, but nothing remotely like a priceless, antique necklace.

I pushed the box back to its cozy home under the bed and sat back on my heels, looking around the room. At the far side of her bedroom was a set of double doors and I got to my feet, going on instinct that they either lead to a bathroom or closet. MJ saw me and followed.

I pulled the handles towards us and was rewarded with a very dark, very large, closet. MJ squinted as he moved into the massive walk-in and felt along the wall. I heard a click and immediately the space was flooded with light. One glance in any direction, and it was very obvious that Nikki Shea would never be lacking in the wardrobe department. "I think she may have cleared out every major clothing retailer on the East Coast," I said, wandering down the wall of clothes and shoes.

"I'd be much more impressed if this was floor to ceiling movies," mumbled MJ.

I glanced back at him and smiled. "Me too."

I made my way to the last section of the closet, which had a sitting area complete with pin-striped lounge chair. Tucked to the left behind the last chunk of clothing was a large bookcase, stuffed with books.

"Wow. She reads. Who'd a thunk it?" I exclaimed, approaching the bookcase and scanning the titles. Some of the bindings looked pretty old and weathered, as if from an antique shop.

I felt MJ come up behind me and reach past my shoulder to one of the books. "CARRIE," he announced, pulling out Stephen King's epic classic about a dangerous teenager who flattens a town. "How appropriate."

"Appropriate for Nikki . . . or me?" I asked, narrowing my eyes at the book in his hand.

"Uh . . . both?" he grinned, sheepishly. I punched him in his arm, determined to be insulted. The only problem was, I probably COULD flatten the town, though I hoped I would never do so simply because I

224

was pissed. I continued looking along the row of books, but then my eye grazed over a petite book with a brown leather binding and my heartbeat began pounding in my ears.

There, sitting between Shakespeare and Poe, was the symbol I had been drawing over and over, engraved on a leather spine. I grabbed for the book and damn near toppled MJ in the process. "Jeez – what's wrong?"

I didn't respond and instead ran to the middle of the closet under the best light and dropped to my knees, the book in my lap. I carefully opened the fragile cover, revealing tons of writing. MJ lowered himself next to me. "What is it?" he asked, as I drew one finger gently over the yellowed pages.

"I'm not sure, but the binding has that same mark Sula drew. The same mark I've been drawing from the gear."

"No way!" he exclaimed, scooting closer to the small book. The writing was faded and appeared to be in French, which might as well have been Klingon for all the good it did me. I took Spanish in high school, thinking that would be the most useful language. Apparently not. "I think it may be an old journal of some sort, but I have no clue what it says. Can you read French?"

MJ looked at me as if I had sprouted the head of a Back Street Boy. "Yeah right. It's a miracle if I can understand any tourist south of the Carolinas! What do you think this is?"

"Damn if I know. This book has got to be important. Do you think Nikki can read it? What if it says stuff about Elizabeth? What if she knows about my family and . . . oh my god, ME?"

MJ's eyes widened, "That would seriously suck. What if she knows

225

about Raef and --" MJs words trailed off as his attention was diverted to something under the bookcase.

"What?" I asked as he leaned to the side and dragged a wooden box from a hidden area under the bottom shelf. He slowly opened it and there, sitting inside, was Elizabeth's necklace. The Devil must've been ice skating, because I knew Hell had to have frozen over.

"We did it," I breathed, totally floored. "We found the damn thing. I can't believe we actually – ." My words halted on my lips as the familiar sound of the ball-finial hitting the floor echoed through the house.

My eyes widened and MJ instantly signaled me to be quiet as he dashed to the light switch and snapped it off. Plunged into darkness, I scrambled to my feet with the book and necklace, grabbing MJ and pushing us both into the depths of Nikki's designer clothes. I prayed we couldn't be seen by whoever else was in the house, now that we were hidden among the racks of long dresses and dark jeans. I slid the necklace over my head and it rested against my chest, pinned in beneath the book I was clutching. My nerves were at DefCon One.

Jail. Prison. The Pen.

I was definitely going to be wearing a striped jumpsuit.

MJ was stone still beside me as we heard the bedroom door slide open wider, the bottom brushing softly against the thick carpet. I swallowed and moved my head slightly to get a glimpse through the open closet doors and into Nikki's bedroom. MJ did the same, but I felt his body tense as a guy stepped around the bed, heading toward the bureau.

Dressed from head to toe in black, the slim, tall figure was not Nikki. As the strange visitor turned, I glimpsed his face. His eyes were dark and his skin pale, with a single shamrock tattooed under his ear. This nut was

226

a robber, and by the looks of him, he was aiming to score some quick money, probably for drugs.

Unlike our careful inspection of Nikki's things, the guy started to ransack her room, yanking the drawers completely out of the beautiful dresser. He dumped her carefully folded clothes onto the floor and began ripping through them, as if searching for something. He yanked the sheets off her bed and managed to haul her mattress off the boxspring and it crashed into her computer. The bedroom, once a haven, became a battleground and it was disturbing to watch.

"That's so not cool," whispered MJ in my ear, as the thief continued to destroy Nikki's sanctuary. He stopped for a moment after demolishing a large portion of her room and looked directly at the darkened closet where we were hiding. He began walking towards where we were hidden, but he halted when the sound of the front door closing echoed up from the first floor, along with the sound of keys being dropped on a granite counter top.

The robber turned slowly to look at the open bedroom door, listening. In the darkness my hand found MJ's and I squeezed it, terrified for whomever had just returned. I prayed that they had all come back together. Safety in numbers, though this guy standing in the middle of Nikki's now ravaged room looked like he wasn't all there. Dangerous, as only a drug-addict can be when obsessed.

Then we all heard it.

Singing, off-key, as if the song-bird was wearing headphones.

Nikki had come home and it sounded like she was alone. MJ's hand clamped down on my own in a vise grip as the silent dude in black pulled a small object from his jacket pocket and headed for the door. The light

227

from the hall caught the glint of a silver blade in his hand as Nikki, on the first floor and unaware, continued to sing.

As soon as the robber left the bedroom, I slammed into panic mode.

"Oh my god! We've got to do something! We've got to - what the hell are you doing?" I demanded as quietly as I could, finally realizing MJ was stripping out of his clothes. He began shoving his things into my arms and I fumbled to hold everything.

"What do you think I'm doing? I'm going to phase and tear that jackass limb from limb! Take my stuff and sneak out and get back to the Bronco. I'll meet you there!"

"No way! I'm not leaving you with – oh jeez!" I snapped my eyes closed as MJ shed the last scrap of his clothing. I held still, listening and not daring to peek in case I got an eyeful of the anatomically correct, human side of my male co-conspirator. "MJ?" I whispered after a few seconds, but then felt a wide, soft head roll against my arm. I opened my eyes and watched as Marsh moved to the center of the closet.

Being a shape-shifter certainly had its perks.

I was about to protest the idea of me leaving him behind, when a terrified scream rang out from the first floor. Marsh shot out of the closet and through the bedroom door to the stairs like a four-footed bullet. I dashed after him, his clothes and shoes tucked into my arms.

I heard Nikki pleading and something smashed, but then I heard a deafening bark and dangerous snarl. The kitchen went silent except for the sound of Marsh's toenails slowly ticking across tile floor and a blood-chilling growl rolled slowly through the house.

I angled myself at the bottom of the stairs and was able to see Nikki on the floor in an ice blue dress, her back wedged against the base of the kitchen island, her forehead bleeding. She watched, wide-eyed and terrified, as Marsh carefully placed himself between her and the knife-wielding intruder. No doubt she was both grateful and shocked to see the local stray in her house.

Marsh had his teeth bared, his hackles raised, and looked like a demon dog with a lust for home invaders. The guy, knife still in hand, swapped his weight from foot to foot. Marsh suddenly lunged and the robber flailed backward, slamming to the ground.

Marsh pinned the sharp blade to the floor, roaring and snapping at the robber's face. For one horrible moment, I actually thought MJ might kill him. The guy struggled with Marsh, who finally let him free. The robber jumped, snatching his knife from the ground as he hauled through the back door.

Marsh snorted and turned slowly to face Nikki, who managed to scramble into a sitting position, though she was shaking. Slowly, carefully, Marsh stepped towards her. He lowered himself to the ground as he came nearer to her, scooting along on his belly and turning himself from vicious attack dog to sweet puppy looking for a friend. He stopped when he was close enough for Nikki to touch him if she chose. For a while, she simply clung to herself as the blood trickled down her forehead, looking at Marsh with confusion and fear painted on her face. Marsh slowly began to wag his tail and flipped his ears forward and back.

Cautiously, Nikki reached out a trembling hand and touched the velvet ears of my friend's furry form and stroked his head softly. "Good dog," she said, her voice a cracked whisper.

Marsh scooted a little closer until his head was in her lap and she continued to tell him he was a good dog until her voice broke. She doubled over into Marsh's thick, black coat and sobbed, hanging onto his massive head as if he was her lifeline. Nikki, scourge of my high school life, looked more broken in that moment than I had ever been after the Breakers.

I saw Marsh look to me and I mouthed the words *good job* to him from my hiding place by the stairs. He rolled his head slightly to bring himself closer to Nikki's shivering body and I silently slipped out through the front door, leaving my friend to comfort Nikki Shea alone.

It wasn't until I reached the Bronco, that I realized I had more than MJ's cod fish boxers and random clothes in my hands. I also had the little book from Nikki's closet . . . and Elizabeth's necklace.

I PUSHED THROUGH THE DOORS to the high school, holding them open for Eila and a few other students as we entered on Monday morning. The sheer volume of students moving in the space never failed to leave me floored. Cape Cod, as small as it was, had an enormous high school that served thousands of students, and hallways that seemed to form miles of tile.

Eila once said the building was so massive, that you could hide a small army within the walls – it was an idea I found worrisome.

Christian was of the mind that no Mortis would ever make a scene inside the school, as our kind only survived by staying below the human radar.

I had never known a Mortis to make a spectacle of himself in a public place, but someone like Eila had not been seen in almost two centuries. If her presence as a Lunaterra was known, I feared that all bets were off when it came to the safety of the high school and the students inside. A handful of my kind could decimate the student body in a matter of minutes and Eila could level the building all together.

My concerns, combined with the fact that the high school was a public building and therefore anyone, human or otherwise, could enter, made me a huge fan of homeschool.

"Are you listening to me?" I heard Eila ask as we reached her locker.

I gave an apologetic smile, "I'm sorry, my thoughts were elsewhere for a moment."

"I asked where you and Kian were going for, uh, dinner tonight?" she asked, glancing around at the students flowing by us. Several were watching us, which wasn't all that unusual, but the looks on their faces were almost . . . accusing.

I started scanning the halls and realized a fair number of students were stealing glances my way, and my instinct switched to high alert. Something was going on, but I smiled back at Eila, refusing to show her my concern. "I'm not sure yet. Someplace probably west of Boston," I replied, fully aware I was lying to her. Kian and I had planned to head to the Lucky Lady again in the hopes of possibly running into Rillin or another Mortis who might buy from him and know his whereabouts. I may have agreed to get information from him, but the reality was I wanted him checked off our To-Do list as soon as possible. I wanted him checked-off permanently.

I felt Eila's cool, delicate hand lace into mine, and I turned to look at her. She had a knowing quirked look to her face. "You are so not listening to me, are you? Something is going through that head of yours and you have tuned into a new radio station."

I brushed her dark hair back over her shoulder and let it tumble

232

down her back. "I'm sorry, I am just hoping that you have a good day – no drama queens with red fingernails and what not." Technically that wasn't a lie. I hoped that both Nikki and Teddy stayed far, FAR away from Eila every day.

She gave me a smile then looked past me and waved to someone approaching from behind where I stood. I glanced over my shoulder and saw MJ and Ana approaching us, Ana's hands waving animatedly as she talked.

Finally they reached us and Ana was still arguing her point about some drummer from a band I had never heard of. She shook her head, her cropped blonde hair dancing around her face. "No, no, no! The drummer in Ozzy's band kills it. I don't care what you say plus I always assumed you were tone-deaf, especially with YOUR playlist! I can't even believe your iPod allows you to download such crap!"

"TONE-DEAF? I think not. I'm not the one with an entire floppy-haired boy band's album on my playlist," replied MJ with a devilish smile.

Ana looked horrified and gave him a shove, "THAT WAS A SECRET!"

Eila laughed as she jammed a final text book in her locker and slammed the steel door shut, spinning the lock. "I actually like some of their stuff," she replied, defending her roommate.

"HA! See? Even Eila likes their stuff! Tone-deaf you are!" laughed Ana, but then she noticed that MJ was also watching the other students. He gave me a questioning look as he realized I seemed to be the center of some unwanted attention. Angry attention.

"What?" demanded Ana, never missing a thing. She started looking around as well and her face fell from amusement to confusion. She leaned closer to me. "What did you do?" she asked me in a hushed tone.

"What's going on?" asked Eila, sliding up next to me.

Ana looked over to E. "Our classmates seem to be pissed, about what I don't know, but the emotion is aimed at Raef."

"I don't know what they are mad about," I replied, taking Eila's backpack from her, and encompassing her hand in mine. Suddenly the hallway seemed more like a gauntlet.

MJ, getting the same impression as me, curled a protective arm around Ana. Because they were my friends, they would probably also be glued to the same bull's eye I was.

"I wonder if there is some rumor going around that we don't yet know about?" offered MJ, but then a voice, loud and demanding, rang out through the corridor.

"RAEF! WHAT THE HELL IS WRONG WITH YOU!" yelled Jesse, storming down the hall right for us.

I pulled Eila behind me, now faced with a sizable, pissed-off football player headed my way. MJ pushed Ana behind him as well and stood shoulder to shoulder with me. In his human form, MJ would be snapped like a tall twig, but I admired his bravery. Eila, never one to be bossed around, tried to squeeze her way around me, but I pinned her to my back with one arm like a band of steel.

"Raef – let me go," she urged, but Jesse was getting way too close for comfort. He was still yelling at me as he came, and the students were quickly getting out of his way, hoping to survive whatever was about to go down. I ran every scenario I could through my head as to why Jesse was so enraged, but I couldn't come up with a single answer. Not knowing put me on edge, but having to fight this kid didn't phase me in the least. Hell – it wouldn't even be a fight. Jesse didn't know what he was in for.

But then I felt Eila wiggling against me, trying to push off my back with her tiny hands, and I realized I couldn't show my true strength in the high school halls.

Finally Jesse was within feet of me and he shoved me hard, but I caught myself so I wouldn't slam Eila into the lockers. I heard her gasp when Jesse's wide palms connected with my chest, and the fact that he frightened her made my blood boil.

"Don't do that again," I warned, trying to rein in my rage.

"What the hell is your problem, man?" demanded MJ, right in Jesse's face.

"Get the hell out of here Williams – this doesn't concern a light-weight like you!" snapped Jesse. To my shock, MJ shoved the massive quarterback right in the chest. Granted, Jesse didn't move, but MJ's willingness to be beaten into a pulp for my sake spoke volumes to how good of a friend he was. Of course, there would be no way I would let Jesse damage anyone.

He grabbed MJ by the shirt-collar and Ana let out a string of curses, demanding he let her best friend go. She also added a few highly descriptive ways in which she would alter his manhood, but I intervened and clamped my hand on Jesse's arm. If I squeezed the way I wanted to, I'd crush his arm and football would be just a memory. I controlled my strength though, and Jesse's head snapped in my direction.

He glared at me as he let go of MJ, ripping his arm away from my grasp. "Don't touch me, O'Reilly. I knew you had a short fuse, but my god - he won't play for the rest of the year! His college rides will probably

235

bail on him! And for what? Because he had a bit too much to drink and got stupid with your girl?"

My body turned into a stone of rage and I felt Eila grip my sides, whispering a warning to me to let it go. To not react, that it wasn't worth it. But all I could visualize was cracking Jesse's head like an egg against the cinderblock wall. It was Ana's voice, however, that managed to keep me sane.

"What are you talking about, Jess?" she demanded, twisting herself around MJ. "Who won't play what?"

"TEDDY! Somebody called Coach and accused him of assault!"

I was stunned, but unfortunately not surprised. Guys like Teddy didn't change and now he had gone and messed up with another girl. I hoped he didn't get too far with whoever she was.

Eila weaseled her way under my arm. "Jesse! Be quiet will you! None of us reported him. I didn't want anyone to know! I don't want his football career ruined over a few stupid minutes of his life."

I was awed by the fact that she could care at all, but that was exactly who Eila was – concerned, even for someone who had done her harm.

Jesse kept glaring at her and it made my hackles rise. He gave her a disgusted smile, "Don't play dumb, Eila. It doesn't suit you."

That's it – I needed to punch his fat head, and would've but E was between two aggravated men. Not a good place to have her if I wanted her safe. I pulled back my burning desire to pummel the quarterback into the lockers.

Eila's eyes narrowed as she appraised Jesse, "Wait – you think Raef reported it? Are you out of your mind, Jesse? He would never do something like that!"

236

"He would for you! I can see it in his face – he would do anything for you!"

Jesse was absolutely right. I would do it for Eila, but I wouldn't have reported it. I would've just killed Teddy and made his body disappear.

I stepped in front of Eila, which put me even tighter to Jesse. "I didn't call. Don't get me wrong – the idea crossed my mind, but it wasn't me."

MJ wrinkled his brow, "Did Teddy accuse Raef?"

Jesse straightened, flexing his shoulder as if he was stiff with tension. "No. But he never did anything like that to anyone else. Look, Eila, he is trying to curb his drinking because of you." He looked at E, his rage falling slightly. "Just so you know, he has no recollection of that night. He only knows because I told him about what had happened. He is trying to change and he is horribly sorry."

Eila let out a deflated breath. She squeezed around to my side and laid a hand on Jesse's arm, which made me tense. "It wasn't Raef."

MJ and Ana nodded.

Jesse rubbed his head furiously, letting out a half growl of frustration. When he finally composed himself, he looked back at me. "I thought . . . with how you looked at the beach . . . Look, I'm sorry, Raef," he finally sighed.

I gave him a brief nod. I understood that his rage was in defense of a friend, even if that friend was a jerk. And yeah – it made sense that I would have been at the top of his list of suspects, but if the night of the bonfire wasn't Teddy's only transgression with a girl, then he was bound to have more enemies.

Jesse now looked fairly apologetic as he stood in front of us. "Teddy said that if he is off the team for what happened that night, then it is what he deserves. Eila, will you talk to him? For me? I know I said you don't have to, but his mind is really in a dark place."

I braced myself for Eila's answer, because knowing her –

"Yeah. I'll talk to him. Just not today, okay?"

Damn. I wanted to hit something.

Something in the shape of a linebacker named Teddy would suit me just fine.

30 Eila

AFTER THE HELLISH MORNING at school, I needed to defuse.

MJ and I had yet to tell our friends about our successful break-in at Nikki's two nights ago. We thought it would be wise to tell everyone at once and then crack open the diary together – as a team. Our goal was to do so as soon as possible . . . if we could get everyone together in one place for ten seconds.

The sucktastic part would be explaining how we had the necklace in the first place.

Ana had suggested we stop by the local store after school and browse for inspiration to help us unwind. My thinking was tacky nail polish and chocolate. Ana's however was more daring, and I wimped out on her suggestion.

"Are you sure you want to do this?" I asked her as she wrapped another old towel around her bare shoulders. I watched her as she began mixing some weird concoction that was guaranteed to change the color of her pixie-like locks.

"I'm sick of being a blonde. I can't wait to go back to my roots. Literally," she replied, laying out all the items that came in the small box. "I still say you would have rocked the purple streaks. We should have got them."

I flipped through the instructions for the hair dye procedure. "If you had put that stuff in my hair, my luck would dictate that the purple turned pink. I'll pass. You will rock the dark color though."

She smiled and began applying some weird goop to her hair.

"Are you sure you don't need any help?" I asked, though I was praying she didn't because the chemical smell was brutal in the bathroom.

I needed a gas mask, for crying out loud.

"Nope. You go hang with MJ before he eats all the candy you bought. I've done this before, so I'm good."

Thank god.

I left Ana in the bathroom while she tended to her alterations and headed down the stairs to the first floor, where MJ was picking through the junk I bought.

He glanced up at me, "How is it possible you didn't get any licorice? You basically got every variety of chocolate, but no gummy-anything! Sheesh . . . Next time, I'm going in the store with ya and guiding your junk-food selections."

I snatched a candy bar and flopped onto the couch. "Chocolate is a food group for females. Get with the program."

He tossed me a look and I balled the candy wrapper, flinging it at him. It drifted to the floor a few feet before him and he made a comment about my lousy aim.

He finally grabbed a small bag of chips and sat down next to me. "Will she be upstairs for a while?" he asked quietly. I nodded, knowing MJ and I needed to chat.

"So what happened after I left?" I asked, referring to the incident in Nikki's house.

"Nothing really. I stayed with her until she dialed her parents, then I split and got back to you in the Bronco. When she was on the phone though, it sounded like her parents were mad at her. Can you believe it?"

Actually I could. The way Nikki acted was probably a result of a loveless childhood.

MJ examined a chip in his hand, his face serious. "Nikki was really upset about losing the necklace. I could hear her parents freaking out about it on the other end of the phone. I gotta tell ya – I kinda feel bad we took it."

After protecting Nikki, MJ had run back to the Bronco as Marsh, meeting me in the florist's parking lot. He then phased into his shivering, human self and proceeded to get dressed, trying not to freeze his butt off as he did so.

Quite frankly, he needed to figure out how to phase without being stark naked. I mean, we were good friends and all, but some things just stepped over the line, like him stripping next to me in Nikki Shea's closet. I consider that a one-time deal only. No do-overs.

I had sat in the front seat while he changed, examining the stunning pendant. It had tiny little gears embedded in the backside, almost as if they were smaller versions of the one Agent Howe had shown me.

MJ turned to look at me as we sat on the couch, "You do realize we

241

are going to have to tell Raef and the others, right? The sooner we unlock the diary, the better, even if it means we are lectured by Kian and Raef until our ears bleed."

I moaned as I sank deeper into the couch, not looking forward to that discussion with Raef. "Any chance you can track the robber? You know – as Marsh?"

"What do I look like? A bloodhound? NO. No I cannot track the robber who is probably going to break into someone else's house the second he can." He finished off the small bag of chips and balled the bag in his fist.

I sighed, "Late last night I got to look through the French book that has that weird atom-thing on it. The whole book is filled with what looks like math equations related to gears and stuff. And the necklace is like the inside of some super-elaborate watch. There are all tiny gears embedded in the back, almost as if they are smaller versions of the one Agent Howe had shown me."

"Well that's just terrific! And what the hell is with that damn symbol?" asked MJ standing up. "Sula had it, you've been drawing it, freakin' Dalca had a gear engraved with it, and Nikki Shea has a book on it. At this rate, half the town will have the symbol and we will be the only ones that can't make heads or tails of it."

Something occurred to me then, "That dealer – Rillin. He had a symbol on his chest, but I could only see part of it. It looked like it was part of a circle."

"Don't even tell me HE had that atom-thing as well!" accused MJ.

"I don't know. Maybe." I stared at my feet, trying to recall the shape that hid under the strap of Rillin's vest.

MJ watched me for a while and then finally threw his hands in the air. "That's it. My brain is toast and I can't think anymore. All of this is just way too confusing for me. Sula, Rillin, Elizabeth, the diary, Christian, a freakin' atom – am I missing anything? Cause seriously, my tolerance for puzzles maxes out with the wooden ones for the pre-K crowd."

I laughed, because it was better than crying. "Yeah – I get ya, trust me."

MJ and I picked up the snacks and brought them into the kitchen. Raef and Kian had left after school to hunt locally. They planned to hunt for a few hours, then we would all meet up over at Torrent Road.

MJ was our guard until then, and he had been walking a fine line with his mother. So far he had been able to balance guarding us with his time in the shop and school, but I could tell it was getting exhausting for him. I needed to find a way to control my power so the guard dog thing could become a hobby, rather than a mandatory job.

As MJ washed a few bowls, I returned to the front parlor to grab the last couple of glasses, but caught sight of someone on the front porch. Startled, I moved carefully to the far window and peered through, entirely shocked to see Teddy standing on my porch and talking to himself while he paced.

Jeez . . .

He was obviously debating whether or not to knock on my door, and I was just going to leave him on the porch, but then I caught sight of something in the darkened tree line on the opposite side of the street. A shadow, once still, was moving along the edge of the bushes towards the porch and Teddy.

My heart launched into overdrive and I ripped open the front door, startling Teddy. He took a fast step back, no doubt shocked I was now standing in the open doorway. "Oh. Hey. I uh . . . I just wanted to say. You know. . ."

"Come on in!" I yelled in his face, grabbing him by the hand and hauling him through the front door as I tried to keep an eye on the deadly shadow, now cruising toward the side of my house. Teddy was an idiot, but there was no way he deserved to be murdered on my front porch. My skin began to crawl at the thought of a killer outside the walls of my home, hiding in the darkness.

"Give me one second. I'll be right back," I said to Teddy, who was still stunned. Looking at his expression, I knew he had been prepared to get the door slammed in his face.

I flew into the kitchen and grabbed MJ, covering his mouth with my hand so he wouldn't speak. He gave me a confused look and I backed him into the laundry room and shut the door behind us.

"Eila! What the heck are you doing?" he asked. He glanced behind me. "Wow – nice skivvies."

I growled and yanked my plain white bras off the drying line, tossing them in a basket on the floor. "Pay attention! Teddy's here!"

"WHAT?"

"I let him in because one of the shadows across the street moved, and not in a Christmas Elf kinda way!"

MJ's eyes grew hard. "I'll phase and go kick its ass. How many did you see?"

"I don't know and you are not going out there. I want you in here with us. Just phase, will ya, and get your furry rear out with me in the front room?"

244

MJ started swearing a blue streak as he began stripping. I left him in the laundry room to phase while I hurried back out to Teddy, who had not moved a muscle since I left.

"So, uh . . ." I began, but then I realized I was stuck with Teddy Bencourt standing in my parlor. I had not thought this through very well.

Teddy cleared his throat and tucked his hands in his pockets, "Listen, I just came by because I wanted to say I understand why you called the coach and I probably deserved it."

"What? No – I didn't call. None of us did."

Teddy shifted his weight, "Really?"

"Really. Look – I just want the whole incident to go away. You were drunk, you don't remember what happened, and Raef made sure it didn't go too far."

The color drained from Teddy's face. He looked like he might even get sick. "Eila, I can't tell you how sorry I am. I want to fix it – to erase that night all together."

Boy, he wasn't kidding. After the whole disaster with Teddy, I had gone back to my car for a clean sweatshirt and ended up getting tossed from the Town Neck bridge by a Mortis. Raef saved my life that night and everything I knew about the world changed forever in a matter of minutes.

"Jesse said you aren't drinking anymore," I replied, trying to mute the visions now running in my head. Looking at Teddy, I knew he would have overpowered me that night. He would've ended up in jail and I would've ended up with scars on my heart that might never heal. We both dodged a life-altering bullet that evening because of Raef.

"No – no more alcohol for me. Ever. I don't remember that night. I

245

don't know if I hurt you . . . did I?" His question was laced with so much shame I actually felt bad for him.

I shook my head, unable to speak.

He swallowed, "Do you think I did that to another girl? Is that why someone left an anonymous call to the coach?"

Anonymous? I didn't know it was anonymous. "The person who called the coach didn't give a name? What about details?"

Teddy just shook his head and I was lost in thought until someone pounded on the front door, causing me to jump. I walked to the window and looked through the glass to see Jesse standing on my porch. Fate totally hated my guts.

Jesse looked pissed, but I remembered I had other visitors prowling around. I ripped the door open. "Hey, Jesse – Come on in!" I said quickly, yanking him inside. The two football players were going to think I was desperate for visitors the way I was pulling people through my front door. Just as I slammed the door, Marsh lurked into the room from the kitchen, his head low as he watched the two footballers. He looked outrageously scary as he moved slowly into the room, scanning our houseguests, though his gaze seemed to focus on Jesse.

"Is that – is that the town stray?" asked Teddy, trying not to show his unease in front of such a dangerous looking dog.

"Uh, yeah. This is Marsh," I said, tossing a hand toward MJ's black form. "He visits on occasion."

"Nikki Shea's house was broken into the other night and she said this dog protected her," said Teddy. Jesse nodded, his eyes narrowed.

Oh man. Nikki had blabbed. "Her house was broken into? Is she . . . alright?" I asked, trying to act shocked even though I knew all the details

246

of that night.

"Yeah. A little shaken, but you know Nikki. She's strong. She'll be back at school tomorrow or the next day," said Teddy.

Awesome.

Jesse, who was still looking at Marsh with a wary sort of interest, finally turned his attention to Teddy. "I thought I told you not to come by Eila's house? I thought I told you she was willing to talk, but to give her time? I called your house and your mom said you had gone out to talk to someone and I thought you wouldn't be nuts enough to come here. I drove by just to make sure you weren't here, and sure enough – your truck is in her driveway!"

Jesse was pissed and while I applauded his attempt to honor my request for space, I also was impressed by Teddy's determination to make things right. It took a lot of guts to come to my home.

Marsh's head snapped toward the staircase as I heard Ana's voice ring out, "Okay, so I know it is a little dark but I really like it. What do you –" Her words halted on her lips as she saw Teddy, Jesse, Marsh and myself all standing in the parlor. "I can't wait to hear the explanation on this one," she muttered coolly, crossing her arms.

I held up a finger to signal her that I needed a minute, then turned back to the two football players. "Why don't you guys head into the kitchen and help yourself to some soda. I just need a moment to talk to Ana."

They gave Ana a wave, which she didn't return, and then headed into the kitchen, Marsh slinking along behind them.

This was a nightmare.

I was now trapped in my house with Teddy and Jesse, unsure of how

247

many Mortis were outside and no clue how to get the quarterback and his teammate safely to their cars. I needed to call Raef, except my stupid phone was in the Jeep along with Ana's. We had tossed them in my backpack and I was so preoccupied with chocolate, hair color, and the Nikki disaster, that I left the bag in my car.

Crap, Crap, CRAP.

Ana leaned against the post, fluffing her newly colored hair. "Soooooo. This situation is interesting."

I rubbed my face, flustered. "Teddy came to the door, but I saw a Mortis in shadow form outside."

Ana stiffened, but then took a deep breath calming herself. She knew as well as I did that the house was safe, and I wasn't inviting those suckers in. "Leaving Teddy outside as a snack would have been the perfect holiday present for Raef."

"Be serious, woman!"

"Fine. I'm just going to fantasize that the only reason he is inside is because you didn't want to have to dispose of his body. And Jesse? How'd he get here?"

"He wanted to make sure Teddy hadn't come by, which he did."

"Well – we are safe inside, and I see MJ has phased. Don't let him try to take on whatever is outside on his own."

"Don't worry. I won't," I said, glancing around the hallway. It was to our credit that neither of us was freaking out about the Mortis lurking around my yard. I chalked up our calm to the simple fact that we had *been there* and *done that* with another uninvited Mortis before. I would brag about our bravery, except it was honed on some seriously messed up experiences.

I looked at Ana, "By the way – your hair looks great in that dark brown."

Ana ran her hand compulsively along the bottom of the banister. "Thanks. Did you call Raef and Kian?"

"Our phones are in the car," I replied, wincing at my foolishness.

"Ah. Well, that wasn't too brilliant," she replied. "It's okay – we'll just stay inside and wait for the guys. The house is safe, so just don't invite any shadows in." I rolled my eyes.

Ana watched me closely as I rubbed the back of my neck, the stress starting to climb inside me. "Eila – are you really okay with Teddy being here?"

Exhausted, I sat on the bottom step of the grand staircase and nodded. Ana slid down next to me, and placed her arm over my shoulders. "Tell you what. Since we are stuck together for a bit, how about I find a game on TV for the guys and you take five or ten minutes and just get your thoughts in order. Raef and Kian will come by here when they realize we aren't at Torrent Road, and it will all be fine."

I looked over at my friend, "Thanks, Ana. I appreciate that."

"Anytime," she replied with a small smile. "Kian and Raef are useful, you know – some of the time."

Kian and Raef had been way more than just useful to us. And I knew that Kian was so much more than a simple guardian to Ana, no matter how hard she was trying to keep him simply as a friend. I looked at my dear pal seated next to me, "Ana, why did Kian call you *Pix*?" I asked, recalling how floored she looked when Kian said the word.

Ana swallowed and fiddled with the edge of her shirt, "It was a nickname. He used to call me Pix last summer. That's all. Just a

249

nickname."

Her mind seemed to drift for a moment, no doubt back to last summer, but then she shook her head and stood with purpose. "All right, enough of this reminiscing crap. I have two idiots to entertain. Now – where's the rat poison for Teddy?"

"ANA!"

31 Eila

I SAT ALONE ON THE BOTTOM of the staircase for a few minutes, gathering my thoughts as Ana suggested. It helped calm me, but it also served to build my anger because I couldn't step outside my house and defend myself, or my friends.

Well, technically Marsh could hold his own, but I needed him here, with us, since I was a flippin' soul-channeling novice.

Aggravating. It was so darn aggravating to be a prisoner in my home. If Raef and Kian were here, they would clear the area and spring us. God, I wish I had my phone and I wish Mae hadn't cancelled the home line.

I sat bolt upright when I realized Teddy or Jesse probably had a phone. I jumped to my feet and was about to go plead for a cellular device, when there was a knock at the front door.

Oh for crying out loud! Was my house destined to be Grand Central Station? I approached the door to open it, but my hand froze on the knob as a voice crept through the wood.

"Ms. Walker. I must speak with you," said a rough voice on the other side of the door. Rillin Blackwood was outside, speaking through the mahogany frame. Holy shiz.

I knew he couldn't cross the threshold to the house, so I gathered all my courage – every last shred of instinct that told me he was not a threat, and I opened the door.

Standing there in a black leather jacket, his wide frame nearly filling the door, was Raef and Kian's dealer and my occasional stalker. I stared at his tattooed skin and the faint scar that ran down the curve of his face. He really was a bad-ass version of Thor.

"Ms. Walker, I apologize for my abrupt appearance and I know you have many questions, but time is critical. I was able to eliminate one hunter who was by the barn, but the others have moved on to what I believe is their current target."

Many questions? More like nine million! But the look on Rillin's face worried me immensely, and his seriousness took priority over any question I had. Plus, he had apparently picked off one of the shadowy visitors that had been stalking my house. That seemed counterproductive if he wanted me dead.

"What do you mean *moved on to their current target?*"

"The two Mortis who bought Blacklist names from me – they are friends of yours? Bodyguards?"

Unease crawled through my body as I replied, "Yes. Why?"

"I believe the Mortis that were here tonight were designed to distract you from their true goal. Your protectors are problematic for them."

"What are you saying?" I asked, my voice faint as fear began to rise.

"I believe your bodyguards are the current target. I need to warn them – you can't afford to lose their protection, especially now. I believe the older Mortis have your details from the Breakers, bought from a man named Anthony Sollen. They've figured it out. They know what you are and who protects you."

All I heard was that Raef and Kian were in danger and my heartbeat pounded in my ears. "They are hunting on Sandy Neck, but I don't know where exactly," I said, louder and panicked. Sandy Neck's beach-side forest was huge.

"I know where they are," announced Ana, coming up behind me, her body tense, but a determined look on her face. "You are Rillin, aren't you?"

The dealer nodded, "Yes, Ma'am. Can you tell me where they hunt exactly?"

"Forget telling – I'll show you."

* * * *

We had basically thrown Jesse and Teddy from the house, without them seeing Rillin, and taken off in MJ's Bronco. Marsh sat in the far back, ram-rod straight. He had tackled Rillin at the house in an attempt to tear his throat out until I managed to call him off, explaining quickly what was going on. Rillin immediately realized I had another guard – a shifter – and he was impressed.

I drove like a woman possessed along Old King's Highway as Rillin followed the Bronco on foot, moving fast in his shadow form along the darkened road. Finally we reached the off-road section of Sandy Neck that Ana had directed me to.

"There's Kian's car!" she gasped from the passenger seat next to me. I pulled in next to the black SUV, nearly snapping the Bronco's key off in the ignition as I scrambled to get out of the vehicle. Ana yanked open the back and Marsh leapt out to the sand.

Rillin stepped out of the darkness towards us. "I'm going to try to locate them – hopefully they won't pick a fight with me before I can warn them. Stay HERE with the Shifter," he demanded, pulling a handgun from his back.

Ana and I jumped back and Marsh growled, but he held it out to me, handgrip first, the barrel pointed at him. "The gun won't kill them, but it will slow them down. Head shots are best if you can. Take it – you've earned this gun."

I reached out and took the oddly familiar weapon in my hand as I nodded.

"The safety is off, Ms. Walker. Shoot, don't hesitate, even if I'm in the way – even if your guards are in the way. Protect yourself, at all costs," he urged and bolted into the woods.

I looked down at the silver handgun in my palm, and finally realized why I recognized it.

It was Dalca's gun.

A gun, which had been pressed to my temple, eliminating all but one option the night of the Fire and Ice Ball.

Ana looked at me, "Are we really staying here?"

"Hell no," I replied, and I started running in the same direction Rillin had gone, Ana and Marsh by my side, and Dalca's gun firmly in my hand.

32 Raef

WE HEARD IT LONG BEFORE we saw it. Motion in the woods, at a distance, but closing fast. Multiple points of action that were not part of the natural landscape headed our way.

"We're not alone," warned Kian, now hyper alert as he kneeled by the deer he had just killed. By the sounds of the snapping twigs and scuffed sand, we weren't alone by a long shot, and whoever was coming towards us didn't care about stealth.

Kian got to his feet just as a Mortis burst through the tree line, smashing into him and driving him into the sand. I ran for him, and plowed into the soul thief who was trying to get a solid arm around Kian's neck to snap it.

I slammed the attacker into a tall pine and managed to drive my elbow into the side of his face hard enough to hear the crack of his neck. He slumped to the sand just as I turned, and was hit in the chest with what felt like a 100-pound knife. I staggered, trying to stay on my feet as

255

I grabbed the shaft of the crossbow arrow protruding from my chest. I yanked it from my body, roaring in pain as the Fallen marks flashed to the surface of my skin. We were under attack, by our own kind. A coordinated assault that could only mean one thing – our identities as Eila's protectors was known.

Kian, now covered in his own dark markings, was going hand-to-hand with two other Mortis, a male and female. I made a move to help him, but was tackled by another soul thief, this one wielding a dagger. He collided with me and we smashed into the sand.

I moved just in time to avoid the dagger being driven into my eye and he buried the sharp blade into the sand next to my head. I fought for control of the blade, while trying to get a grip on his neck, but my arm had become weak from the arrow.

The attacker got the blade over my head once again just as I heard gunfire. The chest of the Mortis above me bloomed red, and his concentration snapped in the direction of the shooter. In that one, fleeting second, I managed to glimpse Eila and my heart froze. She was running towards me, gun in hand.

I reached up and yanked my attacker's neck sharply to the left. He crumbled into a heap and I tossed his body aside, scrambling to get to Eila just as two more soul thieves burst from the shadows and converged on me.

I heard Eila scream my name as the attackers reached me, but they suddenly fell to the ground, dead at the feet of the dealer. I stared at him for a moment, shocked he was standing in front of me and helping me, but then I saw Kian, struggling.

"Go help Kian – I've got to get Eila and Ana out of here!" I yelled and the dealer nodded, throwing himself into the fight with Kian.

I ran for Eila as Marsh bolted past me, throwing himself at another onslaught of soul thieves, swiftly decapitating another female, but the other two broke through, followed by more.

We were horrifically outnumbered, under a full onslaught of Mortis who were trying to kill us.

I ran for Eila, but then felt the familiar knifing punch strike my back, knocking me to my knees as another arrow buried itself in my shoulder blade.

From my point on the ground, I saw Ana running for Kian. She grabbed a crossbow off the body of a dead Mortis, touching his face for a moment, and then stood and aimed at one of the many attackers who had converged on us. She braced herself and fired a clean shot right through his throat, dropping the attacker to his knees.

But the raiding Mortis kept coming, two now headed straight for me. I couldn't reach the arrow in my back and it had weakened my other arm. Eila turned and saw them heading for me, and in her face I saw her power come to life, transforming her soft beauty into razor sharpness.

Her Lunaterra heritage ignited in her eyes, forming a copper ring around the brown, and I screamed at her to not do it. Screamed at her to not call her gift and end her life.

In that moment, my world slowed to a crawl as I watched her throw her hands outward, her dark hair fanning away from her fair skin like a devastating wraith. Shards of brilliant light flew from her body, as she delivered a fatal blow to the fight.

33 Eila

I SAW RAEF FALL to the ground when the arrow struck his back, and my world shattered. Fear and uncertainty, however, were cut down by a blinding rage that crashed through my body and transformed into a lyrical language that tempted my DNA.

Like the sun breaking the horizon, a burning sensation bloomed in my chest, turning hotter as it unfurled through my body and I dropped the gun. My vision brightened, drawing in more light than was possible in the dark winter woods as the power ran down my arms, clawing through my veins like icy talons. My reaction to the brutal sensation was instant and instinctive, and I threw my hands out as if pushing this invisible beast from me, and it transformed into breathtaking streaks of light.

It traveled like a sunburst from my hands and chest, slicing through the Mortis who were attacking us, and rendering them instantly to ash. The ensuing silence felt like its own alternate world, and I dragged in a deep breath, trying to slow my racing heart. I stared at Raef and he looked frozen in place, terrified at what I had just done.

Rillin, who somehow was spared my lethal talent, had been thrown against a tree by my energy. He got to his feet as he steadied himself against the pine bark with one hand, but his scars somehow looked more distinct than before.

Kian was slowly lifting himself off of Ana, whom he had grabbed and thrown himself over to shield her from another Mortis who had launched himself at her. Their attacker was within arm's reach of both of them when I reduced him to nothing more than dust. The remnants of the Mortis had coated Kian's back, and the ash slid from his body like currents of smoke as he staggered to his feet with Ana pinned to him.

"Eila!" shouted Raef and I turned back to him as he got to his feet. I started walking towards him, trying to slow my pounding heart, which was making me light headed and constricting my breath. Kian stepped over to Raef, and yanked the arrow from his back. Raef growled in response, but once free of the arrow, started jogging towards me. "Eila! Are you alright?"

I took another step to him and tried to reply, but my knees buckled and I fell to the cold sand. I felt Raef grab me and pull me into his arms. "NO! Eila! Stay with me! Breathe!"

"My heart . . . is . . . pounding," I managed to gasp between pants. Fear started to weave into me as I realized I was having some sort of heart attack. I didn't want to die – not in Raef's arms. Not like this.

"We need to get her to the hospital!" Ana yelled and she started screaming for Marsh who bolted in from the tree line. Raef began to pick me up, but Rillin appeared beside him, dropping to his knees.

He quickly stripped off the leather jacket from his large frame and laid it over me. "The hospital won't help. She didn't release all of her energy and it's recoiling on her body. It's an overload, but I can fix it," said Rillin urgently.

He reached for me, but Raef grabbed his arm. "Don't touch her!" he snapped, but Rillin was unfazed.

"I get it – you don't know me and you don't trust me. You think I'm a threat, but I just saved your life, as did she. I can do this for her. Let me save her."

My heart was beginning to climb up my throat and I was started to slip into that quiet place of blissful unconsciousness. I closed my eyes as I heard Raef tell Rillin to help me.

I felt someone pulling open my jacket as Rillin gave instructions to keep me warm afterward and something about hypothermia. "I'm going to force a release of the remaining energy you have lingering in your body, but it will drop your body temp," said Rillin, his face near mine. "I swear to you, it will only last a few seconds, so just hang in there."

The moment his rough hands touched my chest, I was thrown into a torturous hell like I had never known before. It felt as though I was being crushed into a box of ragged glass and I screamed as I arched into Raef, clinging to him. The glass pushed deeper into my flesh, and I knew there was no way I could handle the pain, but then it mercifully halted. The glass, the pain – it was gone, as if it never happened. My heart began to slow, my breathing evened out, and I felt Raef pull me tighter to his chest as his fingers traced the artery in my neck, checking my pulse.

"What happened?" I whispered as I slowly opened my eyes. The world came into focus, Raef's bruised face above me.

"Rillin released your power somehow," he answered, a mixture of relief and unease layering over his face as he held me tighter. I turned my head to see Rillin bent over in the sand, his hands pressed to the sides of his head as if he was in terrible pain. The Fallen markings that covered his skin flickered in uneven patterns, like an electrical current that was fluctuating. Had he absorbed my energy? How was he not dead? How was he not killed when I threw my power in the first place?

"Rillin?" I asked as my teeth started to chatter thanks to a strange chill that was funneling into my body.

Dragging himself to standing, Rillin stumbled into the woods, mumbling something about finding us later and keeping me warm.

* * *

Raef had climbed into the far back of the Rover with me in his arms. I was freezing – FREEZING, as if I had been packed in ice. Everyone layered their coats over me, but I couldn't get warm, and I shook violently as my body tried to produce a scrap of heat. My back was on fire as my kill mark once again began burrowing up my back, contorting itself into a larger mark thanks to what I had just done.

Kian drove with Marsh jammed in the passenger seat, while Ana hung over the back seat, trying to stop Raef's bleeding. The puncture wounds from the arrows were already starting to heal, but Mortis blood was toxic to me. Bleeding around me was a sizable no-no.

Ana had managed to get Raef's shirt off and he held me tightly to his warm chest as she used duct tape to cover the holes on his body. It wasn't pretty, but it worked, and I was grateful for the contact with his skin. He watched me carefully, every so often checking my pulse and trying to bring my frozen body in closer with his. He talked to me to keep me awake and at one point he unwrapped some of the jackets from my stomach and raised my shirt to press me to his warm skin. Whatever Rillin had done, he fixed my heart but dropped my body temperature to Siberia.

Once at Torrent Road, Raef carried me into a beautiful bathroom and turned on the shower, kicking off his boots as he did so. I understood what his plan was and I managed to toe off my sneakers, though my whole body was shaking. He grabbed me around the waist and pinned me to his body, stepping into the shower and the fantastic liquid heat.

The water rained down on us, soaking our clothes and hair. I was still shivering, but the water felt like it was slowly warming my bones. Raef wrapped his arms around me, using his own body heat and that of the water to bring my core temperature back up. We just stood there while the water flowed over us, catching every curve of my face and every angle of his chest. Once in a while he would turn the hot water up higher and my body slowly stopped shivering.

I felt exhausted, but focused on his hand that held my shoulder blade, and the simple action of his thumb tracing back and forth over my wet shirt. "I've never seen you kill someone before," I said quietly, as I rested my cheek against his wet chest, and his thumb stilled.

He was quiet for a while, but then he finally spoke, his voice echoing deeply in his chest, mixing with the sound of his heartbeat. "Did it bother you, E?"

I simply shook my head *no*. I knew what Raef was capable of, but somehow I had never visualized him murdering another person – even a soul thief. It made the experience all the more real and a stark contrast to the life I hoped I could lead. I realized then that such pipe dreams of teenage nonsense and movie nights were just that: dreams.

"I killed them," I whispered, guilt beginning to crush me. I felt Raef's arms tightened around me and he rested his head on mine.

"You saved our lives. They would not have stopped until we were dead. You scared the hell out of me, but I am proud of you," said Raef, his words rumbling in his chest.

"I'm a murderer," I replied, my throat burning with the need to cry. I had killed before, the night of the Breakers, but I didn't remember any of it. Seeing what happened to the Mortis tonight when my power sliced through them was just awful. Some of their faces were frozen in fear as their bodies turned to dust.

Raef let me go and brushed my soaked hair from my face as he turned my head to look at him.

"You are a survivor. A selfless fighter, and it wasn't murder. It was self-defense and damn heroic. You're not a murderer, Eila. I am. I kill people for their soul. That day I picked you up with my motorcycle, I had killed a man while you were in school. He was a bad man, had done terrible things, but he begged for his life when I killed him, and I did not show him an ounce of mercy. That is murder."

I shook my head as I traced the edge of the tape on his chest, "I know what you are Raef, and what you do in the name of justice – and to protect me. You're not the one I'm afraid of."

He brought his face closer to mine, gently sweeping the water drops from my cheeks, "Who are you afraid of E?"

"Myself," I replied.

34 Raef

EILA WAS WRAPPED IN LAYERS of blankets as she sat curled up at the end of the couch by a roaring fire. Ana had grabbed her some clothes from my closet, and they hung loosely from her, making her look even more petite than she already was. I did love seeing her in my clothes, illogically believing they added another layer of protection to her.

Christian, who had been searching for Rillin in Boston when we called him, knelt beside her, one hand on her knee as he talked to her. When he learned what had happened, he drove back from Boston, probably breaking every speed limit possible. As he spoke with Eila, I realized he truly loved her, as if she was the daughter he never knew.

MJ had phased back into his human form while we had been in the shower, and I had to give him credit – he fought like a pro out on Sandy Neck. His speed and accuracy as Marsh made him entirely lethal, and the least banged up. He had left a little while ago, heading back to his own home before his mother grounded him for the next century.

Kian looked the worst, covered in fading bruises and slices to his brow, lip, arms, and back. He sat on the floor at the other end of the couch, while Ana, her hair now a coffee color, tended to his back from her perch near Eila's feet. Her tiny fingers worked to cover each cut and scrape with small pieces of bandage, even though Kian would be entirely healed by dawn.

I suspected the need to just *do* something led to her insisting on taking care of Kian. Ana had kept her cool under fire tonight, as had Eila. Neither of the girls, or MJ, were simple teenagers anymore. They were fighters, comrades, and a whole lot more. I listened as Kian pretended to complain about Ana's nursing skills, while Ana told him to *suck it up and deal.*

I handed Eila a cup of hot chocolate, and she wrapped her hands around the wide mug, warming her palms as Christian thanked me. Her body temp was almost normal and her cheeks held a flushed quality that I adored. I thought she was going to die tonight.

I thought her power was going to stop her heart and I would be left with her dead in my arms. It was very probable that that is what would have happened if it hadn't been for Rillin Blackwood. Eila had told me what had happened earlier in the evening and how they all ended up on Sandy Neck. I was not pleased about the human visitors, but Eila seemed to have found an inner peace regarding her and Teddy. I chose not to react to their visit, especially since several Mortis had been wandering around her home in the dark . . . and Rillin had killed one.

Christian finally left Eila's side and headed into the kitchen. I followed him and found him pacing back and forth along the granite island. He was stressed and so was I. Rillin had said he would find us later, and "later" had come and gone a few hours ago.

Could this beast of a dealer really be an ally or was the assault on Sandy Neck a set-up?

"Whoever attacked you knew exactly what they were doing and they were old school fighters," said Christian. "Using weapons during battle was fairly standard in my day – it was the best way to take out a Lunaterra at a distance, or weaken another Mortis so you could more easily kill him. Those that Eila killed must have been tracking us for a while, testing us to make sure we were Mortis. It would explain the slashed tire and you getting hit by an arrow a few weeks ago." I didn't follow his logic on the tire and my incident while hunting and I gave Christian a confused look.

He crossed his arms, the tension flowing through his body. He too could have lost Eila tonight. "I think the tire was to see how fast you and Kian could move, and the *accidental* arrow was to see if you were bothered by it. A human would have been writhing in the sand, screaming."

I sighed, "I think whoever was buying details from Sollen had to be part of the group that attacked us. And I don't think they are aiming to abduct Eila. I think they are out to kill her. To kill us all. They must know what she is and because we protect her, we are traitors as well."

"I agree," replied Christian, rubbing the back of his neck.

What a nightmare.

As the ornate clock on the wall edged on towards midnight, I finally heard a knock at the front door. Christian and I looked at each other and headed into the living room, where Kian was already on his feet, nearly blocking Ana from view. I looked to Eila. "Last chance to leave this guy at the door," I said, hoping she would decide that her leap of faith in

Rillin was an unacceptable risk.

"Let him in," she ordered, wiggling her small frame more upright, a determined look on her face.

I glanced to Kian and Christian and I knew they stood with me when it came to letting this guy in, but he had saved our lives. Savior or not however, if he made a wrong move the three of us would be on him in an instant.

Christian opened the door and there stood Rillin in a t-shirt that revealed numerous tattoos, inked over many scars. The jacket he had lent to Eila was laying over the back of one of the chairs near the girls, and he looked over his apparel, and then the entire room. His eyes finally landed on Eila and he spoke to her, ignoring the rest of us.

"You're looking better, though you should have listened to me and stayed by the car," he said to her from his spot just outside the front door.

Eila didn't respond and the way he looked at her set my nerves on edge. I wanted to instantly build a steel wall around her.

Christian stepped aside, "Come in."

Rillin stepped into the room and turned to me, sensing somehow that I was her lead guard of sorts. "May I check on her?"

I glanced to Eila and she nodded, sliding her feet out from under her. She walked over to where we stood, a blanket still wrapped around her shoulders, and I took up the space immediately next to her.

"Can I have your wrist?" he asked and I tensed, but Eila simply extended her slender arm out in front of her. He took her hand in his, and felt her pulse. "You seem fine – all the excess energy is gone from your system. If you're going to throw the Light, you need to make sure

267

you tether all its pieces, otherwise you can fall into cardiac arrest."

"How do you know that? How did you even know what I was?" asked Eila, tucking her arm back into her blanket.

"The explosion at the Breakers was all over the news, and at first I thought it was a terrorist attack, as the FBI believed. But then certain details emerged, including Mr. Raines' involvement, your injuries, and the FBI's inability to list an explosive. Our meeting in the woods was by sheer luck, but at the football game you were identified as the girl from the Breakers. I started searching for details about you, which linked me to your home and a picture of someone I used to know. You're just like her, you know? She wouldn't have stayed by the car either . . . if we had cars back then."

Christian stepped forward, his face tense, "Who are you talking about?"

"Elizabeth. And she was just as stubborn as Ms. Walker," said Rillin.

35 Eila

WE WERE ALL WATCHING RILLIN, a tangle of curiosity and distrust on all our faces. Christian however, had stilled into a creepy sort of statue the moment he heard Elizabeth's name. He was gripping a mahogany desk so hard, I was sure the edge would have a permanent imprint of his fingers.

"You need to start talking," ordered Raef, placing his hand to my back.

Rillin looked at Christian oddly, clearing his throat. "The Lunaterra are normally trained by their parents to fight. But those of the royal houses utilized enslaved trainers – Mortis – known as Trials. I was one of their Trials."

I heard Christian mutter a curse. I looked at him, "What? Is this true? They had . . . Mortis trainers?"

"Supposedly, though as far as I know, none ever left the palace alive," replied Christian.

I crossed my arms, not buying this ridiculous idea of enslaved trainers for one second. "That makes no sense. Why in the world would the Lunaterra use their enemies to train?"

Rillin leaned back against the door. "The best way to learn how to defeat an enemy is to know the enemy in every way possible. It was a brilliant idea – imprison your enemy and force them to fight, but control how far they can go. Learn and practice your fighting technique with those you seek to destroy. We were a combination of gladiator, target, and personal trainer."

I snorted, refusing to believe such a tall tale. "I don't see how they could force you to obey them."

"Every Trial, the moment they were captured, was fitted with Limiting Link."

"What the hell is Limiting Link?" asked Raef, outrageously tense.

Rillin pulled down the neck of his t-shirt, revealing the left side of his broad chest and the brand I couldn't quite make out before. It was a perfected version of the strange atom that had been haunting us.

I sucked in a short breath. "What is that?" I asked, desperately wanting to run my fingers over the raised mark.

"This is my Limiting Link. It is a bunch of carefully entwined rhodium wires and gears that the Lunaterra implanted in every Trial the moment they were captured. Well, technically a Feon would implant it. They prevented us from leaving the palace grounds and would bring a Trial to his knees if he tried to kill a Lunaterra during training, or anywhere else."

I finally pulled my eyes off his chest, "You mean that's not a scar? There are actual wires under your skin?" Rillin nodded and I suddenly felt itchy, as if such a nasty device was crawling around in my own body.

Kian jammed his hands in his pockets, "I've never heard of a Feon. What are we talking about?

"Feon are very rare, now-a-days. They are humans who have the ability to control and contort metal and its properties. If any survived the Lunaterra Wars, they would have gone into hiding. To control a Feon means you control the key to any vault, lock, bridge, jetliner. If it's metal, it follows their command. The Links bound us to a device inside the palace."

Ana had squeezed in next to Kian, whose protective arm was around her tiny frame, "So basically you had, like, a doggy containment system – the ones that buzz the dog if they try to take off or bark too loud."

Rillin looked at Ana, one eyebrow curved in a curious arc. "You must be Ana Lane," he replied, ignoring her analogy . . . though it actually sounded dead-on. Rather than answer Rillin, she sealed her lips tightly shut and Kian pulled her closer.

"How did you know Elizabeth?" asked Christian, his voice so low my own toes curled.

Rillin eyed Christian warily, no doubt confused as to why he was so tense. "I was her Trial. As a female, she was with a Trial from the time she was eight until she was fifteen. Boys remained with a Trial until 20. Older trials were considered more valuable as we could take more severe hits from a Lunaterra and we wouldn't be killed."

"So that's why my energy didn't kill you when I, uh, threw the Light. You really are like a gladiator," I mumbled, disgusted by my family tree.

Rillin shrugged, "Technically I was a knight. A Templar, when I was still human."

"You were a knight? A real knight in shining armor?" asked Ana, floored. "Like, with the shield and the horse and the maiden in the tower?"

"I do not recall any maidens in towers," replied Rillin.

"What happened to Elizabeth?" demanded Christian, knowing that something had occurred to condemn Elizabeth to die when she was fifteen, but she mercifully escaped execution.

Rillin looked suspiciously at Christian who was boring holes through his head with his stare. "She escaped the palace into the woods, but you know that, don't you? There were rumors that Elizabeth had been taken in by a group of Mortis. Rebel fighters from the north. You were part of that group, weren't you?"

"Yes, I was, and when I found her, she had been beaten. Badly. Left to die!" Christian's anger seemed to literally fill the room, like a smoky layer to the air.

Understanding hit Rillin. "Wait. You think I beat her? Good god no. I was her trainer and she was the most brilliant fighter I had ever seen. She could control her power and literally form it into a physical weapon. I consider training her one of my greatest accomplishments."

"Her family was going to kill her!" snarled Christian.

"And they didn't! I got her out!" snapped Rillin. Both pissed off men started toward one another, but I yelled at them to knock it off. I felt Raef angle himself in front of me and I realized I had forgotten he was even next to me. I had forgotten everyone except Rillin and Christian.

I touched Christian on the arm and lowered my voice, "Can you handle being here?" His jaw was set so hard I thought he might crack a tooth. "I get this is difficult for you. I do, but we need answers without fist fights. So can you be here, or no?"

Christian stalked back over to the desk, leaning against the edge of the curved front.

Rillin looked between the two of us, no doubt trying to figure out what the hell was going on in Christian's head and why he was so upset. He had no idea Christian had been in love with Elizabeth – had no idea I was descended from their affair.

"Just for the record, I didn't hurt Elizabeth. I mean, training she got a few scrapes, but she gave as good as she got. And yes, she was sentenced to death because she killed another Lunaterra – her suitor."

WHOA! WHAT?

I pointed an accusing finger at Christian, who looked just as stunned as the rest of us. "YOU said she was condemned to die because she was feeding the Mortis information on pending attacks!"

"That's what she told me!" protested Christian.

"Wait – Elizabeth was the one who was leaking attack info?" asked Rillin, equally floored. "I thought it was one of the other Trials – somehow getting information to the outside," Rillin swore angrily. "I should have known. She was so unique. She thought for herself. She wasn't just a drone like the rest. She . . . she wasn't linked to the rest, was she?"

Christian shook his head, "No. She didn't connect with the minds of the other Lunaterra, which is how she wandered off when she was little. She was her own person. She followed her heart. Following directions wasn't high on her list of priorities." Christian's voice softened. "You said she killed another Lunaterra. Her suitor?"

Rillin seemed lost for words for a moment, no doubt thinking back to my grandmother when she was young and probably stubborn as hell. "Yes. All Lunaterra females are bound to their assigned suitor on the night of their fifteenth birthday."

Christian drew a careful breath, "What do you mean, bound?"

"Her assigned suitor, a male in his final year of training, would, well, you know. Most females were mothers by the time they were sixteen." Rillin glanced to me.

"By force?" I whispered, horrified.

Rillin shrugged, "Technically they didn't say 'no' since free will was eliminated from the Lunaterra line. They all followed orders blindly – it was mind control on a genetic level."

I swallowed hard. "So they were programmed to not object to being . . . being . . ."

"Damn it," whispered Christian, closing his eyes.

"Elizabeth had come to me the morning of her fifteenth birthday. She was upset about being bound that evening, and I told her to not do anything she wasn't ready to do. When she left my cell, the determination on her face haunted me, because I knew her suitor would take her by force. No Lunaterra said no. No Lunaterra got a choice. That night she fought him, hard. But her determination turned into desperation and she killed him."

Christian snapped the edge off the desk and I jumped.

Rillin glanced at Christian, as he continued, "The palace didn't know what to do with her at first, so they dumped her in my cell with me for days. Her suitor had done a number on her before she smashed his miserable head against the marble floor. She was in rough shape. I tried to keep her warm to prevent her from slipping into shock, but she needed a healer. After a few days, word came that she was to be executed."

"Her Feon friend came to my cell one night and asked if I was willing to make a run for it with Elizabeth if she could shut down the device that kept me linked to the palace. I agreed and by nightfall she had done it, causing the palace to erupt into chaos. I remember picking Elizabeth up in my arms and looking through the bars of my cell door and literally saw mass confusion. I heard the guards yelling for the traitor to be killed. I knew they were coming for Elizabeth and I just went for it. The second they opened the door I was on them, snapping their necks in seconds. The Limiting Link was no longer working, just as she had said, and I ran with Elizabeth in my arms, through the palace and finally to the woods. Somehow her friend had freed me."

"If you saved her from the palace, why did you leave her unprotected in the woods?" growled Christian.

Ana put her hands out, as if to halt all conversation, "Hold up. Where in the heck is this damn palace and how in the world isn't it like, listed on Wikipedia or something? I mean, you can't exactly misplace a palace."

"It wasn't misplaced. It was hidden from the human eye and tucked into a remote area of France known as Auvergne. Much of it was built into the ground and when it crumbled, most of the palace became buried under the land. I was told there were occasional Mortis looters who looked for trophies in the hidden tunnels once the Lunaterra were eliminated. They would sell the remnants on the black market to other Mortis."

"Hidden from the human eye? Yeah – okay. Sure it was," replied

Ana, but Rillin gave her a knowing look. It made Ana shift nervously on her feet. "WHAT?"

"Nothing," replied Rillin.

"Forget the damn palace!" snarled Christian. "Why was Elizabeth alone in the woods?"

Rillin drew a deep breath, "I hid her the best I could, but I feared that the palace could still track me via the Link. So I left her, intending to come back as soon as I could get it removed, but then everything went to hell. Fighting broke out everywhere, the other Trials escaped and turned on their captors. Mortis camps were being raided, rebel clans were being formed left and right, and nowhere was safe – especially for her. It was as if the floodgates had opened and the Lunaterra were on a homicidal warpath. When I was unable to find a Feon to remove the Link, I headed back to where I had left her, but she was gone. Within weeks, the palace was nothing but rubble."

The silence that bled through the room seemed endless. Christian was rubbing his forehead and Raef had woven his hand in mine. Up until this moment, we had only known Christian's version of what had happened to Elizabeth. That he had found her when she was five and had returned her to the palace, only to search for her again when she was a teenager. He had found her, badly injured and sick, in the woods – the same woods where Rillin had left her after he saved her from being executed.

The portrait of my grandmother was slowly being painted by the men who had known her, all of whom were technically her enemies. Christian had loved her. Rillin had trained her. Raef and Kian had befriended her.

I stepped closer to Rillin and Raef moved with me. "Mr. Blackwood.

Rillin. Why are you helping me?"

"A long time ago I left an unlikely friend alone in the woods, and she disappeared from my life. I left you alone in the woods as well, but once I understood who you were, I couldn't leave. Life rarely offers us second chances, Ms. Walker, and I will not walk away this time. If you let me, I can train you so that you may fight alongside your guards, as I suspect Elizabeth did with Mr. Raines. I owe it to her, for she never treated me as a slave. She treated me as a friend and she went on to help my kind."

I looked at Raef and he was tense, hard, and unyielding. I turned back to Rillin, "Why did you leave me the billiard ball?"

"I had followed you to this house the night you fell while riding – I knew something was just different about you. But then I saw Raef help you out of your car. In fact, I thought he might have seen me. I was unsure if you knew that Raef was a Mortis. But after the football game, and meeting Kian and Raef at the Lucky Lady and their reaction to what I said about Christian, I knew something was going on. I started digging for details on you, which led me to the link with Elizabeth. I used the billiard ball to test what kind of connection you shared with Raef and Kian. I wanted them to know I got close to you, knew who you were, but did not harm you."

"Next time leave a note," muttered Ana.

I looked to my friends, then back to Rillin, "You will have to prove yourself to my guards."

"I would expect them to demand nothing less," replied Rillin.

Christian rocked from foot to foot where he stood, his arms crossed tightly over his chest as he thought. Finally he looked to Rillin, "Elizabeth said she had two friends inside the palace. Two people who made her life bearable. If you are who you say you are, tell me their names."

Rillin tucked his hands in his pockets, "Well – she had been friends with Katherine, who she called Keek, the daughter of two metal workers who were kept in the palace, though I don't know what happened to her the day we escaped. As to her other friend, I am hoping she was referring to me."

Christian's jaw pulsed, "I gave her necklace back to her friend Katherine after she died. She had left me a note instructing me to do so. I never knew Katherine was a Feon. She must have been the one to alter the necklace in the first place. That means that Nikki Shea may be a Feon as well."

"Keek – I mean, Katherine, was her friend who damaged the device which freed me."

Christian narrowed his eyes, "Speaking of friends, she never mentioned the name *Rillin*. Ever."

"No – she never called me that."

Christian suddenly looked less suspicious, as if Rillin was headed in the right direction. "What did she call you?"

Rillin's face revealed the smallest touch of longing. "Monster. She called me *her* Monster," he replied quietly.

36 Raef

I TOOK A SLOW, DEEP BREATH as the elaborate chandelier inside Torrent Road came into view far above me. I shifted slightly and the right side of my chest and shoulder screamed and I hissed out a curse. That's when I felt her beside me, her body pressed against mine, and one delicate arm hugged tightly to my torso.

Eila was laying on the floor with me, curled against my body. We had fallen asleep together on a pile of blankets and pillows by the fire, not long after Rillin had left.

I didn't try to distance myself from her.

Not after last night. Not anymore.

Rillin had passed Christian's test, and he had left hours ago to dispose of the body he had hidden in Eila's barn, unlike Agent Sollen, whose body he had hung from a beam. Agent Howe had been right – his partner's suicide was staged.

Rillin said that once he knew Eila had ties to Elizabeth, he started following the FBI. He soon learned that Sollen was selling details of the Breakers to someone, most likely a Mortis, so he killed Sollen to protect Eila's identity. After stringing up Sollen at his Boston apartment, Rillin had found a few more files and Dalca's gun, all of which he took, though he was unable to pinpoint the soul thief who was buying all the details. I was grateful he had grabbed the files before Agent Howe had found them, along with his hanging partner. Unfortunately, Rillin agreed with Christian and me – Eila's identity as a Lunaterra was now known. She would be marked for death by those Mortis who had fought against the Lunaterra. In Rillin's opinion, last night's attack was the first of many. As much as I wanted to distrust him, I believed he was right.

I felt Eila shift and she appeared above me, blocking the chandelier as her hair cascaded over one side of her face and dusted my bare chest. "How are your boo-boos?" she asked, as she traced her hand over the square of tape on my chest.

I reached up and touched her chin. "Boo-boos? I don't get boo-boos."

She sunk down to my shoulder, "They looked like bad boo-boos to me last night. Do you think they are all healed?"

Yes, said boo-boos were probably all healed, just damn sore. "I'm fine," I replied, slowly sitting up and bringing Eila with me. She moaned, as if she didn't want to get up yet. With her wrapped around me, I didn't want to get up either, but I could hear voices in the library.

The early morning sun drifted in through the towering glass windows in the living room, twisting its way through Eila's hair, and catching the mahogany of her eyes. With her warm body nestled to me, and one of her legs twisted over mine, she was beyond tempting.

The tension from the night before eased from my body as I held her, knowing that she was whole and safe in my arms. I ran my hand softly under the fabric of my own shirt that she wore, and along the skin of her back and her kill mark, endlessly thankful that nothing had happened to her. My hand slowly slipped up her spine and she didn't flinch – didn't dictate a line I might be crossing. She closed her eyes as she felt my hand splay across her sweet skin, and I traced the gentle divot of her spine with my thumb, a perfectly centered valley along the small expanse of her back. Her eyes drifted open and she smiled, leaning in to steal my breath with a kiss, but Kian's voice cut through our moment as he appeared from the kitchen with Ana.

"All right already – this portion of the house has a G-rating unless Ana decides to change that with me first," he said, winking to her. She gave him a shove, her dark hair bouncing slightly.

Eila turned a bit pink as she edged away from me and turned to Kian. "Hey! I like your new haircut!" she said, pulling herself off me entirely, ending my chance of a kiss. Some days I really hated Kian O'Reilly.

It was then that I realized he had indeed cut his hair, which had previously reached his shoulders. Gone was the straight, blonde surfer-look, replaced by a respectable, far shorter trim. He looked over to Ana, who had shimmied her way up onto the pool table. The sunlight pouring in through the windows outlined her in a golden halo, despite the bitter cold air outside. She ran her hand through her newly colored hair, "Yeah, well – new beginnings and stuff. I dyed my hair, he asked me to cut his. Blah Blah Blah."

"She tried to take my ear off," said Kian calmly.

"DID NOT," protested Ana, but then she smirked. "Well . . . I may

281

have thought about it."

Eila was already heading for the kitchen, trying to keep my sweatpants from falling off her lean hips as she asked Ana what was for breakfast. Ana hopped back off the table and trotted in behind Eila, as I dragged myself to my feet.

"Is Christian here?" I asked, pulling the tape from my chest.

"No – he left around two in the morning. With everything that's going on, he might be thinking of pushing up that vacation he had mentioned." Kian walked behind me and brutally yanked off the other piece of tape on my back and I growled. Any sign that I had been struck with two arrows last night had disappeared. Even Kian's bruised face was back to normal.

Eila reappeared with her clothes from last night balled in her hands, Ana close behind her. "We're going to get changed upstairs and then get to school," said Eila, obviously delusional.

"Get to school? You can't go to school today. We have things to discuss, and you fired up your ability last night. I want you to take it easy. You're staying here," I said, trying not to sound like an overbearing bodyguard.

She stopped and looked at me. "I have a test today and Ana has to climb to the top of that rope thing for gym. I refuse to stop my life just because, well, you know."

"Because you are being hunted? Because you almost died last night?" I demanded sharply. Ana muttered something foul about the rope climb.

Eila sighed and wandered over to where I stood, "I get you are worried, but I can't live my life in a cage. I want to LIVE, every day. I want to go to school, watch dumb movies while eating ice cream, and maybe even go to prom." She slid in closer to me, bringing her chest to mine, and my hand automatically went to her hip. "I want to be able to kiss the one who loves me so fiercely, without thinking about the rest of the world. I want to experience all that life has to offer, because for me, any day could be my last. I know you want me safe. You want me to survive. But there is a difference between just surviving and really living."

She rose up on her tiptoes, laying a scorching kiss on my lips before heading upstairs with her short-statured co-conspirator. I looked over to Kian, who had a huge, irritating grin on his face.

"Ah, yes. The halls of academia beckon thee. Come young man, and learn thee well."

I glared at him, "Oh, just shut up."

37 Eila

SCHOOL WAS PRETTY UNEVENTFUL, until just before lunch. During English and Ecology, Jesse hadn't mentioned his visit to my place, and I was grateful he didn't bring it up. I had stopped off at my locker to switch books before heading to the Café to meet up with Raef, Ana, and MJ.

I was shuffling books and folders in and out of my locker, thinking about Rillin, when a perfectly manicured hand slammed down on my locker door, nearly shaving my nose off in the process.

I followed the hand back up to the face of its majorly pissed owner, Nikki Shea. I studied her, trying to see if she was a metal maven like her ancestor and, if it was true, why she didn't just make the locker come to life and eat me?

"Where is it?" she hissed, close to my face. I didn't flinch, refusing to move back.

"Where is what?" I asked, though I knew damn well she was asking

284

about the book I borrowed and Elizabeth's necklace. Nikki's book full of gears and equations suddenly made perfect sense if she tinkered in supernatural metalwork.

"Don't screw with me, Walker. I have you on video! Do you really think my computer wouldn't have a webcam? You are some kind of stupid! You and that waste of space, Williams, should be thrown in jail until hell freezes over. Did he jump out a window when the robber came in? He is such a wuss! The dog is the only living being worth a damn in this godforsaken town. Give me back the book and necklace and I won't tell my parents about the video."

WEBCAM?? Damn it! Someone I knew who rocked a fur coat once in a while was now on my hit list. Thank god she didn't see him phase however, which meant the robber must have blocked the camera when he was trashing her room. Thank heavens for small favors, though I was still going to kill MJ. *The house is easy to break into* he said. *We won't get caught* he said. When I find him, he better run for his life, 'cause he's a dead doggie walking.

I looked at Nikki, who had a hard, angry glow about her. Her hand had curled around the combination lock on my locker and she was squeezing it so hard, I could see every tendon in her hand. She knew I had broken in, but she must have also seen the other guy trashing her room. How did she know I took the book or the necklace? Maybe she didn't.

"I didn't take a damn thing from your house!"

I didn't move and finally she snapped, screaming in my face, "GIVE THEM BACK!"

"NO!" I yelled, though stupidly admitting I had the damn things.

285

She leaned in closely and whispered in my face, "I know what you are. I know what he and his brother are as well. After you messed up in the Breakers, my parents had no choice but to tell me everything – about what you are and about Raef and Kian. They told me to leave your sorry ass alone – to stay away, and I have. But YOU are the one who invaded MY space! And I don't care anymore if my parents told me to keep my distance or that Katherine and Elizabeth were pals. I have no intention of ever helping you. Ever. Katherine was an idiot – just a slave to the needs of your damn kind. Why couldn't you just stay dead inside the Breakers?"

I was struck into silence. My mind was spinning as I watched her push away from my locker, warning me to return the book and necklace as she tossed her hair to the side, and turned to stride down the hallway and out of sight.

I stood there, shell-shocked for a moment. Nikki Shea knew.

She knew *everything*. Even worse, she knew about us.

All the blood in my body seemed to plunge to my feet. I needed to tell the others immediately about her, maybe strangling MJ as I did so. Raef was going to be livid that I broke into Nikki's house and just as freaked about the fact that Nikki knew what we were. Just fantastic.

I grabbed for the lock on my locker and went to turn the dial to my combination, but the stupid thing wouldn't move. I gave it a hard yank, but it stayed locked and unyielding, not unlike my crappy luck.

I tried to force the bugger into submission, but it wouldn't give an inch. The bell rang and soon I was the only person left in the hallway, swearing at a five-dollar lock. I needed to get to the Café before Raef worried why I wasn't there, but I needed my books for my next class.

So I did the only thing I could do – I pulled out my flame-thrower and roasted the sucker from the door.

Okay, no I didn't, but the dream was no less tempting.

Instead, I texted Raef to tell him I was okay and then I ran to the janitor for the bolt cutters. I ended up running to my next class as well. By the end of the day, I had logged a mini-marathon inside the beige walls of BHS because I lacked a simple flame-thrower. I bet I could've bashed it off with Rillin's damn billiard ball though.

As the last bell rang for the day, Raef and Ana joined me at my locker, complete with new padlock. I quietly filled them in on the whole breaking and entering with MJ.

"You broke into her house?" asked Raef, upset and a whole lot shocked.

"And you didn't take ME?" demanded Ana. Raef glared at her.

I sighed. "Look – MJ was right. Well, at the time at least. We figured the necklace would allow us to read the diary and maybe throw some light on Rillin. But with everything going on, we haven't had a chance to even use it on the diary. We wanted everyone there when we opened it."

"And you took some French book with a bunch of drawings in it . . . and all of MJ's clothes?" asked Raef, shaking his head.

"Where is MJ?" I asked.

Ana shifted her backpack, "He had to run to The Milk Way to do something for his mom. He will meet up with us later."

I glanced to Raef, who was staring down the hallway at all the students leaving for the day. "You should have told me, Eila. I feel like you never tell me anything anymore."

He was right. I had kept things from him, but I had no more secrets left. "I know – I'm sorry. I was just trying to prove that I'm not a complete, idiotic weakling. I swear to you, I have no more ridiculous secrets though."

Raef moved in close to me and wrapped his arm around my back pulling me in tight. A few classmates saw us and whispered a comment to one another. Raef never showed his affection for me so openly, and our contact made my cheeks flush. "You don't need to prove anything to me, Eila. And I could never, ever see you as a weakling," he said quietly.

"I make stupid choices sometimes," I whispered.

"They are just logically-stunted decisions," he said with a soft smile. But then I totally killed the mood by confessing the tidbit about Nikki getting a fun little history lesson from Mom and Dad. The admission instantly threw Raef and Ana into a tense silence. Between Nikki's knowledge and the attack from last night, surviving seemed like a far more daunting task than ever before, even with Thor on our team.

38 Eila

AS WE WALKED OUT TO RAEF'S TRUCK, my phone rang and I answered it, greeting MJ, whose grinning face appeared on the screen. "I have some rotten news about Nikki that I need to tell you. Can I swing by The Milk Way or will your mom blow a screw?"

"When is any news regarding Psychopath Barbie NOT rotten? And I *was* headed to the shop, but now I am hiding out across the street from *your* house."

I stopped walking for a moment and Raef and Ana halted beside me, giving me a weird look. "Why are you stalking my house?" I asked.

"Because I just saw our friendly neighborhood robber dash behind your home. I think he might be looking to get inside."

Goosebumps climbed along my neck. "MJ – are you sure?"

Raef and Ana came close to me, tilting their heads slightly so he could hear MJ's voice through the phone. "Eila, I'm telling you. I just saw him walk around the backside of your house and he . . . Oh hell's bells! He got in! I can see him inside your house now! He just walked past the downstairs window."

My body started to tremble and my voice shook when I spoke. "Don't go in, MJ. Just watch him. We will be right there." Adrenaline was soaking through my body as I hung up, making every nerve inside me shiver.

Raef had heard the conversation and yanked open the door to his truck as Ana and I climbed in at record speed. He slammed the truck into drive and peeled out of the school.

"Why is he now in my house? MJ said he's not a Mortis, but there is no way he is randomly breaking into my house." I whispered.

Raef never took his eyes off the road as he spoke, "This fool has probably been hired by someone to break in. My guess is his employer is part of the same group of Mortis who attacked us on Sandy Neck."

I clenched my hands. "He was tossing Nikki's room, looking for something. He must be after the necklace, just like Dalca. If he's at my house, then he must know I have it – must have seen me run from Nikki's house to MJ's Bronco." Doubt began to suffocate me. We were never going to get ahead. Never going to be anything less than a constant target. Our lives would be one endless carousel of trying to out-think those who wanted to kill us. Abduct us. Steal from us.

It was never going to end, and that realization crushed me from the inside out.

Ana sat forward from the back seat. "Eila, isn't Mae coming home today?" she asked, panicked. *Oh my God! Mae!*

I dialed MJ and he picked up on the first ring, "MJ, Mae is supposed to be coming home today. Her flight should have landed an hour ago.

She could be home any second." Please God, let her be safe. Please let her plane be delayed.

"I know," he replied, his voice breathless as if he was running. "She just pulled in."

"Stop her!" I pleaded. I couldn't lose Mae.

"I'll do all I can." I heard MJ's voice call out to Mae as the line went dead.

I was gasping for breath, trying to quell my panic. "MJ is going to try to keep Mae from going inside," I said in a near whisper. Raef simply nodded, hauling through the streets like a drag racer as he possessively laced his hand over mine.

Ana turned to me, her own fear thick, "Is he going to shift into Marsh?"

I looked back to Ana, knowing the lives of two people I loved might be on the line. "I don't think so. He doesn't have time."

39 Raef

ANA HAD MANAGED TO CONTACT Kian about what was going down at 408. He told her he would meet us there and he demanded that she stay locked in the car. Ana agreed on the phone, but one look at her face in the rear view mirror told me she had no intention of hiding in my truck. I stole a glance at Eila, who was so pale she looked like a ghost. Her delicate hand was gripped so tightly in my own, I was sure she had lost all sensation in her fingers.

We couldn't stay on Cape Cod any longer. We needed to get away and regroup -- to understand what was going on around us, without the constant pressure of trying to keep ahead of our enemies. I silently pleaded with fate to protect Mae and MJ.

I pulled into Eila's home behind Mae's minivan, sending the crushed seashells in her driveway flying. Eila was out the passenger door before I even came to a full stop and I yelled at her to wait, but it was pointless. I jammed the truck into park, leaving the keys dangling from the ignition as Ana jumped ship as well, racing into the house.

I managed to finally get inside where I found Eila squeezing the life out of one, shocked Mae. MJ came in from the other room, thankfully in one piece. "So, uh, can I bring anything else in for you Ms. Johnson?" he asked, a slight sweat to his brow.

Mae replied that she was fine, while Eila still hugged her tightly. I looked at MJ and he gave the smallest shake of his head. Whoever this guy was, he had somehow slipped out of the house unnoticed.

"Eila, sweetie. Are you alright?" asked Mae as Eila finally loosened her grip on the one and only mother figure she had ever known.

"Yeah. I just missed you." Eila looked over at the three of us. "We all did. How was your trip? Did you have fun?"

I had to give Eila credit – she was terrified in the car, but she was burying her fear and trying to act normal in front of Mae. I did notice a slight shake to her hands, however, and she jammed them into her coat pockets.

"It was fabulous. I think Mr. Raines will be purchasing two of the properties I saw. California is simply spectacular."

Eila looked in the direction of the front staircase that lead to her room. "I, uh, just want to, uh, change real quick, and then you can show me all your pictures. You took pictures, right?" she asked Mae.

"Tons! Wait until you see these places," said Mae, starting her coffee maker. She gave Ana a quick hug, but then her gaze settled on me. I knew what she was thinking and I cut her off before her imagination could wander too far, "Rules were obeyed, Ma'am."

It was a lie, but keeping Mae safe and secure meant a lot of lying. I saw Eila head out of the kitchen with Ana, but then she paused, looking back at me.

"I just need to borrow Raef for a second. I have some winter clothes stashed up high in my closet and he can reach them for me." Thank goodness for Eila's quick thinking. The idea of her going anywhere in the house without me made my skin crawl. While MJ believed this guy was gone, I wasn't buying it until I searched the house as well.

Mae was about to respond, when the side door flung open and Kian and Christian came through, causing her to jump at their sudden appearance. "My goodness, what a welcome home," she laughed, her hand at her heart.

Christian, smooth as ever, beamed. "I heard you have much to tell me! I want every last detail of your report and let's go over the photos and history packets."

"Now?" asked Mae, a bit shocked that work was so pressing.

"If possible, yes. I heard there might be other buyers sniffing around the Art Deco place in Monterey."

Mae pulled herself together and nodded. "Of course. Let's go into the parlor and we can take a look at what I have." She grabbed two leather messenger bags from the table, offering a quick hello to Kian as she passed him. Christian flicked his eyes upward, signaling for me to check the house. As Mae disappeared into the parlor, Kian bolted for the back staircase.

The girls followed me upstairs with MJ, a maneuver that was now easy thanks to Christian's swift move to preoccupy Mae. As we got to the top landing and the girls' rooms, Kian came down from the third floor. "Upper floor and Mae's room are clear," he whispered, his gaze settling on Ana. "And I thought I told you to stay in the car."

294

Ana waved him off as she slowly opened the door to her room. Kian moved in ahead of her and glared at her as he did so, pissed she could have flung herself in the crosshairs of some nut job. MJ tracked into the other two spare bedrooms to double check, while I pulled Eila in behind me, slowly opening her bedroom door.

She sucked in a tight breath at the sight before us. Her room looked as though it was tossed about in the roughest of seas. The mattress was angled off the bed, her clothing had been thrown everywhere, and the pictures from her bureau now lay scattered on the floor.

It was a disaster zone, violated and torn apart.

I felt Kian, MJ, and Ana step in behind me as I watched Eila slowly walk into her room, scanning the destruction. Kian told me that the house was indeed free of the intruder.

Ana squeezed past me and started slowly picking up the random bits and pieces of Eila's world that lay in tatters all over the floor. My heart tightened as I watched E slowly reach down and pick up a cracked picture of her and Mae. She carefully pulled the worn photo from the glass and managed to slide it into the edge of her large mirror, her movements slow and painfully sad.

MJ set a toppled chair back on its feet, returning it to its place under her desk. "Eila - I know the diary is at Christian's, but are the things we took from Nikki still here?" he asked.

Eila got down on the floor by her bed and squeezed her way underneath. When she wiggled back out, she had the French book and the necklace in her hands. "I had cut a hole in my box spring and stuck them inside. I thought it was the safest place," she explained as a rare, determined tear trailed down her cheek.

295

I pulled her close, drying her face with the edge of my sleeve, as I told her she did a good job. Our friends started righting the room so Mae would never know what happened, and I held Eila tightly, rubbing her back as I swore to her it was going to be okay. Swore to her that we would make it through anything together.

I hoped it wasn't a lie.

40 Eila

THE RIDE TO LOGAN AIRPORT was filled with our confusion and concerns over what had happened. It had been 48 hours since we were attacked, 24 since my room was wrecked, and 15 since Mae said "yes" to Christian's impromptu vacation.

Selling the idea of a drop-everything-and-leave getaway to Mae seemed impossible to me, but Christian had worked his magic, no doubt using his megawatt smile and vodka-smooth charm to full effect. He convinced poor Mae to fly out at the crack of dawn with him to Barbados to check on a turn of the century mansion. Even more amazing was his ability to get her to agree to let me and Ana fly down in his private jet to his home in the Caribbean. Well, we'd fly part of the way at least, though Mae didn't know that itsy-bitsy detail.

He told her that Ana and I could meet up with her at his Bahamian home, which was his own private, island named Polaris. It would have been a dream come true, if it wasn't for the fact we were basically running for our lives. Again. Another small piece of info that Mae was unaware of.

Christian had also left out four critical details when talking with Mae. Those details were called Raef, Kian, Rillin and MJ, all of whom were coming with us, along with one other dear pal: Cerberus. Christian's plan was for us to fly from Boston to West Palm, and then grab Cerberus, sailing her the rest of the way to Polaris. Kian however, said there was no way Rillin was coming with us on Cerberus, and I had to admit that having the former knight jammed in with us on Kian's sizable yacht was a little too weird for me.

We decided that Rillin could fly down to West Palm with us, but then we would part company. He would continue on by plane the rest of the way to Polaris once we hit West Palm. I got the sense that Rillin actually wanted to discuss some things with Christian, and he also mentioned readying a few training rooms for us, before we arrived.

Kian, Ana, MJ, Raef and myself would take Cerberus and follow by sea, making the run in a couple of days at most. It was a chance to defuse, to island hop, and to just be the five of us, as we once had been. Of course, Mae would eventually realize the boys were also on "vacation" when she finally arrived at Christian's home in a week or so, and no doubt flip out.

Smooth talking on Christian's part had also convinced MJ's mom and dad that he was looking to get a few opinions on a little gelato café on the main island of Great Abaco, and MJ could help him decide. MJ's parents saw it as a brilliant chance to expand their ice cream empire to the Caribbean and be backed by a billionaire. MJ, however, saw it as the ultimate vacation and a chance to advance his phasing abilities, and we all gave him suggestions. I was totally rooting for something Harry Potterish, like Buckbeak the Hippogriff. Ana wanted something powerful and regal, like a lion, while Kian suggested a fat pink pony with a rainbow on its butt.

One of those ideas wasn't taken too well.

I studied Raef as he drove us in his truck through the Ted Williams Tunnel that led to the airport. The orange lights of the tunnel splashed over him and our three friends in the cab seats behind us, as if we were at a Halloween rave. Rillin had chosen to drive to the airport in his own silver '69 Chevelle, following Raef's truck closely through the streets of Boston. When Ana had seen his car, she nearly swooned at its fine lines and beastly engine. Apparently you could take the girl out of the garage, but you couldn't take the octane out of her heart.

I knew Rillin's decision to follow us was both to ease the tension of Raef and Kian, and to also keep an eye-out for trouble. I believed him to be an asset, but Raef and Kian weren't sold on him yet. Christian, however, had managed to form a strange sort of camaraderie with Rillin. I suspected that Elizabeth in some ways bound them together, though Rillin was still entirely unaware that Christian was my biological great grandfather. The secret that I was a half-breed, both Lunaterra and Mortis, was guarded just as potently as my life.

"It looks beautiful on you," said Ana, leaning forward from her seat between Kian and MJ in the back. Neither of us had ever flown and our lack of wings told me that humans were not meant to fly. I wanted to barf. I reached down and fingered the oval diamond necklace that hung from my neck.

"It does look stunning on you, but I don't like you wearing it. It

STORMFRONT – K.R. CONWAY

makes you a bigger target," said Raef, glancing to me while he drove. I caught a glimpse of Rillin's Chevelle as he switched lanes to keep tight to our vehicle.

"I'll put it and the two journals into Christian's safe once we are at Polaris, but I am done leaving any of them out of my sight until then. I'm not risking having them lost or stolen," I said quietly, though I did lift the necklace and slide the silvery pendant under my shirt. I felt the cool metal slowly warm against my skin.

Raef and I had gotten into an argument about the necklace. He wanted it stashed in the safe inside Torrent Road, but I wanted to unlock Elizabeth's diary once and for all.

Rillin had suggested waiting until we were far from the Cape before I unlocked the diary, just in case it did something weird – like blow the roof off my house. Apparently the metal workers from his days in the palace were quite fond of booby-traps, and the design of the necklace was obviously built by a very talented Feon from Nikki's family tree. The gears in the necklace were so intricately laced and complex, that even NASA would be scratching their heads. It also made me certain that the gear Dalca had kept hidden in a safe was more than just a token from a dead Lunaterra.

After the scream-fest at my locker and Nikki's revelation, I knew that the chances of a truce with her had nose-dived through the center of the earth. My kind, at one time, had forced hers to work inside the palace. A palace where Katherine and Elizabeth had managed to form a friendship, and spark the fall of the Lunaterra Empire. In some ways that seemed so weird to me, in other ways it made perfect sense. They say that opposites attract, and Raef and I were certainly opposite. I suspected Katherine and

Elizabeth were also the most unlikely of friends, though Martians would need to land and declare that pigs could fly before Nikki would be remotely civil to me.

I also suspected Nikki had a few more talents than simply shaking her pompoms and kicking my butt during field hockey. Talents that maybe allowed her to cook my old combination lock into a block of useless metal.

And here I was thinking she had a heart of stone, not iron.

41 Eila

CHRISTIAN'S PRIVATE HANGER at the airport was as polished as Torrent Road. His three jets, all a high-gloss white with North Star's compass rose logo, sat lined up with one another. The largest, however, was lit up, and a curved staircase opened from its side to the ground, beckoning us inside. Parked under the wings of the other two planes were several luxury vehicles, including a Bentley, Mercedes, and a gorgeous looking storm-gray Corvette. Rillin drove his Chevelle to the back of the hanger, parking it alongside the Bentley.

"Holy cow. Looks like Christian got your exact same Corvette," said Ana, glancing to Kian as she walked under the wing of one of the jets, heading for the line of cars. Raef and MJ were pulling our luggage out of the truck, but Kian just stood there, staring at the beautiful sports car. Ana ran her hand along the curve of the car as Rillin got out of his Chevelle, tossing a duffle bag over his shoulder.

I nudged Kian, "Are you alive? Earth-to-Kian?"

"That's not a new car. That's MY Corvette. The one Collette took in trade for the dresses," replied Kian. I had never met his psycho-ex girlfriend, but supposedly she wanted to rip Kian apart piece-by-piece when he stopped dating her, though she was insanely talented as a clothing designer.

"This can't be your car – I mean, HER car, Key," said Ana, apparently using a nickname for Kian that I had never heard before. "I mean, how in the world would Christian even know Collette?"

Rillin headed for the jet, but tossed a glance back to Ana, "Who? Collette Lamoureux? She's Christian's tailor and dealer. She is incredibly talented."

Oh dear.

Rillin dropped his duffle bag by the stairs to the plane and leaned against the handrail. "Christian said he has her traveling with Mae, for protection. How did you guys not know this?"

Kian let loose the longest, most colorful string of curse words I had ever heard in my life. Raef came up next to him, a huge smile on his face, "Hey – look at the bright side. You get to see your car again."

"THAT'S NOT A GOOD THING!" yelled Kian, but MJ and Raef started laughing. Rillin looked at me, confused.

"Uh, Kian is familiar with Collette's many talents," I said, trying not to laugh.

Ana came up next to me and grabbed her backpack from the floor where MJ had set it. "Oh she's got talents all right – most of which are best used horizontally, I suspect," said Ana, entirely pissed that Collette was somehow back in the picture. Kian actually blushed. Ew.

"Too much information!" I demanded, just as the pilot appeared at the top of the plane's stairs. He was young, like Christian, and equally good looking. He wore a full captain's uniform, and walked down the stairs to where the six of us stood.

"Good afternoon. My name is James, and I'll be your pilot. Mr. Raines tells me you are headed for West Palm, and then I will be heading to Polaris with a Mr. Blackwood. Are those plans still in effect?"

Rillin stepped over to the pilot, "I'm Blackwood and yes, those plans stand." The pilot nodded and shook his hand, then he came over to each of us, making introductions and shaking hands. When he came to me, however, he stopped and took his hat off, tucking it under his arm and Raef's eyes narrowed. "Ms. Walker. It is a true honor to fly for you. I am humbled that Mr. Raines has assigned me to you and your team. If there is anything you ever require, all you need to do is ask."

I was entirely lost, "I'm, uh, flattered . . . I think."

James put his captain's hat back on his head. "Mr. Raines informed me of who you are Ms. Walker. I was part of the Northern Rebellion with him and Elizabeth. She was a dear friend. I was terribly sorry to hear of her death. She was a true hero."

I was too shocked to say anything, but I felt Raef place his hand around my waist and pull me behind him. "Christian said nothing about having a Mortis as a pilot."

"Mr. Raines only employs his oldest friends when it comes to specific positions within North Star, but only a few of us were comrades who fought alongside Elizabeth. Miss Walker will only be put in contact with those of us who were friends of her grandmother. Mr. Raines did specify that should you have any concerns relating to me, you are free to call him and he will assign two human pilots for your trip. If you do not wish me to be your pilot, I will stand aside without question."

We all looked at one another, deciding what to do. Finally Rillin stepped over to Ana, and Kian watched him carefully. "Can you read him?" he asked Ana.

Ana gave him an incredulous look. "What?" she asked.

"You are a Sway, correct? A reader of emotions and memories? Just tell me if our captain is being truthful."

"How did you know I could . . .? You know, freakin' never mind. And I have no clue what the whole *Sway* thing is. Secondly, I've never done that with a Mortis," she replied, fidgeting as she glanced from Rillin to James.

James just smiled, apparently fine with this option of a lie-detector test.

Rillin sighed, "Ms. Lane, I saw you read the Mortis on the beach, and he wasn't even alive. In a matter of seconds, you took his knowledge of the crossbow and knew how to use it. If you can reload the dead, under fire, this should be a piece of cake."

"What did you just say?" asked Kian. "Did you just say she *reloaded* the dead?"

Rillin gave him a wary look. "It's not a putdown if that's what you mean. Those Sway who can read the memories and emotions of a person after they have died are known as Reloaders or Bone Readers. It's an incredible talent. Not all Sway can do it."

Kian turned to Ana and they exchanged an unspoken understanding. Kian had told Ana about the reloaded phrase in Sula's notes, which now finally had meaning. Sula Lane had to have been a Sway, which was probably why she was such an asset to the FBI as a profiler.

Kian touched Ana on the shoulder. "You read a dead body? I didn't know you could do that," he said quietly.

She shrugged. "I . . . I didn't know either. But you were in trouble and – I don't know. I went on instinct I guess."

Rillin, stepped aside so Ana could see James clearly. "You can do this, Ms. Lane. Don't over think it. Just let your instinct take over. We only need to know if he is telling the truth or not. I don't need his entire life history."

Kian gave her an encouraging nod and Ana slowly reached out towards James, who bent slightly to bring his face in contact with her hand. Both of them closed their eyes and the hanger fell silent.

Kian watched her carefully and she tilted her head, as if she was listening. After a minute, she drew a deep breath, pulling her hand away from James. She swayed slightly and Kian steadied her with a strong hand.

"He's telling the truth," she whispered. "I could read him."

I gave Ana a proud thumbs up then turned to James, "Get us the heck outta here?"

"Yes, Ma'am," replied James.

42 Raef

CHRISTIAN'S PLANE, LIKE EVERYTHING ELSE he owned, was spectacular.

It was basically a flying lounge from New York's fanciest hotel, with the front half containing a bar, couches, and flat screen. The back, however, was a more private sitting area with a wide, round couch. After an hour of staring at Nikki's strange little book, which we discovered was not French but some unidentifiable language, Eila had gotten sleepy and headed into the back room.

I followed her, and as I shut the door to give us some privacy she turned to me, handing me her phone. "Can you take a picture of my kill mark?" she asked, turning her back to me and raising her shirt slightly.

I stepped over to her and slipped my fingers into the waistband of her jeans, pulling them down slightly to reveal the kill mark that sat near her tailbone. I could hear her breath stagger and the mark glowed in response to my touch. I wondered if the reaction was unique to my hand alone. I snapped the picture and handed her back the phone as she pulled her jeans back up to her hips and adjusted her top.

She looked down at the photo of her back. "It changed again. It's longer than last time," she said quietly. "It doesn't seem to match anything in Nikki's book either."

I cupped her chin in my hand and turned her face up to meet my eyes. "Nothing matches it because you are unique. One of a kind. And I think it's beautiful on you."

She gave me one of her quirked smiles that I loved. "That's just because you have marky-things too. You get all covered with your sexy Fallen marks and I think you are so darn irresistible."

I smiled and pulled her face closer to mine. "You find my marks sexy?"

"Maybe. Just a little."

I pulled her in and kissed her soft lips and she sighed as I pulled her toward the couch.

A while later, Eila had fallen asleep with her head on my lap and my hand slowly traced up and down her warm arm. I watched out the window as the sun sank below the clouds that carpeted the sky below us, throwing pastels of gold and pink against the horizon. In the air, away from the confines of the world, I actually began to relax.

I could hear Kian and Ana discussing where we would stop and dock at night. Ana was so excited, and her happiness meant the world to Kian, who had seen her suffer too much in the past. She was also very proud of reading James, and I was massively impressed that she read the Mortis on Sandy Neck. If she could read the dead, then her potential was endless.

MJ had parked himself in the co-pilot seat next to James as soon as we had taken off, and James seemed to enjoy the company. All the lives which Elizabeth had touched never failed to amaze me. Both she and Eila had a pull about them that attracted the strangest group of allies, forming friendships and alliances, where hate used to dominate. They were peace, personified.

I heard the door slide open and looked up to see Rillin, and the calm that had set over me quickly vanished. "Can I come in? I'd like to speak with you," he asked, so quietly that only I could hear him. I looked down to Eila who was still deep in sleep and then gave Rillin a quick nod.

He shut the door and sat across from me, his arms resting on his thighs, as he looked at Eila. He finally turned his attention to me. "I'm sensing that you are more than just a guard to her," he said.

"I don't see how that is your business," I replied, an edge to my voice.

Rillin leaned back casually. "It's not. I'm just trying to figure out how all of you fit together – and why you and Kian weren't killed by her power out on Sandy Neck."

I studied Rillin, debating answering him. In the end, he would find out anyway, so I simply replied, "We are immune."

He didn't believe me. "Nobody is immune. You can build a tolerance, like a vaccine to a disease, but no Mortis is immune to the Light."

"Kian and I are immune. We have been since Elizabeth's death on October 14th, 1851," I replied as Eila sighed in her sleep. She rolled over, tucking her face against my stomach and her back to Rillin. I pulled a blanket higher on her body as she fell back into a deep sleep. I didn't like him in her presence while she slept. I felt that only I should be with her in such a vulnerable state.

Rillin glanced to Eila and back to me. "You seem to know the date well."

"I should, since Kian and I were there, the night she died inside her own Core Collapse. She killed herself and Jacob Rysse, but her energy somehow made Kian and me immune," I replied.

Rillin shook his head, "You two should have been dead. Elizabeth should have killed you that night. Hell, a Core Collapse would even kill me. Who turned you two?"

"I have no clue. Neither does Kian." The question of who made the two of us into Mortis was one mystery I held no hope of solving. The fact that neither Kian nor I could remember who turned us, however, was puzzling, especially since we were both turned on the same night, as if deliberately.

Rillin was quiet for a moment, but when he finally spoke he seemed more concerned, "Is that what happened inside the Breakers? Did she cause a Core Collapse?"

I didn't want to remember that night. It was too hard, too vivid, but I answered him, so Eila wouldn't have to later. "Yes. We had been cornered by followers of Jacob Rysse who wanted to try to turn Eila into a Mortis."

"That's ridiculous. Why would they think a Lunaterra can be turned? Genetically it is impossible and trying it would trigger a Core Collapse. That's what happened, right? They tried it and her body went into self-destruct?"

I looked away from Rillin and out the window, trying to block the memory of Eila's ragdoll body in my arms. "I did it. They were going to shoot her in the head with the gun you recovered. She didn't think they would make me attempt to turn her, but they did. I'm the one who nearly killed her."

Rillin said nothing, his gaze falling to the floor.

"I think about it, all the time. She said we had no choice, but it haunts me," I said, stroking back her hair from her cheek.

"You love her."

I set my jaw tight, tension twisting inside me. "I just want her to have a life. I don't want her to be a slave to her family's history, or ours."

Rillin crossed his arm, "You want her to have a full life with whatever time she has left. I get it."

Fear started to crawl into me, and I narrowed my gaze on Rillin. "What do you mean *with the time she has left?* She is only turning eighteen, not eighty. She has her whole life ahead of her."

Rillin looked confused for a moment, but then some sort of awareness crossed his face. "You don't know, do you?"

"Know what?" I breathed, my hand stilling in Eila's hair.

"The Lunaterra had been inbreeding for years, trying to keep their line pure. Eventually health problems cropped up. They had to start having babies younger and younger because their lifespan had become so stunted."

I couldn't move. I could barely breathe. "How stunted?"

"Twenty to thirty years, max."

My world seemed to crumble around me. Eila may only have a couple years left to her life and suddenly every second seemed even more precious than before. She had so much she wanted to do, so much left to experience, but vicious Fate would rip her from me.

"Raef – listen to me. Eila is several generations out from the pure-bred nonsense. At this point, she is more human than Lunaterra, so she may very well live beyond the typical lifespan of her kind. Although, the fact that she is more human than Lunaterra, does make her ability all the more unusual."

I looked at Eila, a spark of hope forming that she would be able to live to a ripe old age. "What do you mean?"

"Well, to be able to command the Light, Lunaterra need to be of pure blood. Eila is far from that, and yet she not only called the Core, but she managed to survive it. Not even Elizabeth was able to survive the Core Collapse. That leaves me with only one possible explanation."

I was getting uneasy, as Rillin seemed a bit too smart for his own good. "Do tell."

"I believe Elizabeth did not conceive a child with Captain Walker, who was boringly human, but someone else. Someone who was neither human nor Lunaterra. To survive the Core, Eila would need a powerful ability to heal. Combine that with the scar on her chest, and Christian's protective instincts over both her and Elizabeth, and my guess is that a certain billionaire achieved the unthinkable with a mutual friend."

I didn't respond and kept my gaze level as Rillin drew a breath, "Raef, that mark on her chest is a soul scar. A Lunaterra shouldn't have one, but a Mortis who is struck by the Light and manages to survive, acquires one permanently. You didn't cause that scar – her own body did."

My jaw ticked with tension, "You're covered in soul scars, aren't you? That's why you have so many – from sparring with Lunaterra."

312

Rillin nodded and leaned forward, "Eila isn't just the last of her kind, Raef. She is the only one, ever, of her kind. I am going to be training someone who is unlike anyone I have ever trained before."

Any hope I had of keeping Eila's heritage a secret disintegrated with Rillin's accurate appraisal. "You can leave us now," I replied coldly, my eyes never leaving his. I was done talking.

"I will, but I do have one last question."

I was so not going to answer any of his damn questions anymore. He needed to go soak his head before I went and snapped it off.

"Where's your scar, Raef?"

"I don't have any scars," I replied, confused as to what he was talking about.

Rillin got to his feet, but leaned down near my face and the look in his eyes made my entire body coil on edge.

"Exactly," he replied.

43 Eila

MJ WASN'T KIDDING WHEN HE SAID Cerberus was no longer the biggest fish in the sea. Rows of luxury yachts lined the docks at the Horizon Yacht Club, though Cerberus was still impressive with her ruby hull and sleek lines.

"I think I have died and gone to heaven," moaned Ana, whose bare feet were warming nicely on the teak decking of Cerberus' bow. The towering palm trees that lined the edge of the pool at the yacht club's main building seemed downright tipsy as they swayed in the ocean breeze. We had traded icy New England for sunny West Palm, and I wasn't sure anyone could drag me back to winter, or the chaos that existed in the colder weather.

I started daydreaming about becoming a hermit, living on a tropical island where I painted seashells for the tourists, though they would mock my artistic abilities.

As soon as we had gotten to Cerberus, Ana and I had traded our heavy winter clothes for the few summer items we had managed to bring. Though she had told me I could borrow some of her clothes, which Kian had kept from last summer on board the yacht, I was hoping I would get to shop for a few things on the islands.

While Ana lounged on the front of Cerberus, soaking in the afternoon rays, I headed to find Raef. I passed by Kian and MJ, who were tending to some last minute needs of the yacht, and I gave them a quick wave.

Kian had contacted the yacht club yesterday, instructing them to ready the boat to leave. Not only had they fueled and washed Cerberus, they had also brought in gorgeous arrangements of flowers, and the scent inside the boat was sublime. The smell of jasmine and lily permeated the inside of Cerberus, forming a garden-like oasis that was to die for.

I saw Raef standing on the dock next to Cerberus, talking to a young man with several boxes on a cart. I hopped down onto the deck and walked up behind him, threading my arms around him. He glanced over his shoulder at me as he hugged my arms tighter to his chest. I loved the feel of how solid he was and how my body molded so easily into his back. Yeah, I could stay in this fantasy paradise for a LONG, LONG time.

"Wadda we doing?" I asked, glancing to the kid with the boxes.

Raef pulled me around next to him, keeping one hand snuggled around my waist. "I ordered some provisions for our trip. Sam here works for the marina and has brought us our groceries and a few other supplies." Sam gave a little wave.

"So, Sam, what is the likelihood that there is chocolate inside one of these boxes?" I asked with a wink.

"Pretty high, I'd say. The lady at the Sand Dollar Candy Shop took over one whole box," replied Sam, who looked as though he wasn't much older than I was. "So, you guys on break from college or something? Your yacht is the bomb!"

I laughed. "Thanks, Sam. We are on break," I replied, leaving out the fact that we were in high school, not college.

"I bet you guys are headed to the Outer Islands. Bimini is awesome – really cool snorkeling out there," he replied. I went to speak but Raef squeezed my side, a signal to keep me silent.

"We're heading to a bunch of places. Not sure where we are going first though," answered Raef.

Sam nodded, "Well, if you're leaving now, the only place you can get to before midnight would probably be Bimini. You really don't want to be stuck out there with all the reefs in the dead of night, know what I'm saying?"

"Good thinking, Sam," I replied. "So which box has the chocolate in it?"

Sam pointed to the box beside me, "That one has enough sugar in it to keep ya flying for days!"

I turned to Raef. "Awww. Did you order me an entire box of chocolate?" I asked him in a sing-song voice. I was just a wee bit high on the whole tropical getaway thing.

"Of course, but you may need to hide it or Ana will clean you out in a matter of hours," replied Raef, running a piece of my dark hair through his fingers. It occurred to me that Raef was far more addictive than my favorite candy. Chocolate? Who needs chocolate?

"What am I being accused of?" demanded Ana, jumping down from

Cerberus onto the dock. Kian and MJ joined us, leaning down to grab a couple of boxes.

"Chocolate thievery," I replied.

She gave a dismissive wave, "Oh please, I'm not that bad."

Kian laughed, "Liar. You are some freakish super-criminal when it comes to anything related to a cocoa bean. You're screwed, Eila."

"Hey! Don't go telling her that! Now she really will go and hide all the goodies!" said Ana, pouting. I watched her as she strode over to Kian and tried to peek in the box he was carrying. He deftly lifted it with one hand out of her reach, but she kept trying to make a grab for it, cursing him as he laughed. She lunged for the box, but missed and ended up hugging Kian.

She seemed stunned for a moment and he slowly wrapped his free arm around her back. They simply looked at each other, all amusement falling from their faces, until Kian finally cleared his throat and Ana let go. Kian turned to Sam, "We're going to need some more chocolate, kid."

Sam nodded, "Will do, sir. I'll be right back."

Ana began walking back to Cerberus to climb aboard, but I called her back. "Ana, hang on – I want to talk to everyone for a second."

Kian and MJ set down the boxes and everyone came closer to me, Raef's hand finally dropping from my hip. I instantly missed his electric touch.

"So, I need to lay down some rules," I started, but MJ moaned. I gave him a shove. "I'm serious! Listen, we have three days to just be ourselves. No need to care about our pasts or what we are. So I have one rule: that we forget the world, for just three days, and enjoy ourselves and one another. I want to be plain old normal."

"I thought you wanted to open the diary?" asked Raef.

MJ pointed an accusing finger at Raef, "HA! Rule Breaker! Right there! Time out for YOU!"

Raef rolled his lips, trying not to smile as I crossed my arms, acting pissed. Finally he tossed his hands, "Okay then. No talk of . . . well, you know. Stuff."

"And there is a *ton* of stuff," mumbled Kian, and I shot him a lethal look. I wasn't stupid. I knew that trying to ignore the fact that some jerk had broken into my house and Nikki's and was running around god-knows-where, wasn't going to be easy. I knew that Collette and Christian were traveling with Mae, which made my skin crawl, and that Nikki held our secret over us like a giant stone. I knew that the FBI hadn't given up on uncovering what happened, which was made worse by a damn gear that was somehow linked to me, and I knew someone had bought most of our files from dear, dead Agent Sollen. I knew that I needed to train with a Blacklist dealer who knew Elizabeth, and I knew that Ana's mom was murdered.

I knew that I had died in Raef's arms.

My deal seemed more like Mission Impossible, but it was worth a shot. All our problems would unfortunately still be there when we arrived in Polaris, but for the next three days, we were going to escape.

I stretched out my hand into the middle of my circle of friends, like a team getting ready to play the game of their lives. "I get it won't be easy, but we have a rare chance to just be together, as friends. And I can wait on the diary. I've waited this damn long and a few days won't hurt. The books and the necklace are in Cerberus' safe. So who is with me?" I

318

asked.

"I am!" replied MJ, placing his hand over mine. Ana agreed, adding a requirement for daily doses of candy as she placed her hand on MJ's. Kian followed suit, placing his wide hand over her tiny one.

Raef looked at me, slipping his hand under mine. "Deal," he replied softly, and then he leaned down and kissed me in front of our friends. They all burst into moans and groans, fleeing the scene.

I couldn't help but smile wide with Raef's lips pressed against my own, but the best part was, he was grinning as well. We could pull this off – we could be normal for once. Right?

44 Eila

"IF YOU EVEN THINK ABOUT PULLING me in, MJ, I will smother you in your sleep," warned Ana in an orange tankini as she inspected the crystal clear water below Cerberus' dive deck.

I stood beside her in a far more modest pair of board shorts and long-sleeved rash guard, admiring our finned visitors.

Their numbers were a bit overwhelming.

MJ had tossed some pieces of bagel into the water after breakfast, and the exotic fish of Bimini Island went nuts. There must have been a million brightly colored Nemos and Dorys swarming the silver ladder that hung from the back of the yacht. Their crazy behavior reminded me of Mae after she went on a strict protein-only diet.

Get between her and the rare donut, and you could easily lose a finger.

"Oh you are such a WIMP. They aren't barracuda, for crying out loud. Trust me – they won't bite," encouraged MJ.

Raef and Kian were leaning against the back of the dive deck, watching the two of us with great amusement as we tried to drum up the nerve to go in the water. Their bare chests and arms were downright distracting, and I had to stop myself from drooling over Raef's fabulous body.

I freakin' love the Caribbean!

We had managed to arrive at Bimini last night around 10pm, making the crossing from West Palm in only five hours, beating Sam's guesstimate.

MJ, brat that he was, proved our stellar wimpiness by leaping into the water just after breakfast. He hung onto the ladder, while all the fish formed their own aquatic flash mob around his legs and arms.

I shook my hands in the air trying to drum up the nerve to get in the water. I didn't like seafood, period, and now I was expected to swim with it?

I can do this.

They're just fish.

Little, superfast, squirmy, scaly . . . crap, I can't do this.

I glanced back at Raef, my brain short-circuiting from the sight of him. "Can't you come in too?"

He shook his head, "If Kian or I get in the water, the fish will scatter. Animals don't exactly like soul thieves, remember? Just go in, experience the moment, and when you've had enough of the fish-lips, we'll get in and clear the area."

I looked at Ana, closing off all thoughts of how many fish were in the water. She narrowed her eyes at me, reading my emotion shift from nervous to bold, "Don't. Don't you dare."

321

With one good shove, I knocked a screaming Ana into the water along with me. I surfaced with MJ laughing in front of me, the fish going bonkers around us.

I could feel their little bodies brush against me and I sucked in a squeak between my teeth. Ana popped up behind MJ and latched onto him while she screamed obscenities, though she was smiling. MJ got shoved under water for a second, but then managed to pry her hands off his neck.

"Jeezus woman, you're like an octopus. Calm down," coughed MJ, wiping the water from his face.

"Oh my gosh. Oh my gosh. Oh my gosh," chanted Ana through her panicked laughing, jumping every once in a while when a fish would bump her.

Raef leaned forward on the dive deck with a piece of bagel in his hand. "Here – take this and hold it away from your body. They will eat out of your hand."

I took the bagel from Raef and pushed away from Cerberus, holding the piece of bread above my head. Once I was away from the swarms of fish, I slowly lowered the breakfast snack into the water and was instantly rushed by every guppy in a five-mile radius.

I squealed, and their little lips felt like slimy gummy bears all over my hand. They thundered around my legs and back, bouncing over my arms and tapping my toes. I was engulfed in the living jewels of the Bahamas, splashing and jumping. My life felt amazing.

Kian hoisted Ana out of the water, and she was now walking around the yacht's deck as she gathered our picnic items and towels. Kian was easing three paddleboards from Cerberus into the water near MJ. We intended to paddle over to the nearby private beach and spend the day there.

I looked back at Raef, who was standing on the dive deck like a lifeguard in his red, low-riding swim trunks. He was smiling at me as he watched me float in the ocean.

I loved my friends. Loved everything about them. They were my world, my family, and I'd do anything for them. And Raef? Raef was so much more than my guard, more than just a boyfriend. I felt as though he was a piece of me, his heartbeat shadowing my own.

He was a gift, sent from another era, to stand with me, and face Fate with me, hand-in-hand.

I swallowed back the overwhelming emotion that was building in me – happiness and joy, flooding my mind. "Thank you, Elizabeth," I whispered to the sky, and I saw Raef cock his head slightly.

Even at a distance he had heard me, and he dove off of Cerberus, swimming towards me. The fish hightailed it from the area as he finally reached me and grabbed me by the waist.

"You okay?" he asked, his forehead wrinkled.

"Heard that, did ya?" I asked, taking a breath and he nodded, holding me a little tighter. All my bagel was gone and the warm, blue water around us was quiet except for the sound of Ana, Kian, and MJ laughing. In the arms of the boy I loved, surrounded by the world's untouched beauty, I had found my own earth-bound heaven.

I sighed, "We would have never met had it not been for Elizabeth. I blame her for a lot of things, but the reality is, she made my life complete. Unforgettable."

Raef stroked back my soaked hair, his eyes tracing over my face. He

323

finally rested one hand to my cheek, smiling. "You know you're going to need a time out, right?"

I gave him a curious glance.

"You said no 'stuff' and she-who-shall-not-be-named falls under that category. You broke your own deal, Ms. Walker."

Damn. I did. But then I remember what he said a few minutes ago. "Wait! YOU broke the rule first! You called yourself a soul thief before I mentioned E –."

Raef halted my words with a salty kiss and I entirely forgot what the heck I was talking about. He traced the curves of my lips with his own and ran one hand gently across my back, scrambling my brain. He pulled away, whispering, "Don't say her name, or I will have to stop you again."

I hung onto his shoulders while he kept the two of us afloat.

Somehow he always kept us afloat.

"I am completely down with breaking my deal if *that* is how you intend to get me into line," I replied.

My stunning lifeguard smiled at me. "You're right. There needs to be a lot of rule breaking," he said, but his smile faltered. "I mean, rule breaking that is okay with you. Not rule breaking that goes over the line, or anything. I mean, we can . . . just . . ."

His words trailed off as the Fallen marks subtly appeared on his face and cheeks, which actually had a slight blush to them. I would have teased him about getting flustered, except his face was serious.

The stupid butterflies started to circle inside me and I swallowed as I ran a hand through his wet hair. "If there is a line, we will know it when we get there. I trust us."

Raef cradled my cheek, pulling my face to his, "If?"

"If," I replied, my voice like a feather in the wind, and I kissed him as if he was all that kept me from spinning away into the universe. I could have kissed him until the ocean swept us away, but MJ's voice rang out, demanding we get a room, and I felt Raef chuckle.

45 Raef

I WATCHED EILA AND ANA walk along the water's edge of the secluded beach near where we had moored Cerberus. They hunted for shells and sea glass, comparing their treasures to one another and commenting on how they could make this or that into a piece of jewelry. The southern sun made the salt water crystals on their faces sparkle and every once in a while, Eila would turn to me, holding up a shell, thrilled at her find.

The sight of them, together as friends, was both heartwarming and painful to witness.

MJ slid one of the paddleboards along the sand, dropping it next to where I stood. He flopped onto the board, his long body nearly reaching the entire length. "I need to get me one of these. Paddle-boarding is almost better than surfing," he said, staring up at the branches of a tree near us.

Kian walked up next to me, tossing some driftwood for our fire next to MJ's board. "You can have that one."

MJ sat up, his face surprised. "Are you serious?"

Kian looked at him, "Are you going to question the gift, or shut up and accept it?"

"Nope! No questions! But seriously, thanks Kian," replied MJ, admiring the board that was now his. He ran his hand down the polished edge of his newest toy.

"MJ is easy to please, but you are a whole different story. What's on your mind, brother?" asked Kian, looking at me.

Kian had never called me brother, unless as a snide putdown, but this time was different. I looked at him, "Brother? Since when do you call me brother?"

Kian shrugged, leaning against the bark of a windblown tree that jutted out of the sand. "I saw what you did on Sandy Neck. I got nailed and you came to help me. You ordered Rillin to help me as well. I get that we haven't always gotten along, and most of the time I've wished you *would* break your neck, but you put your life on the line for me that night. So yeah, I can call you brother, but only because the term 'friend' is a bit too cozy for me."

I was shocked, but I got it.

We were part of the same team – the same group of fighters.

We would always butt heads, but at the end of the day we had each other's backs, MJ included. "Thanks . . . brother," I replied, my eyes going back to Eila, who was inspecting something in Ana's hand. The girls' heads were almost touching as they stood together, looking into Ana's palm.

"So, you going tell me what is going on, or not? Because I've never

STORMFRONT – K.R. CONWAY

seen Ana or Eila so happy, but you look like you need a Prozac or something," said Kian.

I finally turned away from the girls, and MJ and Kian watched me closely. "I talked to Rillin while we were on the plane. He knows about Eila's true background with Christian. He figured it out because of the scar on her chest. He must have seen it when he helped her on Sandy Neck," I replied, defeated.

MJ dragged his hand through the sand. "Raef, he was destined to find out eventually. Don't sweat it, although I don't understand how the scar gave her away as part Mortis."

"The scar she has he called a soul scar, and he apparently is covered with them. Mortis who manage to survive a hit from a Lunaterra throwing the Light, end up with a scar, just like Eila."

Kian thought for a moment. "So, she caused her own scar?"

I nodded, "Basically, yeah. She is her own enemy, genetically that is. On the plus side, her healing ability thanks to the Mortis side of her, probably is why she survived the Core Collapse."

"That is seriously messed up," muttered MJ.

"So Rillin knows. Is that such a big deal?" asked Kian.

I ran my hand down the bark of the tree, hoping it would dig into my skin and ease my pain. "I also found out why the Lunaterra were having children so young. I guess after years of inbreeding, they were starting to have some genetic abnormalities. One of the biggest problems was their shortened life spans," I said, turning my attention back to Eila. She and Ana had sat down on the beach and were talking while digging their feet into the sand.

"How short?" asked Kian, now also looking at Eila.

"Twenty to thirty years," I replied, my chest tightening.

MJ swore and looked at me, "Does she know, Raef?" I shook my head.

Kian rested his hand on my shoulder. "Raef, man. We will always outlive them and we can't read the future. She is part Mortis, and that could make her lifespan long and rich. We don't know which set of genetics dictates what inside her, but human lives are not endless. Someday I will say goodbye to Ana and I've learned that no matter how I try to control the future, I have to accept what exists just for today. I have to live with Ana for today, knowing that tomorrow may never come for either of us. Don't dwell on what you cannot control nor predict."

I turned to Kian and he dropped his hand. "What will you do, when Ana's life is over?" I asked.

"I'll be done as well. I've lived long enough, seen enough. When her life ends, hopefully when she's old and gray in her 90's, I'll be sure to end mine as well," replied Kian. "Raef, I know what you tried to do inside the Breakers and I get it. But what would've happened if you had succeeded? Eila would never have recovered from losing you. It would have destroyed her, piece by piece. You can't do that to her. I debated the same thing when Ana told me to leave. I couldn't fathom living without her by my side and I couldn't see her ever forgiving me. I almost did it, but then I realized if she ever found out, she would blame herself. And look at me now. I have her back and she's happy. Had I killed myself, I would have never been able to find this future with her. You would've never come back to the Cape and met Eila. Shit happens for a reason and sometimes you just have to go on faith that it will work out."

MJ looked up at Kian and I, his voice angry. "You two debated suicide? You don't do something like that – you suck it up and deal! You two are my friends as well, and we sure as hell are not engaging in some messed up suicide pact. And as much as I hate agreeing with him, Kian's right. You can't see the future, Raef, and I will guarantee you that Christian never thought he would knock-up Eila's grandma. Eila herself is proof positive that the future is an open road. Heck – this time next year, she could be holding a baby that looks a heck of a lot like you, Raef!"

"THAT future I can avoid, I assure you," I replied, though the idea of having a child with Eila filled me with a warmth that I had never even debated. My mind shifted to a vision of her tucked into my arms, with a little dark haired baby resting on her chest.

So much of what I had always believed were unshakable truths had been shattered over the past few months. My world had been turned upside down, twisted with moments of perfection and desperation. I was a Mortis, but I had a human side as well. A human side that I had completely ignored until Eila fell into my life.

Ana and Eila started calling to MJ and we all turned to see the girls standing on the two other paddleboards on the beach, smiling. They wanted MJ to show them how to use the long boards and he yelled back that he was coming. He got to his feet, looking back at Kian and I as he hoisted his board from the sand. His face was as serious as I had ever seen it. In that moment, he no longer looked like a tall, lean high schooler, but a faithful friend and comrade.

"Listen, you two idiots," he growled, "we live for today. Really live, just as Eila wants us to, because she and Ana deserve it. Hell, we all do. We get one shot at this life. One shot to make it epic. I intend to leave one heck of a legacy and not regret a single moment of whatever Fate says I have left. I sure hope you two will join me, because I suspect you have only survived for the past century and a half. It's time to start living, losers."

MJ turned and jogged down to the girls with his new board.

Kian started walking towards them as well. "Hey – you joining them?" I asked.

Kian looked at me over his shoulder, "Heck yeah. I'm not letting a dog call me a loser, are you?"

"Hell no," I replied, and headed straight for the girl I loved.

46 Eila

WE HAD SPENT THE DAY in our own corner of paradise. I could still feel the subtle tilt of the paddleboard ripple through my body with Raef pressed against me, showing me how to paddle straight as I stood on the board.

I showered in Cerberus' bathroom, my skin salty and sun-kissed and entirely warmed right through to my bones. Everything about the day had been perfect, including the evening bonfire we made. I had leaned back against Raef while we sat by the fire, his hand drawing circles around my shoulder. MJ told stories of shark encounters on the Cape and horrible customers at the Milk Way.

When the moon had climbed to her high perch in the sky, we had gathered all our things and took the paddleboards back to Cerberus. The yacht seemed to float on a halo of light, thanks to the running lamps that were hidden below the dark water line.

We could night swim in the yacht's aura, if we wanted to.

332

We could pluck mussels from the sea floor, if we wanted to.

We could run away for the rest of our lives, if we wanted to.

I sighed, happiness and freedom enveloping my soul. I switched off the water and stepped from the shower, smiling at my new tan lines in the fogged mirror. But then my eyes found the long, thin scar that ran between my breasts, and I knew some pasts could not be erased, deal or not.

I touched it, running my hand down the mark that was roughly five inches long. I had never let Raef see its full length, hiding it under carefully selected tops, including my rashguard from today. To me, it was a symbol of survival. For Raef, however, it could be a symbol of my death. So I hid it, as best I could. Ana knew how long it was, having seen me change, but not Raef.

I wrapped the towel around me and walked across the hall to Raef's room, where all my things had been placed into various drawers. He had given me his room to use for our trip and I loved the idea, though last night he chose to stay up with Kian. I had hoped that he would join me in his room, but he seemed torn on what to do. Rather than push the issue last night, I just told him I was tired and crawled into his bed alone.

Tonight, however, I wanted him with me, so we could reminisce about the day, plan for the next, and he could kiss me until I was light-headed. Ana had left me a silk nightgown, but the low neckline would have shown off my scar. Instead, I chose to wear one of Raef's shirts. I had done the same thing the first night I slept over on Cerberus.

The night before I died.

I carefully selected one of his beautiful shirts, a smoky blue, and buttoned it right up to my neck. It wasn't very comfortable that way, but it covered the scar completely. The ends of the shirt hung low on my thighs, and I grabbed Raef's robe from his closet, slinging it on. I headed for the door, intending to join my friends on the top deck if they were still up, but the door swung carefully open and Raef came in.

His hair was damp, and he wore a pair of cotton pants and nothing else. He looked so casual, so relaxed and human. "Hey. Are you heading upstairs?" he asked.

"I, uh, was going to come looking for you, but here ya are."

He reached out and tugged at the robe, "I see you are still drowning in my clothes. Didn't like what Ana left you again?"

"Well, I just, kinda like your shirts better. They smell like you," I said, my cheeks flushing. Raef stood there, unable to move for a moment. He finally managed to speak, "Do you still want to go upstairs? Everyone is asleep. Well, except Kian. He is on the top deck reading."

"He reads?" I asked and Raef tried to not smile.

"If you can believe it, he likes Tolstoy and Shakespeare," he replied, pulling me closer. "My heart is true as steel," he whispered, quoting Shakespeare, and my body began to heat.

"I've never doubted it," I replied, the butterflies literally forming a mosh pit in my belly. I stepped back from Raef and he watched me as I dropped my robe and climbed into bed, tucking my feet under me. He hesitated at the door, his hand going to the knob to leave, but I spoke up. "Come and talk to me. Tell me where we are going tomorrow and what excitement there will be."

He gave a quirked grin, "You want me to run down your itinerary, Ma'am?" I gave a silly nod, though I was trying to control the rush of nerves that were flowing through my body. He wouldn't cross a line, I knew, but I was nervous because the line didn't seem to exist for me anymore. Raef's hand moved to the lock on the door, and he turned it with a click.

The butterflies rushed the stage, and I twisted my hands together as Raef came over to the bed and climbed in next to me. He pulled me down to rest on his bare chest and began talking about our next stop. He told me about the little open air shops, the steel drum music, and the endless stretch of white sand beaches. As he spoke he ran his fingers gently up and down my spine and I listened to the deep thrum of his voice through his chest.

I traced the angles of his body as he talked, and soon the butterflies had left, replaced by an unshakable sense of safety that I felt in his arms. His hand spread flat against my back and he moved his head to look down at me.

"You feel hot, Eila," he said, his face a little concerned.

I raised myself up off his chest slightly, and tossed my hair over my shoulder in mock sexiness, "Yeah – that's what all the soul thieves say."

He smiled, "I'm not arguing with that, but I mean you physically feel like you are really warm. You sure you don't want to change into something lighter? Boxers and a tank top or something? We are in the Caribbean after all."

The amusement fell from my face as I fingered the top button of the shirt. "I, uh, I'm okay," I replied.

Raef, however, was no fool. He slowly sat up with me in his lap, drawing his hand away from my back and reaching for the top button of the shirt. I tensed.

"It's okay, Eila," he whispered. "You don't have to hide it from me."

He didn't move to unbutton the shirt, however, waiting for me to make the first move.

I slowly unbuttoned the top button, my hands shaking slightly. I knew he had gotten small glimpses of the very top of the scar when a shirt would shift, but I had no idea if he knew how long it was. I knew that he had ridden in the helicopter with me when I was airlifted from the Breakers, but I had no clue what he had seen while I was unconscious, my body drifting between life and death.

I continued unbuttoning my shirt until it left a gap that revealed the first inch of the scar, but nothing else. Raef slid his hand around my shoulder and softly touched the very top of the scar and his jaw was tight.

"It's not that bad," I whispered. "It's not even that long."

"I know how long it is," he replied quietly.

"How?" I breathed. I had been so careful never to let it show.

He brought his hand to my cheek, but his face looked pained. "I saw it in the helicopter. The paramedics were trying to cut the dress off you, but the beading was getting in the way. They needed access to your skin to shock your heart back into rhythm. I . . . I tore the dress off of you."

I swallowed, remembering what my beautiful dress looked like in the FBI's box, ripped and stained. It was destroyed because my guard, my love, had been desperate to save my life that fateful night.

I could almost hear the delicate beads rain down on the steel floor of the helicopter as Raef tried to bring me back from the dead. I tried to not think about what I looked like in that helicopter, but my imagination painted a ghastly scene.

He looked into my face and brushed my hair back from my cheek,

"I'm sorry. I should've told you sooner."

"Why didn't you?" I asked quietly, my fingers trailing over the edged lines of his chest.

"When I was in the moment, nothing registered in my head but saving you. I meant to tell you, a million times, but you were so timid with how I touched you – modest even. And then Teddy was trying to apologize, and there was that line that I was trying not to cross, and Rillin appeared, and I just . . . I couldn't tell you."

I grabbed onto his wrists and gave him a firm squeeze to get his full attention. "Raef. It's okay. You helped save my life. And yeah, I am kind of embarrassed, but on the other hand, it was you."

I looked at his beautiful face and was stunned to see a slow tear run from the corner of his eye. "I can't lose you," he breathed. "Promise me you will live, that you will beat the odds." His desperation seemed all-consuming, and my heart broke for him.

Something potent and beautiful shifted in the air around us, and I leaned my body into his and began kissing him, holding his face in my hands. He cautiously ran his hands up my thighs and under the back of my shirt, and the Fallen marks scrolled over his face, the blackest I had ever seen.

I let the world fall away from me, and all my worries and fears scattered off, like a dandelion in the summer wind. I simply felt him touch me, and how the sounds of our breathing drifted through the darkened room, softly lit by the glow of my kill mark.

I ran my fingers through his hair to his neck and shoulders, and his kisses carefully trailed from my lips to my neck and he eased the shirt off one of my shoulders, kissing the line of my collarbone. Heat bloomed

337

inside me, and I found myself undoing the remaining buttons. Raef, realizing what I was doing, broke from kissing me, and pulled me against his chest, shielding my now naked torso from the room.

The Fallen language was written beautifully over his entire body and he drew a trembling breath as he rested his forehead against mine. "Wait . . ." he breathed. "Just wait. I don't want you to do something because you've just gotten caught in the moment. I need to know that you are thinking this through. Not long ago you had a line. What happened to that line?"

I couldn't form words to answer him, so I moved to kiss him again, but I was shaking ever so slightly from the nerves jumping around in my body.

He placed a hand to my lips, stopping me. "I can feel you trembling, E. This needs to be right for you. I would wait forever for you. Be sure this is what you want. I'd never forgive myself if you regret this because you were not ready."

I looked at Raef and knew, without doubt, I would only want to experience this moment with him. Yes, I was nervous, but they were good nerves. And I had the basics down, thanks to health class, friends, and even Mae, though that conversation was about as mortifying as possible. I was ready, not because of desire or my age. I was ready because of Raef.

He had never seen me as a washashore who lived on the fringes of life. Instead he understood who I was before I even fully understood. He knew me before I knew myself. I loved him, I trusted him, and I knew he would be careful. Gentle and protective as he always was with me.

"I'm sure," I whispered as I began slowly kissing his broad shoulder

338

and his powerful arms wrapped around me, tugging at my hair. He spoke softly in my ear, telling me that we could stop at any time. That it would be okay. I nodded and my nerves climbed higher as the liquid fire in my veins flowed into my tummy.

His hands traveled to my face, and his dark eyes looked into mine, "Promise me you will tell me to stop if you need to. Promise me."

"I will," I replied quietly. But then I leaned forward to his ear, my nerves so intense that I could power a roller coaster.

"Go slow," I breathed.

His arms banded around me, holding me tightly and his voice broke as he whispered back, "I promise."

47  Raef

THE EARLY MORNING LIGHT that slipped through the porthole puddled in golden pools across Eila's bare back. She slept on her stomach next to me, one delicate hand tucked against my chest. Her wild, dark hair was splayed across the pillow and over her shoulders.

She had kicked down the sheets during the night, and now the silky cotton was wrapped low on her hips and legs, leaving the rest of her exposed. She looked like a beautiful mermaid with a white tail, sleeping next to me. A beautiful mermaid, whose back was carved with the cryptic markings of her dangerous heritage.

I laid on my side next to her, my head propped on one hand, while the other played softly with the tips of her hair. I wanted to touch her, everywhere. Feel her satin skin under my hands and how her body moved at my touch.

I wanted to make love to her again and again, forever.

But she needed sleep, so I kept my fingers to her unfeeling hair and listened to her breathe softly. Last night, it took every ounce of strength I had to rein back my demanding need and dangerous instincts. My kind did not make love. We conquered one another during sex, taking only for ourselves, our own needs, and never thinking of the other.

But last night, all I thought of was Eila.

Of how I should physically love her, of where to touch her, and how to stay connected with her mind and her emotion. Something in me shifted last night as I slowly explored her body and listened to her breathe. My own burning demands fell away and suddenly my ability to please her was all I desired. Bringing her body into a rush of sensation felt phenomenal *to me*. Better than anything I had ever experienced in my lifetime.

At times I led her and other times, I followed. We gave and took in equal, thinking of one another, rather than ourselves. We were unhurried as we discovered what made each other ignite. And at one point I changed her body forever. It was the hardest thing I had ever done, for I knew I caused her pain when she gasped and held me tighter. I had asked her if she was all right and she responded by kissing me slowly, and in that one moment, the fibers of my heart unraveled.

I felt her stir next to me and she stretched her body, her hand sliding easily up my chest to my jaw. Then her fingers traveled over my face, as if she were a blind man identifying a friend. Though her eyes were still tightly shut, a beautiful smile spread on her blushing face, and she giggled.

I was cooked. Done. Permanently filleted.

This one unlikely girl, designed as my enemy, set my heart on fire. I leaned down next to her and kissed her soft, pink lips as my hand ventured out of her hair and trailed down her back. Her giggling turned into a soft moan as I ran my fingers along the edge of the sheet near her tailbone. She opened her wide, brown eyes and smiled at me in a way that no one ever had, and I was lost.

"Good morning Mr. Paris," she said, her voice rough with sleep. I laid my head on her pillow so I was eye to eye with my mermaid and pulled her closer to me.

"Good morning Ms. Walker," I replied, bringing my hand up to her cheek and softly pushing her dark hair back from her face. "How are you feeling this morning?"

She drew a sweet, soft sigh. "Adored," she answered, letting her fingers play over my bottom lip. "Different."

I smiled at her and she rose up and pushed me onto my back, sliding her body on top of mine. I could feel the tingle of my markings begin to surface on my face, revealing my desire. Her finger ran along my brow, no doubt tracing the markings, and a wicked smile curled on her lips. "Hmmm, what are you thinking about, Mr. Paris?"

I didn't beat around the bush, and I ran my hands down her ribs, "Making love to you again. Right now." The contrast between the hard lines of my body and the softness of her curves was a graceful concoction of Yin and Yang. I inventoried every one of those gentle curves that pressed against me, burning them into my memory.

She ran her cool, small hand down from my face and along my side, though her hand stayed in neutral territory. She was far more timid about touching me than I was with her, and her uncertainty I found beautiful.

She rolled her hips slightly and I couldn't help but growl. Yes, I wanted to make love to her again, instantly. But last night she gave her

342

virginity to me, and knowing Eila, she wouldn't admit to being sore. Using all my willpower, I gently stilled her hips and rolled her off me. "As much as I want to, I think we should wait and give your body a chance to recover."

She huffed and crossed her arms over her breasts and her scar, "Fine. Half hour, then?"

"Uh, I meant a little longer," I laughed.

"Picky, picky. Forty-five minutes?"

I was about to reply when someone banged on the door. "Eila! Are you awake?" demanded Kian from the hallway. "I think Raef may have gone ashore to hunt and we need to get under way. I need to go and track down his sorry ass. EILA! Are you in there?"

Eila started to rise from the bed, but there was no way I was letting her naked body go anywhere near *that* door. I pulled her gently back down onto the mattress and covered her with the blanket. "I'll get it," I whispered, kissing her lips. She gave me a sweet smile as she tousled my hair.

I pulled on my pants and padded over to the door. Kian was now demanding that he do something insidious to me because I had apparently jumped ship without notifying the captain. "Eila! Woman! Get your fine assssss –."

I whipped open the door before he could complete his appraisal of Eila's rear and his words stalled on his lips. He looked at me, stunned into silence for a second. Then a knowing smirk rose on his face, "Jeez, Eila. You need more beauty sleep. You look like crap."

"Very funny," I replied, not amused. "I did not jump ship."

Kian narrowed his eyes, "This is not your room during this trip. Did

343

you and Little Miss Lite Brite discuss politics . . . or play doctor?"

Because she never did follow directions, Eila slid up next to me, thankfully wrapped up in the blanket. Kian's eyes widened and all sense of humor fell from his face. He glanced at me, darkness on his face, then back to Eila. "Are you hurt?"

"No. Of course not," she replied, confused.

He stepped forward to me, pointing an angry finger at my chest. "You are reckless. Reckless and stupid!" While I didn't think Kian would be high-fiving me, I was taken aback by his level of hostility. I didn't understand where it was coming from.

"I don't have to explain myself to you," I growled back, defensive. I was pissed that he thought I would ever hurt Eila. "She was never in danger with me. I was in control."

Kian stared at me for a long time before he spoke, "Control is an illusion. You, my friend, were just plain lucky." He stepped back from the doorframe, his jaw set in a hard line. Slowly he seemed to regain his composure. "We're leaving. Get upstairs and help out."

I was about to ask what was going on, but Kian just strode away towards the galley. Eila looked up at me and I wrapped my arm around her.

"What was that all about?" she asked.

"I have no idea," I replied.

KIAN DIDN'T TALK TO RAEF ALL DAY as we sailed from Bimini to our next stop in Freeport. I hung out with Ana on the aft deck lounge, creating a few necklaces with the beautiful pieces of the ocean we had taken from the island, and a bracelet for Mae. I kept trying to figure out what happened this morning with Kian, but I couldn't wrap my head around his reaction.

The way Raef looked at me and brushed against me, meant so much more now. A hidden understanding and deeper connection than I ever thought possible existed between us. If his eyes didn't remind me of a few hours ago, the gentle ache throughout my body did. It was a good ache, but he was right – I need a chance to recover.

I had been so caught up in the moment last night that I completely forgot about protection, but Raef didn't. Apparently certain things come standard in the Sail Away kits from the yacht club, including shampoo, razors, and well, safe sex items. My mind kept wandering back to last night, replaying bits and pieces of what we had done together, making me about as useful as a zombie.

"Quit zoning," demanded Ana, bouncing a shell off my shoulder.

I blushed. "Sorry," I replied, focusing back on a necklace I was making for Raef. It was a simple design of braided cotton with a small shark tooth hanging from the middle. It was an awesome find from yesterday, and I knew it belonged on my soul shark's neck.

I pictured him wearing it, and not much else.

Crud – I was going to get NOTHING done.

Ana was faster than I was at making the pieces into necklaces, probably because she wasn't daydreaming about Kian. She had made MJ one already with a piece of twisted beach metal she had found, and he had been wearing it all day. If either of them could tell that I was different, they hadn't said a word.

In some ways, I really wanted girl-time with Ana, to discuss what I had done last night. At the same time however, she believed a soul thief would never make love to a human. A few months ago, I would have been in complete agreement, but after all that had happened to us, combined with how gentle Raef was last night, I knew we had been wrong. If she found out about Raef and me, would it make her question Kian's excuse for not sleeping with her the summer they met?

I glanced at her as she finished off a sea glass necklace for herself. "I can make one for Kian. All the boys should have one," I offered, trying to deviously test her mind as it related to the boy she once loved.

She picked up another piece of sea glass, this one slightly larger but the same color as the one that now hung on her neck. "I'll make him one," she replied, and I glanced up to the flybridge above us. MJ and

346

Kian were hanging out by the ship's wheel, but Kian glanced down at the two of us, no doubt having heard his name with his superior hearing. Why was he so angry this morning?

Kian's eyes connected with mine and he said something to MJ, who nodded in response, taking the wheel. Then Kian made his way down from the flybridge and into the parlor, not saying a word to Ana or me.

Screw the silent treatment. I was ticked that he had acted like a moron this morning and we needed to have a chat.

I got up, making an excuse to get us some drinks, and followed Kian into the parlor. He was by the bar and I came up behind him, giving him a small shove. "What the heck was that all about this morning?" I asked, truly aggravated. I was grateful Raef was in the shower, so I could talk to Kian alone.

He didn't turn to me. "Nothing," he said, rummaging around in the cabinet for something.

"You were mad. Why would you have been mad? That makes no sense to me!"

Kian yanked a pair of binoculars from the cabinet and spun on me. "He could have killed you, all right? What the hell is the point of protecting you if he goes and does something so stupid as that."

"So sleeping with me is stupid?" I asked, now offended.

"Yes! No – I mean. Damn it, Eila – it's dangerous for our kind to sleep with a human. It's always a gamble and a lot of the time the human doesn't fair so well, trust me." Kian was getting angry, but it didn't seem to be aimed at me. The way he spoke made it seem like . . . oh, hell.

"You've slept with a human, haven't you? But Ana said that you wouldn't with her. If it wasn't Ana, then who --?"

347

"My fiancée."

My eyes went wide. "You were getting married? When?"

Kian's shoulders dropped as he let out a sigh and placed the binoculars on the counter. "When I was still human, I was engaged to a girl named Mary. But a few days after I was turned, I went to her house. She let me in, because she loved me and I was the man she was going to marry, have children with, and grow old with. God help me, she trusted me to take care of her, but I wasn't the same man. I no longer loved her, just lusted for her, and I took what I wanted that night."

I had stopped breathing and Kian shook his head, his eyes to the floor and his hand curling into a fist. "Her family found her body in her bedroom the next day."

Good god. I forced away the chill that climbed over my skin as I stepped forward, covering Kian's clenched hand with my own. "Kian, it's not the same. You're not the same," I whispered, so terribly sorry for him and poor Mary.

He pulled his hand away from mine and picked up the binoculars. As he pushed past me, he looked down into my eyes, his face hard. "That's your biggest mistake, Eila. Raef and I are still Mortis. We survive on the lives of others. We are killers and there is no changing that."

He started leaving the room, but I called after him. "Kian – you didn't mean to do it," I pleaded, trying to ease his grief.

He stopped just before the glass doors and he looked at Ana who was holding up her necklace, examining her handiwork. Finally he turned back at me. "Yeah, I did, Sparky," he replied sadly and walked outside.

I watched as Ana said something to him and held up the necklace she had made him. He leaned down to her and she tied it around his neck,

348

turning it so it sat perfectly against his flawless skin. She gave a proud smile and he returned it easily, saying something that earned him a jab in his side from Ana, who laughed.

He loved her fiercely, and despite her reluctance to let him in, Ana loved him as well. Ana wasn't Mary – not even close. Kian had to know that, somewhere deep down and past all the fear. He glanced back at me as he headed for the flydeck and his smile faded.

As he disappeared above me, I realized Kian failed to understand two critical facts: Ana wasn't afraid of him . . . and I, too, was a killer.

49 Raef

I WATCHED, ENTRANCED, as Eila swayed in perfect unison to Bob Marley's song in the middle of the dance floor. MJ had stolen her from my side, and he turned her about in the open air restaurant, among the other yacht owners and vacationers. The pale gray of her sundress dipped into a midnight black, and it slid along her legs as she danced barefoot, a single pink seashell hanging from her neck. I reached up and touched the shark tooth she had tied to my neck when we were getting ready to leave the yacht for an evening of music and dancing.

I remembered how I pressed her against the wall in my room, kissing her deeply as she tried to concentrate on knotting the gift at my neck. I smiled, recalling how her body vibrated as she giggled when I turned my lips to a spot on her neck that was ticklish.

Not far from them, Kian danced with Ana, her lips silently singing the song as she twirled. He smiled as he held her and pulled an exotic flower from her hair, sticking it in his own and she laughed.

"Let me guess. Something to do with the Internet or cell phones, right?" asked a low voice next to me. I turned and saw an elderly man leaning against the bar not far from me.

"I'm sorry?" I asked, my brow falling.

He gestured with his drink to my companions on the dance floor. "I saw you kids pull in on a sweet cruiser. I'm figuring if you guys are that young to be sailing here alone on such a beauty, there is wealth involved. It has gotta be the tech industry."

Dealing with nosy, rich men was never my strong suit. "Something along those lines," I replied, hoping to end the conversation. The reality was, our wealth came from years of hard work, careful buying of stocks, and purchasing land wisely. Kian, however, did invest early in a certain tech company whose logo was a tree-borne fruit, while I favored a start-up known as Google.

"You guys going to be part of the fishing tourney tomorrow?" asked Mr. Nosey.

"We're just passing through," I replied, catching sight of Eila and MJ headed my way.

Eila slid up next to me and I wrapped my arm around her. The heat from her body emanated through the sheer fabric of her dress and sweat had dampened her dark hair around her face. "Did you see me?" she asked, beaming and breathless as she kissed my cheek.

"I did – you guys looked great," I replied, handing her a glass of ice tea.

"Damn straight we looked great!" said MJ, planting a kiss on Eila's forehead. Jealousy stirred subtly inside me, but I knew MJ's affection for Eila was that of a big brother and nothing more.

Eila turned to my chatty barmate. She extended her hand, "Hi. I'm Eila."

Mr. Nosey took her hand and kissed her knuckles. I wanted to snap his lips off. "Pleasure to meet you. I'm Mr. Garrett, owner of this delightful establishment."

"You own this place?" I asked, surprised. This guy dressed like a tourist, complete with garish tropical shirt and cargo shorts.

"That I do. It does me a world of good to see you young folks enjoying the evening here. It can be pretty hard to compete with the fancier places up the coast, but I am glad that I still somehow appeal to kids like you."

With its thatched roof, basic wooden tables, and sand-dusted floors, The Pink Crab wasn't anywhere near five-stars, but it was 100% true to the essence of the island. It also was fairly far off the beaten path, making our likelihood of running into another Mortis pretty remote.

"I think it is just fabulous, Mr. Garrett. Even better is the whole 'footwear optional' thing," said Eila with a laugh, holding up her heeled sandals. She had rid herself of her shoes within five minutes of entering the small bar.

Mr. Garrett smiled at her and pulled a hibiscus bloom from a large bush that was leaning into the bar. He held the flower out to Eila, "For such a beautiful compliment, and an even more beautiful lady." Eila took the flower, tucking the red bloom into her wild ponytail.

"Thank you," she said, but I felt her hand rub my side. She knew I was uneasy with anyone coming near her, my guard instincts relentless.

Mr. Garrett eased his wide frame from the barstool. "Well, you kids enjoy yourselves. And I wish you safe sailing, wherever you are headed.

I've got to see to some business, but have a great evening." Eila gave him a wave as he left.

Kian and Ana were still on the dance floor and I looked down to Eila. "So, do you have enough spark left to dance with me?" I asked, tucking one wayward strand of hair behind her ear.

"Hmmm . . . that wasn't much of a request," she replied, fingering my necklace. I pulled her in tighter to me, bringing my lips dangerously close to hers. "Dance with me," I whispered. "Dance with me now, or I may lose my mind and drag you back to the yacht instantly."

"Is that a promise or a threat?" asked E, hooking her finger into my necklace and pulling me so close that our noses touched.

"Both," I whispered back to her.

"Good answer," she replied.

 50 Raer

"ARE YOU SURE?" I asked Kian as I stared down at the photo of Mr. Garrett on his laptop.

"Look man, this is Rillin's area of expertise. If he says this dude is on the Blacklist for drugs, then he is. I don't know about you, but I could use the hit," said Kian, pulling on a blue, long sleeve shirt.

I had laid with Eila in my arms until she drifted into a deep sleep and then I slipped away from her warm body, not wanting her to know I was about to go kill a man. Ana, however, was aware of what we were up to. She seemed to accept that we were hunting humans, though I was sure the fact that they were criminals eased her mind.

She stood in Kian's robe, her arms crossed over her chest. "I can't believe you two are going hunting now. Can't you just wait until we dock at Polaris in two days?" she asked, playing with a throw pillow from the parlor couch. The yachts nearby had all fallen dark and we had shut down most of our lights as well, so as not to attract attention.

354

Kian pulled a switchblade from his black bag and tucked it into his belt as I removed my necklace, placing it on the bar. Rillin had insisted we start arming ourselves, since the other Mortis had attacked with weapons, but I still felt uncomfortable with the idea. Kian, however, took to the plan with ease.

We were both dressed in dark colors, though our ability to pull the shadows over our body was the ultimate camouflage.

My partner in crime looked to Ana, "We need to go tonight, Pix. Rillin says Polaris has no large game to hunt, except for those with dorsal fins and loads of teeth, and quite frankly, hunting sharks is not fun."

"This hit will last us for a solid week, Ana," I said as MJ came in from the aft deck. He pulled the glass door shut behind him as he entered the parlor.

"So, how long you think?" asked MJ. He was going to be with the girls while we hunted, but we didn't foresee any issues. We were docked at a marina that was fairly remote.

"The Pink Crab is about 10 minutes away by foot. If we locate Garrett and his nephew right away, we can be back in under an hour," I said, tying my black boots as I calculated how long it would take to efficiently murder two men.

"What do you want me to tell Eila if she wakes up?" asked MJ.

"Just tell her the truth – Kian and I went hunting."

"Want me to tell her you went to kill an older man who gave her a pretty flower? Want me to tell her *that part*, Raef?" asked Ana.

I stopped what I was doing and took a deep breath. "Look, I get you don't approve of me sneaking out like this, but she didn't take it too well when she learned we were hunting people. We've had a great trip so far

355

and I don't want to ruin it for her. As for Garrett, Rillin says he is selling a lot more than drinks and fried conch out of his establishment."

"What exactly landed him and his nephew on Rillin's list?" asked MJ.

"Drug smuggling, though his nephew dabbles in the skin trade and high-end theft as well," said Kian. "I've got no qualms removing these two scumbags from the land of the living."

The skin trade, selling people for profit, made me ill. It was almost always young people, usually females, who were bought and sold like animals. Kidnapped from their families, never to be heard from again.

"I want the nephew," I said, thinking of Eila safely tucked into my bed.

"Fine by me," said Kian, starting for the door. He looked to MJ. "You keep an eye out for anything weird, got me? Where's the gun?" MJ pushed up his t-shirt and revealed Dalca's handgun tucked into his waistband.

"You sure you don't want to phase, MJ?" I asked, still not thrilled we were leaving the girls alone with him.

MJ shook his head, "Not this time. I wouldn't get around too good as Marsh in the layout of the yacht. Two feet are better than four inside here. Don't worry, Raef. I got your girl. She's safe with me – Ana too."

Ana snorted, "I can kick your butt when you are in human form, MJ, and you know it."

Kian walked over to Ana and pulled the sea glass necklace over his head. "I can completely see that happening, Pix, but try not to damage MJ while I'm gone." He placed his necklace over Ana's head and it rested against her own piece of the ocean, "Keep my present safe, will ya?" Ana, unable to reply, simply gave a small nod.

We left, heading down the dock silently, and I glanced back at Cerberus. MJ stood on the flydeck watching the night.

I had one hour to kill a man.

One hour to be a monster.

51 Eila

SOMETHING JOLTED ME AWAKE and I blinked into the darkness, listening for a moment.

I rolled over to tell Raef I thought I heard something weird, but was surprised to see he was not in bed. But then I heard the doorknob turn and I smiled, knowing it had to be Raef, returning to bed. It took less than two seconds to realize the tall, slim shape entering the room was not the boy I loved.

The figure lunged at me just as I went to scream, and he pinned me to the bed pressing something over my mouth.

"Shut up," he hissed, yanking me onto my stomach.

Terror was flying through my body as I heard tape ripping and felt my wrists being bound behind my back. I screamed through the tape across my lips, knowing that no one could hear me.

Where was Raef? What had this monster done to my friends?

The man was working at the tape, when the training Raef had put me through kicked in and my fear was replaced by a need to fight – and beat the tar out of this man.

I arched backward quickly, knocking the back of my head into the man's forehead as hard as I could. He hissed out a swear, and his weight eased from my back just enough for me to flip over. I brought my knees up hard and fast, and nailed the bastard right between the legs and he let out a holler, falling over sideways.

I somersaulted off the bed, hitting the floor hard on my knees as my attacker staggered to his feet, still partially doubled over. I scrambled to get my bound hands under my butt and past my legs, so that I at least had the use of my clasped fists.

Just as he stood, I launched myself at him, landing on his back and slinging my arms over his head in the most messed-up piggyback ride ever. I pulled with all my might on his throat and he began gagging, his own hands clamping down on my wrists, trying to release the pressure.

He suddenly pushed backward, hard and fast, slamming me up against the edge of the porthole, and my shoulder screamed in pain as I groaned. He pulled forward to bash me against the wall again just as Ana came flying into the room with a fire extinguisher in her hands, screaming like a banshee dressed in a black t-shirt and hot pink boyshorts.

She jumped onto the bed just as she swung the canister, connecting the heavy red bottle with the jaw of my attacker. The resounding clang spun the man's head to the side and he staggered, falling to the floor. With my hands still trapped around his neck, I crashed down with him, slamming my already painful shoulder into the ground, nearly knocking the wind out of me.

STORMFRONT – K.R. CONWAY

Ana scrambled off the bed to me, her make-shift bat still in her hands. "What the HELL?" she yelled, shaking.

I was still catching my breath and my body twitched from the adrenaline in my veins. I managed to pry my hands from around the unconscious man's head and peel the silver tape from my lips, hissing as I did so.

"Thanks" I breathed.

"THANKS? THANKS! Screw thanks - who is this dirtbag?" she demanded, kicking the man hard in the side. He moaned. "Welcome aboard Cerberus, scumbag!"

"I have no clue what just happened," I replied, trying to twist my wrists out of the makeshift cuffs, but the tape only clung to my skin more tightly. "Where's Raef and Kian? Where's MJ?" I asked.

Damn, my shoulder hurt.

Ana notched the tape and managed to tear it free from my hands. "Key and Raef went Blacklist hunting about a half-hour ago, but MJ . . . MJ should be here," she replied. I scrambled to my feet and headed for the door, yelling for MJ.

Ana dropped to her knees next to my attacker and yanked him over to his back. Blood poured from his broken nose, and a massive bump was forming on his head from Ana's killer aim. She placed her hands on his forehead and closed her eyes.

I nearly asked what she was doing, desperate to search for MJ, when I realized she was trying to read him. Her eyes flew open and she looked at me, terrified as I heard the engine roar to life. "Pirates," she breathed.

My eyes grew huge, "OF THE CARIBBEAN?"

52 Raef

"WE ARE LOOKING FOR MR. GARRETT," I said to the over-sized bouncer at The Pink Crab's backdoor. What was the worth of this guy? That he could squash someone with his two-tons of fat? Humans could be so stupid when it came to security. We had already been frisked by the first idiot and passed the "no-weapons" test with flying colors. Little did they know we didn't need weapons, though Kian was hiding a nice blade.

"Mr. Garrett is busy," said the lump of meat.

"Mr. Garrett knows us." My stomach turned as I recalled him kissing Eila's hand and giving her the flower.

"Trust me – we are the type of clients that Mr. Garrett enjoys doing business with," said Kian, channeling his rich-kid-drug-addict slant. The bouncer eyed us a moment longer and then brought a walkie talkie to his mouth, relaying our request.

The lock behind the bouncer made a double clicking sound and he pulled the large wooden door open for us. "First door on the right, boys," he said with a sneer.

We stepped inside and I quickly realized that the door on the right was the only door in the hallway. I didn't point this out for the bouncer, since I was sure he couldn't count anyway. I opened the door, taking a fast inventory of the room, Kian close behind me. Mr. Garrett sat behind an ornate, cherry desk with a box of Cuban cigars. The smell of the rolled tobacco helped to mask the smell of weed.

"Good to see you boys again," said Garrett, not attempting to stand or shake our hands. He didn't have any guards in his room with him, which meant that he didn't see us as a threat.

"Good to see you, too," said Kian. "We heard you have some outstanding goods for those with discerning tastes, and we were hoping to possibly purchase some of your fine . . . cigars."

Mr. Garrett's mouth twisted into a small grin, believing we were looking to score some cocaine, not cigars – or his life. "Hmmm – you know, boys, I'd like to do business with you. I would. But I am thinking that you might be in over your head, purchasing such high end products from me. Boys like you need to be careful in places like this."

"I think we can handle ourselves, but thanks for the concern," said Kian. "Name your price."

Garrett gave a small chuckle, "So cocky for so young. I suspect Mum and Dad may not be too pleased to learn their sons are throwing away their trust fund money on cigars and pretty young things. Speaking of which, where are those lovely girls anyway?"

I stepped forward, "The girls are none of your concern. Leave them out of this." Unease was beginning to flow through me and I could tell Kian was feeling it as well. Something was not right. Something about the way Garrett was dealing with us. Playing with us.

"You know, beautiful things go missing, even in a paradise such as this. Perhaps you should be more concerned about what you have, or rather did have, than what you want."

All right, I was done. I strode over to the desk and Garrett got to his feet, pulling a gun from under the desk and aiming it at my chest. "Your first mistake was thinking I would deal with snot-nosed brats like you two," said Garrett.

I leaned more forward and the gun pressed against my chest. Yeah, a bullet would hurt, but it certainly wouldn't kill me. "Actually, Mr. Garrett, your first mistake was letting us inside," I growled.

"You're mighty confident, considering I could put a hole through your chest. I bet you wouldn't be so cocky if you understood the true price of doing business with me."

Tired of his rambling, I lunged, easily disarming Garrett and pinning him by the neck to the wall. He looked momentarily shocked, but irritatingly sure of himself. Kian sauntered over beside me. "I don't know, Mr. Garrett. I think we are getting quite a bargain."

Garrett's face twisted into a perverse sort of grin that chilled me to the bone. "I don't think so. You see, my nephew just left to collect a very nice yacht as payment for your evening in my bar. The girls will just be a bonus."

I glared at Garrett. "What have you done?" I snarled through my teeth as Kian yanked his phone from his pocket and dialed MJ. It rang and rang, then went to voicemail.

Garrett offered a perverse smile. "There are pirates in the Caribbean, and my nephew's crew is hunting some very beautiful treasures tonight."

Kian roared at Garrett, "Call him off!"

"Or what, you little shit?" snapped Garrett. "You're playing a game that you have no business being in. You don't have it in you to kill someone like me. You're just a kid!"

Rage consumed me, and all of Rillin's rules about making a hit look like an accident disintegrated as I grabbed Garrett by the neck . . . and removed his head from his body.

53 Eila

CERBERUS LURCHED ONCE AGAIN to starboard and Ana and I tumbled sideways in the hall, banging against the bathroom door.

"We need to get upstairs," I yelled over the roaring engine as I tried to get to my feet and steady myself. The floor of the yacht slanted towards the stern, and dishware slid from the counters, crashing to the floor and scattering down the hall towards our feet. Ana scrambled back as a chef's knife pinwheeled its way past her toes and struck the back wall.

"Go find MJ! I'm going to try and shut her down from the engine room!" yelled Ana. The floor tilted the other way and Ana grabbed hold of the bathroom doorknob, keeping herself from sliding across the hall. The knife came back towards me and I slammed my hand down on the handle, grabbing the sharp kitchen tool from the tile floor.

Now I had a weapon and I was dying to use it on whoever was trying to steal our yacht. They might be pirates, but steering wasn't their strong suit. If they had done something to MJ, I would beat the piss out of their booty.

"Be careful!" I yelled to Ana as more stuff smashed to the floor. She nodded and pushed off the wall, heading for the back of the shuddering yacht and the engine room door.

I bolted for the stairs and managed to get up five steps before the yacht lurched hard and I lost my footing, tossing the knife. I hung on to the handrail, but my body slammed against the wall and my injured shoulder gave a sickening pop as I cried out in pain. I forced myself to my feet, knowing I needed to get to the bridge and stop whoever was controlling the boat before Cerberus fell on her side completely. Before she sank, taking us with her.

The boat leveled, and I pinned my injured arm to my side and dashed to the top of the stairs and the parlor. Standing by the inner controls was MJ, pale with blood streaming down from a slice in his forehead, hanging with all his might onto the steering wheel.

"MJ!" I yelled just as he pulled hard on the wheel and Cerberus leaned sharply to port. I stumbled forward and MJ grabbed me just as I was about to slam into him, and my hand slapped into the stereo system. A rock song began blaring from the speakers at a deafening level

"Eila! Are you okay? Where's Ana?" he yelled over Steven Tyler's screaming voice.

"She is trying to shut down the engine. What the hell is going on?" I yelled back, but the wheel came to life and yanked the other way out of MJ's grip and we fell to the floor together. I screamed as my shoulder took the brunt of the fall, but my pain powered my anger and shut down any trace of fear.

366

I wanted justice. I wanted control. The Lunaterra side of my DNA cranked my inner fatal female to life, and I was ready to unleash the crazy on Black Beard's idiots.

MJ tried to pull himself up to the controls, locking his hand over the throttle, and Cerberus let out a screaming growl as the engine battled against itself. "Some guys knocked me out! When I came to, we were underway, headed god knows where. I've been fighting with whoever is on the flydeck for control of the boat. I'm trying to keep us close to the island," said MJ. "If I keep fighting the guy above us, we are going to tear Cerberus apart!"

"They're pirates!" I yelled. MJ glared at me as if I'd lost my mind.

I managed a glance out the parlor windows and realized we were pretty far from shore. "Raef and Kian are still on the island?" I yelled, pissed that we had left them behind. MJ nodded, his jaw hard. "Where's Dalca's gun, MJ?"

"I don't know. I got hit in the head and when I came to, I no longer had it," he yelled, trying to be heard over the music. From my vantage point on the floor I could see the SOS kit secured under the cabinet. I yanked the red box from its spot and pulled out the flare gun, loading it.

"Eila – the flares aren't going to help us!" yelled MJ over the music.

"Got a better plan?" I argued, scrambling to my feet. "Hold her steady if you can!"

"Where are you going?" demanded MJ, hanging onto the wheel with all his might while the boat lobbed one way, then the other. I staggered back and forth, trying to maintain my balance.

"To get our boat back, captain!" I yelled. Dang – I was actually high on the rush of what was happening. Any clear, shy thoughts I should have been entertaining had disappeared to another dimension.

I was entirely fearless.

MJ swore, "Be careful, Eila!"

I ran in spurts through the parlor, balancing on a couch or chair until I reached the glass doors. I pulled them open and managed to make my way to the ladder that led to the flybridge, my heart pounding. With only one working arm, I held the flare gun in my teeth and started climbing the ladder, hanging on for dear life when Cerberus would jolt. She was tearing up the ocean, tossing up waves and foam that sprayed the side of her ruby hull and slicked the ladder rungs.

Finally reaching the top, I peeked over and saw a man dressed in black, dreadlocks hanging down his back. I leveled the flare gun at his back and fired, but the shot went wide and struck the instrument panel.

The man spun, his green eyes immediately finding me. Crap.

He pulled a gun from his waistband and aimed for me just as Cerberus lurched hard to starboard once again. The man staggered, losing his balance, and his arms flailed. I ducked as he hit the deck hard, his gun firing.

Cerberus' engine moaned one last time and then fell silent.

I hugged the ladder with my one good arm, my eyes still closed, breathing hard as the remaining waves slapped against the hull and Aerosmith abruptly silenced. Then I heard MJ, screaming my name. I snapped out of my frozen mind and realized I wasn't dead. I called back to him that I was alright and I peeked my head up and over the ladder.

On the floor lay our pirate, blood pooling under his body, the gun nowhere to be seen. I suddenly felt hands on my hips and I jumped a mile. "It's just me. You okay?" asked MJ, steadying my body. "I heard a gun shot."

I nodded, "I think . . . I think he may have shot himself. By accident. He looks pretty dead." Reality was slowly filtering back into my mind and I began to realize just how nuts I had been. I had thought I was invincible. I was ready to fight to the death. I began to shiver as the adrenaline ebbed from my system.

I heard Ana, cursing from below us, and I cautiously climbed down the ladder, now valuing my life, while MJ continued up to check on the unmoving man. Ana was slowly lowering herself to sit on the rear lounge, streaks of grease covering her cheeks and arms. "You shut down the engine?" I asked.

She nodded. "Bloody pirates. I shut it down, but I have a feeling it is going to take me a lot longer to get her back up and running. So much for a vacation from being a mechanic."

"Is the guy from Raef's room still unconscious?" I asked.

"Yup – and I used the entire roll of duct tape to wrap him up like a burrito! I'd like to see him get his butt out of that!" I smiled, leaning over and high fiving her with my good hand.

MJ was already on the phone as he climbed down from the flydeck, Dalca's gun tucked back in the waistband of his pants. I could hear Raef on the other end asking what had happened, if we were all right, and where exactly we were. After giving him coordinates, MJ handed his phone to me and went to Raef's room to check on our sole surviving hijacker.

"Are you okay?" asked Raef, the concern in his voice carrying easily through cell.

"Yes. Sort of." Ana looked at me a little funny, wagging one hand to let me know that Cerberus might not be 100% anymore. "Well . . . Cerberus might not be *perfectly* good."

"I don't care about the yacht, Eila. Cerberus is replaceable, but you are not," he replied. "Kian and I are headed your way with a speedboat we borrowed. Well, stole. We should be there in just a minute or two. We can see you guys about a mile away."

I looked out into the dark night and could see nothing but the blackened ocean. "I'll take your word for it," I replied, but I sobered when I remembered why the boys had not been on the yacht in the first place. "Raef? Did you kill someone tonight?" I asked.

The line was quiet for a moment and I heard Raef take a breath, "I did, and Kian or I will dispose of the man who is still alive on the boat."

I swallowed, holding my arm tighter to my body as unshed tears stung my eyes. I couldn't reply, knowing that the man on the deck below my feet was sentenced to die. It was one thing to be attacked by someone, and have the police haul him off, but knowing that Raef and Kian would act as judge, jury, and executioner was difficult to deal with. "Raef – don't kill him."

"Eila, he can't be left alive. For what he has done and what he might know about us, he can't be allowed to live. There is no other way."

I looked at Ana. "There is always another way, Raef."

54 Raef

I COULD FEEL THE COLD SWEAT leeching through the back of Eila's tank top as she sat on my lap, her chest pressed to mine. She was breathing hard and shaking from Kian's third attempt to lift her dislocated shoulder.

She rested her head against my shoulder and I could feel her warm breath curling over my neck.

"I'm sorry," she whispered.

The fact that she was in such pain and I was trying to keep her from moving while Kian hurt her further, was killing me.

She had separated her shoulder when she fell on the stairs, and every time Kian moved her arm, her entire body tensed, making it impossible to push her shoulder back into place.

"It's okay. Let's just, take a break, okay? Let's just sit here for a second," I said to her, kissing her damp forehead. If we tortured her much longer, her body would start to head into shock.

Ana and MJ came up from the lower deck, both covered in grime. "How you doing, Eila?" asked Ana, sitting herself on a chair next to mine. Ana had been slaving with MJ, trying to get Cerberus back up and running. We needed to get the hell out of here.

"Not great," replied E, softly, not moving.

Kian draped a throw blanket over Eila's back, trying to warm her up and Ana looked at him. "Don't we have anything stronger than just regular pain meds onboard?"

Kian shook his head.

Ana sat down next to me, watching Eila. She scooted closer, "Eila? I might be able to block your pain. Can I try?"

"Ana – what are you talking about?" I asked, glancing over Eila's head as Ana got to her feet.

She shrugged, "It's worth a shot. Technically pain is only what the mind translates. If I can block her mind from translating what she feels into pain, I might be able to help her."

"Do it," whispered Eila.

Ana glanced to Kian and he gave a nod. "You tell me when, Pix," he said, coming to stand next to Eila's side again.

Ana placed her hands to Eila's forehead and back, closing her eyes. Eila's tense body slowly began to soften in my arms and her breathing began to even. Ana's face was one of complete concentration, her eyes pinched shut, her jaw hard.

After a minute she gave the smallest nod and Kian carefully touched Eila's hanging arm. Eila took a shorter breath and Kian paused, looking at me. Ana hadn't moved, her face tense and focused. I felt Eila relax again and I mouthed the word *go* to him.

372

Kian lifted Eila's arm, rotated it forward, then up and back to her side. I could feel the slight pop travel through her shoulder blade as Kian successfully reset her arm. He didn't let go however, holding her arm against her side.

I stroked Eila's dark hair, "You okay?"

"Yeah, thank god. You rock, Ana," breathed Eila, slowly easing herself back from me while Kian still kept her arm steady. MJ looped a make-shift sling over her neck and Kian slid her arm inside. Her accelerated healing would repair her shoulder completely within a day, but the sling would help speed the process.

Ana finally let her go and blinked a few times, swaying slightly on her feet. I began to understand why Rillin called her kind Sway. I reached out and quickly grabbed her by the hip to steady her. "Damn – I feel like I rode the carousel for too long," she said, rubbing her face. Her fingers left grease spots on her forehead.

"Are you okay, Pix? You look a bit drunk," said Kian, trying to make her smile, but clearly concerned.

Ana gave him a thumbs up and steadied herself, her dizziness passing. Eila looked up to her friend, "I owe you, woman."

"Pfft – you *always* owe me," replied Ana with a smile. "In fact, I think everyone owes me, because I am pretty sure I fixed the engine."

"Uh, technically you messed it up in the first place, though," said MJ, who dodged a throw pillow when she flung it at his head.

Our three friends began making preparations to get underway and head for Polaris. We had planned to go to one more island before heading to Christian's, but between the pirates, Eila's shoulder, and the forecast of a stormfront moving in, our semi-vacation needed to be over.

Eila remained on my lap, studying my face.

She was paler than normal from her injury, but the pink was slowly returning to her fair skin. When Kian and I had finally gotten to Cerberus, one look at the destruction inside the boat told us that the girls and MJ put up one hell of a fight.

Eila had told me she had used what I had taught her to defend herself and I was proud of her. But when I learned that she had been bound and her mouth duct taped, I only wanted vicious revenge.

We had argued over her attacker's fate -- she wanted him to live, but I wanted him chopped into fish chum.

Ana's Babe Ruth swing, however, had settled his fate for us. The clean strike she had delivered to his jaw and temple, had caused a fatal injury inside his brain, and by the time I checked on him, he had died. We had dumped both bodies overboard, knowing their blood would soon attract the sharks.

Sadly, neither of the pirates were Garrett's nephew, and with Garret having lost his head, I was concerned the nephew might seek revenge. Rillin's idea of us all carrying weapons now seemed like a much better plan.

I looked at Eila and swept a damp piece of her hair back from her face. "Can I get you to bed? You need to rest."

A smile played over her beautiful lips, "Yes you can, as long as you come to bed with me. I mean, I know it is such a burden to share your bed with a blanket hog like me, but do you think you could tough it out?"

"Sleeping with you is mighty hard, you know?"

She pouted. "Oh dear. We can't have that. I guess I'll just bunk in with Ana tonight. I can't have my guard being tortured," she sighed.

"ANA! Can I sleep in your b—,"

I quickly covered her mouth with my hand and a devious smile curled onto her pink lips, sending sparks through my fingertips. I let my hand slowly drop, and trace along her jaw as I pulled her in, mindful of her shoulder as I kissed her.

"I'm thinking you don't mind the torture?" she asked with a brilliant smile.

Nope – I didn't mind at all.

55 Eila

POLARIS WAS A STRIP OF EMERALD in a sea of blue.

Like its namesake, the lush island seemed to be the most magnificent point in the Caribbean, with Christian's home standing proudly atop a hill near the private docks.

We had arrived just as the sun climbed over the ocean, having cruised through the night ahead of the coming storm. The sky now burned red and tumultuous, as a wayward raindrop would randomly fall, braving the way for its friends to follow.

"I could stay here forever," said Ana with a sigh, looking out over the breathtaking landscape from the second floor balcony.

I reached out and touched the fragrant vines that clung to the balcony, sliding my finger along the purple petals of a flower I couldn't identify. Ana was right – I could stay here forever, in Christian's stunning, New Orleans-styled home. That was the biggest surprise for me when I first saw the house – that it wasn't some elaborate fortress or

376

a modern castle, but an antebellum estate. It was *Gone with the Wind* and Bourbon Street.

Massive white pillars towered from the lush grounds to the shingled roof three stories up. Two full balconies ran the entire circumference of the home.

My bedroom, complete with canopy bed, private marble bathroom, and two sets of French doors, overlooked the ocean and the southernmost part of the island's rolling hills. Ana's room connected to mine, and I could see us sitting out on these covered balconies late into the night, stargazing and dreaming. Raef, Kian, and MJ all had rooms on the third floor, directly above us. With a dozen bedrooms and nearly 8,000 square feet of sprawling deep south elegance, the Polaris house was simply magnificent.

The home was constructed as a massive, squared-off U, with the back half open to a huge, outdoor living space with lounging beds, fire pits, and a pool that seemed to tumble off into the ocean beyond. My room and Ana's were located on the innermost part of the U, and our view stretched out over the pool to the ocean beyond, and Cerberus, now docked in her own private harbor.

I watched our faithful yacht and she barely moved in the now rougher seas. MJ walked along her fine lines, checking her ropes to make sure she would weather the storm, while Raef and Kian unloaded some things from her. She would need some small repairs from our encounter with the pirates, but overall, she was a tough seagoing siren.

"Ana? Eila?" called Rillin, in his deep, gruff voice from below us. He stepped out into the open-air room and looked up to where we stood. His face was completely fuzz-free, which caused me to blink a few times

377

in surprise.

"Why, look! It's Thor! And he ditched his beard! How fancy!" said Ana, with a chuckle.

Rillin crossed his arms. "I thought I'd show you two where the kitchen was. You know – so you can make yourselves some breakfast. I'm assuming you didn't grab something on the yacht just now."

Nope. Sure didn't, especially since I was busy snuggling in bed with Raef up until we pulled into Polaris. I will admit that I slept like a rock last night, but Raef informed me that he preferred to stay up and watch me sleep. It was both creepy and outrageously sexy.

"Excuse me, but are you saying that our stay at Casa de Christian doesn't include maid service and a private chef? What type of cheap, two-star establishment is this anyway?" asked Ana, acting disgusted.

"She's joking, right?" replied Rillin.

I smiled, "With her you can never quite tell, but I am happy to cook." I knew Rillin, Kian and Raef would not be eating, but MJ, Ana, and I needed some real food. Christian had made sure the home would be stocked when we arrived, and for his thoughtfulness, I was grateful. He was still in Barbados with Mae . . . and Collette. He would arrive in a few hours, but Mae wouldn't be here for days, and I suspected we would see some major fireworks once Kian's ex descended on us.

A warm gust of wind ruffled the leaves of the tall palms lining the pool, forcing them to fold over, a sure sign that the storm was fast approaching.

"Meet me at the bottom of the stairs and I will show you to the kitchen," said Rillin as he disappeared back under our feet. The rain became more persistent as Ana and I headed back inside through my bedroom.

As I walked by a set of double doors that centered the far side of my room, I caught a glimpse of something glittery inside. I stopped short and Ana nearly collided with me. "What the heck?" she muttered as I turned and headed for the shimmering object.

I pulled the doors open and before me hung rows of stunning dresses, jeans, shirts, and nightgowns. "Oh. My. God." I whispered, walking into the biggest closet I had ever seen.

Ana followed, whistling as she ran her hand along all the beautiful clothing. I pulled the sparkling evening dress that had caught my eye from the rack, holding it up. It was pewter colored, with a devastating slit up the leg and a back covered in metallic-toned lace. Everything looked as though it would fit me.

I knew of only one person on the planet that could make something so beautiful and who knew my specific clothing size. "Collette," I said turning to Ana, but she was holding up what looked like shredded red yarn, wrapped around another hanger. "What is that?" I asked.

"A bikini, I think." Ana eyed the scrap of fabric as if it was a poisonous snake.

"That's not a bathing suit! That's floss with a couple of napkins attached! I'm NOT wearing that!"

"You're right. If you wore this by the pool, Raef would have a heart attack." She winked at me.

The woman was the devil, but her evil ways were rubbing off on me. I narrowed my eyes, snatching the floss from her. "I saw a hot tub not far from that pool. I think my shoulder could use a good, long soak, don't you think?" I asked, wiggling my nearly healed arm that was still in its sling.

Ana smiled in that bad-girl way that I had come to love.

"You know . . . if my room has a fully stocked closet . . ." I started, but Ana's eyes sparkled and she tore out of my room, heading to her own couture oasis. We might be tomboys, but free clothing like this was way too fun to pass up. Breakfast could wait.

"RILLIN ASKED WHERE YOUR SCAR WAS? But we don't have

scars. What the hell did he mean?" asked Kian, walking up to Christian's house. I pulled the huge front door open as MJ and Kian walked through, their arms filled with some of the girls' things.

"I have no clue what he meant. I was hoping you could come up with some insight," I said, stepping into the home's massive entrance. A towering, circular staircase spun upwards to the left, while the right was open to a billiard room, complete with massive fireplace. Chandeliers and pieces of history were everywhere, including paintings and maritime relics. Christian did nothing subtly.

Rillin came around the corner and gave us all a nod, shaking each of our hands in turn. "How was your trip?" he asked.

MJ dropped one of the bags by his feet. "Except for the pirates? Oh, it was fabulous."

"Pirates? What happened?" asked Rillin, his face hard. "Is that why

Eila has a sling?"

I nodded. "Those two from your Blacklist had ties to the pirating community. They tried to hijack Cerberus while Kian and I were off hunting. The girls and MJ managed to take the yacht back, however."

Rillin looked surprised. "I'm . . . impressed."

"Why does everyone seem so shocked that I can hold my own in my human form? I'm starting to get a complex, damn it!" protested MJ.

Kian was about to reply, but then we caught a glimpse of Eila and Ana through the back wall of glass. They were walking past a massive pool and testing the heat of the hot tub with their feet. Eila bit her lip as her toe inched into the water, her arm still in a sling, her torso wrapped in an array of red ribbons that seemed to flow outward from an obscenely hot bikini.

Her scar was easily visible as it plunged down the center of her chest, and one part of me was proud that she was no longer hiding it. The other part of me, however, wanted to force everyone from the building so I could see how long it would take me to unwrap the suit from her breathtaking curves.

I suspected Kian had the same thoughts about Ana, who was in a white bikini, but hers had a web-like strip of fabric that ran from the bottom piece up to the top, covering her stomach. Barely.

Rillin turned to see what we were staring at and caught a glimpse of both Ana and Eila talking and laughing as they lowered themselves into the steaming tub. He cleared his throat, turning back to us. "Collette stocked everyone's rooms with a full wardrobe, bathing suits and training apparel included."

"Obviously," muttered Kian.

I continued to watch Eila, and she eased the sling off her arm and sank lower into the hot tub, resting her head back against the granite edge, her face skyward. The tiny raindrops landed along her cheeks and she closed her eyes as they slid down her face, like tears. "I need to cool off in the pool," I said to no one in particular.

"Me too," replied Kian.

"Absolutely," said MJ.

Kian and I turned to look at him, shock on our faces.

"What? I may be just a friend to them, but I'm still a guy. Sheesh." MJ stomped off, heading in the direction that Rillin specified, no doubt to grab a suit and cool off for multiple reasons.

Kian turned to me, a calm expression on his face. "I just want you to know that if those suits are any indication of what Collette has left for them to wear on a daily basis, then I will be dead inside of a week."

"That makes two of us," I replied, heading for my room and my own suit, which was hopefully NOT a Speedo.

57 Eila

BY NIGHTFALL THE STORM HAD MOVED on, leaving the evening warm and covered in stars. Outside the palm trees barely moved in the light breeze, and the air was clean and floral and far better than any perfume I had ever smelled.

I examined myself in the mirror inside Ana's room as we got ready for dinner. The black, lace dress hung from my body, and the ultra low back showed off my kill mark. I was self-conscious at the idea of going semi-commando, but Ana assured me I looked spectacular, and that with the back so open, I couldn't hide a bra strap. Luckily Collette had built in a little support for the girls in the front, but still – I never went braless.

"If you're sure," I replied to Ana's tenth assurance that I was going to leave Raef speechless.

Ana's floor-length dress was a riot of green swirls, each emerald ribbon spinning around her tiny frame. The halter top was covered in crystals that climbed over her shoulders and formed a single line that traveled down her spine to the dipped back of the dress. I took comfort that she too had to ditch a bra. When I finally meet Collette, we needed to have a chat about making us clothes that allowed for supportive undies. I suspected the French walked around half-naked all the time.

Tonight we would open Elizabeth's diary and Ana thought we should make a special evening of it. She said that for all we went through to get it, for all that Elizabeth had done to protect it, we needed to mark the occasion with a party. Christian had arrived a few hours ago, and we had gotten him up to speed on the pirates. He seemed unconcerned about Garrett's slimy nephew, assuring us he would finish the job as soon as possible, but as always, he wanted to make sure I was all right. Thankfully my shoulder was back to normal and the sling had been flung in the trash.

He also informed us that Mae would be arriving in several days, and while I was thrilled to see her, I was not looking forward to the lecture she would give as soon as she realized Raef and Kian were with us.

"Ready?" asked Ana, picking up Elizabeth's necklace from the bureau. I tucked the diary tighter to my body and gave her a nod. We headed down the curving staircase that lead to the main atrium and the outdoor living area, where our party was supposed to take place.

I stepped through the glass doors with Ana and caught sight of all five guys talking near the edge of the infinity pool. All were dressed in various shades of white linen shirts, though Raef, Rillin, and Christian had rolled their sleeves up to their elbows. The tiki torches had been lit around the area and the chandeliers that hung from beams over the lounges and table all had little white candles that flickered inside their glass jars. It was absolutely gorgeous. Something out of a fantasy world.

I looked around the space, my eyes finally going back to where the guys stood, but Raef had seen me, and he walked towards me, along the edge of the pool. In the candlelight, his flawless face showed no hint of the killer that lived inside him. Every move he made was precise and smooth, and it reminded me of how his body moved with mine that night on Cerberus, as if we were designed to fit perfectly with one another.

He finally reached me, stopping just shy of touching me. "You are stunning," he said quietly, a glorious smile gracing his face. I blushed and held the diary closer to my chest, but he carefully slid it from my hands so I couldn't hide behind its leather binding. He set the book on a table next to us, and his eyes returned to me, trailing over my body. The heat in his gaze flushed every inch of me and I loved the power it yielded in its wake.

I turned slowly, revealing the back to him and he reached out, trailing his hand down my spine and stuttering my heart. He pulled me toward him, one hand on my bare back, the other sweeping slowly down my neck. "I love you, Eila. For this life and the next," he said, kissing me softly as the Fallen marks bled onto his skin. He did it in front of our friends. In front of my grandfather.

In front of the universe.

Christian came up next to us, and Raef pulled me close to his side as his Fallen marks faded. My grandfather looked to both of us, then finally held out his hand to Raef and they shook, exchanging some unspoken understanding that Raef and I would never be anything less that what he had with Elizabeth.

Fate had set us to collide and nothing would ever tear us apart.

Everyone clustered around me at the mahogany table, looking over my shoulder at the pages and pages of Elizabeth's diary, now finally filled with writing thanks to the necklace that was seated in the cover. The words had bled to the surface the moment the diamond pendant had touched the leather, and the little clicking noises it made assured us that it wasn't some kind of magic, but a delicate, word-revealing engine, built by Nikki's ancestor. As for the words inside, they were mostly written by a young girl with a semi-crush on her trainer she called Monster.

At least, that was the first half of the book, and I could have sworn Rillin actually blushed.

But as the pages went on, it was obvious that Elizabeth questioned what her kind was doing. The violence and the one-mindedness to kill the Mortis didn't sit right with her. She wrote of a man she met in the woods when she was little, saying that he seemed like a safe haven for her, though she knew only later that he was a soul thief. In later pages she wrote that he, Christian, once again saved her and kept her safe. She fought next to him and his friends, including James, who showed her how to shoot with a bow.

Realizing I might stumble across some very intimate details of her and Christian, I jumped ahead to the end of the diary, closer to what I knew would have been her death. Christian looked relieved, though Ana protested skimming past the juicy details.

Toward the end of her diary, Elizabeth seemed to have fallen into a darker train of thought. She loved her son, but something seemed wrong. She talked of a Mortis named Jacob Rysse, who she believed was going to try and restart the Gabriel Device for his own purposes. He wanted to wipe the world of both the Lunaterra and any compassionate Mortis. He wanted a precision army to enslave the humans and he believed this device would be the key to absolute power.

"All right – back up," said Kian, rubbing his forehead. "So Elizabeth decided to kill Rysse to keep him from finding and restarting this device thing? What does she call it? Gabriel? I don't understand what this Gabriel device is."

Ha – he wasn't the only one.

Rillin crossed his arms, thinking. "It almost sounds like she is referring to the same thing that kept the Trials bound to the palace via the links – the same device that Katherine disabled or damaged. I just have no clue what it looks like or if it would have even survived the palace collapse. And why in the hell did Rysse meet with Elizabeth and think she could be turned? How does that play into his need for the device?"

I moaned, my brain just about melting. Raef leaned over me, looking at Elizabeth's writing. "Okay – well, let's rethink this. If the device was in the Lunaterras' possession and they had used it to enslave the Trials and god knows what else, then maybe Rysse needed a Lunaterra to control it? Maybe HE couldn't use it because he was a soul thief, but a Lunaterra could."

Christian nodded, "That actually makes sense. So Rysse would've needed a Lunaterra that would be willing to work with him, which was basically no one except Elizabeth. She not only was hated by her own kind, but she was already fighting for us. She would have been the ideal choice and Rysse probably figured she would've wanted revenge on her own family. I still don't understand why Rysse thought she could be turned however."

I flipped through several more pages, but then stopped short when I came across a page full of Fallen markings. They seemed to be organized, like a family tree, with numbers that lined up with each horizontal line. The first line, number 1, had a set of marks that I had never seen on Raef, Kian, Rillin or Christian, but the name Jacob was scrawled next to it. The second line, showed a set similar to the first, but the patterns had begun to change, and I immediately recognized them as those that graced Kian's and Raef's skin. Alongside this line, Elizabeth wrote several names I didn't recognize. There were more sets of Fallen marks, line after line, with each line changing more. Page after page of markings, some with names alongside the lines. Eventually I found Christian's name and the word *Monster.*

"Is this a family tree?" asked Rillin.

Kian nodded, "It appears she was tracking generations of Mortis, but Raef and I are one line below Jacob. That doesn't mean what I think it does . . . does it?"

I looked up to Raef, "You two were turned by Jacob Rysse himself?"

Raef stepped back from the table. "That can't be right. Can it? And why is there no one above Jacob? I mean, where did he come from?"

Christian slid down into a seat at the table and looked at Raef and Kian. "Jacob must have been one of the First Army. The original set of humans who were changed into Mortis by the Fallen One himself. They were considered the purest, most dangerous, of all the Mortis. If you two were turned by him, it may explain why you weren't killed by Elizabeth's power. Plus, her Core Collapse must have been filtered through Jacob before it hit the two of you, lessening its impact. Between what you were

389

already, and the energy she released during her death, you both were basically vaccinated that night. It also means that you and Kian are only steps away from pure, angelic strength."

MJ rolled his eyes, "Don't go telling them they are some kind of superheroes. Kian's fat head will get even bigger!"

Kian smiled broadly.

"Everyone will need to train," said Rillin. "If you two have that type of strength and capability, we need to bring it out. Parts of the Mortis community now know of Eila's existence. She needs to be protected at all times."

"Yeah, but for the rest of my life? I mean, isn't it easier to just tell them that I'm not a threat? You know – I'm a friendly type of Lunaterra? Can't we just ALL get along?" I demanded.

"We could tattoo 'I Heart Soul Thieves' across Eila's forehead," offered MJ. "Maybe set her up with a blog and Pinterest page?" Everyone glared at MJ, but I actually was down with all those ideas.

I sighed and flipped to the last page. On it was another family tree, but this time it was Elizabeth's. Listed with each family member was their date of birth and death. At the very bottom, Elizabeth had written herself and Christian with a line connecting them to each other and another line below them, linking them to their son.

Ana, who was leaning over me to see the diary, spoke up. "Wow. I only see a few people lived past 35. Fighting must have been brutal back then." Raef leaned forward and trailed his hand over the names. He looked to Rillin and something seemed to be communicated between the two of them.

"What? What is it?" I asked. Raef placed his elbows on the table, rubbing his face with his hands and I could see MJ and Kian were tense as well. Now I was getting nervous.

Something was not right – I could see it on their faces. So could Christian. "What's going on?" he asked.

"The Lunaterra had stunted lifespans after years of inbreeding," said Rillin.

My eyes grew wide and Christian got to his feet, alarmed, "How short of a lifespan are we talking?" he asked.

"Twenty to thirty years," replied Raef. I turned to him, and his sad eyes met mine. "Rillin told me on the plane. He also knows about your real background."

Christian froze.

Raef laced his fingers into mine, "Rillin figured out your connection to Christian after Sandy Neck. He saw your scar, which only appears on Mortis after they are hit with the Light. Rillin is covered with them."

I looked to Rillin. "Is this true?" I asked.

He nodded and unbuttoned his shirt, revealing many scars. He touched the deep trio that curved around his side. "These are from Elizabeth. She threw one incredible punch." He touched another deep groove near his shoulder, "This one is from you, the night on Sandy Neck."

My eyes grew wide. I had damaged my would-be trainer. He would carry the mark of my ability to the end of time. "I'm, uh, sorry," I said, feeling bad I had injured him.

"Don't worry about it, Eila. I wear my scars like a badge of survival, as you should with yours."

I looked back to Raef, "Why didn't you tell me? About the lifespan thing?"

"I didn't want you to only obsess about how long you would live," said Raef. "No one should carry that burden. And you are generations out from the inbreeding and you are part Mortis. For all we know, you could live past 100. Mortis are immortal – that could make your life long. Far longer than an average human." I stroked his arm, watching my guard carefully and seeing the desperation in his face.

Was I scared that my life-clock might be ticking towards midnight? Absolutely. But life gave us no guarantees when we were born. There is nothing that says that I get to live past tomorrow, even if I was just human. "Raef – I live for today. For you and me and our friends. This knowledge changes nothing for me, only that the future is a complete gamble and that I wouldn't bet on anyone else but us. All of us."

I slowly shut the diary and slid it to Christian, the necklace still in the cover. He gave me a small smile, knowing I was offering him a chance to read Elizabeth's thoughts in private. I got to my feet, with Raef at my side. "I'm done with the heavy. How about we enjoy ourselves? This is a party after all. Now, who's gonna dance with me?"

"Me!" yelled MJ, grabbing me by the hand and towing me toward the open space near the pool. I laughed as he started dancing like a weirdo next to me as Ana flicked on the stereo. Kian slipped his hand into hers and he pulled her toward us, spinning her out and then back to him.

Ana and I jumped between partners throughout the evening, and I quickly learned that Rillin loathed dancing and Christian could go pro in ballroom. But it was Raef who stole me away from Christian finally, pulling me into an intoxicating slow dance as Otis Redding's soft music flowed around us.

His wide hands held me to him as he moved across the open space and I could feel his body heat melting into mine.

I tucked my face against the chest of my beloved bodyguard, and tried, if only for a moment, to forget all that we were up against.

58 Eila

"I'M TRYING," I GROWLED, sweat soaking through the thin body suit Collette had made me.

Rillin stood across from me in a loose fitting, Asian style outfit, his broad arms crossed over his chest. His scars twisted around his arms and shoulders, like a thorny vine, and his face was hard as he studied me.

"It isn't about brute force, Eila. It is about grace, anticipating the move of your enemy, and feeling the air around you. Right now you are just trying to bash your way through the target, and all you are accomplishing is tiring yourself."

"Well, I'm also getting my rage on, which is what you want, don't you? Feed my anger to flip the switch on my glow stick ability?" I was almost yelling, frustration and fatigue flaring in me. I had been training for hours each day, and I seemed no closer to accessing my inner fighter.

It had been three days since we opened Elizabeth's diary. Since that night, we had trekked across the five-mile island, discovering sweeping flower fields, white sand beaches, and waterfalls.

We also explored the house and Christian's insane collection of antique art and rare treasures. And we had started training, which involved everyone forcing their physical limits and abilities to the edge.

Raef, Kian, and MJ pushed their endurance levels, running around the island twenty to thirty times in one shot and at top speed, though MJ did so as Marsh. They swam, climbed, and perfected hand-to-hand fight techniques. They knew how to assemble a variety of handguns and shoot with precision aim.

They were a supernatural SEAL team of sorts.

MJ worked tirelessly at phasing on the fly and was no longer required to strip out his clothes, thanks to a specialized wardrobe Collette had invented.

Often times, I found him with a stack of anatomy and biology books surrounding him by the pool. I suspected he was working on shifting into something else besides Marsh, though he would not tell anyone anything, no matter how much Ana or I nagged him.

Ana had also been training, both in hand-to-hand techniques and as a Sway. She read constantly and we would volunteer ourselves to be guinea pigs as needed. Her ability was hit or miss, though she did have the whole truth or tale thing down perfectly.

She had been working with Rillin on something he called *blinding*, and though she wouldn't say what it was, she seemed excited about its possibilities. She said it had to do with how the Lunaterra palace stayed so well hidden. I was out-of-my-mind curious.

Of all of us, however, Rillin spent by far the most time with me. At first Raef had insisted on staying in the training room with me, which was

Christian's stunning library, but I found him to be a distraction. Eventually I asked him to leave, and he did so reluctantly.

At the moment, however, all I wanted to do was take a nap and maybe raid the chocolate box.

Rillin had given me a short sword after deciding that my Light throwing style from Sandy Neck favored a blade stroke, which was just laughable.

He said that before I could command my power, I needed to master a weapon that reflected my fighting style and wasn't going to end up throwing me into another heart attack.

I got the logic behind his technique of "training," but I seemed to be a stumbling klutz while attempting to follow the directions of an ex-Templar knight.

He had laid out several types of weapons, everything from daggers to knight-styled long swords. He gave me the short sword, which was a mini version of a knight's blade, and I had proceeded to beat on a headless dummy that was on wheels. Rillin would slide it side to side and I would try to strike it. I missed most of the time, and after 90 minutes, I wanted to aim for Rillin, rather than the dummy.

He sighed, walking over to me as he untied his shirt from his body, tossing it on the ground.

I studied his powerful body. The scars extended over his chest, with Elizabeth's set of three deep slashes tracing his side.

He took the sword from my hand and stepped to the dummy, planting his feet as wide as his shoulders, facing away from me. Covering almost every inch of his back was an owl, its wings spread wide, with the tips of its feathers curling over the tops of his thick shoulders, its talons flared.

A silent hunter, not unlike the man it was inked to, and who I wanted to strangle.

He glanced over his shoulder at me, "Grace, Eila. Don't over think your move. Let your body understand itself and you will bring forth your power, and channel what strength you have to do the most damage."

Not likely, but whatever, Jedi Master.

I watched as he turned back to the dummy and his muscles flexed as he brought the blade to his side, spinning it by the handle. The sword balanced perfectly in his hand, the hilt counterweighted to the shining steel.

But then he stepped and spun, a full 360 degree turn, bringing the blade into a deadly angle as it met the side of the dummy, cutting the target completely in half in one lightning-fast movement. Ninety minutes I had been hacking away at that thing, and in one sweeping motion, Rillin had cut it in half.

The severed upper half hit the floor and wobbled over toward my feet, like a lopsided bowling ball. "Show off," I muttered.

Rillin looked back at me as he placed the sword among the others and picked up a shorter, narrower sword that had a subtle curve to the blade. The length of the steel was engraved with flowers, and the handle was wrapped in strips of leather. I sighed, "What's this one called?" I was resigned that I wasn't getting a break yet.

"This is a Katana," said Rillin, handing the beautiful weapon to me, hilt first. "The Samurai used them in combat. They are lighter and the curve allowed a warrior to unsheathe the blade and slice through their enemy in a single sweeping motion. You cannot swing like a bat with this one, so don't even try it."

I already liked the narrow feel of the Katana in my hand and I straightened my arm, holding the sword horizontally in front of me. The sunlight pouring in from the open library window caught the edge of the steel, sending a streak of light across the high ceiling. "I like this one," I said. "It feels better to me. Lighter. More natural."

Rillin stepped around behind me and suddenly I was very aware of his body in the space of the room.

He reached out over my arm, laying his own massive bicep on top of mine. He curled his scarred hand over my fingers, gripping the sword along with me, and my nerves began to flare. He brought my other arm up to the hilt, and showed me how to use both my hands to hold the Katana. He then took his free hand and pressed it flat to my lower stomach, pinning my back to his front. I jumped when we made contact, but he seemed unfazed.

His voice vibrated through me when he spoke, and suddenly every inch of my body was alive. "Now step with me," he said, and he moved to the left, tightening his grip on my stomach and forcing me to move with him, while his other arm guided the Katana to a sweeping side move.

"You're fighting the fluidity of it, Eila. You have to trust yourself and your body," said Rillin, forcing me to step the other way and rotate the blade again.

"Close your eyes," he said softly. "Feel your way through the movement, of how your body flexes, and how the air sweeps across the blade." I did as he said, closing my eyes, and feeling Rillin's body molded to mine as we stepped back and forth, smoothly like a cat. "Block out the world, Eila. Focus on what you want and what you feel. Command your body to move the way you wish. You are a lyrical form of death. Graceful, precise, and committed to the kill."

I did as he said, relaxing into his movements and focusing on my own body. Believing I was like the wind and water, my movements became more fluid, more natural.

Even with my eyes closed, I began to see the room about me – of how the blade was turning in my hands and how my feet flexed to the floor. I could feel the sun when I stepped into its glorious path, but also the darkened corner of the room, shadowed by the books.

The edge of my vision began to glitter, like cut crystal, and with my eyes still tightly closed the room came into view, like an artist's charcoal sketch. It was hauntingly beautiful and my breath caught as my head turned to scan the room, somehow seeing without my eyes. I could even see the remainder of the dummy, standing near me, half destroyed.

"Do you feel yourself within the space? Can you see yourself moving?" asked Rillin, his voice nearly a whisper.

I nodded slowly and he carefully released me, but I kept moving side to side, sweeping the blade in a slow, deliberate arc.

I stepped forward, still moving in the light-footed motion, both my hands gripped tightly to the leather handle and turning in unison. I focused on what I felt, on what I saw even with my eyes closed.

I was one with the air, with the ground, and with the energy that began to skate across my skin. And then, without conscious decision or command, I took a bold lunge and hauled the blade in a perfect arc, cutting clean through a swath of space in front of me.

I eased out of my stance and slowly opened my eyes and the near blinding light of the room faded. In front of me was just the pole the dummy had been on, shuddering slightly. Beside it lay my target, completely severed from the stand.

I turned back to Rillin, breathless with the effort I didn't realize I had used. "Like that?" I asked, catching my reflection in a massive mirror. The edge of my eyes glowed a brilliant gold, like the outer edge of a solar eclipse.

"Exactly like that," said Rillin, and he studied me, as if he was seeing someone else.

As if he was once again facing Elizabeth.

59 Raef

EILA LAY IN MY ARMS as we watched the subtle movement of her bed's canopy sway with the night breeze that drifted in through the open balcony doors. The house was quiet, everyone having gone to bed, or tucked into their rooms, reading.

I listened to the sound of the palm trees rustle and the ocean roll not far from the house, while I twisted a strand of her wet hair through my fingers. We had all gone for a night swim in the glowing pool, trying to unwind from a day of training, and we ended up betting one another which constellations we could identify. At one point, Ana climbed onto Kian's back and just held on, using him as her own floatation device.

Eila yawned, rolling more into my chest, and I pressed my arm firmly around her back, kissing the top of her head. "You're tired," I whispered.

"Mmm - I'm tired from training and, well, other things," she replied, drawing circles over my chest that still held faint traces of the Fallen marks. They had been black as ebony a little while ago because of what we had done, and this time Eila hadn't felt pain. She had let herself go completely as we made love, and I had felt the rush of her heartbeat rocket through my chest, pacing my own.

I leaned down, kissing her softly on the lips. She sighed and I couldn't help my need to bring her body into tighter contact with my own. I rolled myself on top of her, careful to keep my weight off of her as I caged in her head with my arms. She was going to attempt to throw her power tomorrow, and it hung like a cloud of doom over my head.

"Are you sure you want to throw the Light already? There is no rush, you know?" I asked, sweeping her hair back from her face. I knew every one of her freckles and where her skin would flush when she was embarrassed. I knew how she slept, how she laughed, and where her tears tracked when she cried. I knew her, all of her, and adored everything about her.

Eila nodded and rolled her soft body under mine and my Fallen marks darkened once again. "You worry too much," she whispered, bringing her lips in contact with mine, quickly escalating a polite kiss into a fiery one. God, I could never get enough of her, but even with her pinned under me, her safety was paramount.

"I can never worry enough about you," I replied, locking her delicate wrists in my hand and dragging them slowly above her head, kissing the ticklish spot on her smooth neck. She laughed and squirmed against me, effectively revving my need into high gear. Her giggles faded into deep, slow drags of air as I trekked my lips down from her neck to her scar.

I drew my hand down her body to her hip as she breathed my name, but then a door slammed in the direction of Ana's room. We snapped out of our moment and glanced to the bedroom door, listening. Then I heard delicate footsteps marching past Eila's door, heading for the third floor staircase . . . and Ana, softly crying. E heard it too, causing her to scramble out from under me, and I quickly pulled on a pair of pants while she flung on a top and boxers.

We managed to get out the bedroom door and nearly collided with Rillin, who must have also heard Ana with his supernatural hearing. He gave me a knowing glare, but kept his mouth shut.

"Where's Christian?" I asked. I wasn't going to hide the fact that I was sleeping with Eila, nor was I ashamed of making love to the girl I adored, but this was not the way for Christian to find out.

"He went back to Freeport to try and pick off Garrett's nephew," said Rillin. He motioned in the direction Ana had gone, "Are you two checking on her?" We both nodded, leaving Rillin standing in the hall as we jogged for the stairs and whatever was going on above us.

As we reached the third floor hallway, Eila yanked me back and put a finger to her lips to signal me to be quiet. Ana had not seen us, and she stood before Kian's door holding a piece of paper in her hands, as if debating whether or not to knock.

She roughly rubbed away her tears and raised her hand to the door, but it suddenly opened. Kian, dressed only in a pair of cotton pants, stepped out to her the moment he saw her wet cheeks. "Pix? What's the matter? Are you okay?"

Ana fingered the paper in her hand, looking down at it as she gave a small sniff, "I was using the laptop in my room just now. The one from Cerberus. And I saw this picture."

Kian swallowed and slowly took the paper from her, looking down at whatever was printed on the page. "I, uh, meant to tell you. I was going to take you by the cemetery to see it, but things got messed up so fast, and we had to leave. I'll have the workers remove it if you don't like it," he said, shifting on his feet, as if guilty of a crime. "I'm sorry I upset you. That wasn't my intention. The cemetery said that it was going to take so long to replace his stone and I knew I could get it done faster. I knew I could give your Dad a nice stone like you always wanted to." Kian carefully folded the paper and handed it back to Ana, who nodded slowly.

I realized then that they were discussing Ana's father's headstone, which Kian had apparently replaced. I was stunned he had done such a thing. To honor a man who had treated her so badly must have been the hardest thing for Kian to do, but he did it, for Ana. He did it because he would walk through fire if she asked.

"I'm not upset," said Ana drawing a trembling breath.

Kian reached out and gently wrapped his hand around her narrow wrist. "Pix – but you're crying," he whispered.

She nodded, reaching her hand up to his brow and tracing down the side of his face as he watched her intently. She rose up on her tip-toes and cautiously pulled him down to her as she brought her lips to his, and I felt Eila's hand grip mine. Kian seemed too stunned to react for a moment, but then he finally gathered his arms around her, lifting her off the ground as he kissed her back. But then Ana began to cry freely.

"It's beautiful," she whispered through her gasps, beginning to truly sob. She told him she was sorry for blaming him for her father's death. Sorry that she sent him away and treated him so badly when he had returned.

Kian gently tried to calm her, telling her it was okay. That everything would be all right and that he loved her. He pressed his back against the edge of the doorframe and slowly sank to the floor with Ana in his arms, holding her tightly as he kissed her tears and her lips.

I pulled Eila carefully to my side and she rested her head against my shoulder, wiping a stray tear from her own face. As we quietly backed down the stairs, leaving Ana and Kian alone in one another's arms, I heard Ana whisper to my brother that she loved him.

Forever.

 Eila

I WATCHED AS THE PIECES of literary confetti floated down around us, and cringed. I had correctly thrown the Light for the first time in my life, and had a pretty solid command of the energy.

Unfortunately, Rillin underestimated the damage I was capable of, and Christian's wall of books paid the ultimate price. I had called the Light, remembering the feeling of the Katana sword in my hand from the day before and how I saw without really seeing. I felt the energy travel through my body and thunder to my palms as I swung my hands as if I was slicing the air with the sword.

The Light had exploded from my hands, like a curved blade, and Rillin dove for the floor when it flew past him, smashing into the bookcase, causing the classics to explode. The ornate bookshelf had groaned as it leaned, and the entire top section tipped over and crashed to the ground.

Rillin was getting to his feet just as Raef and my friends burst through the library doors. They had all been waiting outside at my request, and now they took in the destruction of the room, with Rillin and I standing in the center. "What in the heck happened?" demanded MJ, picking up a torn page that had fluttered to the ground near him.

Ana slid some of the broken books aside with her bare foot, "Jeez, Eila! You just murdered Steinbeck!"

"Hey! I didn't know I could do that!" I said defensively, pointing to the now obliterated bookshelf. I turned to Rillin, "Did YOU know I could do that?"

Rillin shook his head as he dusted more paper shreds from his shoulder. "No. That was, well, unexpected."

"Unexpected? UNEXPECTED! I just destroyed Christian's friggin' library! Mae will be here in a few hours and look at this place!" I yelled. Raef came up next to me and seemed to be looking me over for any damage. He placed his hand to my neck, checking my pulse. "I just burned books," I mumbled and Raef smiled.

"We will replace them and I can fix the bookshelf. Were you able to control it?" he asked, somewhat dubious given the room's current state of destruction.

"I was able to form it and throw it, if that's what you mean. I just didn't think it would wreck the house." I turned to Rillin, who was inspecting the broken bookshelf. "How did I do this type of damage? I thought my ability was limited to damaging soul thieves, not demolition work."

Rillin turned back to me, "You took out a sizable portion of the Breakers."

"Yeah, but that was a Core Collapse. Isn't that standard when that

STORMFRONT – K.R. CONWAY

happens?" I asked.

Rillin shook his head. "No, but I wasn't sure what exactly went down in the Breakers – if there was another aspect to your light show that I didn't quite understand. But this," he gestured to the destruction. "This is a different kind of power and it has to be related to what you are as a hybrid. I suspect you channel more than the Web of Souls. More than simply the energy living souls give off to one another. Like your scar, however, I suspect Light casting might be a bit more complicated for you. As both a Mortis and a Lunaterra, you basically damage yourself when you correctly wield the Light. My guess is that is why your hands are now bleeding."

I took a startled step back and Raef grabbed my hands, "Eila! You *are* bleeding!" He uncurled my fingers to reveal a knife-like slash across the palm of each hand. Raef yanked his shirt over his head and pressed the fabric into my palms to stop the bleeding and I winced. "Sorry," he said to me, quietly, then turned angrily at Rillin. "Did you know this would happen?"

"I wasn't sure. It was a possibility. It should heal quickly, but I need to figure out if there is a way to keep her power from rebounding on her," replied Rillin, pushing aside a tattered book with his foot.

"Damaging my granddaughter was not part of the training deal, Mr. Blackwood," said Christian from the library entrance. I didn't even realize he had come back from Freeport.

"Uh, sorry about your books. Did you get your guy?" I asked him.

"I did, but we have a problem. The FBI is in Freeport investigating the beheading of Mr. Garrett, who they had been watching for his drug-trafficking connections. Howe is with them, which is not a good sign. If he has been reinstated, and he is part of the investigation, then there must be a connection back to you two! Which one of you two saw fit to rip the man's head off?" demanded Christian, glaring at Kian and Raef. My stomach sank at the thought of either of them leveling such violence against anyone, even a drug dealer.

Rillin stepped forward, clearly angry. "You guys ripped the man's head off? Are you out of your minds? We can't afford attention like that!"

"It was a momentary lack of solid judgment," said Kian. "He was bragging about hijacking Cerberus and taking the girls and well . . . I may have lost it. It won't ever happen again." Raef was listening to Kian with a somewhat stunned expression on his face.

"We have another problem," said Christian. "Before I took out the nephew, he had been meeting with a slim, dark haired man that had a shamrock on his neck. Does he sound familiar, Eila? MJ?"

I stiffened.

MJ's mouth dropped open, "Are you kidding me? Nikki's robber is in Freeport and he was talking with the same idiot who had his men try to hijack Cerberus?"

Rillin swore, "They have to be human hitmen. Bounty hunters. It isn't unusual to have Mortis run human organized crime rings, I just didn't think that is who was aiming for Eila and the rest of us. They are self-serving, so unless there was a financial gain to killing us, they wouldn't. If Shamrock Man is here, then we are being followed, and it means they are after something they intend to profit off of – something of great value."

"Do you think the Mortis who attacked us on Sandy Neck are also part of this crime group?" I asked, now wishing I too had trained with the handguns.

Rillin was quiet, thinking and looking tense. "I'm not sure," he replied.

"Mae is due to arrive this evening," said Christian. "Eila's ability to practice will be seriously curtailed once she is here. By the fact that I no longer have a library, I am thinking training still has a ways to go however."

Rillin shook his head. "Eila throws with great control, but she channels a different kind of Light. There was no way for me to know that, but I will figure out how to have her safely throw, and quickly. If we are being followed, time is of the essence. It's unfortunate that the Feon training equipment was destroyed in the palace. I suspect such items would have been useful with Eila."

Christian became very quiet for a moment, and when he spoke his voice seemed to be darker than I had ever heard before. "What if you did have the equipment? Would she be able to throw safely?"

"Possibly," said Rillin suspiciously. "Why?"

Christian didn't answer, instead walking over to the remaining piece of the bookshelf. He pressed his hand to the wall directly next to the shelf and a single square of light formed around his hand. It beeped a few times and with a hiss, the wall slid sideways, revealing a dark stairwell that trailed down under us.

"Holy flippin' Hogwarts!" gasped Ana, who had laced her hand with Kian's. After last night's revelation about her father's stone, I had barely seen Ana. She had been with Kian all day . . . and all last night. One could only wonder if Kian had finally put Mary behind him with Ana's help. We needed a girl pow-wow really soon.

"What's down there?" I asked, still clutching Raef's shirt in my hands.

"Everything," replied Christian, and he started down the dark stairwell. We looked at each other, and headed into the unknown behind my grandfather.

 61 Raef

ONCE IN THE STAIRWELL, I switched places with Eila, putting myself ahead of her as protection.

The fact that Christian had a hidden stairwell and possibly items from the Lunaterra made me uneasy. He could have told us before.

Why wait until now?

The bottom of the staircase ended in a small, round room with a black pool and nothing else – as if we were at the bottom of a massive well.

Christian began unbuttoning his shirt and kicking off his shoes.

"Is this a joke?" asked MJ, looking at the water. It was so dark inside the turret-like space that the edges of the pool seemed to disappeared into inky oblivion.

"My vault is accessible only through an underwater tunnel. It is a security precaution, to keep humans away. The entire house is built over a limestone cave, where I keep everything of value to me."

MJ looked at the water in the darkened room. "I, uh, think the invisible hand-pad on the wall pretty much covers your securities needs."

"One can never be too careful when protecting that which is priceless," offered Christian. "We need to go swimming, so I suggest you lose the shoes and whatever else might weigh you down."

I glanced at Eila, who shook her head as she wiggled out of her yoga pants and shirt, leaving on just her boyshorts and exercise bra. I wanted to drape something over her, but she just looked at me and shrugged. "Technically Collette's bikini was far more revealing than what I'm wearing now, don't you think?" I sighed and kicked off my shoes, the other guys following suit.

Ana looked at Kian, and he pulled off his shirt, handing it to her as he smiled. She then ducked behind him and switched into his shirt, which hung to her mid thigh. When she reappeared, she saw that everyone was giving her a curious glance.

"What?" she demanded, her face flushing. "My undies were a bit skimpier than Eila's, okay? Sheesh."

Kian's smile grew.

Eila stepped over to the edge of the black water, looking at its smooth surface when we all heard a splash. Everyone froze except Christian, and I studied the water as a small ripple made it to the lip of the pool.

Then, to my absolute shock, a smooth, gray triangle coasted by, followed by a smaller one.

"SHARKS? I'm not going in with sharks!" yelled Ana. Eila nodded rapidly.

What in the world could be valuable enough to call for hidden doors, underwater tunnels, and sharks? I stepped up to Christian, who had pulled three air tanks from a small alcove under the stairs.

"What's in the vault, Christian?" I asked, darkness threading my words. I didn't trust this man entirely. This seemed like too great a risk.

He ignored my question and handed Rillin and MJ the tanks – one for each of our human counterparts, since we soul thieves could hold our breath for hours.

I grabbed Christian's shirt, pinning him against the wall. "What's in the vault?" I growled.

He yanked my hand away. "Like I said, everything is in there. I thought the diary would be enough. I thought her book would have all the answers, but it doesn't. And now we have Ana. We might be able to fill in the blanks, including why Eila's throwing ability is different."

"What are you talking about?" I demanded, angry.

With the mention of Ana, Kian switched to high alert as did Rillin, and they stepped in next to me while MJ placed himself in front of the girls.

"Tell me what's in the vault! Why would you build a vault this deep under ground? This well protected? What could possibly be worth all this?"

But then I heard Ana's small voice behind me. "Oh my god. She's here, isn't she?" she asked, stepping past MJ to Christian. "You need me because I'm a Reloader. I can read the dead."

I glanced at Eila and her mouth dropped open in shock.

No. It couldn't be. He didn't . . .

Christian took a deep breath, his eyes filled with pain as he nodded, "Elizabeth is in the vault."

DID YOU KNOW THAT THIS IS AN INDIE PUBLISHED BOOK?

DID YOU KNOW THAT YOU – THE FANS – ARE THE ONES WHO CONTROL HOW MANY OTHER READERS WILL FIND EILA'S STORY?

I WRITE FOR MY FANS AND COULD USE YOUR HELP. IF YOU LOVED THIS STORY, PLEASE TELL YOUR FRIENDS, YOUR LOCAL BOOKSELLER, YOUR LIBRARY, YOUR SCHOOL – HECK, EVERYONE!

IF YOU CAN, PLEASE REVIEW US ON GOODREADS, AMAZON, AND B&N. REVIEWS HELP THE BOOK FIND A WIDER AUDIENCE.

GIVE US A SHOUT-OUT ON TWITTER, FACEBOOK, PINTEREST, AND INSTAGRAM AND WE WILL SHOUT BACK! THE MORE YOU TALK ABOUT THE BOOK, THE MORE EILA AND HER CREW WILL FIND NEW READERS!

THANK YOU!

COMING IN 2015:

KIAN & ANA'S NOVELLA
CRUEL SUMMER

THE REBELS WILL RISE
TRUE NORTH

HISTORY WILL NOT BE DENIED.
R U BRAVE?

ACKNOWLEDGMENTS

I can honestly say that UNDERTOW and STORMFRONT would have never existed had it not been for my family, especially my mom, and a gaggle of crazy friends. They were the original cheerleaders who forced me to pursue my imagination into a world of unlikely alliances, warring families, twisted histories, passions, and lies. Many thanks to them all, for they deserve far more than a page at the back of a novel.

To those people who nagged, prodded, and occasionally shouted "WHERE THE HECK ARE THE NEW PAGES?" I cannot thank you all enough. Without you, there would have never been Eila, Raef, Kian, Ana, and MJ. These fabulous people include: my parents, my brother, my kids and husband, Charlotte the Spiderwoman, Kim of the South, Kim of the North, Bethany the Bold, Layla who has everyone begging for more, Crafty Carrie with her nine-thousand origami pieces, Sabine the Saavy, and so many, many other brilliant friends.

As always, many thanks to my "cast" of the UNDERTOW series (those teens from Cape Cod that were brave enough to be photographed for book covers, blogs, character cards, etc.). I will always see you as the original characters. A huge high-five to Leslie McKinnon (Eila), Colby McWilliams (Raef), Christa Mullaly (Ana), Justin Blaze (Kian), Sean Potter (MJ), Megan Jones (Nikki), and Emily Penn (Elizabeth).

Endless thanks to my super talented photographer, Alex Daunais, who never sleeps and must run on gallons of caffeine. And a huge thank you to Cape Cod photographer Carole Corcoran and the stunning landscape shots that she captures through the lens of her camera. Her photographs grace the back cover of the UNDERTOW books. Mad skills, woman!

Many thanks to the local Cape Cod businesses and places that sparked my imagination, including Four Seas Ice Cream, Craigville Pizza, The Chocolate Sparrow, Sandwich Town Neck Beach, Sandy Neck beach, and Barnstable High School.

A shout out as well to the Mercandetti Family, who owned a certain Sea Captain home a long time ago, and which I always found 100% magical.

Many thanks to my fellow writers, including Trisha Leaver, Dean Coe, and many others who would happily shake some sense into me when I got a bit hysterical after rewriting a scene for the twentieth time.

A gold medal must be given to fan Bobbie Jo who convinced me to start a street team (which I refer to as the "pimp-my-novel" project), and librarian Lindsey Hughes who thought up Fallen tattoos for kids, though sadly not real ones. Bummer.

Huge thanks to YA librarian Kathy Johnson as well, who was the first to ever ask me to teach a class for teenage writers. I love doing it.

Lastly, a massive hug to my fans and Cape Cod – this series will always be for you. You are the reason why I work tirelessly to perfect the characters, and I hope they haunt your dreams . . . and maybe your nightmares.